ELLIE PILLAI
IS (ALMOST) IN LOVE

CHRISTINE
PILLAINAYAGAM

Illustrated by Trisha Srivastava

faber

First published in the UK in 2023
by Faber & Faber Limited, Bloomsbury House,
74–77 Great Russell Street, London WC1B 3DA
faber.co.uk

Typeset in Mr Eaves by MRules
Printed by CPI Group (UK) Ltd, Croydon CR0 4YY

A CIP record for this book is available from the British Library

ISBN 978–0–571–36702–3

MIX
Paper | Supporting
responsible forestry
FSC www.fsc.org **FSC® C171272**

Printed and bound in the UK on FSC paper in line with our continuing
commitment to ethical business practices, sustainability and the environment.
For further information see faber.co.uk/environmental-policy

2 4 6 8 10 9 7 5 3 1

You can listen to the *Ellie Pillai is (Almost) in Love* album by scanning in the link below – hear Ellie's songs come to life!

There are song chapters throughout the story that reference specific songs on the album.

For anyone who doesn't believe
they're extraordinary – you are.

1

A Girl Called Ellie

My name is Ellie. Ellie Pillai. And I'm in love with the boy in the yellow rain mac.

Or at least, I think I'm in love. Because I'm only fifteen, and I'm not sure you can love someone enough, or that much, when you're only fifteen. But I think I could be. As in, I *could* be in love with the boy in the yellow rain mac.

They describe love as the sensation of falling. Careering out of control, or drifting gracefully. It could be either. And this is the first time I've been *almost* in love, so, it could go either way.

My name is Ellie. Ellie Pillai. And I'm almost in love with the boy in the yellow rain mac. Or maybe I'm just falling.

falling: *adjective*
moving from a higher to a lower level, typically rapidly and without control.
i.e. *'she was injured by a falling tree'*

1

2

The Universal

The problem is, he's kissing me. And the kissing has been going on for a long time, and now I'm not sure what Happens Next. His hands are in my hair, which is nice, but he's starting to trail his fingers down the back of my neck, which sort of *tickles*, and I think it's possible he may be reaching for my bra hook, but the thing is, I'm not wearing a bra, I'm wearing a crop top. You know, like an Actual Child. Because Dad managed to shrink the only bras I own by washing them on a 90-degree hot wash – which even Mum is suspicious about, because Dad never does my washing, 90 degrees or otherwise, because he believes I am old enough to do it myself. So, *why then* did Dad choose *today*, of all days, to be *helpful* and put a wash on for me?

A Very. Hot. Wash.

And then I realise, my boyfriend (my more-than-just-a-friend-that-is-a-boy boyfriend) is definitely going for my non-existent bra hook. Because his hand is halfway down my back, and it's fumbling at the back of my cropped Nirvana T-shirt (because: Kurt Cobain's harmonic language, not just: it was on sale at H&M), pinching at the material where a hook should exist, but which is instead a neon-pink band that reads 'HELLO KITTY' because I Am Literally Wearing a Child's Crop Top. Which I last wore when I was twelve, when I am now almost sixteen, and I want to die.

Because I have a boyfriend now. A bona fide, real life, practically perfect boyfriend. With dark hair and green eyes and an asymmetric smile that makes me smile, even when I'm just thinking about it. The problem is, now I'm here. On his bed. In my flared cord trousers and custom floral Vans. Listening to Blur, 'The Universal', which should be making all of this feel better, but instead feels like the prelude to something more. It really, really, really could happen, Damon Albarn croons.

OH GOD. What? What could happen? Come on, Albarn. Stop being so sexy and beguiling. Now is not the time for *it* to happen. Not when I'm wearing corduroy flares and a Hello Kitty crop top and I can't remember whether I shaved my armpits. OH GOD. Is this what having a boyfriend is? Having to remember whether or not you shaved your armpits every day? Or just having to shave your armpits every day?

I mean, shouldn't I be wearing something *sexy* (ugh) – or at the very least something where the zip isn't partially stuck and I have to jump up and down in order to get it off.

This is stressful. Like sweaty, unpleasant, band-of-sweat-beneath my-crop-top stressful.

'Ellie?'

'Um, yeah,' I say, as Ash stops kissing me.

'Are you talking to yourself?'

'Er, no?' I answer weakly.

'Because you were kind of gesticulating as if you were talking to yourself.'

'Was I?'

He grins, his faded blue T-shirt the colour of sky, and puts his head close to mine, our foreheads touching.

'You are not,' he says, putting his hands into mine, 'allowed,' he says, kissing my forehead, 'to think about other things,' he kisses my neck, 'when we,' he says, pointing to him and then me, 'are kissing,' and one hand is back in my hair. 'Is that understood?' he chastises gently.

'I'm not,' I lie.

'Good,' he replies, cupping my face in his hands, and this time it's hard to think about anything else except how good it feels to be near him. How I spent months wanting nothing more than for him to be categorically and undeniably mine; and now he is.

But then there are my nipples. My brown nipples. Which a girl once told me, when I was getting changed for swimming, were 'brown! I didn't realise your nipples would be brown; but I suppose it makes sense', and ever since that moment, I have realised that not everyone has brown nipples. I'm not sure why I've suddenly remembered that. But I wonder whether I should warn him. Or whether he has brown nipples, because he's half brown, or whether it doesn't really matter, because his mother is brown, and so surely he has some visceral, instinctive understanding of brown nipples, or . . .

'Ellie?' he says, grabbing my ear and tugging it. 'Earth to Ellie Pillai. Come in, Ellie Pillai.'

4

'Oh God, sorry. Was I doing it again?'

'Yes,' he says, looking slightly concerned, his hand coming down to rest on his washed-out black jeans. 'Are you OK? Is *this* OK? Because we can stop if you want to.'

And honestly, I never want to stop kissing Ash Anderson, it's just that I'm *me*, and sometimes that makes things slightly problematic.

I lace my arms around the back of his head, pulling him closer.

'You,' I say, kissing his cheek, 'don't need to worry,' I kiss his other cheek, 'about me,' I say, feeling the softness of his mouth beneath mine.

And this time, I let Damon Albarn do all the talking; because someone else has to, and my mouth is otherwise engaged.

3

I'm Not Discussing This Over WhatsApp

Jessica:
what happened?

Hayley:
deets. all the deets.

Jessica:
✓ THAT.

Ellie:
what r u 2 blathering on abt?

Hayley:
WHAT HAPPENED?

Jessica:
what is blathering?

Ellie:

not discussing this over WhatsApp

Hayley:

facetime?

Ellie:

no

Jessica:

zoom?

Ellie:

NO

Hayley:

do u want 2 kno what happened when
i went 2 James's house?

Ellie:

YES

Hayley:

i'm not discussing it over WhatsApp

I genuinely hope nothing *actually* happened when Hayley went to James's house, because as she told me last term, she's a feminist vlogger and he's a footballer, which really shouldn't make any sense – it's just, *they do*. But it isn't going to take much for this delicate balance of the universe to tip completely off its axis.

7

Ellie:
FINE. 2m?

Jessica:
☕?

Ellie:
tea

Jessica:
the spoke – 11?

Hayley:
FINE

Ellie:
FINE

Jessica:
drama queens

Hayley:
ty.

Jess:
😄

Ellie:
♥ this new group chat

4

The One

On the way home from Ash's house, The Beatles, 'Drive My Car' is playing on repeat in my head – or possibly in real life – because it's hard to tell the difference between daydreams and reality when you are dating a green-eyed Timothée Chalamet lookalike.

In the back seat, I furtively reply to the messages from Jess and Hayley, while Ash drives, with his mum up front directing him. He's weeks away from turning eighteen and taking his driving test the same day. A week after that, I turn sixteen – and yeah, that feels kind of *big*. Like maybe it's *time*.

And even though it didn't happen today (thanks, Hello Kitty crop top), it feels like when I'm sixteen, maybe it *should*. Because he's kind, and sweet, and maybe even The One. Even though we've been going out for approximately two days since I serenaded him and he met my parents over dinner, today I met his mum too – as in My Boyfriend's Mum, as opposed to just My Favourite Teacher. It's strange how quickly things happen when they Actually Start Happening. How calling him my boyfriend feels completely normal now. Because I, Ellie Pillai, have a boyfriend, and he's kind, and sweet, and maybe even The One.

I smile to myself while trying not to think about Dad demanding we kept my bedroom door open last night, then appearing at random intervals like some kind of sergeant major planning an indiscriminate inspection.

As my phone buzzes again, I roll my eyes. What do those two clowns want now? Although I love the fact that for once I'm the one with *news*, and that finally my two clowns are getting on.

Mum:
ARE YOU OK? WILL YOU BE HOME SOON?

Ellie:
omw now. ash & his mum driving me.

And this is Mum panicking that she hasn't seen me in the last eight hours, because in Mum's head, any number of bad things can happen when she isn't there to prevent them. Which I get, because bad things do happen – like my brother Amis dying of leukaemia. Words I'm only just starting to be able to say in my head without wanting to cry. I just keep trying to explain to her that there's nothing she could have done to prevent that. Because we tried. We tried so hard, for so long.

Mum:
GREAT! SEE YOU SOON.

I clear my throat, trying to let the feeling pass.

Note to self: teach Mum to turn the caps lock off on her phone.

'I can't wait till I get my driving licence.' Ash cringes as he walks me to my door when we arrive. 'So I can drop you home on my own. I can't even kiss you,' he says, squeezing my hand meaningfully.

He's wearing a soft black jumper over his T-shirt now, his jeans loose and cuffed at the ankle – one side tucked unknowingly into a white sock, the laces of his paint-spattered Converse looped round and round their tops.

'But I can kiss you,' I smile, standing on my tiptoes and planting a gentle kiss on his lips – and Mavis from next door's lilac curtains are twitching at the mere hint of this scandal.

'Ellie. What time do you call this?' Dad barks, as he opens the door.

'Er, 6.15 p.m.?' I say, irritated.

'Hi, Mr Pillai,' Ash says, extending his hand.

'Ellie has a curfew,' he says sharply. 'It's 11 p.m. on weekends.'

'YES,' I say through gritted teeth. 'And its 6.15 p.m., Dad. So, looks like we made it . . .'

He opens his mouth to respond as Mum rushes forward.

'Ash!' she cries, enveloping him. 'Where's your mum?' she says, her hand caressing Phantom Baby.

'In the car,' he grins. Because there is nothing to do but grin and squeeze each other's hands while the awkwardness of this nightmare passes.

Mum peers out on to the driveway, waving like an overenthusiastic clown as she approaches the car and hustles Mrs Aachara inside.

Dear gods (any of them), please, just NO.

But my parents being distracted means Ash and I can finally go up to my bedroom without being watched, so I grab his hand and lead him upstairs, leaving Mrs Aachara to the mercy of Mum's hallway interrogation.

I nudge the door closed with my foot, and turn towards him as he nudges it back open.

'What are you doing?' I hiss.

'Your dad wants us to keep it open, Ellie,' he says, twirling a lock of my hair around his finger. 'And as he doesn't exactly love me, I'm not planning to make it any worse.'

'He just doesn't know you yet. When he finds out you're a Bowie fan, he'll love you more than I do.'

'So, you love me, do you?' he smirks.

'Er, no,' I splutter. 'I mean . . .'

Oh God.

What?

What Did I Mean?

'I'm joking,' he teases. 'It's been two days.'

And I know I don't *love* him, love him – but I feel like I *could* love him. Like maybe that's possible. Like maybe that's not so funny.

'Actually,' he says, watching me carefully, 'it's been about three months. Because I haven't thought about much else since the first day I met you,' and now David Bowie, 'Moonage Daydream' is playing – probably just in my head, but who can tell any more – as the boy with green eyes looks at me and the world stands still. Which would be much more romantic if Bowie wasn't singing about an alligator.

'Ash,' comes a low voice from the doorway. 'Nimi wants to know if you'd like anything.'

Dad.

We spring apart.

'Er, no. Thank you,' Ash says, pushing me away from him.

I nod vigorously at him, trying to convey with my eyes: You Must Accept Dad's Hospitality.

'I mean . . . yes?' he says, staring at me, confused.

'What?' Dad says, his eyes trained to Ash's face like some kind of ninja.

'A drink?' he asks, looking at me again. I nod encouragingly. 'And something to . . . eat . . . ?' He trails off.

'Hmmmmmnnn,' Dad says, narrowing his eyes at him before he makes for the stairs.

'Are you regretting this?' I say, suddenly panicked. I bet that Hannah girl who seems to comment on every Instagram he has ever posted doesn't have parents who are either killing you with kindness or food, or just trying to plain kill you. I bet anyone would be less work to go out with than me.

'What do you think?' he smiles, tucking a stray hair behind my ear.

Minutes later, Mum appears at the top of the stairs with a cup of chai and some biscuits.

'Here you go,' she says, placing them next to Ash – and I swear she even winks a little as she closes the door gently behind her.

Dear gods, thank you for making my mum normal.

Even if it's only sometimes.

♡ Song 1 ♡

Verse, Chorus, Middle Eight – Perfect Things

There's a beauty in imperfection. In the incomplete. A story half told and a chance to write its ending.

Perfection is transitory. Momentary. A million moments of perfection, in a life imperfect.

And the sound of being almost in love is the low sweet thrum of an A below middle C; a trouser leg tucked egregiously into a white sock; it's him and me, me and him, a face close to mine in a moon-laced dream.

Somehow it makes sense, even if it doesn't.

They're just stories
You know that you should not believe in
They're not real
There's no such thing as perfect things.

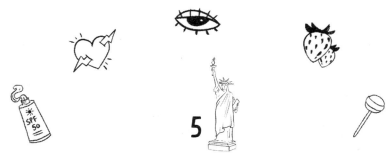

5

New York, New York

The next morning, I've set my alarm to meet Jess and Hayley, but instead I get woken up by screaming.

I run down to the kitchen, my John and Yoko 'War Is Over' T-shirt pulled hastily over the Hello Kitty crop top I fell asleep in. It really is alarmingly comfortable, although disturbing it still fits.

'What's going on?' I mumble, panicked.

'Ellie!' Mum shrieks.

'What's wrong?' I say, my heart racing. 'Is it the baby?'

'Nothing's wrong,' she says, turning to me. 'In fact, everything's perfect. AMAZING,' she says, waving a piece of paper in my face.

'Oh, OK,' I say, sitting down heavily, because this is not the way to be woken on the first Sunday of the Christmas holidays.

'New York!' she shrieks.

'What about New York?' I yawn.

'First-class tickets! To spend Christmas in New York! With Aunty Kitty and Granny.'

'What?' I say, my mouth suddenly open like a Venus flytrap – and my heart is racing again, for all the right reasons.

New York.

'For all of us. We're all going. All the Pillais. Kitty's had a promotion. She's paying for all our tickets and hotel rooms. She said it's a Christmas present for your grandmother.'

'New York,' I mutter again, incredulously. 'New York, Mum? Are you sure?'

'YES,' Mum grins. 'The tickets arrived this morning, and I just got the email from Kitty.'

'When?' I grin deliriously.

'What's all this *noise*?' Dad says grumpily, as he walks into the kitchen, rubbing his eyes.

'New York!' Mum shrieks again, and she repeats the news.

'When?' Dad says, taken aback.

'Wednesday. We've got so much to do!' Mum says, suddenly panicked.

'Calm down, Nimi, think of the baby,' Dad says, leading her to the kitchen table.

'Dover Street Market . . .' Mum whispers, her eyes wide. 'I've always wanted to go. I mean, I know I can't *afford* anything, but I can *look*. I've always wanted to look . . .'

'Wednesday?' I say suddenly. 'This Wednesday? For how long?'

'Two weeks. Until the day before you go back to school, Ellie,' Mum says dreamily. 'Sephora . . .' she whispers in an almost religious fervour.

'So, the whole holiday?' I ask slowly. Because I can't help but think

16

about Ash. About all the time I was hoping to spend with him, away from school, just the two of us.

'For goodness' sake, Ellie,' Dad says distractedly, googling 'Plaza' on his phone – Aunty Kitty appears to have booked us into some kind of celebrity hotel for our stay. I hope the real Timothée Chalamet is there. Actually, I don't. I'd rather have the half-Indian, green-eyed, English version instead. 'It's two weeks. That boy will be here when you get back.'

'That *boy* is called Ash,' I say, dangerously low.

Mum turns to me, smoothing her hands over my hair.

'It's *New York,* Ellie,' she breathes. 'You've always wanted to go. Maybe we can do one of those open mic things Kyra was telling me about last night. I bet they have those in New York. She thinks you need to perform more. What did she say?' She turns to Dad. 'Hone your craft as a performer?'

And I think: oh God, no.

But still.

I've always wanted to go to an open mic night, just to listen. I've always wanted to see the Empire State Building and the Statue of Liberty and walk around SoHo pretending I'm not some hick from a little east England village. Because when you're in New York, you're just *cool,* even when you are categorically Not Cool.

And the more I think about it, the more even the thought of Ash isn't making it any less blinding.

I'm going to New York.

New York, New York.

So good, Sinatra named it twice.

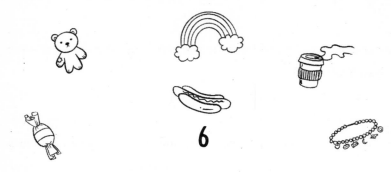

6

I Could Be Happy

On the bus into town, I message Ash.

Ellie:
meet ltr?

Ash:
mine?

Ellie:
mtg jess & hay now – in a couple hrs?

Ash:
♥

And the heart in his message makes me feel warm, and somewhere between happy and a little bit sad, because I know it's only two weeks, but I'll miss him – although technically that would be missing something I've never really had, because it's been *three days*.

I just like the idea that if I want to see him, I can. Which I can't – not in New York.

But.

New York.

It's like my heart is split into two entirely separate pieces, and they both feel guilty for caring what the other one wants.

I step off the bus, my headphones jammed over my ears, thinking about how different the Christmas holidays feel this year, about how different *everything* feels this year. I click into Altered Images, 'I Could Be Happy' and huddle into my oversized brown teddy coat, my sunglasses balanced precariously on my nose as the light refracts off the pavement. I can see my breath in clouds before me as I imagine climbing a tree with Clare Grogan.

This year has been full of surprises. Not just me and Ash, but Hayley, who spent most of her time fighting with James – a footballing know-it-all from our drama group – finally admitting she had feelings for him when he confessed he wanted to do more than just fight with her (obviously, they still argue about *everything*) – and Jess coming out as bisexual when she started dating Elina, Ash's twin sister, who is both incredibly beautiful and seriously terrifying when she thinks you're messing her brother around.

The Jess thing was hard, not least because while she was figuring things out with Elina, they made it look like she and Ash were dating, and for me, developing feelings for my best-friend's-supposed-boyfriend was Not Exactly the Best. And that doesn't even get into Jess's mum walking out on her when she told her about Elina, or the fact she'd been hiding her mum's bipolar disorder from everyone, while she struggled to care for her. All in all, things haven't been easy for Jess, but seeing how happy she is with Elina, watching her thrive at her dad's while her mum gets the help she needs – there are no words. No one is kinder or sweeter or nicer, or more annoyingly beautiful and clever, as Jess. She's the best – and she *deserves* the best. I just wish her girlfriend didn't borderline hate me for not telling Ash how I felt about him as soon as I knew he and Jess hadn't been together. Which is that I almost love him, and I pretty much have from the moment he sent me a link to Radiohead, 'Street Spirit'.

When I reach the Spoke, I press pause on my headphones and peer inside. Jess's wide-leg jeans are making her resemble a *Charlie's Angels*-era Farrah Fawcett, while Hayley's dressed in leather leggings and an oversized red-and-black striped jumper, like a cross between Dennis the Menace and an incognito member of Hole. Their heads are bent low as they talk to each other, the mint tea they've ordered in a pot by the space they've saved for me. A few weeks ago, these two could barely be in the same room, and I can't explain how happy this change in events makes me.

'Hi.' I wave overenthusiastically, my eyes slightly teary as I walk towards them.

'Why are you waving like that?' Hayley asks. 'You look like you're signalling a plane.'

'Nice to see you too . . .' I say, rolling my eyes at Jess.

'Are you *crying*?' Hayley asks suspiciously.

'No . . .' I offer, gulping.

'It's just coffee, Ellie, we're not braiding each other's hair or anything,' Hayley says sarcastically.

'Oh, shut up, Hay, you know you love her,' I say, motioning towards Jessica.

'She's all right,' she admits begrudgingly.

'Thanks . . .' Jess says, raising an eyebrow. 'Anyway,' she says, turning to me, 'we've barely spoken since Friday – what happened with you and Ash?'

'Nothing . . .' I blush.

'Please tell me I didn't drag myself out of bed on a Sunday morning to hear the word *nothing*,' Hayley says crabbily.

'Well, it didn't!'

'You have to give me something to work with here,' she continues, pushing a piece of croissant around her plate with a fork.

'Are you going to eat that?' I ask her. She glares at me, pushing the pastry to the side of her plate.

'Have it,' she says, motioning towards it. 'Just say something other than *nothing*.'

'FINE,' I say, picking it up between my fingers and attempting not to cover myself in pastry crumbs. 'We kissed a lot, and there was some Under the Shirt Stuff, but he couldn't get past my Hello Kitty crop top.'

'You're joking,' Jess says, leaning back in her chair.

'Ha ha,' I say between mouthfuls, and then, 'No. I'm not.'

'Oh God, Ellie. Why were you wearing that thing?'

'I found it at the back of my underwear drawer,' I say, dusting my hands off. 'Are you sure you don't want any of this?' I ask, turning back to Hayley. She shakes her head.

'What were you looking for in the back of your underwear drawer . . . ?' she asks, leaning forward excitedly.

'Nothing. I mean, well, I was looking for something to wear because my dad melted my bras.'

She gapes at me, as Jess grins.

'He put them in a hot wash. Like, ninety degrees or something.'

'Wow. That's passive aggressive . . .' she continues almost admiringly.

'I knew he wouldn't take it well when you started dating,' Jess smirks.

'Why'd you say that?' I demand.

'Have you *seen* your dad anytime anyone even *looks* at your mum, which, by the way, is everyone, a lot. Because, you know, *your mum*. Anyway, he's just overprotective, E. You must know that.'

But Dad hasn't really had a reason to be overprotective before, so I guess I've never noticed.

'He's being so embarrassing,' I sigh.

'Your dad might be embarrassing, but at least he's around,' Hayley says despondently.

'You're right . . .' I admit, sneaking a look at Jess. She's got that faraway look she gets sometimes. The one where I know she's thinking about her mum.

'So, what's going on with your dad then?' I ask Hayley gently. She pushes the last few crumbs of croissant to the side of her plate, piling them up piece by piece.

'Nothing *new*,' she replies, staring into space. Jess and I exchange a look.

'OK then,' Jess says, turning towards Hayley. 'What happened when you went to see Sugar Mice Nipples?'

'Who?' she says, glaring at her.

'She means James,' I mutter hastily.

'Then why did she say *Sugar Mice Nipples*?'

'Long story . . .' I say uncomfortably.

'Sounds like a short story to me,' she responds menacingly. So, we tell her all about the chest pics and a thirteen-year-old James pretending he was Ryan Gosling.

And she laughs, like, really laughs. One of those belly laughs where you can't help but join in.

'I can't wait to use this against him,' she crows.

'So, what happened?' Jess probes.

'I don't know,' she succumbs, 'it's just his house is so *perfect*, and he has these perfect parents and a dog called Hugo, who looks like he should be in an ad for a magazine called *People with Perfect Dogs*.'

Jess snorts and I shoot her a look.

'Sorry,' she says. 'It was funny.'

'I mean, who calls a dog *Hugo*?'

Jess nods along seriously.

'Anyway, when I went to his house on Friday, his parents were there and they were just so *nice*, and they kept asking about my family . . . and the way they are with each other . . . I mean, I don't even know where my dad *is*. I just miss how it was before Nina went to uni – when it was me and Mum and Nina, and I never even thought about my dad.' Her voice cracks as Jess leans over to grab her hand.

'I get it,' she says, smiling.

'Yeah, well,' Hayley says quietly. 'When I win my first Oscar, I'm pretty sure that's when he'll decide I'm the daughter he never had. Except, he has a daughter. He has TWO,' she says forcefully.

'His loss,' I say gently.

She ignores me, so in the silence that follows, I say, 'I need to tell you both something. I'm going to New York. For Christmas. My aunt sent us tickets.'

Hayley's mouth falls open. 'I'm so jealous I could stab you with a fork,' and by the state of the violently dismembered croissant on her plate, this concerns me somewhat. 'Do you think you'll get to see something on Broadway?'

'Maybe,' I smile.

'So, why don't you look happier about it?' Jess queries, inspecting my face.

'I don't know. Ash and I have only *just* started going out . . . it's Christmas . . .'

'Ash? Who cares about Ash? You're going to New York, E!' Hayley says, wide-eyed. *New York, New York.*

'*I* care about Ash,' I say, surprising myself. 'I care about him a lot, Hay. And I know you care about James, so you can't let any of this derail the two of you.'

'Derail us? I'm not a train,' she says, appalled.

'But you're on *track*,' I continue seriously.

24

'For what?' she says, amused. 'Heartbreak and high drama?'

'Listen, Hayley,' Jess says rousingly. 'None of us thought we were going to be in the relationships we're in right now, but we are. Do you like Sugar Mice Nipples?' she quizzes.

'Yesss,' Hayley admits begrudgingly.

'Well, he likes you, and Ash likes Ellie, and I have the hottest girlfriend on the planet – and these are all good things. We just need to embrace them, and if other people don't want to get on board with that, then frankly they can suck it.'

'Suck it,' I respond, holding the spoon from my mint tea aloft.

'Come on,' Jess says, shouldering Hayley. 'What can they do?'

'Suck it,' she says, clinking her fork against my spoon.

And that's it. We've all decided. Anyone who's not on board with this mysterious alignment of the universe can suck it.

Suck. It.

7

The Shoop Shoop Song

On the way out of the Spoke, Jess turns to me.

'You going to Ash's?'

I nod.

'Elina?' I respond.

She grins.

'Great,' Hayley enthuses. 'Just *me* then.'

'Come with us?' Jess says, taking her arm.

'I'm going to James's,' she says glumly.

We hug Hayley goodbye and walk towards the 66 bus stop. Ash and Elina live near the city centre, but it's halfway up a hill, and starting to drizzle.

'How are things with you and Elina then?' I ask, linking arms with her. She's wearing platform boots and I'm in my Vans Old Skools, barely up to her elbow.

'Good. Really good. I like her, E, like *a lot*,' she says emphatically. And I can see that look of worry on her face. Like she knows that liking someone might end up hurting.

'Still not my biggest fan, is she?'

'She'll get over it,' she admits.

Elina and I haven't exactly seen eye to eye – but I'm determined to show her how much I care about Ash, that I'm not going to hurt him.

'I really like him, Jess,' and now it's my turn to look worried.

'I know, E – and I love you, so she'll have to get over it.'

We get on the bus in companionable silence, while in my head Betty Everett is serenading me with 'The Shoop Shoop Song (It's in His Kiss)' as I watch the street signs pass by, rolling my shoulders to the beat.

Does he love me, Betty? Because I do want to know. Even if it has only been three days – *could* he love me? Could someone like him love someone like me? And I imagine myself with a beehive and a form-fitting dress, my arms waving up and down in front of me, like I was in a sixties girl group in another life.

'We're here.' I follow Jess off the bus, waving to Betty on the back seats.

When we arrive, Mrs Aachara answers.

'Hey, girls. Elina's in the living room,' she says, motioning towards the back of the house, 'and Ash is upstairs.' I smile and thank her, nodding goodbye to Jess as I make my way up the stairs.

The Verve, 'Sonnet' is blaring loudly from his bedroom, and I knock loudly, trying to get him to hear me. I push the door open and peer inside. He's wearing a white T-shirt and loose dark blue jeans, with an apron covered in paint, his feet bare on the floorboards.

'Ash!' I shout over the music.

He turns to me, smiling, and gathers me in his arms, picking me up off the ground.

'Hello,' he grins, kissing my nose.

'Hello,' I reply shyly, feet dangling in the air.

He places me back down, and I walk towards his bed and take off my Vans, throwing my teddy coat on his pillow.

'Hello,' he says again meaningfully, as he sits down next to me. My miniskirt is hitching up my thighs and I pull at it awkwardly; his hand beneath the back of my T-shirt, his fingers cold against my skin.

'I have news,' I say, inching away from him.

'What's that?' he says, his fingers circling my back.

'I'm spending Christmas in New York.'

He sits back a little, watching me.

'My aunt sent us tickets. For my dad's whole family. We leave Wednesday.'

'When do you get back?' he asks slowly.

'The day before school starts . . .'

'Oh,' he says disappointedly.

'I know,' I say, taking his hand. 'But it's only two weeks, and just think of the amazing present I'll bring you back.'

'OK,' he says, pulling me closer. 'But you can be my present.'

'So, what are you painting?' I ask, suddenly worried about what being a present entails.

He turns towards the picture; not yet quite anything, but the outline of a shape.

'It's my dad,' he smiles. 'It's a mixed-media collage. It'll be bits of newsprint, part painting, part photography. It's the first time I've felt ready to draw him,' he says animatedly.

'That's great,' I grin, proud of him.

'That's *you*,' he says, his lips beginning to caress my neck.

And I look at him and wonder how someone so soulful and beautiful, and clever and lovely, can be interested in kissing *me* – but before I can overthink it and start gesticulating again, there's a knock at the door.

'Do you guys want to watch a film with us?' Elina asks, rolling her eyes from the doorway. She's wearing a mid-length green floral tea dress with a wide tan belt, and a painter's shirt beneath it. The sort of outfit she's spent approximately zero time thinking about, but looks painstakingly put together. And my Cramps T-shirt tucked into my black miniskirt suddenly feels incredibly basic. Like I should have been refused entry at the door.

'Sounds good,' I say, turning towards her. She eyes me warily, even though beneath the disdain I can at least see she's trying.

'We'll be down in a minute,' Ash says, turning to her; but the way he's looking at me is starting to make me sweat, so I turn to Elina instead.

'Elina, could I borrow a jumper?' Which I know is counterintuitive when you're starting to sweat, but I need to get my Hello Kitty crop top out of this room.

'OK,' she says, beckoning me towards her room across the hall.

'You know you can borrow one of *my* jumpers, right?' Ash says, holding on to my T-shirt.

'I'm just trying to talk to her,' I whisper, as if that was the only reason.

'And *I'm* trying to talk to *you* . . .' he whispers back, holding on to my T-shirt.

'Let go,' I say, swatting at him.

'No,' he says, laughing, and suddenly I look like one of those cartoon mice, tiny and belligerent, a comedy cat's paw pinning down my tail.

'Stop that!' I snort, swatting at him again.

'No. I want you to stay here,' he teases.

'Do you want a jumper or not, Ellie?' Elina asks irritably, stalking up to the door. I widen my eyes at Ash, and he lets go. Nobody wants Elina and me to get on more than he does.

I follow her into her room and stand at the door while she picks her way through a dresser, no doubt looking for a jumper that will make me look as hideous as possible. My eyes pause at the corner of the room, where a picture is sat upright against a stack of books.

'Cool portrait,' I say, pointing towards the painting. It's about the size of an A3 piece of paper, but it's painted on canvas, boxy and solid. It's the top half of a girl, from her head down to her mid shoulders. Wavy black hair and dark brown skin, her eyes fiery. In the background is a kaleidoscope of colours that make her dark eyes glint with life. Like mine, her eyes are a myriad of browns, but they seem almost multicoloured in the picture, like the artist can see something beneath them, not visible to anyone else.

'Thanks,' she says offhandedly.

'Who is she?' I ask. She reminds me of my cousin. Of a better version of me.

'Just an old friend,' she says, not looking at the picture.

She passes me an oversized blush jumper and I pull it on over my T-shirt.

'I love that colour on you,' she says, momentarily forgetting she hates me. I see my reflection in the mirror on her dresser, and I wonder why I don't wear more colour. Why I'm still so frightened of anybody noticing me. And I want to stop that. Stop being afraid of that.

But as nice as she's being, I can't help wondering how Jess feels about the portrait. About the air around it, thick with feeling.

As we walk out of the room, she picks the painting up and pushes it roughly down the side of her dresser.

'It's nobody special,' she says, as I watch her doing it.

8

New York Wednesday

Three days later, and a million hours spent with Ash and a firmly open door (that I've come to realise isn't as annoying as I thought it was), and New York Wednesday finally arrives. I've spent ages packing and repacking my suitcase, trying to put together outfits that are cool enough for the world's coolest city. I'm not sure whether black T-shirts (mostly with New York band references), jeans, black skirts, black tights, black studded ankle boots and my Vans quite live up to this expectation, but I've thrown in a bright pink corduroy boiler suit Jess forced me to buy but I've never had the nerve to wear. Because if there's a place to wear a bright pink corduroy boiler suit, it's New York, New York.

At 4 a.m., Mum, Dad and I drove from our sleepy east England village towards Heathrow airport, on the way fielding a million calls from the uncles, asking questions about which car park we're booked into, who's responsible for taking Granny's supply of Penguin chocolate bars, PG Tips and Marmite, and who's sitting with who on the flight. I'm exhausted, and its barely 9 a.m.

Our flight leaves at midday, and Mum's desperate to hit the duty-free, even going so far as to promise to buy me something if I help protect her from Granny. None of the family know Mum's pregnant yet and we have no idea how they're going to react – but at just under four months, it's impossible to hide. She looks suspiciously like she's hiding a semi-inflated football under her jumper, although being Mum, she's managed to make the look both stylish and flattering.

When we've parked and Dad's wrestled our suitcases on to a trolley, we head towards the check-in desk for first class. In front of us is a bickering brown family, already short from the journey to the airport.

'Delia, I told you *Amma* doesn't like Yorkshire Tea. She must have her PG Tips!' And it looks like Big Uncle is getting started early with his Granny-related paranoia.

'She has enough orange pekoe to drown a man. From Sri Lanka! Why does she want PG Tips? Is substandard compared to our tea.'

'I don't know,' he huffs, 'but you know how she is. She doesn't ask for much, *en anbe*.' His wife exhales loudly. Granny doesn't *ask* for much, it's more the weight of her expectation.

'Benn,' Dad says, tapping his shoulder. 'We have PG Tips.'

'Thank God,' Big Uncle breathes.

Joseph, Peter and Esther, my cousins, are stood silently by their sides: Joseph glued to his phone, Peter playing on an iPad, and Esther, shy and quiet, hugging her mother's legs.

Their bags are put through quickly and they're whisked away to the first-class lounge. I've never flown first class, never even been upgraded, and I am literally as excited as I have ever been about flying on a giant tube in the sky, when I have no idea exactly how it stays up there.

I stand behind Mum and Dad at the check-in desk, my foot tapping the floor impatiently, until I hear my phone buzz.

Ash:

r u at the ✈ yet?

I feel a momentary pang of guilt at my excitement, soon to be replaced by annoyance.

'Can you look up, please?' The check-in assistant is looking up and down at the picture on my passport, then at me, so many times it's starting to make me sweat. Dad says you should never annoy people at airports, even if they're annoying you. That the rules are different inside these strange white boxes, people can shoot you, or lock you up, or stop you from getting where you're going, just because they can. Sometimes, just because you're not white.

'You look different,' she muses.

'I was eleven,' I fake smile. That picture was taken after an argument with Mum, and my face is small and sullen, my eyebrows forming one long arc across my forehead, from the days before I learned to tweeze.

'Ugly ducklings,' the woman smiles, handing the picture back to me. And I wonder what would happen if I told her there's No Such Thing as an ugly duckling, just people who make stupid, thoughtless comments.

When our bags are halfway down the luggage conveyor, I look back at my phone, and try to remember I'm not eleven any more. That I'm almost sixteen. That people can only make me feel the way I *allow* them to make me feel. That I don't have to listen to that voice in my head, the one that tells me I'm not good enough, that I'll never be good enough.

Shut up, voice!

I look at my phone and tap a reply.

Ellie:

omw 2 first class. don't hate me . . . .

Ash:

hate u not being here

And a sudden rush of missing this other person hits me. Like the sensation of falling, when you're completely out of control.

Ellie:

miss u already

Hayley would kill me for this message. She would revoke the FEMINIST badge she gave me on my fifteenth birthday and replace it with one that said PATHETIC CLICHÉ.

Ash:

call me when u get there 💗

A heart. An actual, beating heart.

'Hey, Ellie.'

And there goes *that* moment. That perfect, stood in the airport waiting for someone to run in and tell you they almost love you moment. Replaced with Hope Pillai in the first-class lounge; and I believe that's what's called an oxymoron. Because there is nothing hopeful about spending the next two weeks with my cousin Hope.

'I'm going to get a blow-dry. They're free in here. You can come with me. You look like you need one.'

'Hi,' I manage through gritted teeth.

'Do you wear anything other than black?' she says breezily. Which is annoying, because I planned this outfit for days. My favourite black jeans with a Velvet Underground sweatshirt, studded boots and the shearling coat Aunty Kitty bought for me. I thought I looked like a young, brown Debbie Harry. Which is admittedly mixing my NYC band references, but still.

'We've been here for ages,' she says, as I ignore the comment, and I have to admit her black hiker boots paired with wide-leg jeans, crop top and sand-coloured trench coat make her look like an off-duty supermodel.

Damn. It.

Although a very *cold* supermodel. Because who wears a crop top in *December*?

An off-duty supermodel, obviously.

Ugh.

'I think the aunties were waiting for your mum to get here, so they

36

could go to the duty-free.' When I turn around to look, Mum has fully dumped me for Aunty Delia, Aunty Christine and Aunty Helen – who are all cooing over her baby bump in a slightly hysterical manner, while the uncles pat my dad on the back like a man that's just scored the winning run in a cricket match.

'Mum,' I shout. 'Are you going?'

She hurries over and envelops Hope into a hug.

'Are you excited?' she asks her. 'For New York.'

'I can't wait, Aunty,' she replies, and then 'congratulations' as she hugs Mum again. It almost looks sincere, except I'm not sure that's in her repertoire of stock emotions.

'Ellie, the aunties and I need to pick up some things. You girls are welcome to come – or you could just get your hair done with Hope?' she asks hopefully; and the irony of her *hopefulness* both annoys and kills me. Mum spent an hour last night trying to convince me to spend more time with Hope while we were away – because we're The Same Age, which apparently means we should have Something in Common.

When we were little, Hope and I *were* close. We gravitated towards each other at family events, because back then she was less evil. But then she turned eleven, and suddenly she was the most beautiful thing anyone had ever seen, and I was categorically not. She was popular and stylish and knew the names of all the Bollywood stars, and I did not. We drifted apart – first slowly, then emphatically, then all at once – and after that came the meanness. Comments about my clothes, or my weight, or my inability to speak Tamil, and suddenly the cousin that had held my hand at Amis's funeral was gone. Replaced by some glamazon Bollywood girl who looked right through me.

'I don't really need to get my hair done,' I sulk.

Hope snorts.

'Come with us then,' Mum says distractedly, and I can tell at this stage that she's only interested in getting to the MAC counter.

'It's fine – you go. I need to call Ash anyway.'

'Who's Ash?' Hope says, suddenly interested. 'You can tell me while we're getting our hair done.' She drags me away before I have a chance to argue.

As we settle into our seats and wait for our hair to be washed, Hope turns to me.

'Apparently we're sharing a room at the hotel.'

Oh God, kill me.

Or rather, Don't Let Me Kill Her.

I say nothing, and stare down at the beating heart emoji on my phone.

'Is that your boyfriend?' she asks, motioning at the phone.

'Ash? Yeah.'

'When did you start dating?' – and I wonder why her tone sounds so normal.

'A couple of weeks ago,' I reply – but actually, it's been six days.

'You weren't seeing anyone when I saw you at half-term. Anyway,' she continues, 'it's good we're sharing a room. We can cover for each other. Have some fun.'

And now the breeziness and non-hostility is starting to make sense.

She wants me to lie for her, so she can go out and do whatever it is that Hope Pillai does.

'You have to be twenty-one to get in anywhere, so I don't think we're likely to need covers,' I say slowly.

'We'll see,' she smirks.

She tips her head back as the stylist motions for her to put her hair in the basin.

'Tell me about Ash,' she demands over the sound of running water.

'Um . . .' And I can't really think how to describe him. The boy in the yellow rain mac, who I like/almost love, who gets that I listen to Radiohead when I'm sad and Taylor Swift when I'm trying not to be. So I'm grateful when my stylist takes me to the opposite side of the salon and I don't have to explain him.

Thirty-five blissful, Hope-free minutes later, she sashays over to where I'm leafing through a magazine, her long black hair poker straight and parted down the middle, like an advert for argan oil.

'Wow,' she says, looking at me, which is when I realise I've spent so long avoiding eye contact with her that I haven't even looked at myself. My hair, which is more of a dark brown than her intense black, is curled into beachy waves, its layers hugging my face. Its artful, but at the same time effortless and pretty.

'You look . . . nice,' she manages, choking on the words.

'Thanks, so do you.'

'Let's see a picture of him then,' she demands.

I open up my photos and the first picture I find is a selfie of Ash and me, his face hidden slightly behind mine, the two of us grinning like Cheshire cats.

'He's hot,' she admits. 'Is he mixed?'

'His mum's Indian. How did you know?'

'Everyone I go to school with is, like, from everywhere. Not like where you are.'

It's annoying that she's right. That Hope would never have thought Ash was having some kind of Freudian relationship with his own mother, because she lives in London, where there are more *other* kinds of people. People that look like Ash and me.

'How's Vikash?' I ask, trying to change the subject.

'Fine,' she says, looking away. For a minute, I think she looks a bit upset, but before I can ask, my phone buzzes again.

Ash:

miss u too

I smile, just as she reads the message over my shoulder.

'It's always like that at the beginning.' She smiles patronisingly. 'He won't even remember your name in two weeks.'

And I want to tell her she's a liar. That she doesn't know anything about us.

But I'm too worried she might be right.

9

The Home of
Vampire Weekend

On the flight, I'm sat in the pod across from Dad. He's flattened his seat into a bed and is lying down, his earphones in, staring out of the window.

For a minute, I wish I was little again. I wish I could lie next to my dad, with one of his earphones in my ear. It always felt like we were sharing something so profound; like him letting me hear what he was hearing meant I could see inside him a little bit.

I put my head against the window and look out across the seats, wondering what Dad's listening to. The aunties are gossiping loudly while a businessman tries to sleep; Joseph is asking the air hostess for his fifth Coca-Cola, which does not bode well for his already hyper-annoying personality; and Andrew, my favourite cousin, is reading a book about some kind of skeleton detective.

But mostly, I notice Hope, sat across the aisle, staring out of the window blankly. I heard her arguing with her mum before we boarded.

I close my eyes and think about New York. About bagels and Broadway and the home of Vampire Weekend. I try to remember those things, and grip tight to them, as I ignore Big Uncle's snoring from two rows behind me.

Christmas with the Pillais sounds like a movie. Whether it's a comedy, a horror or a true-crime documentary (*Who Killed Cousin Hope?*) remains to be seen. Whatever it is, it definitely won't be boring.

And then I hear Middle Uncle's snoring from two rows in front, and remind myself it definitely won't be quiet either.

10

Miss Poolah

There are no words for New York City. New York is a city for which there are *no words*. Everything about it feels so . . . *American*. Glamorous, and exciting, and busy – and like Christmas, real Christmas, with snow and yellow taxis and Christmas trees taller than entire buildings in my village. Tom Petty, 'American Girl' feels like the soundtrack to my life, making me take it easy, baby, as we roll into the city.

I have been to America before. A million years ago, when Mum and Dad took Amis and me to Disneyland. Things were different then. Hopeful. We all wanted that holiday to be fun. We went out of our way to make it perfect; as if somehow fun had the power to make everything better, to erase the truth or make it more sanitary.

But being here now feels different. Like we've passed some kind of test, and we're emerging from the other side of a dark tunnel. Bright white snow and lights. I almost don't care that I'm sharing a room with Hope, because at least I can call Ash without Dad's eyes rolling backwards in his head, like a shark before it's just about to kill you.

When we get through the gruelling immigration queues and finally leave JFK, we hail two hundred taxis to ferry the Pillai clan and their luggage to the Plaza on Fifth Avenue.

The Plaza. I can almost forgive Aunty Kitty for every disparaging comment she's ever assisted Granny in making.

When we arrive at the hotel, I'm almost embarrassed by my family's loud, brash behaviour, except New York, it seems, is not. I watch a million other cars arriving at the hotel with equally loud, brash people inside, and accept that this could be the Pillais' spiritual homeland.

The building itself is beyond beautiful, rising majestically from the ground to occupy its space almost perfectly. It feels big and filmic, almost obscene in its opulence, yet it's not ostentatious, just striking and luxurious. We wander in, blinded by it. By the fact we're here, in it.

At the check-in desk, we're allocated our room cards. Hope and I are the only cousins to get our own room, which I can tell annoys Joseph and Andrew, who are both in family rooms with their parents and siblings. But Hope and I are older than them, sitting our GCSEs; at least that's what I tell myself when I feel a bit guilty about it.

'What do you think, Ellie?' Mum whispers, looking around in awe at the giant Christmas tree adorning the lobby.

'I can't believe we're *here*. And my own room! It's amazing, Mum.'

'Not missing Ash then?' She winks. I feel guilty that I've barely thought about Ash. 'I may have mentioned to Kitty that I thought you and Hope were old enough to enjoy your own space. Because I *know* we can *trust* you,' she says, turning to me menacingly. 'Can't we?'

'Of course,' I say, trying to reach my arms around her ever-expanding middle. 'Thank you so much! Not for the Hope thing, but, you know, for everything else,' I grin.

'Be nice to your cousin, please, Ellie,' Mum says, giving me The Look.

And I think: be nice *to her*? You should be telling her to be nice *to me*.

'Fine. But she'd better return the favour,' I complain under my breath.

When Hope and I get to our room, which is opposite Mum and Dad's, we aren't quite prepared for how spectacular it is. Two queen beds sit side by side, with large, ornate gold headboards, and the whitest, softest bed linen I've ever seen.

Hope runs towards one of the beds and springs into the air, landing on it with a muted thud. She bounces up and down, staring around her admiringly.

'Can you believe this?' she intones. I shake my head, walking around, peering into cupboards, then stepping into our bathroom, which appears to have gold taps.

A minute later, there's a knock at the door, and I walk out of the bathroom from where I've been stood, staring at the enormous tub and imagining myself in it. I open the door while Hope continues bouncing on the bed, oblivious.

Outside is what I believe the Americans term a bellboy. He's sort of good-looking, preppy and young, wearing a formal-looking blazer and what I imagine are too-tight dress trousers. Next to him is a trolley with Hope's and my dishevelled suitcases, looking out of place in the Plaza's immaculate corridor.

'Miss Poolaa?' he asks, smiling at me; and the smile is wide and fixed, but in my opinion a bit creepy.

'Poola?' Hope giggles, as she stops bouncing. I watch him watching her, in the way boys watch girls like Hope.

'It's Pill-ay,' I say, correcting him. He smiles and picks the suitcases up, placing them in the room, then stands back, waiting expectantly.

'*Tip him*,' Hope hisses. He looks away, used to the spectacle of two out-of-towners unsure of what to tip. But even as he's looking away, he's sort of grinning, his teeth whiter than I think teeth have any right to be.

'Um,' I say, fumbling in my bag for my purse. 'Do you take English money?'

'Of course, miss,' he smiles, 'but if you don't have anything to hand, I'd happily take your sister's phone number instead.' He grins at Hope like one of those *Wolf of Wall Street* types, with too neat a haircut and eyes the wrong side of black.

She smiles back at him, clearly flattered, then jumps off the bed and grabs a pen, writing her name and number on a piece of paper by the phone. She passes it to him seamlessly, with all the confidence of a girl used to being asked.

When he smiles again, I wonder how old he is. I wonder how old he *thinks* Hope is. I wonder if my parents are going to kill me if she tries to go on a date with him.

'Thanks,' he smirks, winking at her – and she winks back. Just like that. Like there's a code of coolness in this situation, and she's used to obeying the rules, when by this point, I would have fallen over, or spilt something on myself.

When he turns away and I close the door behind me, I look over at her half admiringly.

'Does that happen a lot?'

'Sometimes.' She grins.

'What about Vikash?' I ask, surprised.

'What about him?' She frowns. 'You need to lighten up, Ellie.'

And I think fine, I will. Because actually, I don't really care about Vikash, or Hope, or the Creepy Preppy Bellboy. Because I'm at *the Plaza*. So, even though I wish I wasn't sharing this room with my cousin and her insatiable appetite for drama, I run towards the bed and jump on it anyway.

Hope laughs and jumps back on top of hers.

I'm not sure how long we carry on jumping, but eventually we fall on top of the sheets, burning with laughter – and for a second, I think I recognise my cousin.

The one from before.

11

As God
Is My Witness

I get woken up at around 1 a.m. by a persistent buzzing from my phone. I force my hand out from under the covers to silence it, but every time I press it, another message appears in its place. I squint my eyes at the screen, trying not to let the jet lag take me down.

Hope:
wake up

Hope:
wake uppppppppp

Hope:
going out! come!!!!!!!

Hope:
where u?

I compel my eyes to open and stare at her bed, empty but for the pillows she's lumped under the covers in a makeshift shape. Her messages sound like she likes me. Like she wants me to go out and experience the vivid, dark beauty of New York's nightlife with her. They also sound like the ramblings of a drunk girl. A drunk girl that is out there with gods knows who, doing gods knows what, in Frank Sinatra's city.

Doesn't she know Sinatra was in the Mob?

I'm so tired my brain hurts, but if I don't find her, she'll inevitably get caught – which will inevitably lead to accusations of my complicity, which will inevitably lead to being punished for several decades or until I die, whichever comes first.

I push myself upright and pull my jeans on under the Strokes T-shirt I wore to bed.

This is what comes of sharing a room with Hope Pillai.

Ellie:

where r u?

Hope:

lobbbuy

I'm assuming she means the lobby. As in, the entrance to the hotel. *Discreet.*

I sigh and take the stairs, hoping I won't run into anyone. I'm not exactly expecting my family to be wandering the corridors at 1 a.m., but I once found my aunty Delia washing up when she was still asleep. We called it 'sleep washing' as if it was a hilarious joke, but sleepwalkers get violent when they're woken unexpectedly, and for about a year, I kept having nightmares about her smothering me with a tea towel.

When I get to the lobby, I find Hope exactly as expected, in one of the chairs that make up the waiting area, a concierge buzzing around her, part concerned, part irritated.

'Hope,' I say, descending on her. 'Are you OK?'

She looks at me blankly, her eyes glassy.

'This is my cuzzzzinn,' she says to the concierge primly. 'We're going ouuuuuutttt. Pleazzze get usss a taxxxii caaab.'

He rolls his eyes at me.

'No,' I say apologetically. 'We're not.'

'Don't be sooooo booooorrrrrinnng, Eleeeeannnnooor. When did you get soooo . . .' but she's forgotten the end of her sentence.

'They brought her down,' the concierge says carefully.

'Down?' I hiss. 'Where's she *been*?'

'I'm heeeerrrrre,' she replies, as if somehow affronted that I'm not addressing her directly.

'Hope, we need to get you to bed.'

'They liked my shooooes,' she says, pointing at her feet.

'Who? Who liked your shoes?'

'Twins!' she replies.

And all I can think about is the McQueen sisters, and if they have somehow teleported to New York to ruin my holiday.

'She means the Lennox sisters,' the concierge explains quietly. 'They live on the top floor.'

'People *live* in the Plaza?'

'We were waaattttchhing *Drag Raccccee*. Told them I was niiiinnneeteeeen,' Hope giggles.

The concierge looks away, as if pretending he can't hear her.

'And they just dumped you here? In this state? Lovely friends you've made there.'

'At least I *have* frieeeends,' she slurs.

'Clearly, you have no idea what that concept means,' I respond scathingly. But she's starting to fall asleep now, her chin on her chest, her breathing rhythmic.

'Hope!' I say, shaking her.

'Whhhaat!' she wails.

'You. Need. To. Go. To. Bed.'

'Fiiiinne,' she says, suddenly compliant.

'I'm very sorry about all this . . .' I stutter to the concierge.

He nods stiffly.

I pull her up and walk her to the elevator, because there's no way she's making the stairs, and when we get to our floor, I push her along the corridor, like I'd enjoy pushing her towards a firing line, with the rifles pointed directly at her.

'WHAT THE HELL, HOPE?' I whisper angrily.

'Shhhhhhh,' she says, stumbling.

When we reach the safety of our room, I drop her on the bed like a stone.

'I can't believe you did that! I can't believe you put yourself in that situation! You idiot! You absolute idiot, Hope!'

'You're riiiight,' she slurs, conciliatory. 'I'm an idiot. That's what eeeeveryone says.'

'What do you mean?' I stop: part furious, part disturbed.

'Mum. Dad. Vikash. Youuu. You all think I'm stuuupid, and I am.'

'I don't think you're stupid, Hope, I just think you *did* something stupid. There's a difference.'

'I should be more like yoooou, Ellie, right? That's what Mum says. Be less like *meeee*. Because I'm stuuuupid.'

'No,' I say, my fury subsiding. 'You're not stupid, no one thinks that – but what you just did, it could have ended completely differently. It could have ended really badly. Do you *understand* that?'

She starts crying.

'Hey,' I say, putting my arm around her, surprised. 'It's OK.'

'It'ssss nottt OK,' she sobs, pushing me off.

'What's wrong?'

'I'm not clever or talented or speccccial, Ellie. I'm not like *you*. I'm just pretty, that's all I am. Niiiiccce face, good shoes.' She laughs. 'Mum says it's not enough, but thisssss,' she says, pointing at her face, 'is what I am. And Vikash doesn't even *like* it. He doesn't like how I dress. Or my haiirrr. Or my make-up. Or, like, my whole pesronnnslity.'

'Sorry?'

'Pesronnnslity,' she says crossly; and I realise she means *personality*. Which seems like a harsh number of things to not like about someone you're supposed to be going out with.

I pause, trying to work out the best way to respond. Trying not to tell her that he sounds like the opposite of someone she should care about. That he sounds toxic.

'What about you, Hope?' I say gently. 'What do *you* like about *him*?'

But her breathing has softened into sleep now, her mascara smeared down the side of her face. And I want to ask her who the Lennox sisters are, and why she was watching *Drag Race* with them, and what she was doing in their hotel room when she should have been in bed. But mostly, I want to ask her if she's OK. *Really* OK.

I click into Instagram and scroll through her pictures, looking for signs of the girl I just spoke to. In her latest post she's wearing a green dress, looking happy, surrounded by friends. She looks healthy and young and startlingly, annoyingly, beautiful – but underneath it Vikash has commented:

not your colour babe 😁

I can feel my body tensing with the casual cruelty of it. With the words people say with no thought for the consequences. With the fact she cares what *he* thinks more than she cares what *she* thinks.

And I think: as God is my witness, I will wipe that laughing emoji off your face. Because nobody, but nobody, puts a Pillai in a corner. And as I'm drifting off to sleep, I realise I'm mixing my movie genres, in a possibly not good way. I just know whatever way you look at it, I don't know my cousin at all.

12

Cream Cheese, Lox and a Meet-Cute Bagel

The next morning Hope and I miss breakfast. I tell my parents it's because we're jet-lagged, but it's mostly because I'm holding her hair back while she vomits.

'Who are the Lennoxes?' I ask, as she holds her head over the toilet bowl.

'Eeeeeeeeerrrrrrrrrr,' she wails, her hand pressed tight against her forehead.

'What happened last night?'

'Nothing,' she whispers, as if even the sound of her own voice is giving her a headache. If only she could have been this thoughtful about the headaches she's given me with her voice in the past.

'Looks like it,' I sigh, as she continues moaning. And I want to laugh at her, but it's mostly just frustrating – I thought the two of us had made a breakthrough last night.

She looks at me from beneath her fingers.

'Fiiiine,' she replies. 'I met them in the lobby when I got out of bed last night. They're twins.'

I have a seriously worrying cosmic connection with twins. I used to think they were rare, but they keep coming into my life in a manner that suggests every other person is one.

'OK . . .'

'I was on my way out, and one of them said she liked my shoes. She said New York was boring . . .'

'*Boring?*' I reply, scandalised. 'New York is *not* boring . . .'

'They said they'd been everywhere and seen everything in New York, and I was better off not going out. Especially if I didn't have ID because they wouldn't let me in anywhere,' she continues. 'They're both nineteen, they live here because their parents are, like, really rich or something . . . like hotels, or tech, or something to do with travel.'

'Mmmmnn . . .' I murmur, 'sounds like you really got to know them,' I say sarcastically.

'They invited me up to watch *Drag Race*, so I thought why not.'

'You thought *why not* to some random strangers inviting you to their hotel room?' I exclaim, my voice rising.

'Stop. Shouting,' she implores.

'Fiinnnne,' I hiss. 'But then they got you drunk like an idiot and threw you back where they found you.'

'Sort of . . .' she replies, rocking back and forth.

'For all the gods' sake!' I reply, forgetting to whisper.

'Who are these gods?' she replies with the hint of a smile. Because Hope and I used to talk about all the gods when we were little. We couldn't really understand the white one with the beard who was both a father and a son and died on a cross or was behind a stone or whatever – so we learned about all the other ones and didn't really understand them either. But we started correcting our parents whenever they said 'Oh God' – which was a lot – and saying 'Oh *gods*' plural, because we thought it best not to annoy any of them.

'Hope,' I say, trying to retain my authority. 'If you do anything like that again, I swear I will wake up your parents.'

'I won't,' she says vehemently. And I can tell, just like that morning after the park, when I decided a weird, orange-flavoured alcohol was my new best friend, that she is regretting every sip that passed her lips. Because that's what all those movies with people drinking and looking all glamorous never tell you. That the next day you want to hide under a table.

'So . . . do you remember anything we talked about last night?'

She says nothing.

I pick up my phone and message Mum and Dad to say we'll meet them before dinner at Aunty Kitty's tonight. I imagine my dad reading the message while captive in Sephora, muttering, 'But how many eyeliners *are* there?' Then I google bagels.

'Come on. We need to eat something,' I say, pulling up Google Maps.

Hope throws an outfit together that makes her look like she should be modelling for Yeezy, and I throw on my Vans and a pair of wide black jeans.

'Um . . .' she says, looking at me.

'What?' I say, irritated, waiting for the insults to begin.

'Try this,' she says, throwing a baby tee in my direction. It's lilac, with the words *Baby Tee* written on it. 'And these,' she says, proffering some platform boots.

'I can't wear those,' I say, looking at them. 'I'll fall over.'

'They'll look great with those trousers, E – and we're in *New York.* Try some colour.' And the way she calls me E is just like when we were kids.

'Fiiinnne. But you'd better be there to pick me up when I fall over,' I mutter.

'I will,' she says, smiling.

And I'm smiling back, just like when we were kids.

Outside, the New York pavement is blanketed with snow, and all I can do is breathe it in, my pace set to Ron Sexsmith, 'Maybe This Christmas', and as we pass Central Park, I pull my phone out, thinking of Ash. Thinking of my arm through his arm, the two of us in New York.

I wish. I wish. I wish.

Ellie:

wish u were here

And despite the time difference, his reply is almost instant, like we're feeling the same moment of the same song at exactly the same time.

Ash:

wish u were here

I hug my phone to my chest. I can't wait to see him again. I can't wait to share New York with him, in my bedroom in a little east England village, the door firmly shut.

'Where are we going?' Hope monotones from behind her sunglasses. Since entering daylight, her mood has drastically deteriorated.

'Kossar's. It's a bagel shop. The best one in New York, according to the World Wide Web.'

I hail a yellow taxi like I am a proper New Yorker, and mutter the immortal words, 'Kossar's, please,' as Hope giggles and adds, 'And step on it!' We collapse on to the back seat of the car, cackling like a pair of witches, the driver rolling his eyes at us in the mirror.

When we reach the shop on Grand Street, there's a queue outside. It looks amazing, like the set of a movie, which is exactly how I feel standing outside it, like I'm on the verge of my very own meet-cute. The shopfront is painted a glossy red, somewhere between cheerful and melancholy in colour, with white writing announcing KOSSAR'S since 1936. Through the window past the red-lit neon sign that reads HOT BAGELS & BIALYS, I can see a million types of bagel piled high in wire baskets.

We wait in the queue for a table, and when we're seated, I order two cream cheese and lox bagels (because after much frantic googling I've discovered lox is smoked salmon), and a coffee for Hope. And oh. My. Gods. *The bagels.* Melty, chewy perfection. Like, if the Beatles were a bagel, this is the bagel they would be.

When the coffee arrives, Hope sips it slowly.

'Arrrrrrgh,' she moans, rubbing her forehead.

'Whose fault is that?' I ask piously.

'Because you never make mistakes, do you, Ellie?'

I sigh, remembering her rant from last night.

'I'm pretty much in the middle of one big, long mistake most of the time. I've no idea where you've got this idea that I'm perfect from, Hope.'

She ignores me.

'In fact, I'm the sort of girl who throws up in people's mouths,' I blurt out. 'When I have too much to drink.'

She snorts.

'Seriously?' she laughs, pressing at her brow. 'When?'

'A few months ago. Not my greatest moment.' I smile. 'And honestly, I've always thought you were the perfect one. The way you look and everything . . .'

She's silent for a minute, rubbing her forehead again.

'I'm sorry,' she says guiltily, 'for being horrible to you. Before, I mean. It's just I get so sick of hearing how I should be more like you.'

'Before?' I say, raising my eyebrows. 'Or for, like, the last five years? And when you say *more like me*, you just mean boring and friendless. Not that I'm either of those things – but I'm pretty sure it's what most of the family think.'

'Mum just wants me to stay at home and study all the time,' she says flatly, 'like you do. But it's not who I am. I'm never going to be that person, Ellie.'

'And I'm not either,' I laugh. 'Trust me, if I'd been staying at home and studying, I'd be getting much better grades. I've just been staying at home and being afraid of things, doing nothing – and I really don't want to do nothing any more.'

'That boy hasn't stopped looking at you since we came in,' she says suddenly, nodding towards the counter.

'What boy?' I ask self-consciously. I can only assume I have something on my face, or on the back of my jeans, because I am not the kind of girl that boys stare at.

'Him. With the black T-shirt.' I look up, for a second expecting to see Ash.

I shrug my shoulders, but she's right, he's definitely looking at me.

'He's coming over!' Hope says suddenly, gripping my hand across the table. 'And he's cute!' she says, licking her teeth and trying to smooth her hair back.

And while part of me wants to lecture her about the fact she has to stop caring so much what boys – i.e. Vikash – think of her, I'm starting to worry, because I've read about things like this before. Scams where good-looking men prey on young, impressionable girls, then steal their wallets, or jewellery, or borrow money for some artificial emergency and leave them stranded in some skeezy alleyway – and this is New York, so I probably look like some innocent Bambi type, minus the skinny legs and doe eyes, ripe for the picking.

I steel myself.

'Hi,' he says, as he reaches our table. And OK, he is cute. Seventeen or eighteen. Tall with chin-length dirty-blond hair, blue eyes and a fringe with a mind of its own. He's wearing a Nirvana T-shirt, making me instantly suspicious; most people who wear them can't name a single Nirvana song.

'Hi,' I say, not looking at him.

'This is going to sound weird,' he says, staring at the side of my face, 'but I recognise you.'

'Well, that's original,' I say snootily – and Hope looks at me, unable to recognise this fully in control, street-smart Ellie Pillai.

'I'm not trying to be original,' he says, smiling, 'I just know you.'

'Unlikely.'

'Why's that?' he says, his voice amused.

'Because I'm from literally nowhere, population nothing, so it's highly unlikely we know each other,' I intone, in as grown-up a manner as I can.

'Okaaay,' he says, rolling the word over in his mouth. 'But I do know you. Ellie, right?'

I hadn't imagined he'd be this advanced. He's clearly done his research; he clearly knows my name.

'How do you know that?' I ask ever more suspiciously.

'Like I said, I know you.'

'I'm Hope,' Hope says, offering her hand to him, like he should kiss it, or impale himself on something in worship.

'Hey,' he says, taking her in. What is that *look* people get sometimes, like a spider contemplating eating a fly.

'You go to Bridgewood, right?'

And now I'm convinced he's some kind of professional hitman. Because how does he know I go to Bridgewood, a no-mark school in a no-mark city?

'Who sent you?' I ask, turning towards him, my eyes narrowed.

'Who sent me?' he asks, laughing.

'We don't have any money, you know. We might be staying at the

Plaza, but we don't have any money. My aunt's paying for it. *She* has money but we're definitely not worth any ransom to her, so you can just forget whatever stunt it is you're trying to pull, pal.'

Pal?

'Ellie . . .' Hope cuts in.

'What, Hope? You think he's cute so we should do whatever he says, go wherever it is he tells us to go?'

'Um, I didn't actually ask you to go anywhere . . .' Dirty Blond interjects.

'Well, he is cute! But actually, that's not my point,' Hope replies testily.

'Um, still here . . .' Dirty Blond interposes.

'Well, what is your point?' I ask, infuriated. After all the trouble Hope got us into last night, I'm not likely to be taking advice from her.

'He's *English*, Ellie. The accent? Maybe you do know him.'

I look at him as a dawning realisation strikes me, my face turning slightly purple. I think he might be in that band. From school. The one that played the winter dance, with Hannah, the singer. It's definitely him. I can almost hear him singing Green Day to me while I watched Ash walking away from me at the winter dance.

'Heebbeee jeeebbee.' A sound comes out of my mouth, something strangled and weird-sounding. Like the physical sound of embarrassment.

'What's that now?' he says, staring at me again.

'Come to think of it,' I say, swallowing heavily, 'you, um, do look somewhat familiar.'

'You're the singer – right?'

'Um, heeeheee, jeeebbee.' The words come out knotted and indecipherable.

'Singer?' Hope asks, staring at me.

'Errrrrrr . . .'

'My sister Rosemary. She's in the orchestra. She played that song for you, the one you sang to that boy? I heard her practising. It was good. She said you have an amazing voice.'

'Ummmmm, heeeeebeee jeeebee,' I mumble.

'Anyway, I'm Shawn. I didn't come over to kidnap you, although that might have been fun,' he says, winking at Hope. Why is everybody suddenly winking, like it's the new hello? 'We're looking for a new singer. For our band. I thought you might be interested.'

'Ummmnnnhheh bebejeebee Hannah,' I say, my brain suddenly incapable of normal speech. A band?

'Yeah, well, Hannah and I, we're not, we're . . . we can't be in a band together any more.' And I'm glad to hear him stumbling over his words, so it's not just me that sounds like a babbling idiot.

'I don't think so,' I say slowly, 'but, you know, thanks for asking.'

He shrugs his shoulders.

'See you at school,' he says, turning away.

'Bye,' I murmur to his retreating back.

'What are you *doing*?' Hope hisses under her breath at me.

'Nothing!' I hiss back.

'I KNOW,' she hisses, 'but I thought you didn't *want* to do nothing any more?'

And I think: you're right. But by the time the words are finally out, Dirty Blond is gone.

13
OK, Bye

'So, what's happening now?'

I walk around, trying to find a good angle for the camera on my phone, so I can show Ash our room.

'We're just about to go to my aunty Kitty's for dinner. She lives on the Upper West Side, in some enormous apartment.'

We're on FaceTime, Ash in his room, Nick Cave and the Bad Seeds playing in the background as his painting sits on an easel behind him.

'Sounds fun,' he says absent-mindedly.

'Are you OK?' He seems distracted. Bored even. 'Sorry if this is a bit boring.'

'No,' he says, suddenly paying attention again. 'I'm not bored at all. I've just got some stuff going on.'

'Do you want to talk about it?' I ask, concerned. I want to reach through the video and run my fingers through his curly dark hair.

'No, it's fine.' He smiles. 'I just wish you were here. I miss you, which is stupid, because you've barely been away.'

'I miss you too.'

Hope makes a pretend vomiting sound in the background and fixes me with a glare.

'Look, I'd better go – I have to get changed for this dinner thing.'

'OK.' He looks pensive and worried, his face tense.

'Are you sure you don't want to talk about whatever's going on?' I ask quietly, because I want him to know he can. That even though I'm not there, I am.

'I'm fine,' he smiles.

'OK, I love you,' and then I freeze, because the words came out before I even had a chance to think about them. He freezes too.

'OK, bye,' he says uneasily; and the camera turns black as he disappears from view.

I love you?

OK, bye?

What. Just. Happened?

'What just happened?' Hope asks, mimicking my thoughts.

'Nothing.'

'Did you just say *I love you?*'

YES. Yes, I did.

I don't reply.

'And what did he say?' she continues, watching me closely.

OK, bye.

'I need to use the bathroom – are you done now?' I say, ignoring the question. When I get inside and shut the door, I just stare at myself in the mirror. Why did I say that? WHY did I say that? We've been together five minutes, and I haven't even let him unhook my bra yet. I've

65

just bought a new one today, which is lime green and what I thought might be considered sexy, but is probably just the equivalent of the *OK, bye* of the underwear world.

I try not to think about it. But then Courtney Love is stood behind me, resplendent in a dirty-white vest top, strategically placed holes right beside her nipples. Her hair bleached blonde, her black eyeliner stark against her pale skin, as she sings about crashing and burning, and stars exploding.

Oh God.

Oh God.

Oh God, I think, as the rest of Hole appear in the bathroom of room 1172 of the Plaza, serenading me with 'Malibu', telling me to drive away. Why can't I drive yet?

My phone pings next to me on the sink.

Hayley:
need 2 talk

Hayley:
can u call me?

And I think: I'll call her later. When I've figured out how to get away from the words I just sent out into the universe, hoping for a better reply. And then, as Hope starts banging on the door, saying my parents are waiting for us, I think: *OK, bye.*

14

Are We There Yet?

On the way to Granny's, Dad is squashed up against me in the taxi.

'Nice day with Hope, *en anbe*?' He seems simultaneously uptight, but happy to see me.

'Yeah. It was fine. Good. We went for bagels.'

'Kossar's?' he asks excitedly; Dad and I both like to nerd out by reading the same travel blogs. I nod. 'Your mother spent most of the day dragging me into shops and crying,' he whispers, sighing.

'Hormones,' I whisper, because Mum gets seriously angry when we claim any of her irrational behaviour (and yes, I said it – Mum is emotional and irrational) is down to pregnancy hormones, claiming it's just the patriarchy's way of controlling what they perceive as a feminine problem and infantilising women when they are serving one of the human race's most important functions.

'I think she's nervous about your grandmother's reaction tonight.'

Phantom Baby. I'd forgotten tonight was the night Mum and Dad have to tell Granny.

'Hmmmmn,' I respond sympathetically.

67

'Ellie,' Mum says from the front of the taxi. 'Sit next to me at dinner? I've barely seen you on this trip.'

'Sure,' I reply, as Hope makes eyes at me from across the other side of Dad. I try to make eyes back that say I Won't Say Anything, except I feel like I need to say *something*. At least about Vikash.

'Are we there yet?' Mum asks, as we pull up outside a large, grand building.

'It's just over there,' the driver says, pointing towards a set of heavy dark-wood doors with a smart-looking doorman stationed outside. I can see another taxi pulling up behind us, with Hope's parents and her sister Grace inside, and behind that, at a set of traffic lights, Big Uncle and Aunty Delia with Esther, Peter and Joseph.

We pile out of the cab and wait on the pavement for the rest of the family to arrive, and after a short time, another taxi appears with Middle Uncle, Andrew and Ethan – Aunty Helen is back at the hotel with my cousin Daniel, who isn't feeling very well. I know this last part comes as a bit of a blow to Mum, who was hoping Aunty Helen would work as an ally, should Granny go into attack mode. I take hold of her arm, resting my head against her shoulder – so she knows I'm here, that I'm her ally.

The elevator isn't big enough to carry us all up at once, so we decide to travel in families, with mine going first. The doors open for Mum, Dad and me, directly opposite Aunty Kitty's door. We knock, and when she opens, looking happy for once in her life, she squeals at the sight of Mum's baby bump, and pulls her into a long, tight embrace.

'*Annan*,' she says tearfully, taking Dad's hands into hers. 'What wonderful news. Come in, come in. *Amma* is in the kitchen, I'll wait here for the others.'

We turn towards each other, slightly terrified.

'Noel,' Granny calls. 'Noel, is that you? Come, come. Kitty has not cooked enough, but we will have to manage.'

We walk into the kitchen, all long, cool marble countertops and rose-gold fixtures, to where Granny is sat, looking uncomfortable, and annoyed, on a breakfast-bar stool. Her eyes widen as she takes in Mum's new frame, her tiny, shrivelled mouth making an O.

'Nimi?' she asks, as she turns towards Dad. 'Noel?' she says, her voice cracking.

'We're having a baby, *Amma*,' he says, taking hold of Mum's hand. 'In about five months. Everything's good so far. He's healthy. Nimi's healthy.'

'He?' I ask, suddenly shocked.

'Yes, Ellie, we told you on Monday,' Dad says turning to me, irritated. And I suddenly realise that all I was thinking about on Monday was Ash, and being away from Ash, and missing Ash – so I didn't really hear them, or acknowledge it when they told me; and I'm starting to see why Dad's been finding me so annoying lately.

I say nothing, waiting for Granny to reappear out of whatever reverie she's in.

'*Amma?*' Mum says, stepping forward and gently touching her arm. 'Are you OK?'

Granny turns to her, as if seeing her for the first time. There are tears in her eyes as she grasps forward, her wrinkly hand caressing

Mum's face. 'Yes,' she gulps, and she pulls Mum into a hug and grips her tightly, like she's afraid to ever let her go.

And Dad and I just stand there wordlessly, watching the two of them cry into each other's shoulders.

15

PG Tips v. Orange Pekoe

Over dinner, Granny manages to offend everyone. Which is usual, and not in any way a cause for concern. She forces Mum to sit next to her, and makes a show of clucking over her elaborately, making Dad wait on them both like the queen of an empire, which I suppose she in fact is: the queen of *this* empire. Her family.

Sat on Mum's other side, I manage to benefit from their scraps, as Mum passes on whatever Dad brings to her and I avoid having to fight it out for mutton rolls at the kitchen counter with the rest of the family. When all our plates are full, and we're finally perched as well as we can be around Aunty Kitty's dining table, Middle Uncle raises his glass.

'To Nimi, Noel, Ellie and the new addition. This time next Christmas, there'll be a new member of our family.' We all raise our glasses as Granny interrupts bluntly.

'Yes, yes,' she says, cutting Middle Uncle off. 'Very good. Did you bring PG Tips? I have been looking forward to them very much.'

'I brought them,' Dad says, cutting in. 'And we have enough Penguins and Marmite between us to last until your next trip, *Amma*.'

71

'I do not ask for *much*,' Granny replies piously. 'I give *you*,' she says, jabbing her finger accusingly at the group gathered around the table, 'all the opportunities in world. I leave my country, my friends, my family. All I ask for is PG Tips. Is not *much*.'

Hope and I look at each other, and I have a sudden desire to laugh. Like one of those yearnings you can barely suppress. I can feel it bubbling up inside of me, like a fountain about to spill over.

'I thought your friends sent you orange pekoe, *Amma*, from home?' Aunty Delia says boldly. Granny turns to her, her face hard.

'Pah,' she says, almost spitting. 'Small bag they sent me. Very small bag. I send them nice English husband for daughter, they send me small bag of pekoe. PAH.'

And I want to laugh again, so badly.

'I am good at finding husbands,' she says shrewdly. 'That is what *others* say. Not Kitty. But others. My introductions make good marriages. What *others* say. Not Kitty, but others.'

Aunty Kitty, who for the first half of the meal looked something akin to happy, looks suddenly grey and shiny. Is she angry under there? Is that anger I can see under the surface of that painted smile?

'*Amma*,' Little Uncle cuts in, sending Aunty Kitty a distress signal. 'Did I tell you, Hope's boyfriend, Vikash, is on course for a first-class honours degree?'

She grunts. 'What degree?'

'Dentistry.'

'Is not real doctor,' she says imperiously.

And I can't help it then. I start laughing, the sound escaping like air from a whoopee cushion.

'What is laughing?' Granny turns to me, shocked.

'I'm sorry . . .' I say, trying to control the sound, and I look over at Hope and she's started too, her laughter echoing mine, uproarious and uncontrollable.

'Is true!' Granny says irritably. 'She is very beautiful. She can get real doctor. Or engineer. Not dentist. Chkk,' she says, making that sound of hers, both disdainful and annoyed. Which is unbelievable really, because Hope's mother, Aunty Christine, is an actual dentist, and as usual Granny doesn't really care who she offends.

'Well,' I say, managing to stop laughing. 'Hope's a lot more than *just* beautiful.' Mum looks at me approvingly, rubbing my arm. 'She's smart and talented and special,' I announce to a shocked table; and Andrew and Joseph look like they might keel over from disbelief, because Hope and I have barely said a civil word, either to or about each other, in five years.

'Yes, yes,' says Granny authoritatively. '*Obviously.* She is Pillai.'

Hope and I start laughing again, and this time there is no stopping us as we roll around, trying not to be sick from all the Sri Lankan food we've just ingested.

'You girls!' says Granny, throwing her arms up in defeat at our hysteria. But I could swear she smiles at us almost approvingly.

16

Vikash Said What?

On the way from Aunty Kitty's back to the hotel, Hope travels with her parents, which gives me an opportunity to talk to Mum. I explain everything about the conversation I had with Hope, ignoring the whole *she was drunk* part of the exchange.

'Vikash said *what*?' Mum asks through gritted teeth.

'I just think, maybe, Hope feels like she's got nothing going for her – other than the way she looks. Like, maybe she thinks she deserves someone like that.'

'Well, clearly Thomas needs enlightening about all this,' Dad says about his little brother. 'The way he was boasting about that boy tonight.'

'Noel, he doesn't know what's been going on, and these things go much deeper than that,' Mum says, yawning. 'I'll talk to her, and to Christine and Thomas. Self-esteem is a huge issue for teenagers,' she says in her Therapist Voice. 'It's about teaching them to value their own judgement and not look for validation in others.'

'Learning to like yourself,' I whisper.

'Learning to *respect* and like yourself,' Mum says, kissing my forehead. And I can't help but wonder whether I am therefore ruined, because I know I care too much what other people think. What Ash thinks.

'This whole Vikash thing is a classic example of toxic masculinity,' Mum says, yawning again – Phantom Baby's really taken it out of her this evening.

'Toxic masculinity?' Dad whispers, semi confused.

Everything about telling Mum feels right, and responsible, the way *that* Ellie would behave, the one that's in control. I just wish I knew where she'd been when *OK, bye* went down.

'You did the right thing telling us, Ellie. I'm proud of you, *en anbe*,' Mum says, stroking my arm. Dad smiles distractedly.

'Thanks, Mum,' I say, looking out of the window.

And somewhere, on the other side of the world, Ash is wondering why his girlfriend of two minutes said she loved him; when on this side of the world, his girlfriend of two minutes is wondering why he just ignored it, and she feels so small.

17

Smiley Face with Sunglasses

After the *OK, bye* debacle with Ash, I decide not to talk to him for a couple of days, in a vain attempt to show him I, in fact, do not love him. Every time he sends me a message, I respond with an emoji, which is innately challenging, but satisfying in its brevity.

The thing is, I don't love him. Because I don't actually know him, not really. Just the idea of him, an idea I *could* fall in love with. It's just, I never wanted him to ignore it and *OK, bye* me. I wanted to laugh about it, or talk about it, or anything, other than have him run away and pretend I never said it.

I look down at the last message he sent me.

Ash:

saw this & thought of u

He's attached a picture of a retro Beatles badge, all shiny yellow and chaotic red writing. I'd been looking for one just like it, and I can see it's in his bedroom, on the top of his dresser. I want to feel happy about it, that the badge is waiting for me like a million thoughts wrapped up in one tiny, perfect package, but the unsaid words hang between us, like something even a Beatles badge can't quite paper over – so, I respond with the following.

Ellie:

Which is the best I can do without resorting to a broken heart and a sarcastic *OK, bye.*

'I've got an idea,' Hope says, peering over my shoulder at the exchange between Ash and me. For the last couple of days, since Mum spoke to her, I've noticed a change in Hope. Like a little light just appeared that for ages felt like it had been extinguished. She's being nice to people. Nice to me. And Little Uncle and Aunty Christine seem to be being more careful with her, more aware. All of a sudden her Instagram is no longer public, and they're checking it every day. I don't know what's going on with Vikash, but I think his number may be up.

'I think I've had enough museums and ice rinks to last a lifetime. What if I can get us another day to ourselves?' she asks, trying to tear my eyes away from my phone.

'To do what?' I sigh.

'Anything but stare at that picture of a yellow badge.'

'Sure,' I say despondently.

'We can buy you some more bras ...' she says with a glint in her eye.

'Why?' I say dejectedly.

'Um, I don't know. Because you can only wear that vile Hello Kitty thing for so many more days before I *accidentally* assume it belongs to the last child that inhabited this room and throw it in the bin. Your mum gave us $100 to buy some replacements, Ellie, and you've barely even looked.'

'Whatever,' I sigh.

'Don't worry,' she says, putting her arm around me as I sit on the edge of the bed. 'We'll have fun. I'll make sure of it.'

18

Legends of New York

We're in some kind of boutique, some kind of expensive, cool, I Really Shouldn't Be in Here, New York boutique. I'm wearing the pink boiler suit Jess made me buy, that Hope made me wear, and which until ten minutes ago I thought was cool enough for New York – but clearly isn't, by the reception we received from the women who work in this shop.

A security guard has been following us around since we walked in, and Hope is refusing to acknowledge him as his eyes follow our hands and bags like two well-known criminals or members of an elite Magic Circle that can make things disappear at will.

'What about this?' Hope asks, holding up an oxblood velvet minidress with sheer sleeves and a sweetheart neckline. It has a heavy security tag wrapped around and through it, and I wish she hadn't picked it up. I can imagine steel doors slamming down on us as the lights flash red and Sam Cooke, 'Chain Gang' starts playing.

'It's, er, nice . . . Should we get out of here?' I whisper.

'Why are you whispering?' she asks, tossing her hair back.

The girls working the till have barely acknowledged us, and unlike the rest of the places we've been to, no one's offered to start a dressing room or complimented us on our accents. I feel dirty. Like there's something wrong with me.

'Hope,' I hiss, looking at the price tag. 'It's $800!'

'And?' she says, rolling the word around her mouth. 'We'd like to try this on,' she says sweetly, turning to one of the women.

She eyes us.

'I'd have to get the key,' she says, as if this settles things, 'and I'm not sure we have your size.' I'm suddenly transported to that scene in *Pretty Woman* when Julia Roberts asks how much a dress is in That Shop, and they just keep saying: *verrrryyyy expeeeensssiiiiivee*, which is code for: Get Out of My Shop – and I'm starting to realise we might be a collective Julia Roberts, and this shop assistant the horrible one called Marie who asks her to leave.

'I'll try it anyway,' Hope says from between gritted teeth, and she looks like she's about to climb over the till and get the key herself, when another group of girls walk in. I wait for the security guard to start tailing them, but he stays firmly behind us.

That's when I start to realise why I feel a bit dirty. Why I've come to accept that we don't belong in this shop. Because every other person in here is white; and as the other assistant starts talking animatedly to the new group – offering to start a dressing room, complimenting one of them on her shoes – the realisation becomes an Absolute Truth. An oh-so-obvious truth.

'Hope,' I say, looking at the floor. 'Let's just *go*.' Because I don't want them to win, but I can't stand being in here. I can't stand the way these people are behaving, the way these people *are*. But she's rooted to the spot, staring Marie out; and I have never respected my cousin more.

That's when I see two tall black girls enter the shop. Immaculately made up, about twenty, one in wide, loose-fitting utility trousers and a bright pink trench coat, the other in baggy jeans and a leopard-print bomber jacket. Everything about them, their confidence, their style, makes the shop feel grey and small, and the security guard moves this time, straight towards them, as if greeting them, but not in good spirits.

'Hey – Hope?' one of them questions in the coolest New York accent you can imagine.

Hope looks at the floor, the wall, me, then them.

'Er, hiiiii,' she says, frowning.

'So, I'm assuming you got back to your room OK the other night?' the other one says, laughing.

And *these* must be the Lennoxes.

'Actually, I *collected* her from the lobby,' I reply, suddenly uptight.

'Wow. You are soooooo English,' says Leopard-Print Bomber.

I bristle. Like only an English person can bristle.

'It was rather disconcerting to find her in that state,' I reply, channelling every Jane Austen character, 'as you can imagine.'

Disconcerting? As you can imagine?

'Sorry about that,' Pink Trench Coat replies. 'The girl wouldn't tell us her room number. We trieeeed.'

'She also didn't tell us she was drinking our dad's bourbon . . .' Leopard-Print Bomber drawls sarcastically. 'She was practically passed

81

out in our bathroom. To be honest,' she chastises, 'it was prettttty rude. It was suuuuch a good episode of *Drag Race*.'

I stare at Hope.

'Listen, English, we did try,' Pink Trench Coat states. 'We just figured she'd work it out if we put her back where we found her.'

Hope grimaces while I consider killing her.

So. Much. More. To. That. Story.

Ugh.

Hope!

I glare at her, as if trying to communicate my discontent. It works.

'Sorry,' she hisses. 'I'm an *idiot*.'

And we've come so far, her and me, that I just whisper, 'S'OK.'

'So, what you girls trying on?' Leopard-Print Bomber asks, taking the minidress out of Hope's hand. 'English – this dress would *kill* on you. Have you started a dressing room?'

I say nothing, and look down at the floor, suddenly aware that Marie's still here, giving Marie Vibes.

'We were just about to,' Hope says challengingly.

Marie stares at us, unsure of how to cope with all the BDE in the room.

Leopard-Print Bomber hands her the dress, ignoring the security guard sandwiched between us all for no fathomable reason.

'Is Julia here?' she asks.

'How do you know Julia?' Marie asks slowly.

'She dresses my mom sometimes, for events and stuff.'

'Julia doesn't dress anyone any more, she didn't feel it was right for the brand,' Marie says, unconvinced.

Pink Trench Coat laughs.

'Julia and my mom go waaaaay back.'

She picks her phone up from where it's hanging across her chest like a little bag, encased in black leather with two gold C's on the back of it.

'Julia? Hey, its Carrie. I'm at Sculpt . . . No, with Edie, Mom's in Rome this week.' She laughs. 'We're with some friends, and we want to make sure they have a *really* good time.' She goes silent. 'Oh, that would be sooo great, thanks. I will, definitely.'

She puts her phone down and approximately thirty seconds later, Marie's mobile rings out.

'Julia . . . Yes, of course. We'll take care of them. See you Thursday.'

She puts the phone down and looks momentarily like she might be sick.

'Miss Lennox – is there anything else I can pull for your friend's dressing room?'

Carrie Lennox looks at her, and then at her sister.

'Oh yes,' Edie Lennox says, looking gleeful. 'So many things. But we'll need a drink first – this might take a whiiiiillle.'

Several hours later, we emerge into the bright glare of a snow-covered New York, no bags in hand. We've tried on almost every item in the shop, had so many drinks I've had to pee three times, and watched the scene from *Pretty Woman* where Julia Roberts tells Marie she made a big mistake not waiting on her about forty-five times in front of the other (we're not sure of her real name) Marie. It's been by turns sad, rage-inducing, hysterical and fun.

'Thank you,' Hope says, turning to Carrie and Edie. 'That was *amazing*. Especially after the way I behaved the other night . . .'

'No more bourbon, Sixteen,' which is what they've been calling her ever since I told them her real age. 'And no more wandering hotels at night. You're lucky we weren't axe murderers.'

Why do people always say that? Did there used to be a lot of murdering done by axe?

'But I'm sorry that happened,' Edie says, nodding towards the glass doors at Sculpt. 'New York isn't like that most of the time.'

'Well, it is . . .' Carrie says, raising her eyebrows; and this we understand, because the Maries are everywhere.

'You know, English – you really should have bought that dress,' Edie says, looking at me.

'Eight hundred dollars is a *bit* out of my price range,' I smile.

'Did you find it a bit *disconcerting*?' she says, mimicking my accent.

'Was it not *as you imagined*?' Carrie says, cackling.

'I found it rather displeasing, if one knows what I mean,' I say, mocking myself.

'You're *funny*.'

And the Lennox sisters leave. Legends of New York. And Hope and I just stand there. Watching them go. Until she says, 'Bloomingdale's!' and pulls me along behind her.

19

Two New Bras

An hour later we emerge with two new bras. One black, one red (red!), and matching high-waisted pants which I think make me a look like a 1950s Doris Day type, and Hope thinks make me resemble Granny.

'Where are we going now?'

'Kossar's,' she says, crossing the road efficiently.

'Again?'

'You said you wanted to try one of those cookie things.'

I don't argue. Because I do want to try one of those cookie things.

When we reach Kossar's, we queue again and get a table by the window. I nibble at my black-and-white cookie and watch Hope as she toys with a cinnamon rugelach.

'Are you going to eat that?' I ask, nodding at it.

'In a minute,' she says, looking around.

'What are you looking for?' I ask, my hand inside my Bloomingdale's bag, pulling out my new bras. 'I love this one. I mean it just feels so un-me, but then, it feels so me, you know . . .'

'Mmnn-hmnn,' she says, looking over my shoulder as her face lights up.

'Hi,' she says, standing.

And when I turn around, Dirty Blond is stood behind me, staring at my red underwear.

Oh my God. Oh my GOD. What the . . .

'Hi,' I say, stuffing the bra back into the bag overenthusiastically. The knickers fall on the floor, and admittedly, in the light of day, and not on, they do look particularly enormous.

He leans down to pick them up and passes them to me, while I silently die.

'You came,' Hope says, staring at him. He smiles.

'Let me go order something,' he says. 'I'll be back in a minute.'

'Hope,' I say gruffly, as he walks away. 'What's going on?'

'Well,' she says quickly. 'I knew he went to Bridgewood so I found him on Instagram and DM'd him. He's in New York to see his dad. He really wants to hear you sing, and there's an open mic thing this afternoon at the Bitter End on Bleecker, and we're going to watch him play.'

I look at the guitar case that he's left at the foot of our table and consider putting my hands around Hope's throat and squeezing.

'I'm not singing,' I say stubbornly. 'So, don't even *think* of asking me to.'

'You don't have to, we'll just watch . . .'

'Hope!'

'What? I just broke up with Vikash this morning, and Shawn's cute. Let me live my life,' she says dramatically.

'So, this is just about you fancying Shawn?' I say suspiciously.

'Sure,' she says unconvincingly – and I consider putting my hands around her throat again, but Dirty Blond is back, pretending all of this is fine.

20

The Very Bitter End

It takes us about thirty minutes to walk to the Bitter End, possibly the most ironically titled venue in history given my current state of mind. It takes thirty minutes not because it's a comfortable distance from Kossar's, but because Hope and Dirty Blond have legs up to their armpits, and mine seem to stop about two inches from the ground.

Note to self: Stop being friends with/going out with/being related to tall people.

They walk in front of me, talking and laughing, her hand coming out to touch his arm so often my eyes almost permanently roll to the back of my head.

Note to self: discuss the concept of rebounds with Hope, and explain they are generally perceived as Not a Good Idea.

I can feel my heart racing. Almost like the feel of it is a sound, both steady and unnerving. The sound of Green Day, 'Basket Case', part frantic, part soothing. I watch his guitar, slung across his back, and wonder what it would feel like to be so confident; to be in a new place, a new city, a new country – and to show yourself, your real self, through the cadence of the chords you write, or the key you choose to sing in. In the timbre of your voice. I want to be that person. I want to be *that* Ellie.

'Ellie,' Shawn says, turning around to look at me. 'It's just here – across the street.' We cross over, and as we stand in line, queuing to get in, Shawn glances across at me.

'Have you ever done one of these before?'

'I'm just going to run over to that shop and get some gummy bears,' Hope interrupts. I try to kill her with my eyes.

'You know . . .' says Shawn. 'You're very . . .'

'Weird?' I finish for him.

'Hostile,' he grins.

'Sorry. I'm not a performer. This whole thing literally makes me want to vomit.'

'Right,' he laughs.

Why, gods? Why do I have to choose *now* to be honest?

'Look, I get it,' he says, shrugging. 'I feel like that too.'

'Really?' I ask disbelievingly.

'Yeah. Of course. It's hard to stand up and sing something you've written, and show yourself and stuff.'

I stare at him silently. Wondering how he's managed to convey it so perfectly. That sense of having to be your total and complete self, and not fear the judgement.

'So, how did you . . . you know. Get over it?'

'I didn't,' he says seriously. 'I just let myself feel it. And I try to use it. The fear. To be better. To not be afraid of being afraid.'

'Sounds deep,' Hope says, appearing behind us, gummies in hand.

I raise my eyebrows at him and notice his smile isn't as annoying as I thought it was thirty minutes ago.

When we get to the front doors, they put a stamp on our hands, and we walk into a dark, cave-like room, with a small stage at the front, on which a chair, a microphone and an upright piano sit modestly in a corner.

As Shawn goes to put his name on the list, Hope and I settle at a table with some Coca-Colas and the gummy bears she bought from across the street. I'm finding the whole thing weirdly soothing now; watching all these people tuning their guitars, the air jangling with nerves.

'Hey,' Shawn says, as he sits down next to us and slurps at his own Coke. 'Thanks for coming along. It's good to be doing this with someone I know.' For a second, I almost like him, because actually, it is nice being here, and I like that he gets nervous, I like that he gets it. Maybe one day, I could be one of these people too.

When they start the open mic about ten minutes later, some people are terrible, some people are moderately good, some are OK, and Then There's Shawn.

He swaggers to the front of the stage like he's almost drunk. Like a different person to the one who calmly told me these things still terrify him. He swings his guitar out in front of him, tuning it quickly into the mic.

'This song is called "Ripen/Mellow".'

The start of the song feels bitter and electric, an intro that winds from major to minor, like a sea, angry and foreboding. Then he sings, and the sound of it is exactly like the chords that he's playing, dark and melodic, hopeful and bruised. *I crash, I fall, I stand, I lean. I do it all without you, I do it all without you.*

And I feel the song, in a way I usually only feel *my* songs. Like the notes are in my bones.

They say you'll ripen and you'll mellow, but all you do is fight. You swallow me whole. You swallow my light.

When he stops, for a second the room remains quiet, until a smattering of applause becomes a tumultuous standing ovation, but before he's even halfway back to our table, the compère reads out the next name in the line-up.

'Our next songwriter is a fellow Brit. Welcome to the stage, Ellie Pillai,' and of course he mispronounces my name like I'm actually a type of rice, but there's no doubt who he's referring to.

I turn to Hope, my heart like a drum.

'Go on,' she says, squeezing my hand across the table. 'Go and do *not nothing.*'

♡ Song 2 ♡

Intro, Verse, Chorus, Middle Eight - Raw

There's a rawness when you're singing. A rawness that comes from being flesh and bone; your heart in your hands, your soul in your throat. You're raw, your skin fraying. A moment when you're no longer notes and keys and words but fire.

This song is my fire. The tribal part of me that burns for something more. That asks the questions and no longer fears the reply.

I used to be scared, but now I'm just frozen.
Praying to gods I don't believe in.

I used to be scared, but then a song saved me. It came in cadences and chords, bittersweet and trying. It made me fly, then it set me on fire. *I feel so raw.*

I was not afraid.

I was just me. And I was saved.

21

A Girl Called Ellie

My name is Ellie. Ellie Pillai. And when I sing, the world stands still. Just for me – but still.

For a minute, everything makes sense.

I make sense.

And here are the things I want.

To be the version of myself that isn't afraid to try.

To be the version of myself that isn't afraid to fail.

To be the version of myself that cares what I think, more than I care what you think.

To be myself.

But mostly.

To know who that is.

22

Not Nothing

The applause after I stop singing is deafening. I can feel my breath catching in my throat, my chest heavy with the fear I carried here. The fear that tried to choke me, which I swallowed, and I *used*. The fear I know I *feel*, but which is no longer in charge of me.

I try to blink away the light in my eyes, because even though the piano is in the corner of the room, they're shining a spotlight on it: a spotlight on me. And when I stumbled up here, trying so hard to take my own advice and do Not Nothing, I sat here, in the darkness, until suddenly I was illuminated and there was no turning back. I could hear every breath writ large in the darkness behind me, until the notes played themselves, until I was here, in this moment. Singing in New York.

I stagger back to my seat, people grabbing my arms and pumping my hand.

'Oh. My. GOD,' Hope says, staring at me open-mouthed.

'Your voice . . .' Shawn says, hugging me tightly. 'We should write together sometime. I love your music.'

'Me too, I mean you were just . . .' I gesticulate, trying to convey how much it moved me.

'Oh. My. GOD,' Hope repeats. 'If you two joined forces, you could literally be the new White Stripes.'

And then it's my turn to look shocked.

'What, you think you're the only person with a Y2K Spotify playlist?' she says haughtily. I laugh, the exhilaration of it still carrying me at least two feet above the ground.

'I can't believe I just . . . I mean, I can't believe that I, that *me* . . .'

'Believe it,' Shawn says, dropping a gummy bear in his mouth.

In the words of Hope Pillai, oh my GOD. I do. I do believe it.

23

I Will Follow You into the Dark

'Anyone hungry?' Shawn asks, as we step outside the Bitter End.

'I could eat,' Hope retorts.

I nod along, trying to pretend I'm part of the conversation, but the truth is, all I can think about is What Just Happened, and how I wish I could call Ash and tell him about it in something other than emojis.

Walking next to me, Shawn smiles.

'Well, you didn't vomit,' he teases.

'It was a close call,' I grin.

'I still don't know *why* I didn't know you could do that,' Hope says in awe. And for a second, I can see us both registering how much we've missed. How we've been in each other's lives, and yet we haven't.

I reach over and squeeze her hand. I shouldn't be thinking about Ash. I should be thinking about *this*. Right now. Being in New York. With Hope and Dirty Blond and the feeling I can do anything.

We weave through the city efficiently, crossing roads and pausing at lights, stopping to look in the windows of overpriced clothes shops in the hope we might spot Carrie and Edie. Shawn's dad came to live in New York after his parents divorced, and he treats the city like it's a friend.

'I've spent a lot of time here,' he says, shifting his guitar around on his back. 'I mean, honestly, I wanted to live here when my parents split up, but I couldn't leave my mum . . .' He trails off. 'She wanted to be near her parents, so that's how we ended up—'

'In the middle of nowhere?' I sympathise.

He grins.

'I thought that too to begin with. I hated it. Having to leave all my friends in London to go to some weird backwards city in the middle of nowhere while Dad went off to New York.'

'And now?'

'I like it,' he says, smiling at me. 'I like that people talk to you. That it's green and pretty, and your neighbours pretend to be concerned about you when they really just want to know what you're up to.'

I don't say anything, because I don't know how to explain that you can be in exactly the same place as someone else but have an entirely different experience. That people don't always talk to my family, that sometimes the nosy neighbours are more hostile than they are nosy.

'I don't think that's exactly what it's like for Ellie,' Hope says bluntly.

And the way he looks at me feels suddenly unnerving.

'I'm sorry . . . it's not exactly diverse, is it?' he says uncomfortably.

'It is what it is.' I smile. 'Anyway, where are you taking us?'

'Here,' he says, opening a door and ushering us inside.

Without noticing it, we've ended up in Chinatown, inside a tiny dim sum restaurant called Joy King, lit up by neon signs and peeling plastic posters for char sui pork buns and prawn wontons.

'Hey, Shawny,' a waitress says, coming over. 'Corner OK?'

'Great – thanks, Olivia.'

Olivia winks at him. I wish I was cool enough to wink.

We sit in the corner, and over plates of pillowy steamed buns, crunchy rice-noodle rolls and golden crescent dumplings, we talk about music, and writing songs, and how it feels to be onstage; like there's a different version of ourselves we never knew existed, that fits up there. That belongs.

Hope holds a dumpling up between her chopsticks and sighs.

We take the hint.

'Anyway, maybe I'll move to New York one day,' he says, smiling at her. 'If Mum's OK with it.'

'You should talk to my boyfriend,' I say, and I don't think I'll ever get bored of saying that word. 'He's worried about leaving his mum too. He hates the idea of her being alone.'

'What happened with his dad?' Hope asks, eyebrows knitted.

'He died,' I say flatly. Because that word always feels flat to me; like I can feel it between my fingers to the sound of Death Cab for Cutie, 'I Will Follow You into the Dark'.

'I'm sorry,' Shawn says, looking at the table – and something about the way he says it, pushing his fringe out of his eyes like one of those dogs that's permanently half blinded by its fur, makes me want to stroke his head and offer him a biscuit.

'Poor Ash,' Hope says, shaking her head.

'Ash?' he queries, tucking a stray piece of hair behind his ear.

'Ash Anderson. He's in Year 13.'

And here come the sixties girl group in their glorious gold spandex. Shooping and wooing as I think about his hand on the back of my neck, and his fingers in my hair, and how much I want to send him something other than an emoji. Something that says I Still Really Like You, But I Am Horribly Insecure.

'I know him.' He frowns. 'Hannah and I do.' He signals to Olivia for the bill.

'What's with you and this Hannah girl then?' Hope asks bluntly. 'Is she your girlfriend or what?' I elbow her, my eyes widening in horror at her directness.

'*Ex*-girlfriend.'

'You mention her a lot for an ex-girlfriend,' Hope says, narrowing her eyes at him.

'She annoys me a lot for an ex-girlfriend.' He smiles. 'And we're in a band together. We were, anyway,' he says in an agitated tone.

'Do you wish she was still *in* the band then?' I ask curiously.

'She's a great singer,' he says honestly, 'but I'd love to have someone to write with,' he says, turning to me.

His cheeks dimple a little, and I have to admit, he's even cuter than I first gave him credit for. I can totally see him and Hope having outrageously beautiful children.

Olivia brings the bill over and we split it three ways.

'I'll get the tip,' he says, when we go to look for change. He puts a $20 bill down, and when Olivia walks past, she gives him a peck on the cheek.

I look over at Hope, who seems particularly unbothered.

When we get outside, he turns to me. 'That was fun. I'll see you back at school, Ellie.' He smiles before turning to Hope. 'And Hope, I'll . . .'

'Call me,' she states confidently.

He grins and leans over to kiss her on the cheek.

Take THAT, Olivia.

'So,' I say, turning towards Hope excitedly as he walks away, 'what's going on with you and Shawn?'

She appears to be watching an Unsuitably Aged Suit Man, some lawyer type out on their lunch break, who looks nothing like Shawn.

'Me and *Shawn*?' she says dismissively.

'Don't you like him?' I ask, leaning forward as we walk.

'Er, definitely *not*,' she says, staring ahead of her, suddenly distracted.

'What? Why?' I say, pulling her to a stop. I can't believe she dragged me to that open mic just so could see him again, and now she has absolutely no intention of seeing him again, ever. Except I can believe it, because it's Hope.

'Because there's no point liking boys that don't like you back.' And I want to remind her that Vikash didn't seem to like her very much – because you're supposed to be nice to the people you like.

'But he kissed you!' I exclaim, annoyed. How can she like Vikash and that Creepy Preppy Bellboy, and whatever Unsuitably Aged Suit

Man we now appear to be following, but not someone sweet and talented and Suitably Aged, like Shawn?

'He was talking to *you*,' she says calmly, still staring straight ahead of her, her pace increasing slightly. 'I barely spoke. Which, as you know, is not a very *me* quality.'

'Hehe hee be jee beee,' I murmur indecipherably.

'You should have seen him when you were singing,' she says, rolling her eyes.

'Don't be stupid,' I splutter. 'He just likes my voice.'

'He likes more than just your voice,' she says, dragging me behind her, her eyes fixed to something in front.

'He doesn't . . .' I say, blushing furiously.

'Ellie, will you just *shut up*!' she hisses.

'No, you shut up!' I hiss back. And then I stop suddenly. 'Why are we whispering?' I whisper.

'There,' she hisses triumphantly, as she pushes me behind a dumpster. 'Because of *that*,' she says, pointing towards two people kissing outside a restaurant, one of whom is Unsuitably Aged Suit Man.

And now I can see why she was pulling me. Because the 'that' is a very handsome Chinese man, and the person he's kissing is Aunty Kitty.

24

Not Granny Approved

I'm watching Aunty Kitty kiss a man who is definitely not Granny approved. But who is definitely hot. For a man who is old, and an aunty who is old, and the grossness that comes along with those two subject matters. Although to be fair to Aunty Kitty, in her fitted lilac trouser suit and sky-blue high heels, she looks like the sort of lawyer who might work for Lady Gaga. Like, a less lawyer-y lawyer. A cool lawyer. Like how she probably would look all the time if Granny weren't constantly telling her what to do.

'Oh my GOD,' Hope whispers. 'I thought Aunty Kitty hated men.'

'Why?' I whisper, mesmerised. Old people kissing is gross – and apparently mesmerising, because even though this dumpster smells, I can't tear myself away from it.

'I've never even seen her with one . . .'

'You have now . . .' I murmur. Suddenly Aunty Kitty refusing to be set up by Granny (although seriously, who would want to be set up by Granny?) is starting to make sense. She doesn't want to be set up – because clearly, she can set herself up. Although maybe she can't. Because she's in one of the most iconic, beautiful, romantic cities in the world, and she's kissing a man not far from a dumpster. But then, thinking about it, all of New York could be described as not far from a dumpster. In a good way, obviously.

'I think we should go,' I whisper, suddenly nervous. It feels weird to be watching her like this. Weird and unpleasant. Because who she wants to be in love with, or go for lunch with, or kiss not far from a dumpster, is really none of our business.

'I know, it's just so . . .' Hope says, trailing off. They've stopped kissing now, and started stroking each other's hands, hopping about, trying to keep warm.

'Come on,' I whisper, pulling at her.

'One more minute . . .' she says, her feet rooted to the spot.

'Hope!' I hiss. 'Come ON.'

She turns towards me suddenly, just as I'm yanking her arm with as much force as I can muster. It's brief, and instant, and unexpected; because I'm pulling at her, but she just yields. I fly backwards, my back hitting the snow, immersed in some kind of dumpster juice that is gross and horrible – like watching two old people kissing in the street for no fathomable reason.

'Ow!' I shout, as I hit the ground, dumpster juice spraying all over my pink boiler suit.

'Ellie!' Hope cries, rushing over. She's bending over me, trying to pull me up, as I pull at her, cursing myself for not wearing the ugly snow boots Mum bought me. It's just they make my legs look like tree trunks. Short, stout tree trunks. Like a giant, but very short, sequoia.

'Ow!' she cries, as I pull her down next to me. Not on purpose, but a bit on purpose.

'Sorry.' I smirk. But really, I'm not sorry. Because I am no longer the sole recipient of dumpster juice.

'Thanks a lot, Ellie!' she says, brushing herself down.

'Oh, shut up!' I hiss, exasperated. 'If it wasn't for you, we wouldn't be here in the first place!'

'I came for you!' she cries, outraged. 'For the open mic. And if this is what I get for trying to help you—'

'HELP ME? How is you throwing me under a bus, forcing me to sing, HELPING me, Hope?'

'It got Shawn to notice you, didn't it?' she says, annoyed.

'I don't want Shawn to notice me, I have a boyfriend!'

'Who can't even say *I love you*, Ellie. Seriously, you're better off out of it.'

'It was too soon for me to say it, and anyway, that's none of your business. And who are you to lecture me about boys, Hope. You haven't exactly got the best track record.'

'That's because I prefer *men*,' she replies haughtily.

'What, like that idiot Vikash?' I seethe.

'Ellie?' Aunty Kitty thunders, standing over us. 'Hope?' And suddenly, I realise we stopped whispering some time ago.

We look up at her, our faces frozen mid-argument.

'Hi,' I say slowly.

'Fancy seeing you here . . .' Hope says, looking at the floor.

'Hi,' says the Suitably Aged for Aunty Kitty man, looking moderately amused.

But Aunty Kitty is *not* moderately amused. Or in any way Amused at All.

25

Christmas Eve

The next day, it's Christmas Eve, and we're at Aunty Kitty's apartment again. Granny is in a particularly heinous mood, because she hates Christmas and everything it stands for – like happiness, and joy, and gift giving, and generosity of spirit. Mum thinks it's because she's sad about us leaving, but we've got just over a week, and I don't understand why she can't just enjoy it.

Earlier today, I decided to call Ash. Because I miss him. Because emojis just aren't enough any more; and it's Christmas Eve. A time for happiness and joy and gift giving and generosity of spirit – and Hope has been ignoring me, and I need to talk to somebody sensible. But he didn't pick up, and he hasn't responded to the rambling voice note I left him, which went something like:

I don't think you're OK. And I'm sorry because I feel like I wasn't really listening to you the other day . . . And I'm sorry because of the thing I said, and I'm just SORRY. I want you to know you can talk to me. Also, I'm sorry about all the emojis. Call me back.

So, now I'm forcing myself not to spiral. Because my boyfriend was going through something; he said he had *stuff* going on, which is code for Something Bad Is Happening, and I made it All About Me, by love-bombing him and sending him smiley faces with sunglasses when he didn't love-bomb me back.

When I think about the little yellow Beatles badge, and the picture of his dad, just sat on his easel waiting for his second Christmas without him, I feel sick.

'Ellie, help set the table,' Dad says, motioning to me from across the living room. I walk into the kitchen to get the cutlery, where Aunty Kitty's head is hidden in the fridge, studiously avoiding me.

After the dumpster episode yesterday, she introduced us to Charles as a partner at her law firm, but not as a partner she'd spent five minutes kissing. She looked embarrassed, and angry, and defiant – as if she knew we'd seen everything, but she wasn't willing to admit it. I feel bad. Because I don't want her to admit it – it's none of my business; and I don't want her to think we were trying to make it be.

'Aunty,' I say, tapping her on the shoulder. She turns to face me, her eyes slightly red. She looks pale and weary; dressed like a background character. Like someone who doesn't want to be noticed. Like an entirely different person to yesterday.

'I'm sorry about yesterday. Hope and I didn't mean to upset you.'

She stares at me, her voice hard.

'You didn't upset me. You embarrassed me in front of a colleague. You embarrassed yourselves.'

'Either way, I'm sorry, Aunty. I would never want to embarrass you. Or upset you.' I stare at my shoes, hoping she can sense my sincerity.

'It's OK,' she says quietly, her voice less hard.

I open the cutlery drawer and start taking out knives and forks and spoons; something Granny hates, because we should be using our fingers. Like real Tamils. Not fake British ones.

'Ellie,' she says, more gently this time.

I turn to her.

'You and I, we're from different generations. I'm glad you could come here and have fun, and be in your own room with Hope, and feel independent. But it wasn't like that for me growing up. There are different rules about what's allowed. What your grandmother would accept.'

I frown. Trying to understand why it would be a problem, why she can't just be happy with the Suitably Aged Suit Man. Why she can't dress like Lady Gaga's lawyer every day, and just be herself.

'OK,' I reply, trying to think of something else to say.

'It's just, she wouldn't want me to be with someone like Charles. She wants me to be with someone like us. Someone Tamil.'

And then I finally think of something.

'But what do *you* want?' I ask.

'I want . . .' She falters.

But then Granny is shouting for us, because the dahl's going cold and she's disappointed with the quality of the aubergine curry, and I want to hug my aunty and tell her she deserves to be happy. That Granny will get over it; because this isn't 1952, and she has to. Doesn't she?

Why does love have to be so complicated? What does love have to do with the colour of your skin, or the texture of your hair, or the place you were born in which you had no choice?

And all I want is to tell the boy I almost love that I'm thinking about him. For him to be OK.

> **Ellie:**
> i'm sorry 🖤

> **Ellie:**
> the emojis were flowing like endless rain (into a paper cup)

And I wait, hoping he'll understand. Hoping he'll hear the Beatles, 'Across the Universe' in his head, just as I'm hearing it in mine.

Seconds later, I hear my phone.

Ash:
😄

Ash:
i miss u

If there was a way to reach through my phone and be next to him, I'd be gone, a trail of 1950s Doris Day-style underwear in my wake.

> **Ellie:**
> i'm here. talk 2 me.

Ash:

And there it is again, that beating heart.

But he still doesn't tell me what's going on.

26

Maps

When I wake the next day, it feels strange to be in a hotel room, because it's Christmas Day, and I can't smell pine needles or hear my parents talking in the kitchen. For a second, I think about Amis, because I always do on days like this.

I stare at the ceiling, hoping (ironically) that Hope will be in a better mood today. Until the dumpster incident, I'd thought we were friends again. Now I can't work out how to fix things. What I said that was so wrong, or why she's so angry with me.

When my phone starts vibrating next to me, I look over and see Ash's name on the screen. I fluff my hair and thank the High School Gods for making sure I'm wearing cute pyjamas. A black silky shorts set Mum bought me last Christmas. I press accept on FaceTime and excitedly tiptoe to the bathroom, closing the door gently behind me. The last thing I need is Hope being woken from her beauty sleep. It could lead to the worst Christmas ever given the mood she's been since Sunday afternoon.

'Hi,' I whisper eagerly. 'Merry Christmas!'

'It's good to see you,' he says teasingly. 'I thought you were going to ignore me and send a Santa emoji instead.'

'Hmmmm,' I mumble, embarrassed.

'I miss you,' he says wistfully. 'I keep listening to the Yeah Yeah Yeahs and trying to work out what time of day it is and what you're doing.'

And when he says it, the bathroom fills with the sound of the Yeah Yeah Yeahs, 'Maps'. I've always loved the lead singer. She reminds me a bit of Hannah.

'Well, I *love* you,' I joke awkwardly.

He shifts uncomfortably.

'I'm joking,' I say lightly. 'I'm sorry if I freaked you out the other day – it just came out, I wasn't declaring anything. I mean, I *like* you. But I'm not there yet.'

'Don't be sorry,' he says gently. 'I liked hearing you say it. I guess I just . . . I'm not there yet either.'

And even though I'm glad we're being honest with each other, it still hurts a little to hear him say it.

'Good. So, we're both agreed. No love. Just moderate interest,' I tease.

'More like, mid to above-average interest,' he returns.

'Aha! I knew you were above-average interested in me,' I crow.

'Actually, I'm a little bit obsessed,' and his voice sounds lower and deeper, like it gets just before he kisses me. I can see the neckline of his navy-blue fisherman's knit. The one that feels scratchy and warm when he puts his arms around me. The one he lent me after I fell in the river.

And I wish I was next to him. I wish I could feel it against my skin.

'I'm going to give you the best Christmas present ever when I get home.' Then I realise how that sounds. Like I'm going to offer him my lime-green bra and matching underwear, you know, on *me*, as a Christmas present.

'I mean,' I mumble, 'I bought you a present. Like a real one. From a shop.'

'OK,' he laughs. 'But I didn't buy yours from a shop, sorry. Listen, there's something I need to talk to you about,' he continues.

'ELLIE! Get out of the bathroom,' Hope says, hammering on the door. 'I need to wee!'

'HOPE. I'm on *the phone*!' I hiss.

'Get *out*,' she says, pressing her fist against the door.

'Just a minute,' I whisper to Ash. 'My cousin is the *worst* in the morning.'

I wrangle myself past her as she slams the door in my face, and settle myself against the pillows on my bed.

'Sorry about that. What do you want to talk about?'

'Ash!!' In the distance, I hear someone call his name.

'It's Mum,' he sighs. 'Can we talk later? She's all maudlin about this being our last Christmas at home.'

'Is it weird to say I miss her?'

'I knew you were only dating me for my mother,' he says, amused. 'Call me back if you get time later. And say hi to your family.'

'Hmmn,' I respond softly.

'Merry Christmas, Ellie Pillai.'

'Merry Christmas,' I whisper.

And then I remind myself, Do Not Say I Love You – and I don't.

When I put the phone down, Hope flounces back in. Christmas with the Pillais is happening. Comedy. Tragedy. Drama. Or more probably, a mixture of all three.

27

Christmas with the Pillais

When we arrive at Aunty Kitty's house for lunch, she has actual caterers in. On Christmas Day. People whose job it is to cook our Christmas lunch. Granny is unimpressed, making a variety of snide comments about how she'll never catch a husband if she can't cook her own meals; and I want to remind her that Aunty Kitty works eighty hours a week, and has made dinner for nineteen of us at least three times in the last week.

For the first time ever, I really watch Aunty Kitty when she makes these comments. I used to think they rolled off her, like she was immune to hearing them; but she's pained, and sad – and it makes me pained and sad to see it.

'This looks spectacular,' Mum says, gesturing to the tables. On previous visits, there have been so many of us that kids have peppered the floors, perching around the coffee table, while adults lined the sofas, slotting into any available space. Aunty Kitty's table isn't big enough to accommodate all of us, but the caterers have brought another one and dressed them to match, so we're finally able to sit together. White tablecloths and paper snowflakes, champagne flutes and rose-gold cutlery. I feel like I'm in a picture on Pinterest.

'Harrumph,' Granny mimes critically, as she eyes the caterers suspiciously.

'It looks lovely, Kitty,' Big Uncle says, as Aunty Delia and Little Uncle murmur in agreement.

'GORGEOUS,' Aunty Christine agrees.

'Cool,' Andrew says, while Joseph plays with his iPhone under the table, refusing to acknowledge he needs to thank anyone.

'Like *Frozen*,' Esther whispers, awed.

'It's perfect,' I smile at Aunty Kitty.

'It is,' Hope says, refusing to look at me. It's the first time she's agreed with anything I've said since our falling-out.

'Thank you,' Aunty Kitty says brightly. She looks more like herself today, in a dark green wrap dress and silver sandals. Like the leading character version of herself instead of the one chosen by Granny. 'Merry Christmas, everyone.' She motions to the kitchen as the servers begin to bring out the food. Turkey and stuffing, roast potatoes and gravy, and Yorkshire puddings for Granny, because she's obsessed with the fact Americans don't know how to make them. Each plate is arranged like some kind of restaurant meal, like I imagine lunch at the Plaza would look today.

Just as we're all finishing, sat in a silence broken only by the occasional 'chkk' from Granny, code for I'm Talking to Myself, But I Am Very Disappointed in You All, the bell to the apartment rings, and Aunty Kitty stands up.

She looks over at me meaningfully, and I want to understand why, but I'm too busy trying to get Joseph to stop kicking me under the table. Andrew elbows him, but he seems to think he's being funny. Like we're eleven and this kind of behaviour is still appropriate. I'm wearing a BRA for God's sake. I'm practically A WOMAN. Surely that fact should protect my shins from these kind of shenanigans.

'Stop. It,' Hope seethes at him.

'What?' he grins. 'It's funny.'

'It's not,' she declares imperiously; and he stops immediately.

I smile gratefully at her, but she ignores me until Aunty Kitty returns, with Charles the Suitably Aged Suit Man stood next to her carrying a bottle of wine. He's wearing a navy-blue fine-knit jumper. The sort of thing Ash might wear in twenty years, if he was a lawyer living in New York.

Hope and I exchange a look.

The rest of the family look up: the uncles and aunties and cousins. And Granny.

'This is Charles,' Aunty Kitty offers, her arm waving, as she introduces him to the room. 'Charles is a partner at my law firm.'

'Lovely to meet you, Charles,' Dad says, standing up to shake his hand. 'Merry Christmas.'

'Merry Christmas,' we all murmur. He smiles at us, his teeth straight and white, as he shakes Dad's hand warmly.

'It's lovely to meet you too,' and something in his eyes suggests he really does think it's lovely to meet us all.

'Hello,' Granny says, eyeing him suspiciously.

'Hello,' he replies, smiling at her.

'You are English?' she says, taking in his accent.

'Kitty and I transferred here from the London office at the same time,' he says slowly – and something about the way he says it makes me realise this has been going on a long time.

'I see,' Granny replies. 'Is nice to have friends,' she says to no one in particular.

'Yes,' he murmurs, looking at Aunty Kitty for guidance.

'That's just it, *Amma*,' Aunty Kitty says hesitantly, and suddenly I'm holding my breath. 'Charles isn't just a friend.'

'Yes, yes. Work together also,' Granny says dismissively.

Mum and Dad exchange a look.

'No,' Aunty Kitty says firmly. 'Charles and I are . . . he's . . .' She looks around the room in abject terror. The always-in-control, sensible, trustworthy, known-for-her-good-judgement lawyer.

'Your boyfriend?' I offer. Granny glares at me, as Charles slides his arm around Kitty's waist. Kitty turns towards him and beams, like she's exactly where she's supposed to be, like she knows she's safe.

'Fiancé,' Charles says, smiling at me.

I think Granny might be having a heart attack. She's gone white. A colour a brown woman should never turn.

Little Uncle stands up and starts pumping Charles's hand in congratulations. 'Welcome to the family! You're a brave man!' he jokes.

'A lucky man,' Charles says, his arm tightening around Kitty's waist.

'That goes without saying,' Middle Uncle says, standing up and patting his back overenthusiastically.

But Granny's still ominously quiet, her silence thunderous. So, we fill the gaps with sound. Hand shaking and back patting and wet kisses mingled with congratulations.

'No,' Granny says suddenly, her voice like ice. 'I did not agree this. I did not agree *you*,' she says, pointing at Charles accusingly. 'You,' she says, pointing to Aunty Kitty, 'disrespect your mother. You cannot marry man like *this*,' she hisses. 'Is not our kind. Is no good.'

'*Amma*,' Dad says, his eyes flashing. 'Stop.'

She stands.

'I will not stop. There are rules. Kitty knows rules.'

'What rules?' my cousin Daniel asks no one in particular.

'Stupid rules,' Hope responds loudly.

'I love him,' Kitty says, crying, and I've never seen my aunty cry, never seen her show emotion at anything other than Amis's funeral.

'Love!' Granny says, her eyes flashing. 'What is *love*? I will introduce you to nice boy, you will love him too.'

'No,' Aunty Kitty says firmly. 'I won't.'

Granny sits down again, her breathing heavy.

'How long has this been going on?' she says quietly. 'You wait for me to die. Is this it? You want me to die, so you can do as you wish?' she says dramatically.

'*Amma*,' Middle Uncle says firmly. 'People have to marry who they want. We can't shut out the world.'

'You are all against me!' she says angrily.

'*Amma*,' Dad says quietly. 'Think of what you're saying. In front of the children.'

'They must understand the world is not easy, Noel. Is safer to be with what you know, with what you *are*. It is what is expected. Is best,' she says, appealing to Charles directly. 'Your family, they must agree?'

She looks so old, so fragile, I almost feel sorry for her. Almost.

'My family love Kitty. And they accept us,' he says quietly.

'Chkkk,' Granny says to no one in particular.

'Sounds pretty racist to me,' Hope says angrily.

We turn to look at her. Because she's saying the one thing we all know to be true but can't quite bring ourselves to say out loud. That Granny is being racist. That she's doing to someone else what every one of us has had done to them.

'Racist,' she says, rounding on Hope. 'What do you know of *racist*? I move to the UK in 1978. Am spat on. Laughed at. People will not take money from my hand in shop. They write bad words on our window, smash up my car. Police do nothing. My children are attacked. Police do *nothing*,' she says, shouting. 'I am not racist. I am *realist*. Life is hard. We don't need to make harder. This is not good for them. Is not good for anybody.'

'You think we don't know what it's like to be spat at?' Hope says, angrier still. 'You think I haven't been told to go home, when I was *born* in England, Granny? You think we don't know what it's like for people to judge us? We know life is hard, but what you're saying is wrong. It makes it all worse.'

'Hope . . .' Aunty Delia says quietly.

'No,' she says, turning to her mother. 'We all know she's wrong.

So, why don't we just say it?' I wish I was as brave as she is. I wish I was as strong.

'You all misunderstand me,' Granny says angrily.

And Christmas pudding is sat waiting on the kitchen island, while the servers pretend not to be listening.

Granny pushes her chair back, haughtily exiting the room as Aunty Kitty sobs quietly into Charles's shoulder. Dad and the uncles follow Granny, while Mum and the aunties crowd around Kitty, saying Granny will get over it, that she just needs time.

I walk over to Hope, just as the other cousins have made their way to the TV remote control.

'That was amazing,' I say, sitting down next to her.

'For someone with a *track record like me*?' she says angrily.

'I'm sorry,' I plead. 'I'm sorry I said that. I'm sorry we argued.'

'I know you think I'm just some silly girl who only cares about make-up and clothes and boys, but I'm not stupid. I made a mistake with Vikash, the way I let him talk to me, the way I talk to myself sometimes. The thing is, I'm not stupid. And I've decided I'm not going to let anyone make me feel like I am any more. Not even you.'

'I don't think you're stupid,' I beg. 'I think *Vikash* is stupid. You, you're one of the smartest people I know.'

She smiles.

'I am,' she says, looking a bit teary, 'and don't you ever forget it.'

And I hug her tight and think: I won't.

28

Where's Granny Going to Sleep?

A week later, and we're flying home from New York.

And Granny is flying with us. Because Mum needs looking after. You know, because she's pregnant. At Her Age.

When Aunty Kitty drops her off at the airport, Granny doesn't even hug her goodbye; no happy new year or hopes for the future, just silence between them, cold and foreboding.

I want to understand love. To know how it comes in so many forms. Like this one, that seems riven with hate and judgement and rules, when I thought love was gentle and kind and accepting, or at least tried to be.

As we disappear into security, I look back at Aunty Kitty and think two things.

How can choice cause so much pain?

And where's Granny going to sleep?

29

Our House

When we reach the front of our house, I'm so relieved to see it, I consider falling on the floor crying and hugging the earth – but it would ruin my new wide-leg white jeans.

Granny, who sat two rows behind me on the flight home, spent several hours shouting over the head of the person in front of her, telling me to sit up straight, to read instead of watching my iPad, to walk up the aisle every twenty minutes to avoid deep vein thrombosis, some kind of old people disease, and of course, to get me to deliver whatever it was she needed at any given moment, even though there were air hostesses, whose actual job was to do that for her.

And this, is the start of my new year. Happy being optional.

On the car journey back from the airport, my headphones were jammed over my head, playing Madness, 'Our House' on a loop, as if the sound of jubilant saxophones could somehow destroy the feeling of dread that was creeping into every bone of my body.

Granny is going to be living with us.

Granny is going to be *living* with us.

Kill me.

Kill me now.

When I open the car door, I breathe a sigh of relief at the fresh air in my lungs; then out of the corner of my eye, I spy a little blue car parked right by Mum's Mini.

I turn and run to him as he appears out of the driver's side, his curly hair swept to one side, wearing the jumper. That Jumper, the one where all I want is to wrap myself inside it with him. I throw myself at him, burying my head in his shoulder as he puts his arms around me.

'Hello,' he grins, as he emerges from my hair, and I think he might be as glad to see me as I am to see him. 'Happy new year.' he whispers.

'Hello, Ellie,' his mum says, peeking out from across the passenger side of the car. Mrs Aachara. My Favourite Teacher/My Boyfriend's Mum. Both of which are excellent, but also slightly mortifying to bear witness to at this moment.

I slide out of his arms and on to the ground.

'Ellllieee,' Granny calls, and I turn around, suddenly remembering Mrs Aachara isn't the only witness to this display.

'Who is that?' she calls.

'Granny?' Ash asks, under his breath.

'Yep,' I murmur through gritted teeth. I walk back towards the car, Ash's hand wrapped around mine, and await the judgement and potential Aunty Kitty-style fall out.

'Granny, this is my boyfriend Ash,' I say, waving my hand towards him.

'Mrs Pillai,' he says, leaning down to shake her hand. 'It's lovely to meet you. Ellie talks about you all the time.'

And not in a good way.

'You may call me Cecily.'

I might be choking on my tongue.

'Come here,' Granny commands, as she beckons him to her level. He leans over, and she grabs a handful of his cheek between her fingers, pinching tightly. 'North Indian,' she states, squinting.

'My mum is . . .'

'She is over there? In car? Children must always respect their mothers,' she says pointedly.

'Er, yes,' he says, as surprised by her acquiescence as I am.

'She will come. I will talk to her.' Mum, who's behind her, hulking bags out of the car, looks at me and rolls her eyes in sympathy.

'Let me get that,' Ash says, taking the bag from Mum's hand. Granny looks approvingly at him, while Dad shoots him a look of irritation, muttering under his breath about feet under tables.

'Thank you,' Mum says, impressed – and for the next five minutes, Ash helps Dad unload the car, while I attempt to warn Mrs Aachara about Granny. But she doesn't seem to need warning; she knows exactly how to make Granny feel listened to and respected, and she even seems to *enjoy* talking to her.

I creep up the stairs with Ash, leaving the door ajar as we sit down on the bed and debrief about our respective holidays. Me – the world of Aunty Kitty, Granny and a newly nice Hope, him – getting used to Christmas without his dad. Then I get his present out of the suitcase he's carried upstairs for me, and hand it to him.

'I haven't had time to wrap it, but I figure I'm saving the planet,'

I smile, handing him a bag, inside of which is a large, flat object.

'You didn't need to get me anything,' he says, looking down at it. I smile as he kisses me again. 'Yours is at home.'

'Open it,' I demand. He opens the bag and pulls the object out slowly, and carefully, with just the right amount of enthusiasm.

'Oh, wow. Ellie, it's . . .' and he doesn't say much, just turns it over and over in his hands.

'Don't you like it?' I ask quietly.

'Like it?' he says softly. 'I think it might be the nicest present anyone's ever given me.' I blush, because it isn't *that* nice. Just a vinyl of David Bowie, *Young Americans* that Hope and I spent an afternoon trying to find in a record shop I could literally have lived in, had I not been forcibly thrown out of it when it closed. I know it was his dad's favourite album, and that he grew up listening to it, so he probably already has it; but this copy is special. A remastered version from a few years ago that I know he's tried to find.

'I found it in this record shop in SoHo. The guy that owned it looked like an old Jeff Buckley. In fact, I thought he might *be* Jeff Buckley, other than the fact, you know, Jeff Buckley isn't alive, and actually, he was sort of short, and I always imagined Jeff Buckley would be taller, not that I have any evidence to back that up; you just sort of *assume* people who are that talented are just *bigger*, don't you?' And exactly why am I talking about dead musicians when the only similarity the owner of that shop had with Jeff Buckley was longish hair and a sort of tortured look that was probably more to do with the number of questions I asked him about Jeff Buckley?

'It's amazing,' he says, pulling me close. 'I can't tell you how much I love it.' And in my head, Bowie is singing just for us.

'So, listen,' he says, sitting back for a second, 'my mum has a friend of hers staying with us for a couple of weeks.'

'Ash!' I hear Mrs Aachara call to him from down the stairs. 'We have guests, and we need to pick up Elina!'

'Coming!' he shouts back down.

'OK,' I say. 'That's nice.'

'Yeah, it is . . .'

'Ash, come on!' Mrs Aachara shouts again, and I can hear Granny murmuring about the fact my door looks closed.

'We'd better go,' I say, standing up.

'OK,' he says heavily. 'But about Mum's friend . . .'

'You can't have people over while she's there?' I finish.

'Kind of . . .' he says, waving his arms around in annoyance.

'It's fine,' I say, pecking him on the lips. 'It's just a couple of weeks, right?'

'Right,' he says, leaning down to kiss me again.

We walk down the stairs together, where Granny gives his cheek one final, brutal pinch, as Dad disappears into grunt mode.

At the very end of the day, when I get into bed thinking about exams and school and life as I used to know it – I don't even mind the thought of school, just as long as I get to see him.

I put my new lime-green bra out as a reminder to myself to wear it, and tuck the Hello Kitty crop top into the back of my underwear drawer.

Then I tuck the rest of my new underwear into a different drawer.

Just in case Dad gets any ideas.

30

Earth to Ellie Pillai

Jessica:
r u alive?

Ellie:
✓

Hayley:
where have u *been*?

Ellie:
NY, NY

Jessica:
do they have phone signal there??

Ellie:
sorry. only allowed several secs of non-fam time a day

Hayley:

assume u used them on ash

Ellie:

. . .

Hayley:

hmmmmmmmmmmmnnnnnnnn

Jessica:

hmmmmmmmmmmmmmmmmnnnnnnnnnnnnn

Ellie:

should i keep ur NY xmas presents then?

Hayley:

prepared 2 accept mine

Jessica:

will allow it

Ellie:

ur angels . . .

Jessica:

h – do u still want 2 go 2 Cinema 2m?

Hayley:

i will if u will

Jessica:

😎

Ellie:
what cinema thing?

Ellie:
r u hanging out without me?

Ellie:
hello?

Ellie:
hello??

Jessica:
tell u 2m

☺

Note to self: smiley faces are the opposite of reassuring.

31

The Word You're
Looking for Is *Racist*

'Ellieee!' Jess comes bounding up the school corridor towards me and pulls me into a hug. 'How was New York? Tell me everything!' she demands.

And I tell her about Granny and Aunty Kitty and the fact my grandmother is now living in our spare bedroom and sounds like a bulldozer while apparently Sleeping Peacefully.

'Wow. So, they're still not speaking?' she asks quietly. 'You really weren't joking when you said she was traditional . . .' She trails away.

'Racist, Jessica. The word you're looking for is *racist*.'

'I mean, yeah, it's not great. How do you think she'll be about Ash?' Ugh.

'She met him yesterday, and she *seems* to like him.'

I still can't quite work that bit out. Maybe it's because he's part Indian, or it doesn't matter as much because I'm not her daughter. The truth is, I don't want to question her about it, even though I know I should.

'How did she meet him?'

'He was there when I got home from the airport.' I beam. She nods vigorously, as if in approval.

'Of course. Good. And everything's OK between you?'

'It's great.'

'Good,' she says overenthusiastically.

'And you?' I ask.

'Well, Elina met Dad and Alfie and Barb. Barb thinks she's hot, Dad thinks Barb's inappropriate . . . so, the usual.' She smiles.

'That's great,' I say warmly. 'Also, this *hair*,' I say, leaning forward and running my fingers through her new fringe, 'is giving me major Bardot Vibes. Because you and Elina needed to be a hotter couple. Your hotness was in question, so you just had to push the dial.'

She rolls her eyes. 'Sometimes I think you talk just to fill the silence, E. Anyway, I have to get to registration, and I have Chemistry Club at lunchtime, so after school?'

Chemistry Club? Why?

'Do you want to meet before you go to the cinema?' I ask faux nonchalantly, because I can't believe she and Hayley haven't invited me yet.

'It's Cinema,' she says as if I'm hard of hearing.

'That's what I said. Before you go to the cinema.'

'It's not an *actual* cinema, Ellie, it's a venue. You get stamped if you're under eighteen but you can get in to watch bands and see art exhibitions and theatre and stuff. It's called Cinema. Elina's doing a DJ set there in a couple of weeks.'

'Oh. So, you and Hayley . . .'

'We talked about it when we met for coffee last week. Things with her and James are a bit weird. I thought it might be fun to go together.'

'On a school night . . .' I mock gasp.

'I know,' she says worriedly, 'but Hayley needs cheering up.' I look at her and wonder at what point over the last few weeks Jess started caring about Hayley. Not that it's a bad thing, because Hayley's amazing and Jess is amazing, and I want them to be friends, it's just I don't really want them to be friends *without me*.

'One night off from studying isn't going to kill you,' I smile, trying not to be jealous at this new state of being: I will be a new, mature, better version of me.

'Hi.' And then Ash is next to me, kissing me in the corridor.

'Hi,' I reply dreamily. I'm starting to see how, at times like this, I'm less of a mature, better version of me and more of a really, really annoying version of me. Why do I have to look at him like I'm Julie Delpy staring at Ethan Hawke as her train disappears at the end of *Before Sunrise*? Why is he permanently surrounded by pearlescent lighting and a shimmering sixties girl group? Why am I being so . . . ugh?

'I'll leave you to it,' Jess says, looking at Ash pointedly. Even though I know I'm still doing it, I can't seem to stop myself.

Snap out of it, Pillai!

'Walk you to registration?' he asks, holding out his hand.

His hand.

You are a disgrace.

I try not to care that everyone's staring at us because the last time we were here nobody knew we were together yet – but now they do, and it's weird and unnerving to think people have opinions about that. Opinions about *me*.

'Hey, Ellie,' and suddenly James Godfrey is in step with us. 'Ash,' he says, nodding solemnly in his direction – and I have to admit, I'm a bit grateful for the distraction. 'You look nice,' he says distractedly.

'Oh, er . . .' I say, unsure of how to respond. I'm wearing the blusher Hope gave me for Christmas, which she said made me look like a snack. I said I didn't want to look like a snack, but she said it was a good thing.

Ash glares at him.

'How was your Christmas?' I ask, deciding to ignore the comment.

'Fine,' he says, scratching the back of his head. Why is everyone suddenly behaving like they have nits? 'Um, how's Hayley?'

'She's your girlfriend,' I say, staring at him. 'You tell me.'

'She's been really busy,' he says, looking miserable. 'She's barely had time to talk to anyone.'

This. Is. Bad.

'Can you ask her to meet me for lunch?' he asks quietly, and there's something weird and pleading in the way he says it, like he's afraid to ask her himself.

I stop outside the form room I share with Hayley and look at him.

'Why don't you ask her yourself?'

'Lunch?' Ash whispers, his finger drawing a circle on the top of my hand.

'Yes,' I smile, kissing him quickly.

'Alone?' he adds acerbically.

I nod. I'd much rather be alone with him than have half the school staring at us.

I turn my attention back to James as Ash walks away.

He looks so good walking away.

Stop. It.

'Go on,' I say, pushing James towards Hayley. I want to be more encouraging than just shoving him over there, but she looks spiky today, like her edges are sharper somehow.

'Hay,' I say, standing over her. 'James is here.' I extend my arm towards him.

She looks up, then straight back down again.

'. . . How was your Christmas?' I continue through gritted teeth. Because she isn't making this easy.

'Fine,' she says nonchalantly. I look up at James and shrug my shoulders.

'What were you saying about *lunch*, James?' I ask, nudging him viciously because he appears to have lost the ability to speak.

'Ow!' he exclaims, massaging his ribs and glaring at me.

'I can't have lunch,' she says without looking up.

'You know, Hayley, if you don't want to do this any more . . .' he says softly, just as Mr Gorley arrives, dishevelled and loud.

'Are you in my form?' he asks, glaring at James. 'Are you *new*? There are too many people in this class already, I can't take anyone else on,' he says dramatically, clattering his battered leather briefcase on to his desk.

'Sir, I've had you for physics *for four years*,' James says, appalled.

'I'll see you in *physics* then,' Mr Gorley says, waving him away.

James turns to look at Hayley as he leaves, his eyes hard; but she's staring out of the window, pretending he doesn't exist.

'What's wrong?' I whisper.

'I called my dad . . . I found the number in Mum's phone.'

'OK . . .' I encourage her gently.

'He's married.' She smiles bitterly. 'He got married again, and he never even told us. He didn't bother to invite his own kids to his wedding. Who'd want to marry *that*?' she says angrily.

'Oh, Hay, that's awful, I'm sorry.' And the spikiness makes sense now. The way her fringe is skimming her eyes, and how underneath, they look dark and tired.

'You can't trust anyone, Ellie, not really. They're all liars. They'll all let you down.' She looks so sure of that fact, so broken, that all I want to do is hug her and say he didn't deserve to have her at his wedding. That he doesn't deserve her at all. But instead I say:

'James isn't your dad, Hay.' But she just shrugs again.

When Mr Gorley pulls out the register, I open my phone and type a message to Ash.

Ellie:

hay in mess. need 2 have lunch with her.

A second later, he replies.

Ash:

love how much u care. don't love the fact
we have no alone time together. ever.

Ellie:

love – or mid to above average
fondness for how much i care?

Ash:

ha ha

Ellie:

after school?

Ash:

ur house?

Ellie:

granny = ✗

Ash:

cinema?

Ellie:

haven't been invited

Ash:

u have now

Ellie:

who invited u??

Ash:

it doesn't require an invite weirdo

Ellie:

u like weirdoes

Ash:

i like u, weirdo ♥

I message Jess and tell her I'm inviting myself to Cinema – and she replies that I didn't need an invite – then I message James to tell him Hayley's going, because they need to talk.

Note to self: fix friends' relationships, because mine is pretty close to perfect. Other than the no alone time and Hello Kitty crop top.

London Cousin – Annoying:

did u wear the blush?

Ellie:

✓

London Cousin – Annoying:

London Cousin – Annoying:

London Cousin – Annoying:

32

Yes

We've gone to Jess's dad's to get ready and it's the first time I've been over here since she moved in. But coming straight here after school rather than going home first is causing me a number of problems.

Jess is insisting we study and is now forcing me to do something unspeakably boring with the periodic table, which I'm sure I'll be thankful for come exam day but is currently bleurgh.

I have to borrow something to wear when she is at least a hundred feet taller than me (four inches).

Hayley's on her way over, and I don't know how much to divulge of what she told me earlier, or whether to admit I invited James.

'So, Ellie, why does iodine have a higher boiling point than chlorine?' she asks, as if I have the remotest clue of what the answer might be.

'I invited James,' I blurt out. I can't tell whether it's panic at the idea that I haven't told Hayley this fact, or because I have no idea about iodine or chlorine or why anyone would want to boil them.

'For God's sake, Ellie! When are you going to learn to leave people alone?' Jess sighs, frustrated.

'If I'd left those two alone in the first place, they would never have been a "two" at all,' I say huffily.

'Yes, I know,' Jess says slowly, 'it's just Hayley has a lot of stuff going on right now. Her dad, the exams, James – honestly, I'm worried about her.'

'How do you know about her dad?' I ask, surprised.

'She told me over the holidays.'

'Oh.'

'She did try to get hold of you in New York, E,' she says quietly.

Bleurgh Pillai.

I put my head in my hands.

'I'm being one of *those* people, aren't I?'

'No,' she says kindly. 'Just remember, you were a person *before* you were in a relationship.'

'I can't help myself,' I say, shamefaced. 'It's like, even when I'm not with him, I'm thinking about him – and with Mum and Dad and the baby, and you guys, I'm not really paying attention. I'm being a bit . . .'

'Annoying?' she says, laughing.

I throw a pillow at her.

'So, what are we going to do about James and Hayley?'

'Nothing,' she says, looking at me seriously. 'He was probably going to come anyway – if he wants to talk to her, let him talk to her. But do NOT get involved, Eleanor.' And she only calls me Eleanor when it's Serious.

'Fiiinnnne,' I mutter under my breath.

I sneak a look at her in her new surroundings. She's always stayed in this room when she's at her dad's, but it feels more permanent now. There's a new writing desk and a fluffy beanbag chair in the corner under the window, a poster of the periodic table on the wall and some of Elina's drawings pinned to a corkboard with ticket stubs and ribbons like a map of her life over the past few months. It makes me feel simultaneously happy and sad for her; the ease of it, the way this new life seems to fit her so perfectly, and yet there's a picture of her mum in a turquoise frame by her bed – there, but not there – and I wonder why this is the first time she's invited me over.

'So, how are things with Elina?'

She beams.

'She told me she loves me,' she admits shyly.

'WHHHHHHHAAAATTT?'

'And I told her I love her back.'

'WHHHHHHHAAAATTTT?'

'I'm really happy, Ellie,' she says, smiling at me. 'For the first time in as long as I can remember, I feel *really* happy. I honestly didn't know what this feeling was when I felt it. It's like I'd forgotten.'

'Jess,' I say quietly, going to sit down next to her on her bed. 'I wish you'd been able to talk to me before. I hate the idea that you've been miserable all this time.'

'Not miserable,' she says thoughtfully, 'just, not really there. I couldn't be myself. I couldn't think about anything other than Mum and making sure the bills were paid, and food, and school, and . . .' She trails off.

'Never just you,' I respond gently.

'I know I'm being selfish,' she states.

'You're not selfish, Jess. All you do is think about other people. *Selfish* is not bothering to call a friend when they ask you to,' I say glumly, thinking about Hayley's messages while I was in New York.

She takes my hand.

'Love you,' she says fiercely.

'Love *you*,' I say back just as fiercely. 'And you're allowed to be happy, Jessica.'

'Even if Mum isn't?' she says quietly.

'What do you mean?'

'She wants me to go home.'

'What does your dad say?' I ask, alarmed. Because the thought of her alone in that house frightens me.

'He says she's not ready, and that I need to focus on me – at least until the exams are over.'

'And what do you think?'

'I'd like to think about me for a bit too,' she gulps. 'I know I'm being—'

I cut her off. 'You're *not*.'

She hugs me, and I let her hold on to me for as long as she needs to. Because that's what best friends do. They listen, and they're there, and they think about stuff other than their boyfriend, and what they're doing, and what they're listening to, and whether or not they've noticed you're wearing a new bra.

'Now,' I say, as she pulls away, sniffing, 'can we stop talking about ions and decide what we're wearing to this thing?'

'OK,' she smiles.

'Music?' I ask seriously.

'Something upbeat . . . and optimistic . . . and FUN,' she replies thoughtfully.

'OK,' I say rubbing my hands together, because this is my superpower. The only thing I can offer my beautiful, a little bit broken best friend. A song to make it all feel better. 'Got it,' I say, clapping my hands in glee.

I type the words into my phone, and strings start playing high and strong and joyful. McAlmont & Butler, 'Yes'.

We're jumping up and down, doing aeroplanes as we fly like children around the room, the music inside our bones, like a chemistry we can't explain. And when it stops, it's like there's a little bit of magic still inside us.

She hugs me, and I promise to remember who I was before. A girl called Ellie, who was always all right.

33

Beautiful Ones

I'm wearing a skirt of Jess's that is indecently short on her, and reasonably short on me, and we've borrowed* (*see: 'taken without permission') a shirt from her dad's wardrobe and put a vintage gold belt around the middle of it. I'm wearing bright red lipstick and Jess's gold ankle boots, feeling like a brown Madonna, circa *Like a Virgin*, while Jess is channelling Glastonbury Alexa Chung Realness in denim shorts, a sequin top, Converse and a parka.

Hayley – who's dressed like Wednesday Addams in an oversized short black dress and Dr Martens, is understandably annoyed with me when we're stood outside Cinema and I tell her I've invited James. Technically, he was already going, so maybe I'm less guilty than I thought I was, except I can't be, because Hayley's still annoyed with me.

'Why are you talking to him, Ellie? I thought *I* was your friend, not *him*,' she says huffily, as we stand outside queuing.

'I'm sorry, Hay. I shouldn't have got involved.'

She glares at me.

'But he was coming anyway, so maybe it's a good time for the two of you to talk?' I continue. Jess looks at me warningly, as if to say: Please Just Stop. But I can't. Because I'm me.

'You know, James isn't your dad.'

Shut up, Ellie. Shut. Up.

Her eyes look suddenly huge, or maybe it's the fact her face looks so small. I wonder if she's going to kill me.

She says nothing, staring straight ahead of her.

'Chocolate?' Jess says, trying to deflect, pulling a packet of Rolos out of her bag. 'I hear sugar helps relieve tension,' she says seriously.

'Is that true?' I ask, from a mouthful of Rolo.

'Hayley?' she says, offering her one. She shakes her head darkly.

'Look, here comes Elina,' Jess says awkwardly, trying to fill Hayley's silence. But when I look to where she's pointing, I notice her face fall – because Elina isn't alone, she's with another girl. Older than us. Maybe seventeen or eighteen. A tall, beautiful South Asian girl, and they look good together. Really good.

There's this Suede song Ash loves called 'Beautiful Ones'. This sort of perfect Britpop anthem. All guitars and scratchy vocals and bouncy, happy drums, and I can hear it in my head as I watch them walking towards us, Ash and Elina and this other girl. The beautiful ones.

I can't work out why I recognise her, until I see it as she turns her head a little. The eyes from Elina's painting; the eyes that seemed to speak in ways I didn't think eyes could talk, as Elina shoved the canvas down the side of her dresser.

I look over at Jess again, and she looks annoyed and confused, her eyes flashing angrily.

144

'I can't believe they brought her,' she mutters to no one, and Hayley and I turn to each other, our mouths forming silent O's.

'Hey,' Elina says uncomfortably, as she approaches us.

'Hi,' says the nameless girl with kaleidoscopic eyes and green velvet flares over her long, skinny limbs. 'I'm Rebecca.'

And Rebecca is me. Or rather, the me I wish I was. The better version of me. The cool, confident, gorgeous, tall South Asian girl. And suddenly I feel like I'm dressed for an eighties-themed disco. And not in a good way.

'Ellie.' I wave. She looks me up and down.

'Hey,' she says, cocking her head to one side. 'How *old* are you?' she asks curiously.

'I'll be sixteen in a few weeks.'

She laughs like you might imagine a fairy would laugh, high and melodic.

'I feel about a thousand years old,' she jokes, widening her eyes. 'I must be the only one here old enough to drink.'

'So, how do you know Ash and Elina?' I ask tetchily. Because I want to get it out there. I want to understand why this girl is here, standing between my best friend and her girlfriend. Because Jess has been through enough. Is Going Through Enough, and I'm not going to let anybody hurt her, or take away the happiness she's worked so hard for.

'We're old friends,' she smirks. 'We grew up together.' She turns a dazzling smile on Ash and Elina. I want to turn the dazzle back on her. Like a mirror into the sun. So maybe she can blind herself or turn into dust.

'I mean, I suppose we were a bit more than friends once, weren't we?' she says, smoothing a tendril of hair back from Ash's face. 'It's so cool of you, not to mind me staying with him,' she says casually. And now I think I might be confused. Because she said *him*. Because she seems to be picking nits off my boyfriend's head, talking in some kind of weird, sexy voice, while accusing me of being *cool*.

'Ellie, can I talk to you?' Ash says pleadingly.

'What?' I reply, turning to him robotically.

Jess's boots are starting to hurt my feet, and my lipstick feels like it's stuck to my teeth. It was *his* picture. His painting. Elina didn't know it was there until I pointed it out to her. That's why she looked so surprised, so uncomfortable; he'd put it in there before I came over. He was hiding it from me.

'Nice to meet you, Rebecca.'

My voice has reached an unknown pitch, a sound only dogs can hear. So, I back away and start walking. Because he lied to me. Because he left me in the dark again, and I don't know why – I just know I'm not going to cry, because this make-up took forever, and I may look like an eighties reject but I feel like *me*, and I don't care, I don't care, I don't care.

Just as I round the corner and think, maybe I do care – because the tears are directly behind my eyeballs now, leaking like the pipe my dad tried to fix before he caused an all-out flood in our kitchen two years ago – I hear him.

'Pillai?' And James Godfrey is behind me, looking nervous and slightly perplexed, but mostly just concerned. 'Looks like you're having a worse night than I'm about to have.'

When I see him, I actually throw myself at him, like a child who's just seen their mum on the first day after school.

'Whoa, whoa, whoa,' he says, patting my back awkwardly. 'Let's go in. We may as well have a terrible night together.'

And I think: OK. Because I really don't feel like running any more.

34

Cinema

I've got eleven missed calls from Ash and about the same number from Hayley and Jess. I finally pick up the phone in the girls' toilets and call Hayley, assuming they'll be together.

'I'm in the toilets,' I murmur pitifully.

'On our way,' Hayley says officiously, and seconds later, they arrive.

'Ellie, I'm so sorry,' Jess says, descending on me. 'I told him he *had* to tell you she was staying with them. I assumed he had. Even Elina thought he'd told you.'

'I don't understand what's happening,' I say, staring at them blankly.

'Rebecca's mum – and Kyra. They're best friends, E,' Jess says gently. 'They all grew up together. Ash and Rebecca went out on and off for a few years. Elina hates her, but it's like she's part of their family or something. It was a last-minute thing, her deciding to come with her mum,' she says lightly. 'Neither of them wanted her to come,' she says, trying to make me feel better. But nothing can make me feel better, because I still don't understand.

'But why didn't *he* tell me that?' I whisper. 'Why are *you* telling me?'

'I don't know, Ellie,' Jess says quietly.

'Because you can't trust anyone, Ellie,' Hayley says bluntly. 'People lie and cheat and steal and do horrible things, and that's all fine, as long as you know. As long as you expect it, and never expect anything better – because that's when it gets you. That's when it hurts.'

And when I turn to her, I realise how small all of this is. Ash and his lies, Rebecca and her stupid kaleidoscopic eyes.

I hug Hayley and she feels so tiny in my arms. And I say, 'No. Not all people are like that, Hay. We're not. Jess and me and James. You can trust us.' And she has a good cry on my shoulder, until Jess shakes us and jokingly tells us she feels left out.

'You know what?' I say, turning towards them.

'What?' Hayley says, sniffing.

'Ash Anderson can *suck it*. I'm not going to let him ruin our night. You two could barely stand each other a month ago, who knows how long this group will last.'

'I agree,' Hayley says animatedly. 'He can definitely suck it.'

'Good girl,' Jess says, patting my back overenthusiastically.

'And my dad,' Hayley says suddenly. 'He can suck it too.'

'That's the spirit,' Jess says, patting her too. Hayley looks at me, her eyes wide, as Jess clubs her on the back.

'I'm not *choking*,' she says, staring at her.

'Sorry,' Jess says guiltily.

'Doesn't know her own strength,' I say to no one in particular, because I have often internally referred to Jess as She-Hulk.

'That Rebecca . . .' Jess says, narrowing her eyes. 'It's so *cool* of you,' she says, mimicking her voice, 'to be OK with me staying with him.'

'Hmmmn,' Hayley says venomously.

'Who does she think she *is*?' Jess fumes. 'I feel about a thousand years old,' she mimics again: and Jess is a bad mimic. 'Your . . . *face* is about a thousand years old, Rebecca.' Hayley and I exchange a look, because this is not a good comeback line, because Rebecca's face doesn't look a thousand years old. It looks like an advert. For MAC make-up.

And even though my heart hurts, I refuse to care about that fact. He lied to me, but mostly, I just lied to myself. Because nothing and no one is perfect, and that's what love is, I think. It's accepting that.

Even when you really, really don't want to.

35

Crimson and Clover

Outside the bathroom, Cinema is a lot better than I thought it would be, given I've only been able to judge it by its toilet cubicles so far. It's dark, with velvet curtained walls, a bar running the full length of the room, and a stage at the front, on which a band are setting up. At the moment, a DJ is playing the kind of electronica designed to wash your brain, and there are large neon signs placed at random throughout the room, making statements like, It Was All a Dream and If You've Seen It All Before, Close Your Eyes.

We walk up to the bar holding hands. Like the Witches of Eastwick or the Spice Girls. Like we're all Girl Power and Feminism, and We're Going to Cast a Spell on You If You Come Anywhere Near Us.

The barman looks at Jess, ignoring all the warning signs, and winks unattractively.

'What can I get you?' he asks. He's the kind of man who likes to think of himself as boyish. The sort of man-child Hope might find alluring, while the rest of us look on in horror.

'I've been looking all over for you,' Elina says, spotting us at the bar. She pecks Jess on the lips as the barman stares at them. I can hear Radiohead, 'Creep' whenever he looks at them.

'Ellie,' Elina says, looking at me. 'Can I talk to you for a minute?' They seem almost indivisible to me just now, and I can see Hayley staring at them in the same way I am, because they seem to have something we don't. Something easy and comfortable and contented.

But I don't really want to talk to Elina – because what is there to talk about? He lied to me. He's here with his ex-girlfriend. The one he never told me about.

'Please, E,' Jess encourages me gently.

Elina takes hold of my hand and leads me away from the bar, and her hand feels just like his, except smaller, with less secrets.

'I'm sorry about Rebecca,' she says, as she stops in a corner, tucking her hair behind her ears. 'She invited herself at the last minute. It's a very *Rebecca* thing to do.'

Her pixie crop is starting to grow out at the sides. I can see the colour of it changing at the roots. She's wearing a purple spandex bodysuit with black leggings, giving her a distinctly Bowie vibe. As always, I can't help but like her, even if she can't stand me.

'I just wanted you to know it feels different with you than it did with her. He's different. Better.'

'They were together for years,' I say quietly.

'You mean she made him into someone he wasn't, for years,' she says bitterly.

'Why didn't he tell me about her?'

She shrugs guiltily. Maybe even angrily.

'Why is she here – if it's over?' That's when I realise why I feel so numb, why I haven't completely dissolved inside the leak behind my eyes. Because they used to belong to each other, and I can't compete with that. Someone he above-average likes.

'*He* broke up with *her*, Ellie, not the other way around.'

'It doesn't matter.'

'Do you want to be with him or not?' she says, frustrated.

And she's asking me to fight for him – but I've already done that. I did it the day I sang to him, and every day since, when I've questioned why someone like him would be with someone like me. Now I don't know whether I want to fight any more. Whether the universe is telling me, nice try, but no cigar – and I don't know what that means, but Dad says it all the time, despite being a fervent anti-smoker.

'I can't think about this right now, Elina.' I want to pretend Rebecca isn't here. I want to pretend Ash didn't lie to me. I want to pretend I'm having a nice time, until I actually am having a nice time.

'He loves you,' she states quietly, and I want to tell her that he categorically and undeniably does *not* love me, because he told me so.

'I'll talk to him tomorrow,' I acquiesce. 'I just can't, not right now.'

'If it helps, I don't feel much like talking to him either.' She grimaces. She takes my hand and squeezes it. The way a friend might. The way I hope we might be friends again one day.

When we walk back to the bar, Hayley is laughing at Jess's attempts to be polite to (all) the people who've asked her to dance.

'Is it always like this?' she whispers, watching Jess in wonder.

'*Always*,' I laugh, rolling my eyes.

'Dance?' Elina says to Jess, taking her hand. She nods, and they head to the dance floor, just as James finally makes his way across the room.

'You OK now, Pillai?' he says awkwardly, and I nod gratefully.

'He doesn't deserve you,' he says, glancing at Ash and Rebecca.

'That's what I said,' Hayley replies.

'So, what's going on, Atwell?' he asks, looking at her.

And I don't know what they're going to talk about; whether they're going to work things out, or not work things out, I just know I'm not supposed to be here when they do it.

I step away from the two of them and in the opposite direction to Ash, wondering if I can call Dad for a lift home.

'Ellie?' a voice queries. I turn towards it. He looks weird here, displaced. Like his face belongs to a different life, a different time, but he looks pleased to see me, which is a step up from the panic and confusion and pity that has surrounded every other interaction I've had this evening.

'Shawn!' I reply excitedly, reaching up to give him a hug. He grins, brushing his fringe out of his eyes, wearing a red Nirvana T-shirt paired with black jeans and yellow Converse.

'I'm playing tonight,' he says, motioning towards the stage.

'The band, or just you?' I ask, awestruck. I can't even imagine having the courage to be up there.

'The band,' he says, grinning. I look over and try not to seem too impressed at how band-like they appear – long hair, bored expressions, clothes that seem somewhere between straight off their bedroom floors and out of a magazine. 'Any requests?'

'I'm probably not the best person to ask.' I don't know why I'm telling him this. 'I'm feeling a bit . . . you know.'

'Everything OK?' he asks thoughtfully. 'Hope told me about your aunt.'

So, he and Hope are still talking. Interesting. Very interesting.

'Probably just jet lag,' I smile.

'Come on,' he cajoles, 'I need inspiration. I want to do something sort of . . . bluesy.'

I conjure my superpower, the one that is not the ability to have awkward conversation with my boyfriend's ex-girlfriend, who is two foot taller than me and whose waist is the circumference of my head.

'I was listening to Tommy James and the Shondells, "Crimson and Clover" on the way to school this morning,' I say contemplatively. 'I love that guitar lick at the start, it's so moody. But you probably don't know it,' I say, embarrassed.

'I do, as it happens,' he grins. 'Thanks for the tip.' And there go those dimples again. The ones that make him look like a stray puppy. One of those cute scrappy ones.

Then comes the voice I don't want to hear.

'Ellie?' And when I turn around, Ash is stood behind me. 'Can we talk?' he pleads.

'No,' I say bluntly. Finally, the pearlescent lighting and sixties girl group are no longer with him – and I'm not Julie Delpy and he's not Ethan Hawke, because he already has a Julie Delpy, he just never bothered to tell me.

155

'Don't you have a guest to look after?' I say, motioning towards Rebecca.

'Let me explain,' he begs. 'Mum told me to bring her and there was no time to tell you.' He's looking at me with those eyes. Those green eyes and those long dark lashes against a brown striped polo shirt, like a tennis player from the 1970s.

'You've had plenty of time to tell me.' He looks miserable as I turn away from him, but I don't care any more. I don't care how he feels.

'Ellie, please . . .' He leans forward, grabbing my arm.

I feel a sudden jolt as Shawn pushes his arm away.

'She said – she doesn't want to talk to you.'

'It's OK,' I say, turning to Shawn. 'Ash is my . . .' But I trail off, because we're having a fight, and he's here with his ex-girlfriend. His stupid, beautiful, better-version-of-me ex-girlfriend.

'Shawn!' Someone onstage is calling out to him.

'You sure you're OK?' he asks, leaning down to me, and as he leans forward, his hair is suddenly on my face.

'I'm fine,' I say, embarrassed, but as he's walking away, I can see him watching me, his eyes darting from Ash to me, then back again.

'Who was that?' Ash asks stiltedly.

'A friend,' I say curtly.

He turns towards me, his head in his hands.

'Ellie, I'm sorry. Bec coming to stay, it was all so last minute. You were away, and I didn't want to tell you over the phone, then I didn't want to ruin things when you got back.'

I don't reply as he stares intently at the side of my face.

156

'She's just a friend, Ellie.'

'A friend you were in love with?' I ask tersely.

'A long time ago.'

And I want to question him about that statement, and what it means, and why he didn't tell me before. Because he loved her, and he's probably seen her underwear on multiple occasions – and I've never loved anyone, so that's big. What they felt for each other. What they were. And how can I compete with that – the girl with the emojis?

I consider crying, but I don't. Because there's a soft bluesy rhythm coming from the stage. A bass guitar weeping into the silence for me.

We turn towards the stage, to where the band are playing the opening riff to 'Crimson and Clover', Shawn leaning down into the microphone.

'It's been a while since I played this,' he says to the crowd, 'and I'm not sure I remember the words.' He stares out over the mob, the band repeating the refrain over and over. 'Ellie,' he says, catching my eye. 'Do you think you could help me?' He's beckoning to me from the stage, my body temporarily frozen. All I can see is Hannah, their ex-singer, the ex-girlfriend of my new friend the stray puppy, the artist formerly known as Dirty Blond, staring at me disdainfully, her mouth curved into an unpleasant smile.

I feel terrified, and hot, and hurt, and tired, and there's only one thing I know that can fix that feeling.

'You should go,' Ash says gently.

And so I do. I make my way up there slowly. Like a zombie, just following the chords; and when he leans down to pull me onstage, I feel lost and strange, but like I'm coming home too.

When I stand in front of the microphone, it's too high for me. I try to adjust the stand, but it comes clattering down, an avalanche of sound. I can hear Hannah struggling to contain her amusement, her head turned towards some red-haired girl, her eyes rolled skywards. I can see Jess and Elina, and Hayley and James, and Rebecca; Rebecca and her kaleidoscopic eyes, watching me from the crowd. I turn to Shawn, panicked, but he's just watching me. Not trying to save me, but waiting for me to save myself. I adjust the microphone again, pulling it up to my chin.

The band are playing that refrain. That moody intro, over and over, until my eyes are closed and I feel it. I feel like I can fix myself. Like the alchemy of the music and my voice and the lyrics is all I'll ever need.

When the song finishes, I hear Shawn say to the rest of the band: 'I told you she was good.'

And even though Ash is gone, it actually doesn't matter.

Because I'm almost fixed, instead of almost in love.

36

A Girl Called Ellie

My name is Ellie. Ellie Pillai. And this is what I know.

That working out who you are and what you want is scarier than never actually knowing. Because knowing means there's a risk of failing. Of falling. Of knowing you might never be good enough. Of caring enough about something that The Something can actually hurt you.

My name is Ellie. Ellie Pillai.

And I'm going to fix myself.

I just need to work out what's broken.

37

Must Study

London Cousin – Annoying:

wtffffff?!!!!!!

The next morning, I'm messaging Hope from bed when I hear Mum knocking, the type of knock that feels both gentle and annoyingly insistent; a classic Mum manoeuvre.

'Ellie? Are you up yet? It's eight a.m., *en anbe*.' She's stood over me, looking somewhere between irritated and concerned, poking at me with a wooden spoon, her belly protruding from beneath a floral midi dress.

'OK, OK, I'm up,' I mutter, my head still obstinately under the duvet.

'Are you drunk?' she asks furiously, poking at me again – and it's starting to feel like she's doing what Granny would call *tenderising*, which appears to be code for bashing at something in a slightly violent and grotesque manner.

'No,' I hiss. 'I'm not drunk every time I sleep past seven a.m., Mother.'

'Fine,' she sighs dramatically, 'but you're running late, and your grandmother's asking questions about where you were last night . . . and your father is, well, he's being a bit . . . reactive.'

No, High School Gods, just *no*. With everything that happened last night, I'd temporarily forgotten that Granny is our semi-permanent house guest and Dad is now running my life like some kind of South Asian dictator whose job is to hunt down all fun and ensure it desists, immediately. Not that I'm having fun, because I'm arguing with my boyfriend, and I'm late for school, and Mum is tenderising me with a wooden spoon, while Granny awaits like one of those sharks circling a bloodied limb in the water.

I sit up in bed and stare at her. Or at something. Possibly a wall.

'Ellie!' she says, waving her hand up and down in front of me. 'Are you sure you weren't drinking last night?'

'Not unless you count ginger beer,' I reply sullenly.

'Then why are you being *so* . . .' she asks, waving the spoon around, exasperated.

I release the breath I've been holding for the last twelve hours.

'Ash brought his ex-girlfriend last night,' I reply, rubbing my forehead.

'Oh,' she says, sitting down next to me suddenly. 'What does *that* mean?'

'I don't know.' Because I've never had a boyfriend before, let alone one with a beautiful ex-girlfriend, whose mother is best friends with his mother, and who is probably right now asleep in the bedroom next to his, in her underwear, or *naked*.

'Oh,' she says again, and in the silence, I can sense her thinking. 'Did you talk to him about it?' she asks.

'Not really,' I mutter. There goes that silence again.

'Perhaps you should,' she suggests gently. 'It might not mean what you think it does. In the meantime,' she says more briskly, 'you need to get to school. I'll drive you, but you need to be downstairs in ten minutes.' She looks at me firmly, but with something akin to sympathy.

'Fine,' I reply, irritated, 'but why are you carrying a wooden spoon?' She checks over her shoulder, as if fearful she's being watched, lowering her voice till it's barely audible.

'Granny thinks you should have a *proper* breakfast in the morning, because I don't have a full-time job, or anything else to do with my day,' she states grumpily, shaking the wooden spoon at me.

'But why is it here, in my bedroom?' I ask, perplexed.

'I was stirring the eggs with it, and I needed to leave the kitchen. Quickly.'

She looks serious now. Like she's about to get a headache. The kind she gets whenever she hears Dad's family are coming to visit, or the school asks us to make something for a bake sale.

'Dad got an email this morning ...' she whispers, looking around her again. 'Aunty Kitty and Charles's "Save the Date". For the wedding.' I look at her, unsure of whether to laugh or cry or, better still, be happy for them. I just know this information is not likely to go down well with Granny. Or is currently in the kitchen, not going down well with Granny.

She rolls her eyes into space, as if I can't see her doing it. My parents haven't made their real opinion known to either me or Granny; I just know they think Aunty Kitty should be allowed to be happy. In fact, I overheard Mum muttering to Dad about how Granny thinks we should all live by Sri Lankan rules, when they're not in Sri Lanka any more. When the world's moved on, but she hasn't.

But honestly, I get it. I get Granny. Not because I'm a closet racist who thinks we should all stick to Our Own, or whatever weird, warped way she had of explaining it – but because I understand that feeling of not being able to move on. Of the world changing, and always being that bit behind.

Mum sighs heavily.

'Come on, Ellie,' she says, turning to me. 'Get changed, and we'll make a run for it.'

I message Hope again when she leaves.

Ellie:

don't know what 2 do

London Cousin – Annoying:

☒

Ellie:

ty. v. helpful

I force myself out of bed and into the shower, the sound of drums and a melancholy, high-strung guitar riff playing over and over in my mind as Radiohead, 'High and Dry' serenades me.

I watch Thom Yorke in the mirror behind me. A diversion as the world falls apart. Then I draw on my eyeliner flicks and think: I Am Ellie Pillai. And I Don't Care About Love.

When I get to the bottom of the stairs, I throw my bag over my shoulder and call out to Dad and Granny.

'Bye, Dad! Bye, Granny!'

'Ellie,' Granny says, emerging out of nowhere, and Mum's holding her breath, staring daggers at me. 'You must study. Exams are coming. Is very important time.'

'*Amma*, she was studying with a friend last night,' Mum says quickly. 'Jessica. Very bright girl. On course for all 9s. Wants to be a doctor.' And I wonder how Mum would describe me. 'Ellie. Very average girl. On course for very average grades. Wants to be . . . *something*.'

'Yes, yes,' Granny snaps. 'Ellie is very bright too.' It's one of the things I love about Granny. The way she considers any kind of compliment for anyone else a personal affront to the people *she* loves. People far superior to whoever the so-called compliment is being paid to – then at some later date, she'll tell you what she really thinks of you.

'Must *study*, Eleanor,' Granny says menacingly.

'Yes, Ellie,' Dad says, also materialising out of nowhere. Because that's how things roll in this house these days; disapproving adults lurk in every corner. 'Wednesday isn't a night for going out, but ever since you started dating that boy . . .'

'Mum. Said. It. Was. Fine.'

'Enough, Noel,' Granny says, cutting in before he can respond. 'There is no point argue.' And Mum and I look at each other in disbelief. Because she's arguing so much with her own daughter, she has literally moved to the other side of the world to avoid her.

'Eleanor will be home later. You will both go to work. I will make dinner,' she states.

'*Amma*, that's not necessary . . .' Mum interrupts.

'You are tired,' Granny says something akin to kindly. 'Pregnancy is stressful at your age.'

And the last thing I see as I strap myself into the car is Granny. Stood at the door waving, or possibly shaking her fist at us, as we make our way down the driveway.

I just wish Dad could see that it's not about me going out, it's about me *trying*. About how far I've come. Not because of Ash, but because of me, and who I'm becoming. Last night I sang a song, onstage, in front of people – and it felt good. Like I was invincible, not invisible. So, if I'm changing, I have to believe it's into something better.

Don't I?

38

Landslide

I'm listening to a lot of Fleetwood Mac at the moment. They're Mrs Aachara, or *Kyra's* favourite band, and I love the way she worships Stevie Nicks; that whenever she feels sad she blasts *Rumours* over and over.

On my way out of the car, I turn and wave to Mum absent-mindedly, unable to recall whether or not we've spoken in the last twenty minutes. She waves back absent-mindedly, like we're both somewhere else. Then I jam my headphones over my head and click into Spotify. To Fleetwood Mac, 'Landslide'. To that twangy guitar intro, and Stevie's introspective, melancholy voice.

I walk towards form room, trying to ignore the fact Jess and Hayley have been messaging me all morning, but Ash hasn't.

I can feel the music inside of me, like it's thrumming in my veins. Like it's carrying me somewhere, making everything all right. And I thank the High School Gods for introducing me to Stevie Nicks, for letting me date Ash long enough to call Mrs Acahara *Kyra* and discover the genius that is Fleetwood Mac.

But suddenly my heart is beating faster. Like there's a drum inside of it. A drum that someone is hitting violently and grotesquely, like my heart is being tenderised. I pull the headphones off my head mid-chorus, because right outside my form room a crowd is gathering around a picture. I don't know what the picture is, or who or what it's of; I just know the last time anyone crowded around my form room, it was because someone had scrawled the word 'paki' over a piece of poetry I'd written that my English teacher, Mrs Fry, had misguidedly displayed in the corridor.

We'd been told to write about a season. So I wrote about summer. About the heat. About the one time I went to Sri Lanka, not long after Amis died, and the colours and sights and sounds and smell of it all. How I felt alien, but somehow like I was home.

I approach the crowd cautiously, 'Landslide' crescendoing in my brain. Trying to see my way around the bodies, to whatever it is they're looking at. Praying to any god that this isn't about me.

And then I know it is – but it isn't what I thought it was, even though my heart's still beating like it is.

It's a canvas, half the height of the door and maybe a little wider. A picture of the little yellow Beatles badge, but big. Big enough to take up most of the frame; but instead of saying *Beatles* in chaotic graphic red, it says *Ellie* in the same chaotic graphic print. And you wouldn't think something so simple could have so many details. Could be magnified to that size and still have something to show you. Because it's beautiful, and strangely poetic. Every brushstroke painstakingly real. The texture of it, funny and warm and inviting and honest. Every facet of it, from the pin to the tinge of rust around its outside.

There's a little bit of breath catching in my throat, because it feels exactly like me. Like something I made up, that only I could see; except someone else saw it. Someone else saw me.

When I feel his arm around my waist, we just stare at it from a distance. Two outsiders, watching the crowd.

'I'm sorry,' he whispers, his lips on my ear; and he smells like paint and musk. I can feel his mouth on the top of my head, kissing my hair. I want to hate him. I want to throw the canvas at his head and tell him he isn't forgiven. That it's not OK to lie and hide Julie Delpy ex-girlfriends, naked, in the room next to him.

But I can't. Because it might just be the most romantic thing anyone's ever done for me. Or maybe – the only romantic thing anyone's ever done for me. And even though the earphones are no longer on my head, I can still hear Stevie singing that the landslide will bring it down.

So I turn to him and say, 'It's OK.' Even though it isn't.

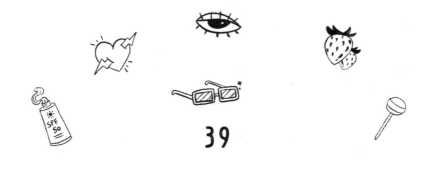

39

The Julie Delpy Wannabe

'So, that's it then?' Hayley says, staring at me at lunchtime.

'What?' I say, pretending to be interested in the ground. Which is hard. Because we're at the back of the library, and I'm staring at black asphalt and a number of crumbling grey bollards.

'He paints you a picture of a badge, and you've forgiven him for lying to you.'

'Technically, he didn't *lie* to me, he just didn't tell me she was staying with him.'

'*Really*, Ellie?' Hayley says spikily. She looks tired and annoyed and, quite literally, spiky.

'You should eat something, Hay. You're getting grouchy,' I say, trying to deflect.

'I'm not hungry,' she practically barks.

'OK, OK . . .'

'I literally Can't Believe You. You were so upset last night, E. You shouldn't forget how he made you feel.'

That's when I lose my temper, because really, I don't want to remember that feeling at all.

'Don't make this about me,' I snap. 'Let's talk about you. You and James.'

'James and I broke up,' she says quickly.

'Oh,' I say, stunned. Because I'd expected some kind of dramatic reconciliation. Some romantic gesture like a painting outside her form room, or a Shakespearian soliloquy in the canteen.

'We're still friends,' she says evenly, but as far as I'm aware, Hayley and James only have two modes: enemies, or much more than friends.

'Why?' I breathe.

'Because I've got *stuff*, Ellie. Stuff I need to sort out on my own.'

'But you like him . . .' I say, unwilling to let it go. All the romantic movies I've ever watched tell me this isn't how it should go.

'It's not fair for him to wait around for me,' she says quietly.

'Why not?' Because I'd wait around for someone I liked. For someone I thought was worthwhile – and I know how much Hayley likes James, and how much he likes her, so every part of me, every Audrey Hepburn movie, every Doris Day film (apart from that depressing one with Frank Sinatra) is railing against this information.

'You know, Ellie,' she says, irritated. 'I'm not desperate to be in a relationship. I'm OK on my own.' The way she says it feels slightly accusatory, like she's saying I *am* desperate to be in a relationship, that I'm *not* OK on my own.

'What's that supposed to mean?' I bark.

'Take it how you *want*, E.'

We stare at each other. Two wrestlers ready to launch ourselves against the ring.

'Hey, Ellie.' I turn at the voice. A welcome interruption to our silently locked eyes. Dirty Blond and the drummer from last night.

'Hey, Shawn,' I say shyly. Because the person I was yesterday, when I was stood on that stage, feels like a million miles away from the me I am now.

'Last night was great,' he says, grinning at me.

'Thanks.'

'It was,' Hayley says semi warmly, a truce momentarily formed. The drummer, who is huge, and looks almost as menacing as Hayley did a minute ago, smiles as he looks her up and down.

'We want you to come to a rehearsal. See how it feels. We meet on Fridays – the school lets us use the main hall to practise.'

'I, um . . . I, well . . .' I try to form a coherent sentence, or at the very least, the word *no*.

'She'll be there,' Hayley replies.

'Cool,' he says, as if I've actually replied. 'Four thirty, OK?'

'Fine,' says Hayley, blithely ignoring me. Or maybe she *is* me, because I'm no longer sure where I am, or if I'm in control of my body. Maybe it's like the film about that actor, the one who has people living in his brain, controlling him. Maybe Hayley's in the control room, on a stepladder, forcing my head to nod up and down like one of those dashboard toy dogs.

'Great. See you Friday,' he grins, tucking a stray bit of hair behind his ears.

When they've gone, Hayley turns to me.

'Now THAT I can get behind,' she sighs.

'What do you mean?'

'You, in a band, instead of just *someone's girlfriend.*'

I turn away from her, choking on the feel of the words in my throat.

'Right. Thanks, Hayley,' I manage quietly. I don't understand why she's so angry with me for forgiving Ash. Because she and James broke up? Well, that's not my fault. Her wanting to be on her own is not my fault. I don't want to be on my own. I don't want to break up with him because of *her.* The Julie Delpy wannabe. Rebecca.

'I'm sorry,' Hayley says, looking at my face. 'I didn't mean it, E. You should do what makes you happy.'

And when she hugs me, I hold her tight, and try to remember what it is that makes me happy.

Ellie:

auditioning 4 shawn's band on fri ....!

London Cousin – Annoying:

London Cousin – Annoying:

🐾

40

There She Goes

After school, Ash is waiting for me at reception, blocking my view of Mr Green, who in my head spent the holidays running shirtless up a snow-covered mountain, wearing one of those pointless sexy bandanas.

I know I shouldn't be thinking about this when I'm stood with my boyfriend – but as he has his Naked Ex-Girlfriend (and I *really* have to stop thinking about her naked) living in the room next to him, I don't feel morally culpable for thinking Mr Green would look *nice* in a bandana.

'Hey,' he says, leaning down to kiss me. He's carrying the canvas with him. The Ellie canvas, with the blown-up Beatles badge and chaotic red writing. And whenever I see it, I hear Paul McCartney singing 'Love Me Do'. Which feels a touch desperate.

'Hey,' I reply, kissing him back.

'Can we talk about last night?' he asks nervously.

Only if we have to.

'You should have told me about her,' I say slowly, 'but if you say there's nothing going on between you, I believe you.' He sighs gratefully and puts both arms around me, pulling the canvas against my back.

'I'm sorry,' he says quietly. 'Bec didn't say she was coming until the last minute, and I just panicked. I know I should have told you. I *know* I'm an idiot,' he says vehemently.

'Hey,' I chastise him gently. 'That's my boyfriend you're talking about.'

He smiles, pulling me tighter.

'Can you come over?' he whispers.

'I can't,' I reply awkwardly. 'Granny's on a mission to have a family dinner tonight.'

'OK,' he says, kissing my forehead. He looks disappointed.

'I can go for a walk now, though?' I say, taking his hand.

We walk out across the playground, swinging our arms like two kids wielding a skipping rope, the feel of it is so different to yesterday, when everyone was staring at us with a thousand unanswered questions, most of which centred around the word how. Today, they're too busy telling me how great I was last night, how they never knew I could sing; smiling at me and saying hi, like Ellie Pillai Is Someone.

'So, how did it feel?' he asks gently. 'Being up there last night.'

'I didn't realise you were still there?' I say, surprised – because when I was finally brave enough to open my eyes, I'd looked for him, but he wasn't there.

'I was,' he says, looking down at our hands. 'But it was your night, so I left.'

And when he says things like this, I realise why I like/almost love him.

'Bec thought you were great too,' he says uncomfortably.

'Did she?' I say through gritted teeth.

'We really are just friends,' he says gently, 'but we *are* friends, Ellie.'

'OK,' I reply despondently.

'She thinks you're cool – and I think you'd like her too, if you got to know her,' he says, side-eyeing me.

But I am now physically biting my tongue. Because when you think someone is *cool*, you tend not to laugh in their face when they tell you how old they are and then announce you used to date their boyfriend by touching him incessantly.

'OK,' I manage.

'How about Friday? We could all go out together, give you a chance to meet properly?'

I want to say no. But it turns out, I'm really, really, bad at that.

I exhale loudly – which sounds something like: fiiiiiinnnne.

But even my exhale can't distract from the sound of grunting I hear behind me. I wonder whether someone's following me around making pig noises again, like James Godfrey's friends in Year 7 until Jess threw her backpack at them.

But the source of the sound is Mrs Aachara. Grunting and sweating and swearing as she struggles to load a prop into her car.

'Miss!' I shout, as I let go of Ash's hand and rush towards her. 'Can I help?' I attempt to wrestle a lion's head out of her hands and into the car.

'Thanks,' she says gratefully, wiping her forehead.

'Got it,' Ash says, grappling with it.

'Can I help?' Mr Green asks, sliding it into the boot with ease. He's been suspiciously rearranging basketballs in the back seat of his car for the last ten minutes. Like he's been waiting for a chance to speak to her.

I wish he was wearing a bandana.

'I had it,' Ash says tersely.

'Thanks, Will.' Mrs Aachara beams.

'No problem. You should have asked me to bring it out for you.'

'That's what I'm here for,' Ash says bluntly.

'You're both being ridiculous,' Mrs Aachara says, rolling her eyes. 'The concept of the helpless female is so 1762.' Mr Green blushes, while I try to remember that line for Hayley.

'Do you need any help at the other end?' he asks magnanimously.

'I can help,' Ash says again irritably, but William Green is completely ignoring him. Not deliberately, but because I genuinely don't know if he can see anyone but her. Somehow, I get the feeling that a sixties girl group is singing in his head while Mrs Aachara smiles at him in slow motion.

'Bye, Mr Green!' a group of Year 12 girls chorus as they walk past, hips swaying, legs up to their armpits. He ignores them too.

'Bye, Ash,' one of them says, turning around to wave at him coyly. To his credit, he doesn't look either, but possibly because he is too busy eye tenderising Mr Green's face with a violent and slightly grotesque look.

'I have a friend,' Mrs Aachara says, waving her hand dismissively. 'So, there's someone at home to give me a hand.'

'A friend?' Mr Green says quizzically.

'My best friend Anika and her daughter Rebecca. They're staying with us at the moment.'

'Oh,' he says, and it's hard not to notice the relief in his voice.

For a minute, they just stare at each other, like Ash and I aren't actually here. Like we're two awkward teenagers chaperoning our own parents, who aren't our parents, but are our teachers; or are one of our parents and one of our teachers, or something like that.

'Anywayyyyy . . .' I say uncomfortably. 'We should go . . . Ash?' I say, nudging him sharply.

'OK,' he says distractedly.

'Bye, miss. Bye, sir.'

'Bye, Ellie,' Mrs Aachara says, turning to me. 'Tell your mum I'll come and see your grandmother soon. I promised I'd show her my wedding sari.' And I wonder how on earth, in twenty minutes, Granny managed to invoke this level of promise from a woman she'd never even met before, and, if I had my way, would never meet again.

'OK.' I smile. 'Come on,' I say, pulling at Ash again.

'See you later, Mum,' he says, ignoring Mr Green entirely.

'What was that?' I hiss, as we walk away.

'What?' he hisses back.

'Er, you and Mr Green.'

He looks at me as if it's obvious. As if Mr Green is a monster, as opposed to an exceptionally good-looking PE teacher.

'He's only a few years older than I am,' he says, appalled. I want to laugh. He sounds like Rebecca and her unrealistic grasp on age.

'He's in his thirties, Ash.'

'Mum's forty.'

'I'm sure she'd be thrilled you're telling people that.'

'I mean, he's a bit young for her, isn't he?' he queries. 'It's embarrassing. She's clearly not interested.' I want to point out that it isn't obvious she's not interested – although it isn't obvious she is either.

'Yeah,' I say slowly. Because truthfully, I know this isn't about how old or not old Mr Green is, or whether his mum's remotely interested in that fact. It's about his dad. About the fact he misses him and isn't ready to think about his mum with anyone else. Like me and Amis and Phantom Baby.

My heart tugs for him.

'How's the picture of your dad going?' I ask carefully.

'Good,' he says quietly. 'I want you to see it.' He turns a crooked smile on me.

'Me too.' I smile back.

And that's how the rest of the hour goes. Me and my boyfriend holding hands. Walking around with takeaway cups of coffee and green tea, talking about art, and exams, and music, and life, my Ellie canvas perched precariously under his arm.

'I missed you when you were away,' he says, standing at the bus stop, waiting for Rex or one of his cronies to arrive and drive me back to the village.

'It's weird,' he says, shaking his head. 'It feels like we've been together for ages. Like you know me,' he says, kissing my nose. Honestly, High School Gods, I could do this forever.

'Are you calling me weird again?' I tease.

'Come here,' he says, pulling me closer.

'Let's see. What do I know about you?' I say, ticking the points off on my fingers. 'You have an unhealthy obsession with Britpop.' He kisses my cheek. 'You've permanently got paint in your hair.' He kisses the other cheek. 'And your ex-girlfriend is living in the bedroom next door.' He kisses me on the mouth for what seems like forever.

'She's not you, Ellie Pillai.'

'Too beautiful,' I joke.

'Not beautiful enough,' he says, staring at me.

I punch him on the arm.

'Ow!' he exclaims, rubbing it.

'Stop,' I state, annoyed.

'What?' he demands.

'I know what I am, and I know what I'm not, and I'm *not* . . .' I say, turning away from him.

'I hate it when you say things like that,' he interrupts – and I'm just grateful at that moment that I can see Rex driving towards us, his disdain evident, as I take my Ellie canvas out from under Ash's arm and get ready to board the bus.

As I slide into my seat, my phone buzzes.

Ash:

The La's, 'There She Goes'

I wedge the canvas between my knees and the seat in front, clicking on the link.

The melody racing through my brain, a feeling I can't contain.

♡ Song 3 ♡

Verse, Chorus, Middle Eight – Dust

When I think about love, I think about risk. Negotiation. What you're willing to give, and what you're willing to accept. When I think about him: the thing that scares me most is how little I want. How little I need. Like, I'd take anything; the tiniest fragment of dust, the merest speck of *something like* love, if it was just him giving it to me.

And that feeling is minor, and major. Melodic and soothing. A ballad and a pop song.

> *It's a little bit of dust, just a little bit like love.*
> *If you close your eyes and just pretend hard enough.*

And when I sing it, it sounds like pleading, and forgiving, and loving and not knowing, and all of the things that exist in between.

Because right now, I'm just a little bit of me.

I'm not quite *me*.

Not yet.

41

Family Dinner

Family dinner goes something like this:

Granny: interrogating Mum over how she's feeling, what she's eating and whether or not she should be working, given she's pregnant, At Her Age.

Dad: interrogating me over anything, everything, and all points in between.

Mum: trying not to offend Granny by saying she doesn't actually like masala dosa, when Granny is under the impression it's her favourite food and has made it because she needs to be properly nourished, given she's pregnant, At Her Age.

Me: trying to appease Granny by telling her Mrs Aachara is going to bring her wedding sari over.

Granny: saying she likes Ash and Mrs Aachara, and how she wants to meet Elina, because when you get married, you marry a family. And Sri Lankans should know that. That the whole family marry The Whole Family.

Dad: trying not to choke on his masala dosa and saying it's a bit ridiculous to be talking about marriage when I'm not even sixteen.

Granny: telling Dad not to call her ridiculous, because she's his mother and it's disrespectful – and then reminding him I'm going to be sixteen soon – and she wasn't much older than me when she got married, which I suspect isn't that helpful, in the context of this conversation.

Mum: asking me how revision is going and what's happening in drama.

Granny: appalled at the concept of me taking drama, although not actually sure what drama is.

Dad: saying he has indigestion and is going to bed early.

Me: wondering if I have indigestion because I definitely feel a bit sick too.

Mum: saying she needs to go and check on Dad.

Finally, when it's all over and they've left the table, Granny turns to me and says:

'Thank God I'm here now. You are all mess.'

And I wonder: is she right? Because I thought things were better. But I don't think they are.

42

Granny Gets It

Jessica:
can't u come over here???

Ellie:
dad says i can't go out during week

Jessica:
to A's? or anywhere?

Ellie:
mostly A's ....

Jessica:
bec making herself at home! ☹

Jessica:
u should b here

Ellie:

they're just friends

Ellie:

we r all going out 2m

Jessica:

don't u have the band thing?

Ellie:

after that

Ellie:

ru and E coming?

Ellie:

me + R + A = 😫

Jessica:

will ask

Ellie:

😎

Jessica:

we're coming

Jessica:

bec mum had to leave for a work emergency, but she's still here!!

Jessica:

exactly . . . . !

It's Thursday night and so far, the week's been OK. Ash and I have an hour together after school every day. When I get home, I tell Granny I have to 'study', which means I can hide in my room without fear of interrogation. It's OK. I mean, I want to see him more, but at the same time, I can't help feeling relieved that we don't have any actual alone time. You know, Sexy Underwear Alone Time. Because his ex-girlfriend is beautiful and womanly, and I'm *me*. Which is something I'm trying to be OK with, but it isn't as easy as I thought it would be.

Now this new information is freaking me out. Rebecca's mum is gone, but she's still here. *Why?* Why is she staying at her ex-boyfriend's house when she should be back at uni, or working, or whatever it is she should be doing with her life that isn't with My Boyfriend.

Then there's The Other Thing. The fact I haven't really talked to Ash about meeting Shawn in New York or agreeing to audition for the band on Friday, and I Don't Know Why.

Later that night, Granny comes into my room with chai.

'Are you OK, Eleanor?' she says, placing the steaming cup on my bedside table. 'You must stay hydrated when studying.'

'Yes, Granny,' I reply meekly.

'Maths?' she asks, craning her neck over my laptop.

'Yes,' I reply. Because there's not much else to do when you're banned from seeing your friends during the week and your grandmother is guarding your room like a witch from a Grimms' fairy tale.

'I am good at maths,' she says, pleased with herself, 'if you need help.' Granny was the accountant at her shop in South London, before she bought it when Dad was a kid.

'I am worried,' she says, sitting down next to me on the bed.

'What about?' I ask, sitting up.

'Your mother. The baby. Your father working too hard. Too long hours. He is very tired.'

And I think: why would the baby be worrying? The baby's fine. Mum's healthy. We're all healthy. Everything's OK. Isn't it?

'The baby's fine, Granny.'

'You will never know,' she says quietly, 'until you have baby of your own. You will never stop worry. Especially not your parents. With everything they have lived through.'

I can hear a sob in her throat. A sort of tremor, like she's finding it hard to swallow. That's when I realise there's a sob in my throat too. Because I do know.

Maybe it's just in the back of my head. Maybe I'm too busy trying to be fifteen. Maybe I push it down, and try to pretend I don't notice it, that constant feeling of fear, of never knowing whether everything will be OK again, or what OK even means. Because I lost someone too; and I get scared, and I get worried, and sometimes I don't know what to do with that either.

And it's like Granny of all people does understand. Because she puts her arms around me suddenly, closing me into her bony chest.

'Of course you know, my darling,' she croons. I'm crying now, and I hadn't even noticed; folded like the tiniest square of a square of a square into her arms. Because she's right. We are a mess. But she's here, and everything's going to be OK.

Somehow, she'll make sure of it.

43

Liam Gallagher's Haircut

'I feel sick. Like, physically sick. I'm going to vomit,' I claim, clutching at my stomach. Hayley and James roll their eyes at each other over my head, clearly unaware – or worse still, unbothered – I can see them.

'I can *see* you,' I intone accusingly.

'What?' James says, shrugging innocently.

'You don't believe me!' I cry, sat in the corner of the drama studio, my arms enveloping my stomach.

'Did you have any lunch?' Hayley asks unsympathetically.

'No. I told you, I don't feel very well.'

'You haven't eaten either,' James says to Hayley. 'Shall I grab you both something now?'

'No, but I'm fine. We need to sort Ellie out before she runs home like a big baby.'

A big baby?

'Ellie, you're nervous. You get nervous. We all know that . . .' James says, as Hayley shoots him a look.

'Come on, Pillai,' she interrupts. 'Just man up. It's going to be fine,' she commands. 'Now get up. We need to finish this scene.'

'We need to challenge terms like "man up",' James states. 'That whole acting like a man equals being *braver* thing. Not to mention the pressure it puts on men to conform to a particular ideal of masculinity.'

Hayley shoots him a look somewhere between respect and irritation.

'Wow,' I say, staring at James. 'Someone's rubbing off on you. I mean, you must be spending *a lot* of time together for you to come up with that little gem –' because James's usual approach to life does not include the querying of sexist terminology. 'Not that I disagree with you,' I finish.

He looks down, suddenly embarrassed, and it's possible Hayley may even be blushing too, it's just hard to tell with that spiky fringe covering most of her face these days. Even though they're broken up now, they still seem to be spending a lot of time together, just without the kissing and hand holding – which Hayley says is called Friendship, but looks to me more like Denial.

'You're right,' she mutters to him.

'You're losing your Woke Credentials,' I crow, as she stares at me. Her eyes seem bigger than usual, like she's trying to unnerve me.

'Just to be clear,' I clarify, clutching at my stomach again, 'I don't actually *care* about your Woke Credentials. I just need to go home. Because I'm not very well.'

'Big Baby,' she states.

'OK, Pillai,' James says, pulling me up by my arms. 'So, you're auditioning for that Kurt Cobain wannabe's band tonight – don't worry about it – you'll be fine. You always are.'

'What do *you* know about Kurt Cobain?' I say grumpily.

'The real one, or the wannabe one?'

I shoot him a look.

'He was in Nirvana,' he says unsurely.

'Name a Nirvana song. Not "Come as You Are" or "Smells Like Teen Spirit".'

'I didn't realise I was being tested,' he mutters, folding his arms over.

'Ellie's very touchy about Nirvana. And pretty much everything else today,' Hayley says in explanation.

'Snap,' I say, looking at her. Hayley is permanently grouchy these days.

'Whatever. He's got the hair, you know,' says James, smoothing back his own nineties Gallagher brother haircut. I mean, for all the gods' sakes, every one of these people is dressed like the music I listen to, and yet they have no idea who they're actually imitating.

And just as I'm about to give him a lecture on the provenance of his slightly too long, mullet-esque haircut, using the emergence of Oasis, pre-recorded for *The Word* at Teddington Studios, dressed in M&S jumpers looking like they'd just eaten a lemon, Hayley interrupts my thoughts.

'You're not clutching your stomach any more,' she says, narrowing her eyes. 'You must be feeling better. Let's get back to work. Jeffrey Dean is trying to rewrite my script. He thinks he's Spike Lee, but white, and living on a farm.'

Note to self: do not engage in conversation about Britpop when faking stomach pains. Am not good at pretending I don't care.

The Concept of Groupies Is Completely Disgusting, Not to Mention Outdated And Sexist

Ellie:

going in now . . . .

London Cousin – Annoying:

say hi to u kno who

Ash:

5.30?

Ellie:

in reception ❤

'Ellie, we're just going to set up.' Shawn nods briskly at me as he walks past, his hair tucked neatly behind his ears. He's wearing ankle-length grey trousers and grey Vans with a bright yellow Ramones T-shirt. In the short time I've known him, I'd bet my entire record collection it'll be seconds before his hair is directly in his eyes again.

'OK,' I reply, and I wonder if it's obvious that I have no idea what Setting Up entails, or whether I have any need to engage with it.

Shawn and the rest of the band, who are currently nameless to me, are plugging things into other things in the main hall, while Hayley and I stand in a corner, mostly trying not to be sick. By which I mean *me*, obviously, because Hayley's just her usual casual, unbothered by anything, confident self.

'Should I *do* anything?' I whisper to her awkwardly.

'*Talk* to them,' she encourages, nudging me forward.

'Oh God, I can't,' I hiss. 'What am I going to say?'

'Hello?' she intones sarcastically.

I look at her, panic-stricken. Suddenly unable to work out how to form the word 'hello' in my mouth. Maybe I can say it with my eyes; I've been told they're quite expressive. Perhaps they can have whole conversations without me saying a word, ideally to anyone I haven't known for at least four years or am unrelated to.

She pushes me forward.

'So, how long have you guys been a band?' she asks Shawn, rolling her eyes unsubtly at me.

'About eighteen months,' Shawn says, looking to the drummer for confirmation.

'Pretty much since Shawny here turned up,' the boy retorts,

and even though we met yesterday, he does nothing whatsoever to acknowledge my presence.

He's a solid kid. Tall and dark, his hair cropped close to the skin, like an army recruit in one of those adverts that claim Your Army Needs You. The size of him feels almost physically intimidating, but there's something gentle, maybe even a little comical about him. 'Shawn started the band. The rest of us were just kinda making noise until he turned up.'

He looks over at Hayley and winks.

'So, who are *you* then?' he asks, staring at her. 'We're not auditioning for groupies yet, but if you find me later, you can have a one-to-one try-out,' he says, licking his lips lasciviously.

'I think not,' Hayley says, glaring at him. 'The concept of groupies is completely disgusting, not to mention outdated and sexist.'

'Sexist,' he says, running his hands up and down his 'OPEN UP – FBI' T-shirt. 'Say it again. Slower.'

'Shut up, Benji,' one of the guitarists mutters. 'Sorry,' he says, looking at us, 'he has no control over anything that comes out of his mouth.'

'But I know how to control my *sticky sticky sticksssss*,' Benji screeches, drumming erratically on his kit.

'I'm Elliott,' the guitarist says, turning back to me. 'I play rhythm, that idiot is Benji, this is Lucas –' a red-headed boy with glasses looks up at me and nods – 'he's bass – and Shawn, you already know.' I nod in thanks at his introductions. 'And you're *Ellie* – the singer from the other night.'

'That's me,' I mutter.

'So, who are you?' he says, frowning at Hayley.

'I'm Hayley – a friend of Ellie's. Here to lend moral support and, more importantly, ensure you're not serial killers. Definitely *not* a groupie,' she says, shooting Benji a dirty look. 'Hopefully that's OK.'

I shoot her back a dirty look, because why is she asking if it's *OK*? What if it isn't OK? Because while my eyes are expressive, they're not capable of singing, or speaking out loud – and I'm definitely not capable of singing or speaking out loud if she's not with me.

'Fine with me,' Elliott says, smiling at her. I think the sigh I emit may actually be the exhalation of every breath that has ever entered my body. Which gives me just about enough courage to look at Elliott for more than 0.05 seconds.

He's about average height, with sandy-brown hair cut like he's in The 1975. His jeans are so tight they look like they've been spray-painted on, and he's wearing them with a fitted green buttoned-up polo neck and battered white Converse. He looks like a boy in a band. A cute boy in a cool band.

For the hundredth time today, I wonder how I'm going to deal with cute boys in a cool band. Because they've got the kind of coolness that comes with wearing short jeans and too-long hair and ironic T-shirts and trainers that look like you can skateboard in them, although I'm sure they probably don't. And they're all in the *sixth form*, so they're, like, grown up, or at least a year or two older than I am. Or a thousand, as Rebecca would put it – when I feel twelve.

'So, Shawn said you play the keys?' Lucas, the bass guitarist, asks me. He's serious looking, his clothing all black, like he's auditioning for the Beatles when they were going through their Hamburg phase. It makes his hair look even redder, like his head's on fire – and I wonder whether that's what my face looks like. Like a red flag, screaming, I'm Here, But I Don't Know If I Should Be.

'Um, yeah. I mean, kind of. I play the piano. A bit.'

'More than a bit,' Hayley says, looking at him. 'She's really good. She writes too.'

'Oh yeah,' Shawn says, looking up suddenly, 'I just remembered. Mrs Mason said it would be fine for us to borrow one of the school keyboards for you. I'll go get one now.' He disappears out of the room before I even get the chance to say *WTFFFFFFFFFFFFFF.*

'So, Ellie,' Benji says, eyeing me; and something about the way he says it feels a little bit dangerous. 'What kind of music are you into?'

'Er, everything, I guess . . .' I mutter like some kind of personality-free zone.

'Yeah, but what *kind* of everything. Like, who's your favourite band?' he asks, narrowing his eyes. They're all staring at me, waiting for me to answer. To make some terrible, horrible choice they can judge me about. I hate that. Because music is supposed to be joyful, and for all my joking around, I would never, ever judge anyone for what they listen to – because your music is what makes you, you.

'Um, I guess if I *had* to choose, it would probably be the Beatles.'

'Why's that?' Lucas asks, tuning his guitar.

'They're just . . .' I pause, because I don't know how to find the words. How to describe the music that made everything make sense

195

when I was nine and it felt like the world was closing in around me. When Dad sang 'Blackbird' to me every night before I fell asleep, and we danced around the kitchen to 'I Am the Walrus' on the day of Amis's funeral, because he used to love that song, and pretended he was a walrus when he didn't even know what a walrus was.

They're all looking up at me. Expectant.

'They're just,' I repeat, '... *everything*, you know. Pop and experimental and modern, and, like, iconic, old-school rock 'n' roll and heartbreaking ballads and anthemic indie and just the *lyrics* ... they were so before their time, and every band, ever after, are just trying to be that ... *everything*. I mean, imagine having three songwriters as prolific as Lennon, McCartney and Harrison in the same band? Who all met organically? Who lived, like, streets away from each other growing up? It's just ... I don't even know how to describe it.'

'Yeah,' Lucas says, looking back at his guitar. 'I'm with you.'

'Shame about Ringo ...' Elliott quips.

'It's always the drummers ...' I say, letting the words drift into the abyss. Elliott and Lucas laugh.

'Burnnnnnn,' Lucas says, poking Benji with the end of his guitar – and Benji, somewhere between shamefaced and respectful, nods at me begrudgingly.

'Who burned who?' Shawn says, reappearing with a keyboard under his arm.

'Ellie here just put Benji in his place,' Lucas replies concisely.

'Practically part of the band already,' Shawn says, winking at me – and while I'm not unhappy to have passed this particular test,

I can't help noticing its almost 5.10 p.m. and I haven't actually sung anything yet.

'So, er, should we, um, get started?' I say, waving towards the keyboard, and Hayley looks at me, impressed, because for some reason, I now appear to be embracing this situation. Mostly because of the fear of Ash and the Julie Delpy wannabe waiting around for me, falling back in love with each other while I cringe my way through this audition.

'So, you write your own stuff then?' Elliott asks, as Shawn puts up the stand and plugs the keyboard in.

'I mean, I do. It's not that good or anything, but I try.'

'It's good,' Shawn says, turning towards Elliott and smiling.

'So, play something for us? Do you have any of the chords written down? We could try and join in. It's how we work with Shawn's stuff, we just kinda play along and see what happens,' Lucas says, as he moves closer to the keyboard.

I can feel my face pulsing, my mouth drying up like a tiny vacuum's sucked all the moisture out.

'I . . . uh . . .'

'What about the song you played in New York?' Shawn says kindly. He's watching me, like he knows how this feels; like I'm naked, or standing in my lime-green underwear in front of a group of complete strangers – one of whom actively wants me to fall on my face because I just called him Ringo. And not in a good way.

I look over my shoulder at Hayley, who smiles supportively.

'Um, well, I've been working on something new. It's kind of a bit pop, I guess,' and I can see Benji rolling his eyes in the background, his sticks gently tapping his drums. 'It's basically a classic C, G, D kind of thing – it won't be hard to play along if you get a feel for the first verse.'

'Cool,' Elliott says, smiling. For a second, I just stand there, terrified and possibly paralysed, till I feel Hayley's bony fingers pushing me towards the keyboard.

I take a deep breath, and will my heart to beat at a normal rhythm. For the sweat that I know is pooling in my hairline not to make its way down my face.

And I try to remind myself that *I can*. Because this is who I am, this is what I want – and before I know it, my fingers are bouncing staccato-like against the plasticky notes, my voice lifting, to rise and fall with the rhythm of the keys.

I don't even notice when the bass guitar starts playing too, gentle and deep, the notes vibrating as they merge delicately into mine. Or when the acoustic guitar starts thrumming, filling the sound, until my staccato is swelling with a rhythm I didn't even know it needed. But I hear the drums. I feel them. Because that's the moment when a song starts to fly.

There's a wholeness to it all. A sound I didn't even know I could make. Despite all of the stumbling and wrong notes, it feels alive. Real. Beautiful.

I'm almost enjoying it now; Shawn picking up on my harmonies, his raspy, syrupy voice blurring into mine. When I stop, they all carry on playing until they suddenly stop too, discordant and out of time.

'Nice,' Benji says, starting to drum enthusiastically.

'Yeah, cool. I like it, Ellie,' Lucas says, beaming at me, and Shawn puts his arm around my shoulders and squeezes, as the rest of the group give him what I can only assume they consider a subtle nod.

'Welcome to the band,' he says, smiling. They're all smiling. Even Benji. Which feels good, and scary, but mostly like something more than that. Like I'm a series of jigsaw pieces, finally coming together.

'You two meeting in New York,' Elliott says seriously, 'was fate.' He's scribbling down the chord progression I've just played, making notes on it, and playing with the rhythm.

'New York?' Ash questions. When I look up, he's stood there, with Rebecca and Jess and Elina at the door.

'We heard you singing,' Jess says weakly. Oh God, why didn't I tell Ash about this audition? Why am I so weird and secretive and stupid?

'More groupies,' Benji says, staring at the girls. 'Niiiiice,' he says, gaping at them and pretending to tweak his nipples.

'You really are a pig,' Hayley says in disgust.

'Say it again. Slower,' he says, closing his eyes and continuing to rub his chest like an ape.

'Ugh,' she intones.

'So, you two met in New York?' Ash repeats, staring at me.

'We ran into each other. In a café. With my cousin,' I say, suddenly aware Shawn's arm is still around my shoulders.

'Well, you sounded great,' he says, looking at me; and if the last time they met Shawn hadn't basically accused him of Bothering Me, this would be somewhat less awkward.

'I thought you already had a singer?' he asks, turning to Shawn suspiciously.

'Not any more,' Shawn replies tightly; and his arm is starting to feel like a dead weight. I wriggle out from underneath it and walk towards Ash, Rebecca staring at me.

'I'm sorry,' I say, turning to the band. 'I have to go. Let me know if you want me to come to another rehearsal.'

'You'd actually have to stay for the whole thing next time, though,' Lucas says, sounding annoyed – and I want to press pause on the last five minutes. Go back to when I was part of something. Just me, not Ash's girlfriend, or Jess's best friend, or Hayley's less confident friend, but me. Ellie Pillai. When Lucas didn't look annoyed and Shawn didn't look disappointed and Ash wasn't staring at me like someone he doesn't recognise.

'I know,' I say quietly, 'it's just, we've got plans tonight, otherwise I'd stay.'

'Stay if you want to,' Ash says, looking at me, and he doesn't seem annoyed, not really. A bit quiet, and a bit confused, but not annoyed. I shake my head.

'I have to go,' I say to the band, who are definitely, definitively, annoyed.

'What's your number, Ellie?' Shawn asks, pulling out his phone.

I wince, giving it to him, even though it's completely legitimate, because now Ash does looks annoyed. Even though it doesn't mean anything, even though honestly, this isn't About Him at all.

As we move towards the doors, Ash puts his arm around me.

'So, you're in a band now?' he asks quietly, as we walk down the corridor; and Rebecca's too close to our conversation for me to feel comfortable talking to him.

'Maybe, I don't know,' I respond quietly.

'I thought you'd tell me if you were doing something like that,' he says softly.

'There are things I thought you'd tell me too.'

'Look – I'm *sorry*,' he sighs.

'I know,' I respond, 'and honestly, I'm OK with it. I was going to tell you about the band, I just hadn't *yet*.'

'But you told Jess and Hayley . . .' he says, looking forward; and it's a statement of fact, not a question. I don't reply as we walk towards the school gates.

'I'm sorry,' I say, squeezing his hand meaningfully. Because I don't know what else to say. I know I should have told him; I know I don't want to keep secrets any more.

'No, *I'm* sorry,' he says, squeezing mine back.

'We really need to stop saying sorry,' I grin.

'We should do something else instead,' he says, turning in my direction and kissing me.

I put my head against his shoulder and hug his arm.

And I want to tell him I love him, but I have to remind myself, I don't.

♡ Song 4 ♡

Verse, Chorus, Middle Eight – Happy/Not Happy

It's sort of happy. Ecstatic really. The sound of first love, and furtive kisses; your parents at your bedroom door, listening for unfamiliar noises. It's the sound of my heart, the way it feels when he looks at me. Like it's beating in a different rhythm, time measured only by its sound.

And now that I'm caught in you,
I need to know if you're lost in me.

It's the sound of his hands in my hair and his lips on my neck. Of feeling like a grown-up, but also still a kid.

It's the bit of me that belongs to him, even when it knows it shouldn't belong to anyone except me.

Happy/not happy.
Am I happy now?

45

The £14 Prawn

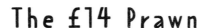

I'm sitting next to Rebecca at dinner, because Ash made me. He's on one side of me and she's on the other; an Ash Anderson Sandwich of Awkwardness.

Why? Why do I need to get to know this person?

I just don't want to be here, and nor, I suspect, does Elina – because she keeps shooting looks at Rebecca which are almost as venomous as the thoughts I keep having about Rebecca; even though so far, she's been completely Pleasant and Normal. Complimenting me on my eyeliner and telling me what a great singer I am, and how my voice sounds so wise when I sing, which is weird, given I'm so young and obviously inexperienced. By the time I realise she isn't being Pleasant or Normal, it's like I've been stung by a jellyfish, multiple times, and am in need of someone discreetly weeing on me, either to relieve the pain or, at the very least, give me an excuse to leave this dinner.

'You OK?' Ash whispers in my ear – and I'm mid wince from Rebecca's latest invective about my Big Voice, when I myself am So Small, or as she puts it, Have Such a Recessive Presence. Jessica is aggressively trying to understand what she means by a recessive presence when I turn my attention to Ash.

'Ordinary people can have extraordinary talents,' I hear her say silkily.

'Ordinary . . . ?' Hayley repeats menacingly.

'I'm fine,' I reply, wondering how he can possibly think anything about this dinner is fine when everyone at it is literally on a knife edge, or trying not to use a knife, to kill his ex-girlfriend. Elina has barely uttered a word, and Jess and Hayley appear to have mastered the art of speaking entirely through their teeth.

We're sat in a restaurant, which is frankly a bit fancy, having *dinner*. Because Rebecca organised it. Jess is basically stabbing her chicken, while Hayley has left her entire meal uneaten, moving it around in circles while trying not to explode with rage.

And eating out for Hayley and Jess and me usually involves a pizza, or some kind of fried chicken, or at the very least a hamburger – but we're eating something called New British, which basically involves someone charging me £14 to eat a prawn. I'm not sure how a prawn is either new or British, but it all seems a bit of a con to me.

'She's nice, isn't she?' Ash says seriously, and I wonder whether he's still in love with her, because only love could make you blind to someone so unpleasant, which upsets me – but not as much as this overpriced prawn does.

'If you say so,' I reply, irritated.

'You said you wanted to come tonight, Ellie. I didn't mind you not telling me about the band – can't you just be nice to her?' he sighs.

Nice to her? *Nice to her??* How about she tries being nice to literally *anyone*. Even the waitress, who she snidely showed her ID to when she wanted a glass of wine with dinner, and then asked if she could recommend a good red, then proceeded to tell her that nothing on the wine list would constitute a good red.

'Mmmm,' I murmur, trying not to let my anger escape me.

'Ash,' Rebecca calls from across the other side of me. 'Do you remember when we went to that gig in Brighton, and you lifted me over that fence to get out? We were so drunk,' she laughs. 'We missed our train home, remember?' She sounds like a twinkly fairy instead of a conniving witch. 'Didn't you end up kissing that girl? The one who gave us a lift home?' I want to say she looks innocent, but it's written all over her face. The fact she's bringing up that he used to drink, when he doesn't any more, that he was kissing someone else back then – multiple someone elses by the sound of it.

He half smiles, his discomfort evident.

'That was a long time ago, Bec.'

'No,' she says pointedly. 'It was about a year ago. You know, back when you had a life.'

Elina sits up, her eyes fiery.

'What the actual . . .' she cuts in bluntly.

'Elina, *don't*,' Ash says firmly.

'Why not?' she says, her voice shaking. 'I can't sit here while she brings that stuff up. Can't you see what she's doing? The way she's talking to you. It's pathetic. *You're* pathetic,' she says, turning to Rebecca.

'Whatever, Elina,' Rebecca says, her eyes flashing. 'Maybe you're happy with your little baby supermodel here, but Ash isn't. That's why I came here. He's not happy. You're not happy – are you?' she says, turning to him accusingly.

And I feel like I've been slapped. First with an apparently British prawn, and now with this. My unhappy boyfriend.

'Tell her,' Rebecca says, her voice rising as she stares at him. 'You called me before Christmas. You said you weren't happy. That things weren't working out. You wanted to move back to London. You wanted to know if you could stay with me and Mum.'

'That's not . . .' Ash says, turning to me. 'That was before . . .'

'Oh, come on, Ash,' Rebecca says, glaring at me. 'I mean, she's perfectly *nice*. Yeah, she can *sing*. Great. But what do you actually *do* together?' she asks, turning back to him. 'She's fifteen. You haven't even slept together yet.'

And its only then that he finally loses it. Just when I'm about to prove my maturity by screaming in her face that I'm sixteen. *SIXTEEN IN THREE WEEKS.*

'You know what, Rebecca, I didn't ask you to come here and I didn't ask for your opinion, and I am happy. So, either be nice, or leave,' Ash says angrily. But I can't stand this any more. I can't stand this lovers' quarrel. Not when the lover is my boyfriend, and the other lover isn't me.

'Don't leave on my account,' I say, standing. 'You two clearly have a lot to talk about.'

'Ellie, don't. Please,' he says, following me. 'It's not what you think.'

'We haven't even slept together?' I whisper. 'Did you tell her that?' I want him to say no. I want him to call her a liar and say it doesn't matter that we haven't. But he doesn't. He's just staring at her, and then at me, like he's confused, like he's trying to choose.

'Well, I'd be delighted to leave,' Hayley says, standing up to join me. 'This risotto is not worth the fourteen hundred calories, particularly when coupled with your personality.'

'And me,' Jess says, following suit. 'By the way,' she says, looking at Rebecca, 'I actually hate your lipstick. It makes you look like an extra in a Twilight film.'

'You might be too *mature* to know what that is,' Hayley says, glaring at her. 'It's about a bunch of vampires, so you'd probably enjoy it – or at the very least, empathise.'

The entire restaurant is staring at us now, the pretend grown-ups at their pretend grown-up dinner, and it feels like this is all too hard, because I never understood why this was happening in the first place. Why we were supposed to get to know each other at all.

'You know, Ash,' Rebecca says, her voice wavering. 'You may not like what I have to say, but I care about you, and I don't deserve *this* . . .' she says, gesturing to Hayley and Jess and Elina. 'I came here to make sure you were OK. I thought we were friends. I thought you knew me. Maybe this is coming out wrong. Ellie – I'm sorry,' she says, turning to me, 'you seem fine, nice. But you don't understand people like us. People like Ash and me. You don't get it. You're not right for each other.' There's so much force, such stubborn belief in what she's saying, that I almost believe her.

'Stop it, Bec,' Ash says furiously.

'I'm sorry,' she says, looking down at her lap, 'but she isn't. She isn't right for you.'

'What – and you *are*?' Elina offers violently. 'Because I have never, ever seen my brother as miserable as he was when he was with you, Rebecca.'

'That's not true,' she stutters.

She's crying suddenly, her body convulsing with tears, and I don't know how she's doing this. Making it look like she's the victim here when every time I meet her, she's rude and condescending and nasty, and he doesn't even seem to notice.

'I'm going,' I say, turning to Ash.

'Ellie, don't, please.'

I don't wait for his reply, or for Hayley and the others to collect their coats. I'm just glad I had the good sense not to check mine into the cloakroom, to be able to throw it over my shoulders right now as I head over to our waitress, as maturely as someone who is only fifteen can, and hand her a £20 note for the world's most expensive prawn.

'Keep the change,' I whisper, as Hayley finally catches up to me, grabbing me by my arm. Because someone, I think, looking at the waitress and her inability to choose a good red from an apparently not good enough wine list, deserves to have a decent evening.

Leaving the restaurant, the air hits me like a slap to the face, because he's not with me, he's not behind me: he's with her. But then I hear him, the door clinking behind him, as he runs to catch up with me.

'Ellie,' he says, grabbing my arm. 'Wait.' I spin around to face him, Hayley a step behind.

'I can't just leave her here,' he pleads. 'She's really not in a good place, and I can't . . . I can't be that person. I'm sorry. I don't want you to think this is about you, or about us. It's about her.' The way he says it, so desperately, with such honesty, makes me want to believe him so much.

'And what she was saying,' he continues, 'it isn't true. I promise. I am happy. *You* make me happy.'

But I don't even know how to make myself happy.

'I was lost before Christmas, I was lost before us, but now I'm not.'

'Why is she the one that's leaving then?' Hayley asks angrily.

He turns to her, unsure of how to respond, then back to me again, his green eyes pleading.

'I just need you to trust me, Ellie. This isn't about you, or us. It's about my friend, having a hard time, and I can't just leave her. Please don't ask me to.' I can feel my heart tugging at me, telling me it's OK, telling me to trust him – and I don't know why, I just do.

'Stay,' I reply.

He leans into me, until our foreheads are touching.

'I'll call you later,' he whispers. He leans down to kiss me, then walks back towards the restaurant, just as Jess and Elina appear from inside to stand next to Hayley. And in that moment, all I want is for him to turn back and look at me. For them to understand what's passed between us, and know he isn't choosing her. But he doesn't.

They're watching me as I watch him, and I can't stand the way they're looking at me. I can't stand the way it's making me feel.

'I have to get the bus,' I state, turning away, my hands buried deep in my pockets.

'Do you want to talk about it?' Jess asks quietly.

'No,' I say firmly. And I walk into the night, the cold wind like a blanket.

46

A Girl Called Ellie

My name is Ellie. Ellie Pillai. And I'm afraid of the boy in the yellow rain mac.

Because love is being afraid. Love is questions, to which there are never any answers. Like, what *is* love?

Does it start with me – or did it start with him? Or Mum? Or Dad? Or Phantom Baby?

Does love die? Does it disappear when you're no longer there to feel it? Is Amis still loved?

Can you love someone when you can't forgive them?

Is love Granny and Aunty Kitty and choices and no choices and having to do as you're told by the one person who says they love you most?

TELL ME, gods, tell me what love is.

And I want to make sense of all this: of him staying, and me going.

But just like a £14 prawn, it doesn't make any sense.

47

The Dark Hour

I lie in bed listening to the sound of my heart, waiting for the familiar buzz of my phone. It's one of those dark hours. The ones that go on and on, the minutes folding in on themselves.

London Cousin – Annoying:
a prawn 🦐 saved the little mermaid

Ellie:
that was a lobster

He never calls.
But I never really think he will.

48

Stranger Danger

The next morning, I wake up feeling hungover, even though the last time I drank was months ago, when I classily threw up in someone's mouth (they deserved it). I just wish there was a more tangible reason for why I feel this horrible.

My brain is a soup of thoughts. The dark hour. Ash as he left me. Jess and Elina and Hayley as they stared at me sympathetically; and Rebecca, somewhere between angry and unrepentant, telling me I wasn't right for my boyfriend.

I take a sip of the water Granny has taken to creepily depositing in my room while I'm sleeping, fearful I'm not hydrating enough (very important for study, Eleanor), then examine my phone, lit up with messages from the faces I don't want to think about.

I sit up straight, fluffing my pillows against my back, and click on a message from an unknown number sent a few minutes ago.

+44 7825 834681:
ru in or not?

I stare at it.

Ellie:
who is this?

But I have a horrible feeling I know.

+44 7825 834681
dirty blond

Ellie:
oh

+44 7825 834681
hope told me abt ur nickname

And I think, Classic Hope. She can find the time to message a boy about me, but she can't find the time to tell me what actually happened with Vikash – although I believe the word Mum used was 'toast'.

Ellie:
dirty the colour, not *dirty*

+44 7825 834681:
got gigs coming up & need 2 rehearse

Ellie:
not sure i'm a good fit tbh

+44 7825 834681:

u r

Ellie:

. . .

I can imagine the ellipsis at the other end of the phone as I keep trying to type something that makes sense. That feels honest. I save his number and reread the message I'm going to send him. The message that says, thank you, but no thank you. It's me, not you. The message that's annoying me, because it's not who I want to be any more.

Dirty Blond:

don't overthink it

And it's a bit like he's reading my mind. Or I'm just very, very predictable.

Dirty Blond:

what ru doing?

Ellie:

thinking. sorry.

Dirty Blond:

i mean 2day. where do u live?

Ellie:

ru trying 2 kidnap me again?

Dirty Blond:

ha ha pal

Oh God, he remembers.

Dirty Blond:

go 4 a drive & talk about it?

Ellie:

stranger danger

Dirty Blond:

not sure how 2 respond 2 that

I think about last night. About feeling confused and lost and a little bit broken. About the release music gives me, and the song Shawn sang in New York and how connected I felt. It makes me want to push myself. To feel uncomfortable and afraid – because this, I can control. Not whether Ash calls me, or whether he loves me, or Rebecca loves him and he loves her back – but this. Me. How I behave, what I do.

I type a reply before I let myself overthink it.

Ellie:

my dad can b weird. meet round the corner?

Dirty Blond:

3?

Ellie:

fletcham – by cricket sign on green

Dirty Blond:

😎

I put my phone down for a second and think about what I've just done. I'm meeting Shawn for a drive. To talk about the band. To talk about *being* in the band.

Ellie:

should i do this band thing????

London Cousin – Annoying:

✓

London Cousin – Annoying:

met someone . . . . hot body, hot face, hot brain (is that a thing?)

London Cousin – Annoying:

questionable taste in girls . . . . . .

I smile.

Ellie:

excellent taste in girls. obvs

London Cousin – Annoying:

true. i'm a catch

Ellie:

wud granny approve?

London Cousin – Annoying:

hard no

And despite Ash and the Julie Delpy wannabe, suddenly I'm smiling, and I don't know why.

49

Sri Lankan Eggs

When I get downstairs to eat breakfast, Granny is busy cooking eggs. We're not much of a breakfast-eating family, so anybody cooking anything in the morning feels pretty much wrong.

'Sri Lankan eggs,' she says, turning to me as I enter the room – and I notice there are green chillies and onions in the scramble, which partly makes my mouth water and partly makes my stomach turn.

'Your mother is still asleep,' she says, spooning some eggs on to a plate for me. 'It is good she rests,' she says wisely.

'Where's Dad?' I yawn.

'Bike ride,' she says, placing a fork in my hand and motioning towards her face semi violently. This is Tamil for: eat. Now.

'Oh,' I say, disappointed. Because Saturday mornings are when Dad and I listen to the radio and drink copious amounts of tea while watching travel documentaries. We like to *um* and *ah* over the exotic foods while eating something equally uninspiring, like toast or Weetabix. Although he currently appears to be obsessed by some kind of disgusting green smoothie that he makes daily with something called *spirulina*. Which smells even worse than it sounds.

I suppose I shouldn't be surprised he doesn't want to watch travel documentaries with me. I just want to explain to him that I'm still his Ellie, I just need to be my Ellie too.

I take a bite of the eggs, Granny watching me anxiously.

'Mmmmmm,' I intone, making a face of enthusiasm. She smiles, satisfied, then turns back towards the hob as I desperately spit the eggs back on to my plate. It's like there's more green chilli than actual egg in it.

'I make good breakfast,' she says sanctimoniously, as she stirs the eggs again. But I'm not sure I can actually hear her, because there are tiny fires erupting all over my tongue, even though there are no longer any Sri Lankan eggs in contact with it.

And then, thank the many gods I quasi-pray to, the doorbell rings – and she turns to answer it.

'EAT,' she says menacingly, as she turns back over her shoulder, motioning towards her face again. I grimace and type a message to the only person who will understand this predicament.

Ellie:

sri lankan egggggggggsssss!

London Cousin – Annoying:

As soon as she disappears out of sight, I stand up and walk, panic-stricken, to every corner of the kitchen, desperately looking for a place to hide the eggs. The food recycling seems too obvious: I can imagine Granny, some kind of old brown detective – Miss Marple in black-and-brown technicolour – noticing a green chilli floating near the top of the container, and pledging personal accountability for hunting down the Pillai responsible, and punishing them with her I Was Lucky to Have One Egg a Week When I Was Growing Up speech. Then there's the bin, so close to overflowing Mum and Dad must be having a stand-off about whose turn it is to take it out – and then I think: the stand-off is with me, because it's *my* turn to take it out, and I curse myself for being so annoying and lazy, because if the bin was empty, I could definitely get away with hiding the contents of this plate without inciting Brown Marple's suspicions.

Note to self: I am my own worst enemy, almost *all* of the time.

I eye a pot plant, its dark soil gleaming invitingly, and wonder whether I can hide the eggs and come back for them later.

'Ellie, your friend is here,' Granny says, appearing in the doorway, her voice suddenly prim. I turn around guiltily, my position compromised, hunched over Mum's yucca plant like some kind of creepy, plant-sniffing weirdo.

'What are you doing, Eleanor?' Granny asks suspiciously.

'Umm,' I mouth, 'this plant just smells so . . . nice . . . and fresh,' I say, standing up straight.

Why, gods, why? Why is he here, in my kitchen, when I'm wearing the world's oldest pyjama bottoms and a stained Led Zeppelin T-shirt, hunched over a yucca plant with a plate of Sri Lankan eggs? Why?? I bet Rebecca's pyjamas are silky and perfect – you know, when she bothers wearing pyjamas, because she mostly sleeps naked and prefers to walk around naked, like the world's sexiest naturist.

'Hey,' Ash says, smiling. He's wearing a light blue sweatshirt with a sheepskin-lined denim jacket, black jeans and his paint-splattered Converse. He puts that jacket on me when I'm cold. I want to throw something at his head. Like the yucca plant, or some Sri Lankan eggs.

'Hi,' I say stiffly. Because I've had time to think about last night now. About the dark hour, waiting up until 2 a.m. for him to call me – and I don't want to be the kind of girl that waits up until 2 a.m. for someone to call me. I want to be the kind of girl who sings in a band and doesn't care whether anyone calls her.

'You are hungry,' Granny says to him. She has the ability to make a question sound like a statement when there is never really any choice.

'Yes, thank you,' he says, sitting down at the table.

To his credit, he has at least realised that the easiest answer when offered food in this house is to respond with a yes. Offence will be taken if you decline, food and/or drink will be presented regardless – only then it will be accompanied by an irate aunty, stationed next to you until said food or drink is fully imbibed. Accept your fate – accept your plate.

'Sri Lankan eggs,' she says, putting the plate of scramble in front of him.

'Looks great,' he says, manfully spooning forkfuls into his mouth.

'You might want to slow down,' I say quietly.

'Healthy appetite,' Granny says approvingly. 'Is good.'

He continues eating, each forkful bigger than the last, and at first, he seems OK; but after a while I can see his eyes watering, his nose running as he delicately dabs at it, trying to stem the never-ending flow of snot that is the hallmark of any good Sri Lankan meal. And I know that inimitable green chilli heat is building in his mouth, like the third and fourth movement in Beethoven's Fifth Symphony, the one Miss Mason is obsessed by and insists on playing over and over, until you understand the concept of a crescendo. Clearly, Beethoven ate Sri Lankan eggs.

I can almost see him choking on it, trying so desperately to be polite while Granny eyes him admiringly. There's a part of me – the part that feels angry and humiliated and hurt – that almost thinks he deserves it. To be undone by some Sri Lankan eggs. But then, as I fear the tears are about to start falling, I take pity on him.

'Granny, didn't you say you wanted to send a bottle of sambal to Ash's mum? Maybe you should get it. You know, so you don't forget.'

She huffs.

'Am not old woman, Eleanor, I am not forgetting everything,' she replies haughtily; but I can tell she's thinking about it, because actually, she forgets a lot these days. Everything other than grudges.

'But I will get now,' she offers, 'so it is done. Am very busy today,' she says, bustling out of the kitchen importantly.

I walk to the fridge and pour him a glass of milk.

'Don't pant,' I advise, 'the air will only make it worse.'

'It's like there's no egg in it at all,' he says, grabbing for the milk and pouring it down his throat. 'Is this some kind of test?' he asks, looking up at me desperately.

'If it is, I've failed too – hand it over,' I demand, as I start scraping my eggs into the yucca plant. He hands his plate over, his eyes darting nervously towards the door.

'It'll take her a couple of minutes, but stand by the door, just in case.' I scrape his eggs into the soil and rake it over. I can only hope I haven't sentenced this yucca plant to death by green chilli.

'Done,' I hiss, throwing the plate back at him. We listen for Granny's footsteps in the hall, then scramble, un-egg-like, to our seats.

She walks in and places the jar of sambal by his side, then looks at our empty plates, gratified.

'Thank you,' he says, picking up the jar.

'You will have more,' she says, gesturing to our plates and heading back towards the stove.

'NO,' I shout, pulling my chair back abruptly. She turns around, eyeing me suspiciously. 'I'm full, and Ash has to go, don't you, Ash?'

'Actually, I was hoping we could go for a bike ride,' he says, standing – and he has a very unnerving way of making unavoidable eye contact.

'I can't,' I say, avoiding it. 'I have to study.' I hope the excuse will be enough for Granny to get rid of him for me.

'It's the weekend, Eleanor. Go with your friend,' Granny says disloyally, motioning us towards the door. 'You study later. In afternoon.'

'I have plans this afternoon,' I say uncomfortably.

'Take day off then. Must not work too hard,' Granny says robotically, and I'm sure these words have never left her mouth before.

'But I can't even *ride* a bike,' I say dismissively.

'I thought I could teach you,' he says softly. And there are those eyes again. Those intense green eyes with their long inky lashes. Stupid expressive eyes. Stupid long inky lashes. Stupid inability to look at him and not want to scream from a rooftop somewhere that he's my boyfriend while The Lightning Seeds, 'Pure' plays on repeat in my head.

'I, um . . .' I say, running out of excuses. 'I . . .'

'She will change,' Granny says, turning to him. I try to find a way to say no. Any way of saying no.

'You will wear something nice, yes, Eleanor,' Granny says in her usual statement/question mode. I open my mouth to reply, but nothing comes out.

'Ellie always looks nice,' Ash says, staring at me. And I hate myself for caring that he says it. That he's defending me against Granny's belief that all women should permanently look like they've stepped out of a Bollywood movie (see: brightly coloured, bejewelled occasion-wear). Because I want to be the one who has the courage to say that. To feel it. To know it about myself.

I try to remember how I felt waiting for his call last night, in the early hours of the morning, when the world was dark. But I can't. Because he's here. Eating Sri Lankan eggs and talking to my grandmother, just so he can teach me how to ride a bike – which he will never do, because Dad tried for months and could never get me to stay upright.

So, I don't say anything. I just walk upstairs and leave him in the clutches of Granny. I figure if he's still here when I get downstairs, then the least I can do is let him watch me fall off a bike.

50

The Cardinal Rule of Any Make-Up-Wearing Person

When I get downstairs, Ash is waiting in the hallway, clutching the jar of sambal.

'You look nice,' he says nervously. I've put mascara on, and a little lip gloss, my hair pulled back from my face – you know, so I can the see the ground clearly, just before I hit it. I'm wearing a pair of dark blue jeans, with some tall black cowboy boots Hope talked me into buying, and a yellow jumper with a weird big collar that I bought in New York.

'Thanks,' I mumble.

'Not that you don't *usually*,' he says painfully.

'Right . . .' I trail off, embarrassed.

'So, your mum mentioned you had a bike in the garage . . . the last time I was here.'

'Mum?' I ask. Mum hates the garage and complains she has no idea what's in it. Secretly, I think she quite likes the fact I can't ride a bike, because it's one less way of me getting hurt.

'She said it was at the back?' he continues stiltedly.

I stare obstinately at the wall beside his head.

'Next to hers.'

It's true we all *have* bikes, from the days when Dad fantasised about family bike rides, but Mum refused to do them, and gravity refused to let me.

'She said it would probably be OK still, size wise,' he persists.

I shrug. I haven't grown much, not vertically at any rate, not since I was thirteen – which is the last time Dad tried to bribe me into learning by buying me one of those cool, retro bikes with a basket – which unfortunately ended in a trip to A&E, three stitches and a hysterical version of my mother.

'I told her I wanted to teach you,' he states, trying to fill the silence between us. 'She said your dad's always asking you to go out cycling with him.'

I open my mouth, but nothing comes out. Like one of those fish in a fish tank that you just stare at, imagining they're trying to say something.

'You said things between you and your dad have been weird,' he says quietly. 'I thought it might help.'

And it's impossible to hate such good intentions. Such thoughtfulness. But somehow, I manage it anyway.

I walk past him to the front door.

'We don't have to do this, you know,' I say, as I walk outside and turn down the side of the house.

'Do what?' he asks, putting his hand on my shoulder.

'THIS,' I say, turning abruptly and shaking him free. 'Teach me to ride a bike. Try to make things better with my dad. You don't have to feel guilty if you're going to break up with me. We don't have to do THIS.'

He grabs hold of my hand.

'I want to,' he says firmly. 'I want you and your dad to get on. I want you to be happy.'

'Because you feel sorry for me?' I say, tears springing to my eyes.

'No,' he says, frustrated. 'I don't feel sorry for you. I feel sorry for *me*. Because I keep messing things up. But I need you to trust me. I can't keep explaining that I want to be with you. You have to believe me, Ellie.'

I let go of his hand and turn away from him, then walk towards the garage and pull the door up, the sound of it instantly gratifying: metal grating against rails, loud and sharp and guttural.

I step inside and pretend to look for the bike. But in the darkness, all I can do is hope I'm not going to cry, because I'm not wearing waterproof mascara today: the cardinal rule of any make-up-wearing person who's feeling emotional. Jess said she wore waterproof mascara every day when she and Elina broke up.

'Ellie?' he says questioningly, as I start picking up boxes for no apparent reason. 'What are you doing?' he asks, gently placing his hand on my shoulder again.

'How can I trust you?' I ask, shrugging his hand off me. 'After everything Rebecca said last night – when you stayed with her and not me.'

'You told me to stay,' he says desperately.

'You said you'd call me,' I reply angrily.

'I'm sorry. It got late, and I didn't want to wake you. But I came first thing this morning, I'm here now,' he says quietly. I can feel his eyes boring into the back of my head, but I'm still stacking boxes, packing them into random places, unable to look at him in case my mascara gives up on me.

'She's my oldest friend,' he says, starting to pace behind me. 'She can be overprotective, and she can be a bit of a nightmare, but she's family, Ellie. And I don't have much of that. I don't have what you've got.'

'You haven't answered my question,' I reply frostily.

'Please, I don't want to lose you.'

'Then tell me the truth,' I say, turning to him.

He sighs and looks downwards.

'We've just always had each other,' he says, looking up at me, 'when things went wrong.' He looks guilty then. Like maybe he's a bit disappointed in himself. 'She broke up with her boyfriend before Christmas, and I guess we've always been each other's fallback plan. She can't handle seeing me with you. She's never been great when I'm with someone else.'

'That doesn't give her the right . . .' I rage.

'I know. And I told her that last night. I told her how I feel about you. How much you mean to me.'

'So, she's still in love with you,' I state quietly.

He doesn't argue.

'How do you feel about her?' I whisper.

'Like I have to take care of her.' He shrugs.

'Why?'

'Because her dad left, and then my dad, who was like a dad to her – she lost him too – and I need her to be OK, Ellie. I need her to be happy. She just doesn't make *me* happy.'

I stare at him.

'But you,' he says, stepping forward, 'you do make me happy, and I just want to teach you how to ride a bike so maybe your dad can see I'm not trying to take you away from him, so maybe we can *all* be happy.'

He looks small for a minute. Forlorn and scared and tired and sad. Like there are too many things he has to take care of. Too many people.

And I get it. I don't want to – but I do. She's family, however much I wish she wasn't. If he cared less, if he didn't try, he wouldn't be him. The him that makes me feel like this.

'It's OK,' I say, reaching up to him suddenly; and he holds me tight. Like maybe he should be wearing waterproof mascara too.

'You can talk to me, Ash. You don't have to do everything on your own. You don't have to look after everybody, you know that, don't you?' I say, stroking his hair. He pulls me tighter.

'I promised Dad I'd take care of them,' he says, his voice breaking. 'I promised.'

I pull him tighter.

'I'm sure he wanted them to take care of you too,' I say gently. 'And I'm here. I'm here for you, OK?'

He puts his hands on my face and kisses me, and it feels like the whole world disappears until he lets go and steps back a little.

'So?' he asks, looking down at me, his hands wrapped around mine.

'So, what?'

'Can I teach my girlfriend how to ride a bike?'

'You can *try*,' I say cynically.

'Anything's worth a try,' he smiles.

51

A&E, Three Stitches and a Hysterical Version of My Mother

I've fallen over roughly five thousand times. There's a hole in my favourite jeans, and the cowboy boots I thought made my legs look marginally longer are clearly the incorrect footwear for trying to maintain grip on a bicycle pedal.

My basket is bashed, and Ash keeps trying to tell me I can cycle – when clearly, I can't.

'But I let go of you,' he exclaims, 'and you didn't fall over!'

'My jeans would beg to differ,' I huff.

'Come on, Ellie, you've almost got it,' he says encouragingly, as I wobble off again, his hand holding on to my back.

'Don't let go!' I shriek, pedalling as fast as I can.

But it's too late. I'm flying, the breeze in my face as he pushes me into the road, the bicycle moving soundlessly. I'm upright. Almost in control. ME. I am *almost* riding a bike, the sound of Queen, 'Bicycle Race' playing on repeat in my head.

Bicycle, bicycle! Freddie sings operatically.

I try not to scream. I try not to overthink the idea of A&E, three stitches and a hysterical version of my mother.

Suddenly, another bike appears in my peripheral vision, and I'm no longer in control. I'm veering. Moving sharply from side to side, getting lower to the ground with every second I fly forward.

'Just keep pedalling!' Ash shouts. 'Don't slow down!'

Don't slow down??? I couldn't if I tried.

'Aarrrrrgggggghhhhhhhhh!' I shriek, turning the handlebars to the left in an attempt to avoid the maniac careering towards me. I jam on the brakes, the bicycle halting abruptly as I tip forward over the front wheel. 'Owwwwwwww!' I exclaim as I hit the ground.

'Ellie! Are you OK?' Ash shouts, rushing over. My bottom half seems to be caught beneath my mint-green children's bike, my cowboy boot stuck somewhere in the back wheel.

'*En anbe?*' Dad says. 'Ellie?' he says, leaning over and peering into my face. All I can notice is that Dad's cycling gear is a bit too tight – and that he seems to be wearing leggings. That are too tight, in too many areas.

Dad the maniac cyclist. A maniac in spandex.

'How many fingers am I holding up?' he says, waving three fingers in my face. I consider lying. Perhaps Ash will think I'm concussed and we can finally end the Ellie Pillai Knows How to Ride a Bicycle charade; but Dad looks concerned. Concerned enough to divulge this incident to my mother, which will inevitably lead to hysteria and a long, unnecessary visit to A&E.

'Three,' I say flatly, as Ash attempts to rescue my boot from the wheel. I would be wearing a pair of socks that read Dirty Socks. Like a child. Like an actual child.

'You looked quite good out there for a minute, *en anbe*,' Dad says, impressed, as I hobble to my feet. 'A bit more practice, and you'll have it.'

'That's what I said,' Ash says, turning to him. 'She just panics, thinks she can't do it, and stops.'

'She's very stubborn,' Dad says to him sympathetically.

'Cycling again then, Dad?' I say, trying to keep the conversation going.

'Trying to get healthy,' he says, poking his stomach. 'With the baby coming and everything.'

'Maybe we could all go out together sometime,' I say begrudgingly. 'When I've practised a bit.' Dad looks so pleased I hate myself for not trying earlier.

'That would be great,' he smiles. 'Do you have a bike, Ash? I have one you can borrow. It's only an old mountain bike, but it does the job.'

'That would be great, Mr Pillai,' Ash says, smiling, even though I know he has his own bike – he came here on it today. He looks so pleased and happy not to be subjected to Dad's usual silence and irritation.

'Good, good,' Dad says, walking off. When he's far enough away, Ash leans down to kiss me.

'I *told* you you could cycle,' he says, putting his arms around me.

'Again,' I say, pointing at the hole in my knee, 'my jeans would beg to differ.'

'Should we practise some more?' he says, kissing my nose. I wish I wasn't meeting Shawn in an hour. I wish I could stand here all day, kissing my boyfriend and learning how to ride a bike – which are two thoughts I never thought I'd have, either simultaneously or individually.

'I really do have plans this afternoon,' I say guiltily.

'Jessica?' he says, playing with my hair.

'Hayley,' I say, lying.

Why am I lying?

'OK,' he says disappointedly.

'But I could come over tonight?' I add quickly. 'Or is that a problem, with the whole Rebecca thing . . .' I say awkwardly.

'No,' he says firmly. 'It's not. I'd love for you to come over.' He trails his fingers down the back of my jumper. 'No more secrets,' he says, pulling me into his chest. 'I should have been more honest about Rebecca. I just thought all this drama would be too much for you. That you'd think it wasn't worth it.'

He kisses me again. A lot. Until I spot Dad watching us out of the living room window and we stop, before we undo our good work and make the hole in my favourite jeans for nothing.

But I keep asking myself why I'm the one who's keeping secrets, why I'm the one not being honest.

And how he could think he wasn't worth it.

How he almost sounds like me.

Dolly Parton Tribute Act

An hour later, I'm skulking around the village green like some kind of plant-sniffing weirdo again. There's a bank of flower beds down the side closest to the road, and to give myself a reason to be stood here, I keep leaning down and pretending to smell the rhododendrons. This is difficult on a number of levels. It's January, so there's nothing but rhododendrons in bloom, not to mention it's freezing, and frankly, there are only so many times you can lean down and sniff the same plant. Which matters because Karen, our neighbour from The Villiers, a weirdly ornamental house with a carp pond in the front garden, is stood outside her house, quite obviously watching me, as if she *wants me to know* she's watching me, her hand poised over her mobile, in case I'm one the of the 'thugs' that keep defacing the village bench. Because in this part of the world, being young and brown makes you a potential mugger/thug/defacer of local property – even when you're wearing lipstick and a pair of cowboy boots, like some kind of Dolly Parton tribute act.

I know.

I'm wearing *lipstick*.

I Don't Know Why.

When I went upstairs to get ready to meet Shawn, somehow, I ended up putting on lipstick and liberally spraying myself with the Chloé perfume Mum bought me from the Heathrow duty-free; a guilt purchase, from when she dumped me for the aunties on the way to New York. It's like I want to impress him. It's like I care what he thinks of me. It's like I want him to *like me*.

No.

I'm just trying to show him I'm cool enough to be in his band.

Or am I? Do I want to be in his band? I don't know. I'm busy. I've got exams and a boyfriend that's leaving in a few months, who I want to spend more time with, not less.

'You can't pick that!' Karen shouts at me from across the road.

'Sorry?' I say, cupping my hand around my ear. Obviously, I can hear her perfectly.

'I said,' she shouts irritably, 'that's council property. You can't pick that!' She points to the flowers.

I shrug innocently.

She narrows her eyes and continues watching me as I deliberately lean down for longer and longer stretches of time. I can hear her breathing accelerate as she angrily mutters under her breath; and all I can think about is the yucca plant and when I can get to it for long enough to remove Granny's Sri Lankan eggs. Because I am not a plant killer. Or a mugger. Or a thug. Or a defacer of local property.

Just as it looks like Karen's about to march over the road and demand I unhand the Fletcham Horticultural Society's Prize

Rhododendrons, a battered VW Golf appears, and Shawn leans out of the driver's seat.

'Jump in,' he says, indicating the passenger side.

'One second,' I say, still standing next to his window.

Across the road, Karen looks apoplectic with rage.

'I can see you!' she screams. I'm not sure what she thinks she can see – Shawn's car is blocking her view, and if she could see anything, it would probably be a sign that read 'Nothing to See'. I crane my head over the top of the VW and shout back.

'He's from the council,' I indicate, pointing at Shawn. She looks like she's about to lay an egg. 'He's checking the flower beds. Apparently, the ones in Wilton are looking much more . . . bloomy.' *Bloomy?*

'Bloomy?' she shouts, concerned. 'I need to talk to him. Wilton are using a non-verified fertiliser!'

I look down at Shawn and try to stifle a giggle.

'She needs to talk to you,' I whisper.

'She's coming over,' he says, horrified. And when I look over, I can see Karen crossing the road towards us, waiting impatiently for the bus to pass.

'Quick, get in!' he hisses.

I jump in the car and Shawn pulls off quickly, the two of us slightly hysterical.

'What was that about?' he says, half laughing, half incredulous.

'Nothing,' I smile, as I watch Karen shaking her head in the rear-view mirror. And I can't tell whether she's relieved I'm gone, or angry that I am what I am.

53

California Soul

We're still laughing about Karen's face halfway up the road, and I fear snot may be forming for which I have no receptacle. Why do I never carry tissues?

'She was . . . *intense*,' Shawn states, as we both start giggling again. 'What's her obsession with those flowers?'

'They're a symbol of all that is good and pure and British, don't you know,' I say, eyeing him.

'I feel like I should be wearing a monocle and top hat, and waving a Union Jack.'

'Karen would love that.'

'Karen?' he laughs.

'I know . . .' I smile.

'You look nice,' he says, gesturing at me. And it's such an abrupt change of subject I snort, and snot comes flying out of my nose.

GREAT.

'Tissues,' he grins, pointing at the glovebox.

'Thanks,' I reply, covering my nose until I can get some paper to it.

'So, what's with your dad?' he asks, indicating down a side road. And I suddenly realise I have no idea where we're going, and I'm in a car with a boy I barely know, who carries tissues in his glovebox and who possibly has a clown suit hidden in the boot and is going to murder me and bury my body in the woods. Which is a concern.

Note to self: do not lie about where you are to the people who will stop you from being murdered.

'Um . . .' I say, wobbly. 'He can be a bit awkward. At least he is now I've got a boyfriend.' Shawn laughs.

'That I understand. My mum HATES Hannah. It's one of the *many* reasons we broke up.'

'Dad doesn't hate Ash,' I backtrack, 'he just worries, that's all.'

'Ash An-der-son,' he says slowly.

'Why are you saying it like that?' I ask.

'Aren't half the girls at school in love with him?' He smiles.

This is a fact I prefer to avoid thinking about.

'Well, I think he's pretty amazing.'

'But you're pretty amazing too,' he says seriously.

'Um . . .'

And I have been repeating the word *um* for about ninety seconds now.

'Anyway. Where are we going?' I ask cautiously, looking around for a blunt instrument. Something that could either kill him, or at the very least give him a bad headache.

'A little spot by the river. I've got some tea in a flask. I thought we could sit and have a chat about the band.'

'Tea? In a flask?' I laugh. 'For a chat? You sound like my dad.'

'What?' he says, laughing. 'I'm very particular about my tea, and this way it doesn't get cold.'

'You're a strange boy, Shawn, erm . . . what's your surname?'

'Kowalski,' he says, smiling. 'It's Polish.'

Ellie Pillai missing. Shawn Kowalski last to see her alive. Distraught boyfriend cries outside house, while brown Julie Delpy lookalike comforts him.

'Kowalski,' I say, trying it out. 'You're a very strange boy, Shawn Kowalski.'

'Music?' he asks, ignoring the comment.

'Sure,' I say, looking out of the window.

And the sound of Marlena Shaw, 'California Soul' begins to fill the car: gentle and soulful and serene.

I lean back in my seat and bask in the sunlight. It's one of those perfect January days, the car warm with snaps of sunshine. I can hear him singing along, harmonising to the horns and their delicate bluesy beat, his voice raspy and bitter. I join in a bit and we look at each other, rolling our shoulders to the beat and grinning. I decide both the flask and song choice make him an unlikely clown serial killer.

'We're here,' he says, pulling into a car park. He opens my door and I step outside, the air icy as I walk towards the water.

'I don't think I've been to this part of the river before,' I shout over my shoulder, as he retrieves a bag from the boot.

'It's great, isn't it? Hannah and I found it a few weeks after I got my licence.

'Come on,' he says, sweeping past me with a blanket and thermos flask. We walk a few minutes further and he throws the blanket down for us to sit on, proceeding to open the flask and pour two cups of tea into two lids, producing an unopened pint of milk from his pocket.

'Wow . . .' I say, laughing.

'What?' he exclaims, grinning.

'Nothing,' I say, shaking my head. 'You just really like your tea how you like it.'

He smiles.

'Are you cold?' he asks, as I shiver.

'A bit, but it's a good cold. Fresh.'

'OK,' he says doubtfully, 'but I can grab another blanket if you like?'

'No, no, I'm fine,' I say, wrapping my arms around my knees and refusing the milk as I take a sip of the black tea. He's right. There's something incredibly comforting about hot tea from a flask.

'So, the band,' he says, sipping his tea. 'We all like you, and we want to do more original material. So, what's the problem?'

'I'm not sure they all *liked* me . . .' I trail off.

'They didn't love you leaving after an hour,' he says directly.

'I know, but like I said before, I get really nervous about stuff like this – and I'm just not sure I fit into your . . . look.'

'Because you're a girl?'

'Because I'm me.'

He scrunches his face up and looks at me questioningly. Like there's something on my face, and he's trying to find the nicest way of telling me.

'What have you got to lose? The more you perform, the easier it'll get.'

'I've got my exams, and Ash is leaving in September, and I don't know if I've got the time to be as committed as you need me to be.'

'Rehearsal is once a week – twice on gig weeks. Ash can hang out any time we do. It's just a way of making some cash and getting better on our instruments. It'll look good on your uni applications too.'

I stare into the distance. Thinking, thinking, overthinking.

'I can see how happy it makes you,' he says, looking at me, 'and when we're good – we make other people happy too.'

And the idea of that feels like a drug; or what I imagine a drug might feel like, if I had ever taken or ever intended to take a drug – which I don't, because I experience paranoia and hallucinations without any outside assistance.

'I'm not sure . . .' I say, sipping my tea.

'You are,' he says obstinately.

'GOD, you're annoying,' I say, pushing him lightly.

'Never heard that before.' He grins.

'So, what's with you and this Hannah then?' I ask seriously. 'You'd better not be messing my cousin around.'

'Hope and I are *friends*,' he smiles, 'and Hannah is just *Hannah*. I am very much not in a relationship,' he says, looking at me.

Note to self: not in a relationship.

'So, you'll come on Friday?' he says, seizing his moment. 'We're playing the spring dance so you need to get familiar with the set.'

'*Fine*,' I say persuaded. 'I'll come.' And I'm glad he's being pushy. I'm glad I'm pushing myself.

For an hour after that, we just sit there. Chatting about his mum and his sister and his grandparents; his dad's new girlfriend, who he thinks is much too young for him. About my parents and Granny and the situation with Aunty Kitty and Charles – and I can't help feeling he's the best friend I never knew I needed.

'I have to go,' I say, looking down at the time on my phone. 'I promised Ash I'd be at his for dinner.'

'Want a lift?' he asks, standing up and brushing himself off.

'Thanks,' I reply.

Because it's time to face the music – in a totally non-ironic way – and tell Ash the truth about this afternoon.

'OK, let's go,' Shawn says, gathering up the blanket, thermos in one pocket and milk in the other.

And for a second, weirdly, he catches hold of my hand – but lets go of it just as quickly.

'Sorry,' he laughs awkwardly. 'I used to come here a lot with Hannah. It was a reflex thing.'

'S'OK,' I mumble, purple-faced.

But truthfully, it didn't feel that weird at all.

54

I've Never Done This Before

When I arrive at Ash's and he opens the door, I turn around and wave to Shawn as he drives away.

Ash stares at the car.

'I'm sorry,' I say, looking up at him. 'I lied to you earlier. About who I was meeting. I wasn't seeing Hayley; I went to meet Shawn.'

He watches me, his eyes soft and unreadable.

'To talk about the band,' I gulp. 'I don't know why I lied to you. It's just, I've never done this before,' which I want to believe isn't completely obvious. 'And I don't know whether it's OK for me to hang out with Shawn. Whether you'll mind or whether you're *allowed* to mind,' I say, gesticulating wildly. 'I just know I really, really like you, and I don't want to lie to you about anything, or for you to feel like you need to lie to me,' I breathe. 'But I'm in his band now, and I'm terrified and excited and I really want to share that with you. And I want to be OK with you being friends with Rebecca, and for you to be OK with me writing songs with Shawn, and I want for us to be a proper us, and . . . and . . .'

'Are you finished?' he says gently.

'Yes,' I exhale.

'OK,' he smiles.

'OK?' I ask shyly.

'Yes. I'm glad you told me.'

He puts his arms around me and picks me up off the step, carrying me into the house like an awkward-shaped parcel.

'Why do you always pick me up?' I laugh, relieved.

'Because you're small. And cute.'

'Like a kitten . . .' I intone sarcastically. So, he picks me up and throws me over his shoulder like a fireman.

'Aaaaaaaarrrrrgggggghhhhh,' I shriek from upside down.

'Is that better?' he asks, amused with himself.

'Nooooooo!' I giggle, as he starts tickling me.

As he carries me up the stairs, Mrs Aachara smiles and waves at us from the sofa in the front room. I try to ignore Rebecca next to her. Not smiling and not laughing. Just looking at me. Like something she wishes didn't exist.

55

Birthday

Ellie:

The Beatles, 'Birthday'

Ellie:

they say it's ur birthday . . .

I send him the link and put the *White Album* on my record player. Disk two, side one. Best. Birthday song. Ever.

I dance around my bedroom, headbanging to the intro, the sound of clanging guitars and blues riff harmonies carrying me around my room.

It's Ash's birthday today. Ash's and Elina's birthdays, to be precise. They're turning eighteen – and in a week, it's my birthday too. Sixteen. Which feels like a moment. A big number. Like something special or important should happen, but I'm not really sure what. Or maybe I am, but I'm too nervous to think about it.

I let the music take me places as I brush my hair and put my eyeliner on. Things with Ash have been great lately. Holding hands under the table in the library, meeting in empty classrooms during free periods; furtive kissing and holding hands in public, having that one person you want to talk to when there's something you want to share.

Tonight, the whole group are coming to our band rehearsal before we go to Cinema, and that feels good too. The merging of these two different parts of my life. Like we're all friends. Like I've suddenly doubled my friendship quota.

Ash:

it's my birthday 2, yeah

I hug my phone to my chest momentarily, wishing it was him.

Ellie:

ru at the test centre yet?

He's taking his driving test today – mostly, so he can do more to help his mum out, but also because we want to be able to see each other without the need for a chaperone.

Ash:

waiting with mum

Ellie:

♥ can't wait 2 c u

The thread goes silent, which I imagine means some serious-looking person in glasses with a big clipboard and red felt-tip pen is taking him to do his test now.

I pack some make-up and a change of clothes into my school bag, lift the needle off the *White Album* and head towards my bedroom door. Granny is hovering in the hallway outside.

'Breakfast,' she says, shoving a piece of toast at me.

'No time,' I say, pointing at my watch.

'Eat! Eat!' she says, motioning towards her mouth, and I put the toast to my mouth and chew quickly, hoping if I finish it, she'll let me go.

'Must get up earlier, Eleanor, and eat breakfast before school. You cannot study unless eating properly. Chkkk.'

'I was revising until late . . .' I exclaim, trying to procure a sympathy vote.

'Chkkk,' she says again. 'Is bad for brain to study late.'

'OK,' I say between mouthfuls of toast.

'You are home late tonight?' she asks suspiciously.

'It's Ash's birthday,' I say, smiling.

'Hmmmmmn,' she says quietly.

'Is everything OK, Granny?' I ask, watching her. Because Dad seems to be working late a lot these days, and when he's around he seems distant; and Mum basically does everything she can to avoid Granny alone time, claiming she's trying to get everything in order before she goes on maternity leave, but last night I caught her watching *How to Get Away with Murder* with her headphones on, when she was supposedly reading case notes in her office.

'Yes, yes,' she says, waving her hands. 'Fine, fine.' But I can tell something's bothering her. I wonder if she's lonely. Whether she misses Aunty Kitty and wishes she could take it all back.

I shove the last of the toast in my mouth and lean down to hug her; she's the only person in the world I have to lean *down* to hug.

'Love you, Granny,' I whisper. 'Thanks for the toast.'

I make a promise to myself that this weekend I'm going to have some Granny time – and that I'll force Mum and Dad to have some Granny time too. Then I'll call Hope and find out what's going on with Aunty Kitty's wedding, and if there's any way I can reason with Granny about it.

With that thought in mind, I bound down the stairs, shout goodbye to Mum and Dad, and head out the front door.

As I walk towards the bus stop, a car starts crawling alongside me. I try to ignore it, expecting some idiot to shout something idiotic at me, before driving away at top speed. But my boyfriend is leaning out, his mum in the front seat next to him.

'Morning,' he says, smiling.

'I thought you were at the test centre?' I ask, confused.

'I just *came* from the test centre.'

'What?' I say, grinning.

'He passed!' Mrs Aachara says, lighting up.

'Wait. What?' I repeat, grinning even more manically.

'I passed!' he beams.

'Congratulations!' I exclaim, leaning down to kiss him.

Mrs Aachara gets out of the front seat and walks towards the back of the car.

'Get in,' he says, motioning to the seat next to him.

'What, in the front?' I say, embarrassed.

'Yes, the front,' he laughs.

I jump into the car as he starts the engine, grinning from ear to ear.

'Put some music on,' he says, motioning towards his phone. 'The code's 8055.'

I tap into Spotify and put the *White Album* on as he turns towards me, his hand suddenly on my thigh as Mrs Aachara asks me whether this might be a good weekend for her to come and see Granny.

And everything about this moment would be absolutely perfect, if it wasn't for the message I see come up on his phone.

Bec:
happy birthday baby! 🫦

Bec:
c u tonight

Bx

Baby?

Who's she calling baby?

56

Tell Me the Truth

I arrive in the main hall earlier than everyone else. I've done one full rehearsal since the last time Ash awkwardly interrupted my 'audition' and I'm glad I've gotten to know the boys a little better on my own.

Even though I still feel nervous about being here, about being part of this band – it's hard not to notice that they don't really care. That they don't notice that I'm nervous, or that I keep getting the words mixed up – they're just focused on the music, on how things sound. They treat me like I'm one of them. Not a girl or a brown girl or a Year 11 brown girl, just a singer and occasional keyboardist in their band.

'Hey, Ellie,' Shawn says as he walks in, holding the keyboard under his arm. 'You're early.'

'Ash had some stuff to do with his mum, so I came straight here. He'll be along in a bit.'

'Cool,' he says, smiling and blowing his fringe out of his eyes. 'Actually,' he says, turning back towards me, 'as you're here, you can help me with something.'

'OK,' I reply, intrigued. 'What kind of something?'

'A song,' he says, watching me. 'I wrote it for the two of us – but I need some help on your vocal bit and the lyrics.'

'So, you want me to *write* my vocal bit, and the lyrics?' I ask, laughing.

'Pretty much,' he grins.

'OK,' I agree. 'Do you have the chords written down?'

'Yep. Just give me a minute to get the keyboard plugged in.'

After a couple of minutes, he gets his acoustic guitar out and tunes it. Then starts strumming a couple of slow, gentle chords.

When he sings, the quality of his voice always surprises me. It's raspy and metallic; gritty with just the merest hint of soul. It reminds me of Ray LaMontagne and Damien Rice, with a bit of Lewis Capaldi thrown in for good measure. And his music is sort of slow and thoughtful, maybe even a bit folky, hidden under an indie heart.

Cos you lie, and you lie, and you lie
I won't cry any more

I close my eyes and let the sound of it wash over me. The chords are written down in Shawn's scratchy, illegible handwriting, so after a while, I open them and try to add some keyboard to it.

'Then,' he says, stopping suddenly, 'I want your vocal to kind of answer mine. I just need to figure out the story. What she's trying to say.'

He starts playing the chords again, and I listen to them.

'How about . . .' I say, waiting for a break in the rhythm.

You're with her, I'm all right, I'm all right
I'm all right – on my own

'That's great,' he says enthusiastically, as I write the words in even less legible scrawl next to his.

'This is the chorus,' he says, going into a more rhythmic section.

Not ready for the shallows, not ready for the heights
Don't know if we're ready, just know that tonight
Our mistakes aren't over
Any more than they're made
Tell me the truth
If you want me to stay

'I love it,' I whisper.

'Sing it with me?' he asks. When he does it again, I try to find a way to match his voice. To sing something different that also somehow fits. It's sort of bitter, and a little bit sweet; anthemic and promising, soulful and broken.

'I've been working on that for *weeks*,' he says when we stop, 'and you made it work in minutes.'

I blush.

'Hardly,' I murmur.

'We make a good team.' He smiles softly. And I want the smile to be something I can turn away from, something I can ignore.

'Let's try it again from the start,' I say awkwardly. When he starts playing his guitar, I add some simple keys to it; and when he sings the first verse, I really listen to it. I try to imagine how he feels. How I feel, this girl he's singing to – so that when I sing back to him, I can mean it. I'm so inside it, I don't even notice when we're no longer alone.

When we stop, I hear clapping, as Elliott and Lucas walk in with Ash and Rebecca just behind.

'That was beautiful,' Rebecca says, smiling. Or rather, she's smiling at Shawn. Like a spider contemplating a fly. She's wearing tiny leather shorts with a cropped white T-shirt and knee-high boots; a sixties go-go dancer with abs. *Abs.*

'Thanks,' he replies, staring at her. Because everyone's staring at her. Even me.

'Hi.' I wave.

'Hey.' She waves back. Because we've said 'hey' at least ten times since she told me I Wasn't Right for Ash Because No One Can Understand Him Like She Does, but never anything more.

'Is it OK if I . . . ?' I point towards Ash. 'Sure,' Shawn says, looking down at his guitar, 'we'll work on it another time.'

'Hey,' Ash says, as I lean up towards him for a hug. 'That sounded great.'

'Missed you,' I whisper, as I watch Rebecca mime faux vomiting from the corner of my eye.

'Are you sure you're OK with Bec being here?' he asks nervously, looking from her to me, then back again.

'It's your birthday, and she's your friend, so provided she's not going to profess her undying love or tell me I'm not right for you again,

I'll be fine,' I smile. But truly, why in the name of all the gods is Rebecca still here? Doesn't she have a life somewhere to be getting on with?

'Looks like she's making some *new* friends,' he grins, motioning towards Rebecca, profusely flirting with the entire band, their jaws hanging down as they stare at her. Ugh.

'Does Shawn have a girlfriend?' Ash asks, watching them.

'Ex,' I say tripping over the word. 'Hannah. Their old singer.'

'I think Bec likes him,' Ash says abruptly.

'She doesn't even know him,' I say through gritted teeth.

Thankfully, at just that moment, Benji walks in.

'ELLIE,' he screams in his usual brusque, slightly aggressive way. 'Let's go!'

Rebecca uncurls herself from around Shawn and walks towards Ash as I head back to the band, the two of us forever moving in opposite directions.

When I'm behind the microphone, Hayley appears at the back of the hall.

'Who's that with Hayley?' Benji whispers to me.

'James,' I whisper back.

'He looks like an Oasis reject,' he replies bluntly; and I don't want to tell him he looks like an Ultimate Fighting Champion reject, crossed with Pete Davidson, but he does.

'Is she feeling OK?'

'Yeah – why?' I ask, distracted, because Rebecca is whispering in Ash's ear while Shawn stares at her.

'Let's try "One Hit Wonder",' Shawn says into the microphone.

And I don't have time to think about Rebecca any more, because I'm a pop song inside a pop song, Shawn's raspy, metallic voice grating against my harmonies – so I don't even notice she's falling.

Stumbling forward, folding in on herself suddenly, out of nowhere, to a soundtrack of guitars and voices and keys – but no drums, because Benji is no longer behind his drum kit. He's pushing past everyone, an urgency in his gait like he can see something we can't, just in time to catch her.

'Hey, groupie,' he says gruffly, as she falls into his arms.

And it's part brisk, part gentle.

'Hey, sexist,' Hayley replies quietly.

'Say it again, slower,' he mutters.

The smile doesn't quite reach his eyes.

57

Goosebumps

Hayley's sat at the back of the hall looking cross and tired, barking 'I'm FINE' to anyone who approaches her.

'Are you sure you're OK?' I ask again worriedly.

'I just forgot to have lunch,' she sighs irritably. 'Jeffrey Dean is messing around with my script again – it took me the whole of lunchtime to make even *part* of it make sense.'

'You can't just *forget* to eat, Hay. You'll get ill. Should I call your mum?'

'No. She'll just freak out and not let me go out tonight.'

I consider this as I watch Rebecca hanging off Shawn's guitar. I need all the allies I can get this evening.

'Eat something now then.'

As if on cue, James appears with a cereal bar in his hand.

'I keep these in my locker,' he says, brandishing it in Hayley's direction. 'For football practice. They're high protein. High calories. Like a meal replacement.'

'Smells disgusting,' she says ungratefully.

'Eat it,' I threaten, 'or I'll call your mum.'

She inspects the ingredients on the back of the packet.

'You all right now, groupie?' Benji asks, kneeling to look at her. He puts his hand to her forehead and frowns. 'You don't have a temperature.'

'That's because I'm FINE,' she repeats, glaring at him.

'Nothing wrong with your facial muscles,' he grins.

'Anyway,' James says stiltedly. 'Thanks for catching her.'

'She already said that,' he replies dismissively.

'Well, she's still my . . .' he leaves the sentence hanging, 'friend, so thanks.'

'So, you two are *friends*?' he queries.

'What is this, the Spanish Inquisition?' she asks tetchily.

'Say it again, slower,' he replies.

She laughs.

'Should we go?' James says irritably. 'We can get something to eat on the way if you don't want to eat that.'

She wrinkles her nose and passes the bar back to him as she stands up.

'Call me if you feel sick again, OK?' She nods.

'See you later!' Benji calls, as they disappear off down the hall. And something tells me he'll definitely be seeing them later – as in, he will seek them out and make himself part of whatever later becomes.

When rehearsal finally finishes, Ash rushes off to meet his mum. It's his and Elina's first legal drink with her – and Rebecca goes too, because apparently, she's Practically Family. So Shawn, who's putting the band's instruments away in the hall cupboard overnight, agrees to wait for me while I get changed, so Elliott and Lucas can go ahead and attempt to stop Benji from doing whatever Benji does.

'That was a good rehearsal,' he says, as I search for my make-up. 'We haven't sounded that good in ages,' he says, lugging the drums into the cupboard.

'Not even with Hannah?' I grimace, trying to free my dress from the bottom of my bag.

He sticks his head out of the cupboard as I raise my eyebrows at him.

'It's *different*,' he replies.

'Ten minutes, OK?' I ask, waving the dress at him.

'Take your time,' he says, ignoring me, because whenever the word 'Hannah' gets mentioned, Shawn goes somewhere else.

I run to the changing rooms and take my school clothes off, bundling them into my bag; then pull on the floral fit-and-flare dress, wiggling to get the zip done up at the back. It's garishly bright in a kind of cool way, neon green and orange flowers, with a skirt that puffs out, hitting at the top of my thigh. It makes my legs look longer than the actual two inches they are, assisted by the single-strap silver sandals Mum lent me and made me promise not to ruin on Pain of Death. I pull my hair into a ponytail and put some red lipstick on after I've removed my eyeliner: because Jessica says the cardinal rule of make-up application is to accentuate lips OR eyes, never both, for fear of resembling a Kardashian.

When I trip out of the girls' toilets ten minutes later and back into the main hall, Shawn's still shoving amplifiers and microphones into the cupboard.

'Ready,' I say, taking a smaller shoulder bag out of my school bag and throwing him the rest of my school stuff to put in the cupboard. He takes the bag without even looking at it and shoves it under the keyboard, forcing the door shut.

'Done,' he says, breathing heavily.

'Cool,' I reply, slipping the black leather jacket I've also borrowed from Mum over my dress. 'Should we go?'

'OK,' he says, turning around and suddenly staring at me.

'What?' I say, self-conscious. 'What are you looking at?' And I wonder if there's lipstick on my teeth, or if it's *that* obvious I can barely walk in these shoes, or that I'm not entirely sure I have the thighs for this dress; but like everything in my wardrobe lately, I'm blaming Hope, and her ability to convince me to try almost anything.

'Nothing,' he says, shaking himself out of it.

'What?' I demand, pulling at my skirt. 'Tell me.'

'You look . . .'

'What? What do I look?' I say forcefully.

'Gorgeous, as it happens,' he says seriously.

And for some reason Vampire Weekend, 'We Belong Together' starts playing in my head; and I'm Danielle Haim (oh, how I wish I was Danielle Haim) and he's Ezra Koenig, and we're bowls and plates and days and dates – but We Can't Be.

'Should we go?' he asks quietly, pointing to the darkness outside. I nod.

'So, Rebecca,' he says casually, as we walk through the main door. 'Boyfriend? Girlfriend? Anyone I should know about?'

'She's single,' I reply awkwardly.

'Cool,' he smiles.

'I mean, she split up with someone recently . . .' I counter.

'OK,' he says earnestly.

'So, I don't think she's looking for anything. You know, *anyone* . . .'

'Right,' he says again seriously.

A minute or two later our Uber pulls up outside. I sit completely still as he slides in next to me.

'You've got goosebumps,' he whispers, looking down at my leg

But he's still Ezra Koenig, so I can't tell whether it's the cold, or the fact he's sat so close to me.

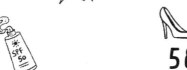

58

Mariners Apartment Complex

When we arrive outside Cinema and I see Ash stood waiting for me, for just a second, my heart stops. Like fully freezes, ceases to pump, I may actually be going into a coma, stops. Because when I look at him, when I think about the fact he's *mine* . . .

But then there's Ezra Koenig sitting next to me. His long legs in his black jeans, his head turned towards the window, barely a word passing between us. And I don't know why this feels so awkward. Why my breath is catching in my throat and I want to start hyperventilating into a paper bag. Because my boyfriend, my beautiful boyfriend, stood, admittedly, with his beautiful ex-girlfriend, is right outside my window. Waiting for me. And Shawn is just someone I'm in a band with. Someone I can write songs with, and talk to about being nervous. Not someone whose nearness should be making me feel like I want to put my head between my knees and start deep breathing.

When we stop, Ash opens my door, giving me his hand to pull me up.

'Hey,' I whisper, smiling.

Because it's him – it's always been him.

'You look beautiful,' he smiles.

I blush.

'Ellie – I'm going to find Benji,' Shawn says uncomfortably. 'I'll see you inside.'

'OK,' I say, relieved. Because this is starting to feel weird now. Like I'm about to kiss Ash in front of my dad. My long-haired, too attractive, eighteen-year-old, blond dad – and this feels awkward in a way it really shouldn't.

'Shawn,' Rebecca purrs, appearing next to him. 'Where are you going? Can I come?'

He smiles, half looking at me, half looking at her.

As they walk away, Ash turns towards me, placing his arms around me.

'*Finally,*' he says, smiling, 'I have you all to myself.'

'And I have you all to myself,' I say clumsily – and I'm not sure why I feel so distracted.

'Are you OK?' he asks, kissing my neck.

'Yes,' I reply, jolted back to the present.

'Good. Because this is the best thing about today,' he says, his fingers trailing down the back of my neck.

'How was the drink with your mum?'

'OK,' he says uneasily. 'She just gets so anxious when I drink, I couldn't really enjoy it.'

'I understand why she's nervous,' I say, stroking his arm, 'but she knows she can trust you. You just need to trust yourself.'

'I do,' he sighs. 'I just . . .' And he trails off, his arms slackening around me.

'Just what?' I ask gently.

'I don't know . . . Bec being here. It's just a reminder of how I used to be. Of who I used to be.'

'Don't worry about anyone else, just keep reminding yourself that you need to like you. It doesn't matter what anyone else thinks,' and the wisdom of my words only strikes me when they're fully out of my mouth.

'And you,' he says, grinning. 'I quite like you, liking me.'

I beam at him.

Because it's him – it's always been him.

Him with his black-and-white striped T-shirt and dark red jacket. Him with his curly brown hair and green eyes. Him. Just him.

'Stop,' I say, pushing him jokily. 'You're making me go red, which is not the look I was going for with this outfit.'

'You look . . .' he says, pulling me towards him again, 'gorgeous.' Why did he have to use that word? The same word Shawn used, the same Shawn I can't seem to stop thinking about. The Ezra Koenig to my Danielle Haim.

Dear gods, *no*. Do not let me realise I have a crush on Shawn, on my boyfriend's eighteenth birthday.

'Stop,' I squirm. 'I'm no good with compliments.'

He picks me up suddenly and holds me there, my feet hovering several inches above the ground.

'Learn.' He grins.

And in that moment, there's no one there but him and me.

'Do you want another fireman's lift?' he asks, laughing.

'Not in this dress!' I shriek.

'Then the words you're looking for are "thank you. I am gorgeous",' he says, lifting me higher in the air.

'Ash Anderson, when I get down from here . . .' I attempt to yelp threateningly.

'Say it,' he demands, laughing.

'You are IMPOSSIBLE,' I squeal, because it tickles, and I am snorting like some kind of pig.

'Say it,' he says again.

'Thank youuuuuuu,' I shriek, as he starts jiggling me up and down, the tickling even more intense, 'and . . . I am gorgeous!' I scream.

He puts me down and smiles, satisfied, while I punch his arm.

'I love you, Ellie,' he says suddenly.

And the world feels silent – except for the sound of Lana Del Rey singing the chorus to 'Mariners Apartment Complex', because I've always thought if love had a sound, it would be her flat, nasal voice, sort of rich and full of sadness, but hope and desire too, saying if you're lost, I'll find you.

'I love you too,' I say, reaching up to him.

Because I do.

Because it's him – it's always been him.

And I'm lost. In that beautiful guitar, gentle and a little bit bitter, those delicate piano refrains, high and sweet and wanting.

Because right where he is, is where I am. Where I'll always want to be.

59

Smile Like You Mean It

I float into Cinema at this point, his arm around my waist.

'E!!' I turn at the sound of Jess shouting my name, Elina stood next to her, looking irritated.

'Hi,' I shout back, heading towards them, pulling Ash along by his hand. 'Happy birthday, Elina!' I say, leaning forward to hug her.

She looks beautiful, in the way only very cool people can. Effortlessly. In a long, tight denim skirt with a split at the side, and a one-shouldered black crop top, her hair slicked back; Jess channelling Farrah Fawcett in a halter-neck denim jumpsuit and fluffy blonde hair.

I love this look for her. The hair, the clothes, the hot girlfriend, the happiness.

'Thanks, Ellie,' Elina says, squeezing me back. And I feel like we're friends, because I'm in love with her brother, and he's in love with me.

He's in love with me.

I beam.

'I'm going to the bar. Anyone want a drink?' Ash says, looking at the three of us.

'Coke, please,' I say, turning to him.

'Not for me.' Jess smiles, shaking her head, while Elina ignores him.

He turns away from us and moves towards the bar, the room heaving with people.

'Are you OK?' I ask Elina carefully. Because it's her eighteenth birthday, and she doesn't seem very happy, and an unhappy Elina can be a very scary thing. I would know. The unhappiness has been directed at me on more than several occasions.

'Ask your boyfriend,' she snaps. I raise my eyebrows, the truce I thought we'd formed over as soon as it started. 'Sorry,' she responds. 'It's just, if I have to look at Rebecca's smug, annoying face for *one more day* . . .' she says darkly. 'I mean, I thought she'd invited *herself* to drinks with Mum and Ash and me, but no, turns out *he* invited her. I mean, for God's sake. Can they do *anything* separately?'

Now it's my turn to look irritated. Or confused. Or maybe both.

Jess nudges Elina violently.

'Oh God, sorry, Ellie,' Elina says apologetically. 'I don't mean it like that. It's not like *that* between them, I just mean . . . I can't work out why she's still here. Why he defends her so much.'

And this is not the conversation I was hoping to have after my I love you/Lana Del Rey moment. In fact, I was hoping that, for once, Rebecca wouldn't be part of this moment, or any moment remotely connected to it.

'Have you seen Hayley?' James asks, appearing next to us.

'Sorry,' I say, shaking my head.

'Isn't she with that guy from your band, Ellie? The tall one?' Elina says helpfully.

'Benji?' I say, watching James's face. 'I don't know, I haven't seen him either.'

'Will you tell her I'm looking for her?' he asks. 'If you see her.'

'Just tell her how you feel,' I whisper.

'I did,' he says resignedly, 'and now she's *missing*.'

'Oh.'

He wanders off while Jess and Elina smile sympathetically at him.

'Well, there she blows,' Elina says, pointing at Rebecca, downing shots at the bar.

I watch her. It seems like a lot of shots. It seems less like fun, and more like drowning her sorrows.

'Give Ash a break, Elina,' I say firmly. 'He just feels a bit responsible for her. He's not trying to annoy anyone – he just wants to keep an eye on her. Looks like she needs it.'

Jess raises her eyebrows at me, as if impressed by my maturity and ability to use my mother's countless hours of Therapy Talk in this new and profound manner.

'Maybe,' Elina huffs, 'but honestly, you should have heard her earlier, trying to harass him to drink more. Even Mum almost lost it.'

'Hey,' Jess says, placing her hands over Elina's wrists. 'Stop ruining your own birthday. Come on, let's dance,' she says, tugging at her hand.

'Fine,' she concedes, because it's impossible not to capitulate to almost anything when Jess smiles at you. She is a sunbeam in human form.

'Coming, E?' Jess says, grabbing me – and clearly, I have no choice when it comes to the human sunbeam either.

We walk towards the dance floor and throw our arms in the air to a remix of the Killers, 'Smile Like You Mean It'. Holding each other's hands, twirling round and round, laughing and jumping and headbanging.

'Have you seen Hayley?' Benji shouts over the music as he approaches us.

'No,' I shout back.

'She's probably with the Oasis reject,' he says sarcastically.

'Probably,' I say, rolling my eyes at Elina and Jess, who seem deeply amused at Hayley's love triangle.

'I told her I like her,' he says out of nowhere.

'Did you?' I say uncomfortably.

'Yeah. And now she's gone missing.'

Note to self: find Hayley and discover how Benji tells someone he likes them.

'I'll tell her you're looking for her.'

'I'm worried about her.'

'She's fine,' I soothe.

Probably just hiding from you. And James.

'She doesn't eat much, does she?'

'I mean . . .' But I'm cut off by Elina elbowing me, pointing at Rebecca now dancing with Shawn. Hanging off him, clearly a bit drunk.

'Is he your friend?' Elina asks the two of us over the music.

'Er, kind of.' I blush.

Benji looks at me and raises his eyebrows.

'You should warn him about her,' she shouts seriously. 'She's a *nightmare*.'

I nod, but I can't think of anything else to say. Because I don't want Shawn to be with Rebecca, because *I* like him; but then, that's not really a reason. That is the *opposite* of a reason. Because I have a boyfriend I am genuinely in love with, and I shouldn't care who Shawn goes out with.

'Ash is taking ages,' I shout back eventually. 'I'd better go find him.'

Elina and Jess nod as Benji disappears.

When I'm off the dance floor, I head towards the bar. From a distance, I can see Ash with Hannah the Singer/Shawn's Ex, stood next to him, talking intensely.

'Ellie!' I turn at the sound of Shawn calling out, stood just behind me.

'Erm, Rebecca's a bit . . .' he says, when he's got my attention, 'out of it. Maybe Ash should take her home?'

And that sentence, and everything it stands for, annoys me in a way I can't quite explain. Why does Ash have to take her home? Why is Rebecca Ash's responsibility? Why is *her* home where *his* home is? *WHY IS SHE HERE?*

'Or I can take her home?' he says, watching me closely. 'If you let me know the address.'

I gulp.

'Are you OK?' he asks, watching me.

'Um, yeah, fine,' I say, shaking it off.

'So, what do you want me to do?' he says slowly.

'I don't know,' I snap. I look up at him. 'Sorry, I didn't mean to snap at you. I'm just bored of talking about Rebecca.'

He grins. 'She strikes me as the kind of girl who is a definite conversation starter,' and the way he says it is almost affectionate. Like he's in awe of the fact she's a complete nightmare. Like it's cute.

'Why don't you just put her in an Uber?' I ask, annoyed again.

'Because I need to make sure she gets home safely,' he says, looking disappointed. 'I thought you two were friends?'

'Not exactly,' I say, ashamed. Because I know I'm being horrible. I know someone needs to look after her. I just don't want it to be Ash. Or Shawn. Or anyone I love/have a teeny-tiny crush on.

'You're right,' I sigh. 'You should take her home – I can give you the address. It's Ash's birthday so it would be nice if he didn't have to.'

'OK,' he says quietly. 'No problem. She's in the girls' toilets though, so you might have to get her for me.'

I grimace.

'OK,' I say, turning away, 'but Shawn,' I say, turning back. 'Be careful. I don't want you to get hurt.'

'Then you should be careful too,' he says seriously.

'What does *that* mean?' I challenge.

'Anyone can get hurt, Ellie,' he says, looking straight at me.

'I know that,' I say, annoyed. 'I just meant, you seem like a good person, and I'm not sure . . . I don't know if she is.'

'Why do you care?' he asks defiantly.

'I, I, don't . . .' I stutter. 'You can do what you want.' He's looking at me like he can see right through me, like I can see right through myself.

Because I do care. I know I do.

I just don't want to accept why.

♡ Song 5 ♡

Verse Chorus, Middle Eight – Spinning Out

It's a song about everything and nothing. Nothing and everything. The moments between knowing what love is and not being quite sure.

It's the sound of falling. Gracefully and frighteningly, fluttering and tumbling. Of trusting yourself too much, and then not at all.

It's slow and syncopated, the way he is with her – the way I am with him. It's a song about belonging – but knowing it should be to yourself.

And who you are with her
Is that you?
And who I am with him
Is that wrong?

60

Rebecca

'Rebecca!' I shout, as I head into the toilets. 'Rebecca! Where are you?'

It's crammed in here, with bleary-eyed girls who clearly shouldn't be drinking, and the rest of us just trying to find a way out.

'Bec!' I shout again. 'Bec?' Because Shawn seemed pretty sure this was the toilet she disappeared into.

'Ellie?' Rebecca says, poking her head out the door of one of the bathroom stalls as the girls queuing to use a cubicle glare at her. 'Come in,' she says, drunkenly beckoning me.

'Er, OK . . .' I say, shimmying past the collective sound of rage that is a group of girls in need of a wee on a night out.

I slide into the stall and shut it behind me, while Rebecca sits down heavily on the toilet lid.

'Hey,' she says, pulling at her hair.

'Are you OK?'

'Some guy just called me the *p* word,' she laughs, somewhere between angry and dazed.

I shake my head angrily. I wish she was joking. But it doesn't surprise me; it never surprises me.

'How do you doooo it, Ellie?' she says, looking up at me, her eyeliner smudged. 'How do you live somewhere like this, where people just staaaare at you all the time?'

'I guess . . . I'm just used to it,' I stutter.

'It's OK. I'm used to it too,' she says defiantly.

'Even in London?' I reply, shocked.

She laughs.

'Even. In. London,' she says, slurring slightly. 'You're so fair,' she says, leaning up to smooth the skin on my cheek.

'I'm not,' I reply, thinking about the many comments Granny dispenses about wearing sun hats and long sleeves and staying out of the sun because I'm too dark.

'Much fairer than meeee, anyway,' she hiccups.

And I haven't really noticed it before, because she's so beautiful and her skin is just part of that, but she is dark skinned. Much darker than me, and shades more than Ash and Elina, who pass for white.

'But you're so . . .' I say, trying to find the words.

'Ugly?' she says matter-of-factly.

'Have you *seen* yourself?' I ask, confused. 'You're gorgeous, Rebecca. Everywhere you go, people look at you. You must know that.'

'Still *dark* though, right?'

'What's wrong with that?' I ask.

'Ever been out without a sun hat, Eleeaannooor? Or factor fifty sun cream? Ever lie on a beach to get a taaann?'

'No,' I say in a small voice.

'You know,' she says, leaning forward. 'You,' she says, poking her finger in my face, '*know.*'

And she's right. I do know. Subconsciously, always, that I've been taught that white is better. In everything. From the films I watch to the books I read, that aren't just part of Western culture – but in Bollywood films, and in my own home, with my own family, in my own brown culture. We cover ourselves up. We avoid the sun. We're told we're *better* if we're *whiter.* Fairer. Lighter. Closer to those that call us those words; and I feel ashamed that I know. But I do know.

'Do you know what it's like,' she says, sitting back a bit, 'to be told, you'd be so *pretty* if you were light. To have your whole family, your whole life, tell you it's a shame. A waste. That you're ugly.'

'But you're not,' I say, trying to take her hand.

She pushes me away.

'I *know* that, Ellie, I just . . .' And I think she might be about to be sick. 'I'm so sick of caring about it. So sick of noticing it when I look at myself. You know my ex? His mum said I was too *dark.* That she doesn't want *dark grandchildren.* And he . . .'

'He what?' I whisper.

'He said *nothing.*'

'Rebecca,' I croon.

'I tried to bleach it once,' she confesses, the back of her hand to her mouth as she rocks back and forth. 'It buuuuuurned. Like my skin was on fire.'

'Rebecca,' I say, grabbing her arms; her eyes are glazed and there's a bit of sick on the side of her mouth. 'You are *annoyingly* beautiful. Mostly annoying, but incredibly beautiful.'

'Geeeeee, thannnnnks,' she says, her head rolling backwards.

'And we're both dark. I'm dark – and you're dark – because we're both *brown*. We're not *white*. And that's OK. We have to stop thinking that it's not OK. We have to stop telling ourselves that we should be something other than what we are.' I sigh. 'I need to go out without a sun hat. Hats looks terrible on me anyway. My head's too small.'

She starts laughing, and then seems suddenly contrite.

'I know you hate me, Ellie.'

'I don't hate you.'

'But I love him,' she says, looking up at me brazenly.

And if this goes any further, I may have to withdraw my previous statement.

'He's my brother.'

'I didn't realise you could kiss brothers,' I reply boldly.

'It's not liiiike that,' she says dismissively. 'Or like sometimes it is. Sometimes I THINK I love him like that. When I'm sad. Or lonely.'

'Are you sad or lonely now?' I ask carefully.

'My EX,' she says, ignoring the question, 'is on my course at uni, and I can't face it. I can't face *him*. I thought I'd never be That Girl,' she says, laughing bitterly. 'I thought I was above all that craaap. Caring about boys who hurt you.' She stares at me. 'Ash would never hurt you,' she says, looking at me directly.

'Anyone can hurt you,' I say quietly.

'Ellie,' she says, looking at me, her voice wavering. 'He loves you. So, I have to love you too. OK?'

'OK,' I acquiesce, because there's clearly no point in arguing with her. Not in this state.

'Shawn's HOT though, isn't he?' she says suddenly, resting her head against the cubicle wall.

'I suppose so,' I say, trying to pull her up as she slides down the toilet lid.

'You're not what I *thought* you were,' she slurs.

'What do you mean?' I ask, expecting a diatribe about my Big Voice and Recessive Presence.

'You're . . . cool.'

'Oh,' I reply, shocked.

'. . . *lovely* actually.'

'Thanks,' I whisper guiltily, because minutes ago I'd have sent her home on her own, a mess in the back of a cab.

'I've had siiiiiiixxx tequilas,' she whispers.

'Why'd you do that?' I chastise gently, tucking a stray hair behind her ear.

'Because it's ov-er,' she sing-songs.

'You don't need him, you know. You don't need anyone, Rebecca. He doesn't deserve you.'

She stares at me.

'You don't have a recesseeeeeeee presennnnce, Ellie,' she slurs, holding on to my shoulders.

'Thanks,' I smile.

'I know you think I'm horrible,' she continues, 'but they're my family. I'd do anything to protect them. Even if Elina haaaaates me,' she finishes, looking upset.

'She doesn't hate you,' I soothe, stroking her head as she leans against the cubicle wall again. 'She just doesn't want Ash drinking like he used to. None of us do.'

'I don't want him to drink like that eeeither,' she says, trying to sit up. 'But he shouldn't have to be *someone else* to be with you. Some Perfect Person. It's OK that he's NOT PERFECT,' she says, jabbing her finger at me again.

'I don't want him to be perfect,' I reply. 'I just want him to like himself.'

'Do *you* like *your*self?' she says, suddenly sombre.

'I'm trying.'

'I feel weeeird,' she says abruptly.

'Try putting your head between your legs.' I read somewhere that's what you should do when you don't feel very well.

'*Huuuuurrrrrggghhhh.* I think I'm gonna . . .' she says, from in between her legs.

She jumps off the seat and pulls the lid up, just in time to deposit her head by the rim of the bowl.

I pull her hair back from her shoulders, making a ponytail in my hand.

'It's OK,' I murmur, as she throws up. 'It's all right.'

And then, next door, I hear the sound of someone else throwing up.

'Are you OK?' I ask gently, tapping on the wall between us. 'Hello? Are you all right in there?'

'I'm fine,' a little voice whispers. A little voice I recognise.

'Hay, is that you?' I ask worriedly. 'Are you OK?'

'I'm *fine*, Ellie. Don't worry about me. Sounds like you've got your hands full,' she says tensely.

'Are you sick? Should I get James?' I offer anxiously. 'Or, um, Benji . . . ?'

'No. I'm fine.'

Rebecca sits back on her haunches, her hair matted across her face.

'I'll be back in one minute,' I say, tucking her hair behind her ears. She nods.

I emerge out of the cubicle at just the same moment as Hayley, who moves to the sinks to wash her hands.

'Hay?' I say, putting my hand on her arm. 'What's going on? How much have you had to drink?'

'Ellie, I'm *fine*,' she says again aggressively. And that's when I notice she is fine. That she doesn't seem drunk at all.

'Hayley, you're sick. You passed out earlier, and now you're throwing up. We need to get you home,' I say, trying to take her arm.

'I said, I'm *fine*,' she says, shaking the water off her hands.

And when she turns to walk away, it only takes me a second to realise I can see the top of her spine through the back of her vest top, her arms bony, her wrists so delicate they seem liable to snap.

'Hayley!' I shout, as the door slams behind her.

And in an instant, I know. I think I always knew. I just didn't *see*. I chose not to.

No lunch. Never any lunch. Her food piled up on the corner of her plate. The fact she seems to know the calorie content of everything I've ever eaten.

Why didn't I see this before? Why didn't I notice? How her new-found spikiness has an almost skeletal quality to it. How she never looks well any more. Even Benji noticed, even *Benji*.

She doesn't eat much, does she?

I want to run after her. To have it out with her, and understand what's going on. To be a good friend, like the one that should have known this was happening in the first place.

What kind of friend am I? What kind of stupid, selfish, horrible person am I?

I knock until Rebecca lets me in again and pull her hair back from her face.

Ellie:
out in 10

Shawn:
OK

Then I look down at Rebecca's shiny, annoyingly perfect hair, and think: I might actually like you.

And then I think: damn it.

And then I think: oh God, Hayley. Where have I been?

61

Stop Thinking About Kissing

I wake up in the early hours of the morning, my brain whirring. After Shawn took Rebecca home, Ash and I looked everywhere for Hayley but couldn't find her. I keep asking myself what I saw. If I'm imagining how thin she looked or the fact she was being sick for no fathomable reason.

I feel like I've been walking around with a blindfold on. Not to have seen how out of character she's been behaving. How actually, over an innumerable number of lunches, I haven't seen her eat; maybe in months, maybe even longer.

I know I've been distracted. I know it was Ash's birthday and he told me loved me. I know lots of things, but it also seems like I don't know anything.

I look over at my phone, glowing in the darkness beside me.

Two messages.

Dirty Blond:

bec home. see u mon

Ash:

did i mention i ♥ u?

A few weeks ago, it was all I wanted to hear. The *only* thing I wanted to hear – but now it's here, and Hayley's sick and Mum and Dad and Granny aren't right either, and it isn't enough. I thought it would fix everything. But all the problems I ever had, they still exist, just alongside the fact he loves me – *if* he loves me. Because I don't know if I believe it. Whether I even really know how to love him.

And here's the thing: can you love someone when you're thinking about what it would be like to kiss someone else? Or when you think about their ex-girlfriend, and wonder whether all the romantic films you've ever watched suggest it's *them* that should be together, not you.

And these are the feelings you feel at 5.29 a.m., when you think one of your best friends might have an eating disorder, and you've been too worried about being the plot twist in someone else's love story to really notice. When you're worried you might not be very nice.

I twist and turn for what seems like forever, and finally creep downstairs to make some chai. When I get to the kitchen, Dad's already awake.

'Hi,' I say sleepily. 'What are you doing up so early?'

'Couldn't sleep,' he says, rubbing his eyes.

'How long have you been here?' I ask, looking at him carefully.

'A few hours,' he says sheepishly. 'What are you doing up, *sina pillai*?' He beckons me towards him.

'Couldn't sleep either.'

'Hmmmnn,' he intones.

I never think of my dad as having an accent, but I know he does. Mostly because it's what other people tell me – like the time I invited a friend over when I was little, and she kept looking at me whenever he spoke, like she was in need of a translator. His English is perfect, but he spent the first twenty years of his life in Sri Lanka, so I guess he sounds Sri Lankan. It's just after years of being in England – thirty years longer than he was in Sri Lanka – he's perfected this other voice. This Sri English voice, where he's a little bit of both.

But there's something about when Dad's feeling sad or angry or melancholy; when his emotions are heightened and he can't really control it, when his accent gets thicker. And I can hear it now. At 5.35 a.m. on a Saturday morning.

'Is everything OK, Dad?'

'Getting old,' he sighs, rubbing his chest, 'that's all.'

I slump next to him at the table and put my head on his shoulder.

'Something's wrong with Hayley,' I whisper.

'Have you talked to her about it?' he asks, putting his head on top of mine.

'Not yet.' Just the thought of talking to her about it puts me in a cold sweat. Hayley can be scary and defensive and spiky and non-talkative at the best of times; and the fact she hasn't responded to any one of my million voice notes, messages or missed calls can only lead me to assume she doesn't want to talk. Or she's lost her phone. Or it's run out of battery. Or she's looking at my name appearing on it, and muting it before throwing it at a wall somewhere.

'That's where you need to start,' he says wisely, and I wonder why *he* doesn't talk to *me* then. Why lately, it always feels like he's somewhere else.

'I guess . . .' I mutter.

'Go back to bed, *sina pillai*. You need to sleep.'

'OK, but so do you,' I yawn. I'm starting to feel sleepy now, just being near him. Warm and safe and contented, my head buried beneath his.

And the next thing I know, I wake up in my own bed. The covers tucked beneath my chin, just like they were when I was a child. I think about Dad carrying me up the stairs, panting and heaving, trying so desperately to pretend I'm still five.

The thought makes me smile – because whatever Dad says, or doesn't say, I know he loves me. Which is when I finally understand, or finally *choose* to understand, what's been wrong with Hayley. How I heard her when she was talking about James's family, and how it made her miss her dad, but I didn't really listen.

Note to self: *listen.*

And.

Stop thinking about kissing Ash Anderson.

Or what it might be like to kiss Shawn Kowalski.

In fact, stop thinking about kissing at all.

62

Rebecca Likes Shawn

Ash:

bec likes shawn. we should set them up

Ellie:

& ☀ to u 2

Ash:

🖤

Ellie:

u had me at 🖤

Ash:

what do u think?

Don't take too long to think about this, Pillai. Taking too long = thinking about Shawn and Rebecca kissing. Which leads to thinking about Shawn and you kissing. Which leads to weirdness and things

which are not good to think about, when you promised yourself you
would think less about kissing.

Ellie:

Ash:

mum coming to c granny. go 4 a drive
after i've dropped her off?

Ellie:

can u give me a lift to H's? 🫣

Ash:

...

Ash:

do i get you 2 myself after?

Ellie:

🖤

Ash:

u had me at 🖤

I really need to try harder not to think about kissing Ash Anderson.

63

There's No Need to Shout

'Granny!' I scream. 'Mrs Aachara's here!'

'You can call me Kyra when we're not at school,' Mrs Aachara whispers. I giggle weirdly. I can't call her *Kyra*. That would make us *friends*. *Friends*.

'Eleanor,' Granny says harshly, appearing almost instantly. 'Is no need to shout.'

No need to shout? My grandmother speaks at a volume that can be heard several thousand miles away. Dad often jokes that she doesn't need a telephone to communicate.

I look at Ash through gritted teeth as he tries desperately not to laugh. She's even shouting, telling me not to shout.

'Ah, ah, Kyra,' Granny says, beckoning her in. 'Come, come!' she says, taking her hand. 'Sit down, I will bring tea.'

'Thank you,' Mrs Aachara says, smiling and rearranging the garment bag she's brought over her arm.

'Wedding sari,' Granny says excitedly. 'NIMI,' she screams. 'NIMI! KYRA HAS BROUGHT HER WEDDING SARI.'

Ash and I stifle a giggle.

'*Amma*?' Mum says, appearing at the top of the stairs. 'What's going on? Are you OK?'

'Yes, yes,' Granny says dismissively. 'Kyra is here. She has brought wedding sari. Where is yours? Must bring and show.'

'*Amma*, I'm sure Kyra isn't interested in my wedding sari,' Mum says apologetically.

'I'd love to take a look,' Mrs Aachara says, looking up at her. 'I'll show you mine if you show me yours,' she quips.

Mum beams for what seems like the first time in ages, because just like Dad she's seemed distant lately. Worried and tired. But if there's one thing that can lift Mum's spirits, it's clothes.

'I'll get it.' She smiles happily. 'Ellie, can you make the tea?'

'No, no. I will make the tea,' Granny interrupts. Which is code for a full china tea set with cubes of sugar and a tiny jug of milk, served with the fish cutlets she made last night for just this occasion. The aunties serve meat patties and fish cutlets and mutton rolls with afternoon tea, not sandwiches or cakes or scones – but I always think tea was Sri Lankan before it was English, so I figure the English have it wrong, not us.

'OK, we're going out,' I say, grabbing Ash's arm and turning away before anyone – i.e. Granny – can stop us.

'You must stay,' Granny objects. 'Is good for young people to know traditions. Traditional is best,' and I can't tell whether that's designed to be a dig at Aunty Kitty or me. At the idea of a non-traditional granddaughter or her daughter's non-traditional wedding to a non-traditional groom.

'I have to see Hayley, Mum. It's important,' I plead.

'Go, go,' Mum says, brushing us away with her hands. 'They don't want to stay here with us old people, *Amma*.'

Granny, who is as archetypal an old person as it is possible to be (I love her, but today she resembles a raisin) looks hurt, so Ash leans forward and says the words all Sri Lankan grandmothers need to hear sometimes.

'Something smells good,' he says, sniffing dramatically.

She smiles, leaning up to pinch his cheek. Hard.

'My cutlets,' she says, satisfied. 'I make not too hot for you.'

'I can eat hot,' he says, suddenly embarrassed.

'Hmmmn,' she says, smiling, and I swear I can see a twinkle in her eye. 'I make for you and your mother – but mostly for you,' she says, winking.

Ugh, a granny wink. Weirdly uncomfortable to witness.

'Thanks,' he blushes.

As we walk out the door, he turns to me.

'Do you think she knows about the eggs?' he whispers.

'Why do you care?' I ask, relieved to have escaped.

'I've never had a grandmother approve of me before,' he says jokily. 'I'd quite like not to lose it.' There's something un-jokey about the way he says it, something sad and a little bit serious – and I think about his grandmother. His mum's mum. The one who has nothing to do with them, because his mum dared marry a non-traditional, non-Indian white man – and really, I think, how is that different to Granny and Aunty Kitty and Charles?

And I've been wondering whether Granny thinks Ash's dad was Indian too. That he's just one of those super-fair Bollywood-Indian types. The ones who could pass for slightly tanned Swedish models. The ones Rebecca and I have spent a lifetime being compared to, and being told we're too dark in comparison. And that's just wrong. Because there is no such thing as *too* dark. That, I have decided, is a concept that is categorically, undeniably, empirically wrong. The insinuation that dark is bad and light is good, because brown culture has to stop 'aspiring' to whiteness, when it is the literal opposite of what we are. And I wish I could have this conversation with Granny, but she's a thousand years old and thinks we should all stick to our own, like some kind of militant dog breeder.

I've tried not to think about that too much. About the fact that once she knows the truth, she might not like Ash as much, that she might think less of him. Because that would mean having to admit she's racist. The word Hope used in New York, which I've tried my hardest to pretend isn't the case but seems more and more like it might be.

I look over at Ash in his green sweatshirt and feel a sudden rush of love towards him. I just want to believe that she can see him for who he really is. Because he's kind and sweet and lovely, and more importantly than that, he understands that Diana Ross, 'Chain Reaction' is one of the greatest love songs of all time.

'She doesn't actually *approve* of you,' I say, linking arms with him. He looks perturbed. 'She *adores* you. Honestly, it's annoying.'

He kisses the top of my head, his smile hidden in my hair.

'So, where are we going?' he asks, as he opens the car door for me.

'I'll Google Map it,' I say, typing Hayley's address into my phone as I slide into the front seat, throwing my/Mum's leather jacket into the back.

I angle the phone on his dashboard, and press Go just as a message pops up.

Dirty Blond:

what r u doing?

I grab at it, desperately hoping he didn't see whose name came up.

'Was that Shawn?' he asks, as we pull off. 'Ask him about Bec,' he says eagerly.

'You know, I was thinking about that . . .' I take my phone down and put Hay's address into his. 'I'm not sure it feels like a very good idea, given Rebecca lives in London and he lives here.'

He looks at me out the corner of his eye. 'It doesn't have to be anything serious. It's up to them what they want it to be – and who *knows* where Bec lives any more.'

And however much something shifted with Rebecca and me last night, that sentiment just irks me. Because where *does* Rebecca live? Is she staying here forever?

'What if he doesn't *want* to go out with her?' I say stubbornly.

'Why wouldn't he want to go out with her?' he asks even more stubbornly.

'You know,' I say, suddenly angry, 'just because she's YOUR type doesn't mean she's everybody's type.'

And there it is. Right there. Beneath the surface, scratched away at, so easily visible. My insecurity.

'What's that supposed to mean?' he replies agitatedly.

'Nothing,' I mutter under my breath – and I have no idea how this escalated so quickly.

'You know, Ellie, I get you being upset about Bec being here. I get you being upset that I wasn't honest with you. What I don't get is why you're upset she wants to go out with Shawn. Wouldn't that be better for all of us? Or is it just that he's YOUR type?' he says heatedly.

'Heeebeeeejeebebbbee,' I reply incoherently.

What. Is. Happening?

'You met him in New York and never even told me about it,' he begins. 'You lied to me about being in the band, then about meeting up with him – now you're spending all this time together, and he's always there, wherever you are, *looking* at you,' he continues, annoyed.

'We met in New York because of my cousin!' I say fiercely. 'I didn't lie to you about being in the band, I just didn't want to tell you until I knew myself if I was going to do it – and he isn't always looking at me – it's Rebecca, always looking at YOU. Or you looking at her, or whatever it is you two do.'

Why am I saying any of this? Why do I care whether Rebecca goes out with Shawn? I love Ash. Not almost, not quite, but really, truly, as much as I know how to love anyone that I'm not related to. It's him – it's always been him. I just can't get past this feeling. The one that keeps telling me I'm not good enough for him. The one that keeps trying to ruin everything.

'When are you going to stop with the Bec thing?' he says, throwing his hands off the wheel momentarily. 'I don't care about Rebecca like that. I love *you*.'

And the words *I love you* have a slightly soporific effect on me. Not that anyone's ever said them to me before. Not really. Not unless you count Berat, the Turkish boy I spent a few weeks kissing on holiday last year, which was more to do with his questionable grasp of English than any realness of sentiment. I mean, he kept saying he loved sun loungers – and no one loves a sun lounger that much.

'I love you too,' I say softly. I let go of the feeling, watching it drift away from me. He loves me. He loves me. He loves me. 'I'll give Shawn Rebecca's number. Honestly, I don't care.'

He puts his hand on my leg momentarily, and turns towards me, smiling.

It's sunny. I want to kiss him.

These are the last things I remember before the world goes dark.

64

A Hairline Fracture, the A&E and a Hysterical Version of My Father

'It's a hairline fracture. Strap it up for a few weeks, and she'll be fine,' the doctor says for the hundredth time.

'But the concussion,' Mum says, 'what about the concussion?'

'We're going to send her for an MRI, just to check – but it's really a formality,' the doctor says kindly. He's cute. In a kind of spotty, almost looks like a teenager way. Dr Yi. I wish I'd shaved my legs this morning.

Dad looks at him suspiciously, a look I can almost instantly read as a request to see someone older. Someone who looks more like an adult.

'Let me check where we are with getting her seen today. I'll be back in a minute,' Dr Yi says, as he makes some notes on a clipboard.

'Where's Ash?' I ask for the millionth time since I woke up. I have a vague recollection of him stroking my hair. Of flashing lights and sirens, and someone crying. 'I need to see him. Is he OK?'

'You should never have been in that car with him,' Dad thunders.

'Mum?' I plead, turning towards her.

'Ellie, your father's right,' she says guiltily. 'He's a new driver. We should have been more mindful.'

'But *where is he*?' I ask shrilly.

'*He's* fine,' Dad says in a low voice. 'You, on the other hand, are in hospital with possible brain trauma.'

'Dad, I'm fine!'

'Ellie,' Mum says quietly, and I can hear that tone in her voice. The one that's begging me to be reasonable when all I want to do is scream. 'You need to understand how we felt when we got that phone call. We're all tired and upset. Dad sent Ash home. He's been in an accident too. He needs to rest.' She looks grey.

'Rest,' Dad mutters venomously.

'What do you mean, you *sent him home*?' I ask, my voice rising.

'I mean,' Dad roars, 'I didn't want to sit and look at the boy who almost killed you.'

'Chkkk,' I spit disgustedly. Damn Granny and her *chkk*ing. It's clearly catching. 'You're being melodramatic.' I can see him heavy breathing, his eyes starting to bulge out of his head, the way they do when you leave too many lights on.

'Ellie,' Mum says calmly. 'You need to rest. Noel, can you get me a glass of water?'

'Are you OK?' he asks, suddenly anxious. 'Is the baby OK?'

'Everything's fine – we all just need to calm down,' she says firmly.

Dad shoots me a look that seems to say This Is All Your Fault.

Then Dr Yi walks back in and announces I have to stay in

overnight, because they can't get me an MRI until tomorrow and I need to be observed.

I observe Mum and Dad eyeing each other, as Dr Yi tells them the police are coming in to talk to me.

I observe this day keeps getting better and better.

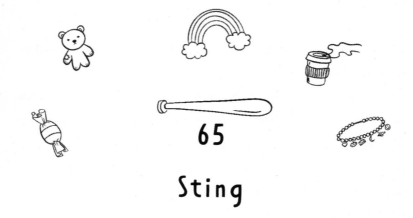

65

Sting

London Cousin – Annoying:

r u OK??? mum said u were in an accident???

The two police people are talking to me, but I'm not sure if I'm really listening. They've given me some kind of medication for the pain in my wrist, and it's making me woozy.

'Do you like Sting?' I ask the female one.

'Um . . .' she says, looking confused.

'You know, and the Police,' I titter.

Dad rolls his eyes and glares at me. It's like being drunk with a completely free pass.

'Bit of a dad joke, that, isn't it?' the male one says, amused. I quite like him. I think he is appreciative of a good dad joke.

'I'm just an oooooooold soul,' I trill.

'So, the other car,' the policewoman says, looking at Mum. 'The driver was an older gentleman. He's admitted he wasn't wearing his glasses and he miscalculated the timing. He pulled out on an amber, and that's when he went into the side of the car.'

'An older gentleman?' Dad says angrily. 'So, an older, *white* gentleman drove illegally, caused an accident that almost killed someone, and what? What happens now? He walks away with a slapped wrist while my daughter has to have an MRI to check she isn't brain damaged?'

'It'll be a lot more than a slapped wrist, sir. We take this sort of thing very seriously, I can assure you,' the policeman says, trying to look authoritative. But like everyone today, he looks like he left high school six years ago.

Dad paces back and forth angrily.

'Do you have children?' he asks the two of them. They shake their heads. 'Because I've spent a lot of time in hospital with a sick child, and trust me, until you know what it's like to have a child, to worry about a child, to live and die for a child, then you don't know A THING about taking it seriously. She could have DIED.'

Mum steps forward and puts her arms around him, just as the floodgates open. Just as my solid, reliable, dependable dad starts to cry. The policemen look at each other, uncomfortable and unsure how to respond.

'He's very emooooosshtional,' I slur. 'Because of my brother. He dieeed,' I explain.

The room's starting to feel uncomfortably hot now, and a bit far away. Like I'm watching it through one of those tin kaleidoscope toys, full of fake, shiny jewels; blurry and colourful and slow.

My arms feel heavy and shapeless. Like they're made out of water, or sand. Or something else. Something arms shouldn't be made of.

And I just feel weird.

Like really, really, super, I-no-longer-have-any-dad-jokes-and-this-isn't-fun-any-more weird.

And the world's going dark again.

Dark. Dark. Dark.

Dark.

66

Motorcycle Emptiness

'Ellie, Ellie, can you hear us?' There are lights flashing above me, and I can feel myself moving quickly. Like I'm flying. Everything feels bright and white. But sometimes red, and maybe even orange.

I can hear everything. Maybe even see it too. But I can't seem to speak. I can't seem to let them know.

Everything's slowing down now. Like every motion is exaggerated. Every voice an operetta, long and loud and whimsical.

Mum's crying – I can hear it. Dad's breathing heavily, his voice foggy and distant, but low, there. Like something to hold on to, something to move towards.

I can feel hands on me. People shouting 'You can't come any further', while Mum sobs.

My heart is a drum. My head is a cloud. My love is my love is my love is my love. Manic Street Preachers, 'Motorcycle Emptiness', is playing. It was playing in the car when the world went dark.

I'm living life like a comatose.

'Stand back!'

I wish I'd shaved my legs today. I wish I'd bothered to pluck that annoying eyebrow hair I saw this morning, right under the arch of my left eyebrow. Because if you die, you don't want to be the girl with the unshaved legs and the unplucked left eyebrow hair, and I'm concerned about the people that do your make-up when you're dead – about whether they have the right foundation shades, because I don't want to be orange, or yellowy-white. I want to be brown, because I Am Brown, and I Am Brown, and I Am Brown.

'Clear!'

I wonder what happens to you when you die, or am I dead already? Is Richey here, from the Manics? Is Richey Edwards my spiritual guide to the afterlife? Because I think I'd like that. I think I'd like Richey from the Manics to be my spiritual guide. I think I'd just like to know he's OK. That he's not sad any more.

'Clear!'

Although I think, on reflection, as much as I'd love to meet Richey, I think I'd prefer to live.

'Clear!'

And it's like when you see one of those time-lapse videos, where ten years of the sun in rotation of the earth can be boiled down to just one minute, because everything speeds up again. Faster and faster and faster, every detail a millisecond of something so much bigger.

Is Amis here, Richey? Where's Amis? Can you tell me before I go? Where he is, and what he's doing, and if he's OK, Richey? Can you tell him I love him? That he'll never, ever be replaced. Can you tell him Granny's driving me mad? Can you tell him, Richey, can you?

'Ellie, Ellie, can you hear us?'

And Richey's been replaced by James Dean Bradfield singing about lungs sucking on air: as my lungs suck on air. Is survival as natural as sorrow, sorrow, sorrow?

I try to signal that I can hear them; my eyes wide open, my throat cracking.

What does neon loneliness look like?

'Your heart stopped, Ellie.'

My heart stopped, Richey.

'You had an allergic reaction to your pain medication, but you're OK now.'

I'm OK now, Richey.

I can hear a collective sigh across the entire room, the beep of monitors and the sound of shoes as they shuffle back and forth through billowing doors.

I once heard an allergy described as the body's overreaction to a particular stimulant. Which is just me, all over. The world's greatest overreactor.

But I can't complain.

Because I'm alive.

I'm alive, Richey.

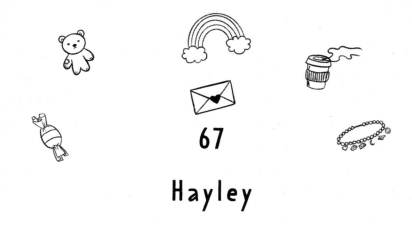

67

Hayley

The weird thing about almost dying is how quickly you're alive again. Eating bad hospital food, and watching bad television, rolling your eyes at your parents as your grandmother tries to force-feed you mutton rolls.

London Cousin – Annoying:

> don't die before i teach u how to do ur hair properly

At least some things you can rely on.

I had my MRI this morning, and everything seems clear, but they're keeping me in overnight again. A hangover from my overreaction.

In the afternoon, I manage to convince Dad to take Granny home. I want him to take Mum too, but she refuses to go.

'I'm fine,' I soothe them all.

'That's what you said an hour before your heart stopped,' Dad says worriedly.

I sigh.

'The doctors said we would never have known I was allergic until

I was exposed to that stuff,' I say matter-of-factly. 'And I'm lucky it happened now, when it was such a low dose. Now they know, it's on my record, and it was all very scary, but these things are a learning experience, aren't they, Mum?' I turn to her for confirmation.

She laughs.

'My big girl,' she says, smoothing my hair back. 'When did you get so strong?'

'Always been strong,' Granny says fiercely. 'Always.'

'Hi,' Hayley says, poking her head round the doorway at us. 'Is it OK if I come in?'

'Yes. They were just leaving . . .' I say, glaring at them all.

'Actually, I'm just going to the canteen,' Mum says pointedly.

'And I'll be back once I've dropped *Amma* home,' Dad says, kissing my forehead.

'I'll pack you some food,' Granny says determinedly. 'For tonight. You must eat. Keep up strength.'

'I don't think they like you bringing in food, Granny.' The mutton rolls have already given the ward a decidedly spicy smell.

'Chkkk,' she replies.

When they all finally leave, I turn towards Hayley.

'I'm sorry I didn't call you back,' she says quietly.

'That's OK.' I yawn. 'I was actually on my way to see you. When the accident happened.'

'I know,' she says guiltily. 'I'm sorry. I shouldn't have ignored your calls. If you hadn't got in the car to see me, this would never have happened . . .' Her eyes fill with tears.

'Hey, hey, hey,' I say, sitting up.

'Don't sit up!' she screams.

'Why?' I say, confused, and slightly deafened by her response. Turns out, I'm not the only overreactor in this room.

'You might . . .'

'Might what?'

'I don't know,' she says, crying now. 'Die or something.'

'Hayley, stop. I'm fine.'

'Your heart stopped,' she sobs.

For all the gods' sake. How many people know this fact?

'Yes, but it's fine now – and you know why I was coming to see you, so why don't we just talk about that instead.'

She looks at me. Somewhere between scared and defiant.

'There's nothing to talk about,' she says bluntly; and the old Hayley, the spiky, scary, angry Hayley, is written in every single word of it.

'But my heart stopped,' I say, lying back on my pillow and trying to look pathetic; which, in this case, doesn't take much effort.

'That's not fair,' she sighs.

'Hayley, you're sick . . .' I say quietly.

'I'm not,' she says in a small voice. And I leave the silence there for her. I let her fill it with her own discomfort. Because we both know something's wrong. We both know.

'I've been reading about it,' I say after a while. 'Not eating and making yourself throw up like that. Over time, it affects your heart. It can kill you, Hay. It can make your heart stop.'

'It's just something I do sometimes,' she says in that tiny voice. 'When I feel out of control. When things feel weird or bad. I don't know. It just makes me feel better. It's hard to explain.'

'Does it make you feel in control?' I ask quietly.

She shrugs.

'You're not well,' I state again. I want to shake her, or hug her, or call her mother, but I can barely find the energy to stay upright. 'I can't pretend I understand what you're going through, Hay, I just know I love you, and I don't want anything to happen to you. Who am I going to move to London with if your *heart stops?*' I say firmly.

'Who am *I* going to go to London with if *your* heart stops?' She smiles.

'Promise me you'll talk to someone, Hay. Promise me you'll get some help. Please.'

She looks at me, and nods. A tiny, almost imperceptible nod.

'You *scared* me,' she whispers.

'You're scaring me,' I say, taking hold of her hand.

'Ellie?' Jess bursts into the room, causing Hayley to let go of my hand abruptly. 'I came as soon as they let me.'

'Did Ash tell you what happened?' I ask desperately, because I haven't heard from him since the accident and I don't know why. 'It really wasn't his fault – it was all the other driver. Even the police said so.'

'He must have been camped out here all night. Where is he?' Hayley asks, looking around her. 'Or has he gone home for a bit?'

'Dad told him to go home after the accident,' I reply quickly. 'He hasn't been back since. He's probably not feeling very well.'

She stares at me, while Jess pretends not to have heard me.

'What, he hasn't been back since the car accident? Since after the heart thing?' Hayley asks incredulously. 'Have you spoken to him?'

'No,' I say, annoyed, 'but I like I said, he was in the accident too, and he's probably not feeling very well.'

'He's not the one lying in hospital having almost *died*,' Hayley says angrily.

'Stop it, Hayley,' I say, leaning back into my pillow. 'I'm too tired for this.' But it's not because I'm tired, it's because I might cry. Message after message after message – and nothing. Dad sent him away, I remind myself; he's just doing what he was asked to do. It'll be fine when I get home. Fine when I see him at school.

'*Shhhh*,' Jess says, glaring at Hayley. 'We can talk about this later. When Ellie's feeling better.'

There's a gentle knock at the door, and we all turn towards it, grateful for the interruption as a mop of dirty-blond hair appears.

'Hey there,' Shawn says, looking around the room awkwardly. 'I heard what happened. How are you?' he asks gently.

'Come in,' I beckon, sitting up.

I must look horrible. A hairy, unplucked physical manifestation of the word 'ugh'.

'You're busy . . .' he says, smiling at Jess and Hayley. 'I just wanted to check on you. Rumour is, you were dead for ten minutes,' he jokes softly.

'Thirty seconds.' I smile.

'I've been dead inside for years,' Hayley jokes gruffly.

'Oh, and I brought you these,' he says, embarrassed, producing a bunch of yellow tulips from behind his back.

No one's ever bought me flowers before. It feels so grown-up; although ideally, I'd have preferred them for a reason not related to me lying in a backless green hospital gown with a half-plucked eyebrow.

'They're lovely, thank you.'

'I'd better go,' he says, sticking his thumb out behind him.

'Oh, OK,' I say, suddenly aware of my nakedness beneath the backless green gown.

He walks towards me and puts the tulips down on my bedside, bending down to hug me.

'I'm sorry,' I mumble. 'I smell horrible.' Because he smells lovely. Like apples, or Calvin Klein. He leans into me, his hair brushing the side of my face.

'No, you don't,' he whispers.

And there goes that stupid heart of mine. Stopping again, for all the wrong reasons.

68

Sweet Sixteen

Mum and Dad make me stay home from school for the next four days, and I have to beg them to let me go back on my birthday, despite the fact they have repeatedly told me this is the Most Important Year of My Scholastic Life, and There Is No Reason I Should Be Missing School. It turns out, my parents are where I get my classic overreacting from.

I keep telling them you only turn sixteen once – and I'm pretty sure you shouldn't spend it bedridden, with your grandmother force-feeding you soup.

The truth is, it's not school I'm missing. I haven't seen Ash since the accident, something Dad is still entirely blaming him for, even though there is a police report and a *confession* (a signed confession!) concluding he was entirely *not* to blame.

We've spoken a sum total of once, awkwardly, for five minutes, while Dad hovered over me, threatening to take my phone away.

On Friday, almost a week after the accident, I shower and wash my hair, then stand in front of the mirror and look at myself. It's my birthday and I'm sixteen. I look different; I *feel* different. Or maybe I don't, and

I just wish I did. Either way, I've decided things have to change. I've almost met Richey from the Manics. I've *seen* things.

I've begged my parents to let me go out this evening, and while they've said yes, I've been told in no uncertain terms: no alcohol, no dancing, no fun. I keep telling them I'm fine. That Dr Yi said I'm fine, but it's only thanks to Jess's persistence and promises sworn on Pain of Death that I've been given permission to go out at all.

I put my make-up on slowly. Carefully. Filling each eye socket with colour, and a tiny, almost imperceptible flick of liner. When I've dried my hair, Granny piles it on my head in a pretty, wispy bun. It makes me look older, sophisticated, like I haven't really tried, even though it's taken twenty minutes of her twisting and pulling at my hair, her bony fingers poking into the back of my head like a knife as she hisses at me to sit still. Granny is good at hair, and as I've eaten all the weird, random things she's put in front of me this week, this is my reward.

When I finally stand up and head downstairs to the kitchen, my legs feel weird. Like I'm a toddler and I don't know how to use them yet.

'Happy birthday!' Mum screams, startling me so much I fall into the kitchen wall. For a woman so obsessed with my cardiovascular activity, she's definitely not seeing the irony in almost causing me a heart attack.

'Happy birthday, *en anbe*,' Dad says, kissing me on the forehead.

'Yes, yes,' Granny says, put out. 'Is no need to shout, Nimi.'

We collectively roll our eyes at the shouting that accompanies this statement.

'Do you want your presents now, or later?' Mum says excitedly.

Every year for the past six years, Mum's treated my birthday like something icky to be held at arm's length, and I can sense how hard she's trying to make this year feel different, to not think about Amis.

'She's going out later,' Dad says.

'So, now then,' Mum says brightly.

'I promise,' I say, smiling at Dad, 'we'll celebrate tomorrow. Jess has something organised tonight.'

'With your friends,' he says grouchily, which is code for: That Boy That Almost Killed You. And I want to say, it's my birthday, Dad, can't you at least *try* to look happy? And also, That Boy That Almost Killed Me (which he didn't, because it wasn't his fault) doesn't appear to have had anything to do with my birthday plans, or me, so, you know – you win.

'Here,' Mum says, passing me a small box. 'It's from Granny too.'

I look at it with no idea what could be inside. Maybe an Apple Watch; I've always wanted one.

Maybe there's nothing like a near-death experience to guilt your parents into buying you a good present. Maybe I should have asked for a new iPad. Or one of those close-up make-up mirrors that the Kardashians are obsessed with; Jess says you can practically see inside your pores with one. I imagine tiny people inside mine, screaming to be released from my weird, dry skin, or singing a musical number about my need to tone before I moisturise.

I tear it open, expecting to see a white box with a sleek picture of a watch on the outside; but the box is leather and padded, and inside is no watch but a necklace, delicate and gold, with a vintage-style 'E' dangling from it.

'It's beautiful,' I breathe.

'Jess picked it.' Mum smiles. 'Do you like it?'

'I love it,' I say, my eyes welling up. Dad puts it on for me.

I don't really own any jewellery. Not unless you count the Jesus medal sewn into a small pillow-shaped thing my parents make me wear pinned to the inside of my jumper, which I know is weird, but it's a Sri Lankan, Tamil, Catholic *thing*, and therefore has no reasonable explanation. But this necklace is perfect. Just the right length to see the E when my shirt is slightly unbuttoned at the collar, the chain like delicate gold thread against my throat. It feels dainty, and grown up, and pretty, and sure of itself, like all the things I want to be. That maybe I will be. Now I'm sixteen.

'Thank you,' I say, hugging them all.

'There are more things,' Mum says, smiling, 'but we'll save them for tomorrow, when we get to see you properly.'

'OK,' I say, shovelling my breakfast down, and staring at my wrist where I once hoped an Apple Watch might live. On reflection, I think Apple Watches are overrated. In fact, all the people I know who own Apple Watches are annoying, and overrated. 'I'd better go,' I say, through a mouthful of blueberries, 'or I'll miss the bus.'

'I'll drive you,' Dad says quickly.

'You're going to have to let me do something on my own at some point, Dad,' I say gently.

'Not on your birthday I don't,' he says, going to collect his car keys.

And as I pass the mirror in the hallway, I think I hear the tiny people in my pores singing; and I think: OK, fine. I'll take the overreacting if on this occasion it means I don't have to face Rex, the Bus Driver Who Hates Me for No Fathomable Reason (Or for One Very Fathomable One), on my way to school today.

After all, it is my birthday.

69

They Say It's
Your Birthday

London Cousin – Annoying:

happy bday cuz!

Ellie:

♥♥♥

When I get out of the car by the school gates, I can see Hayley and Jessica waiting for me at the bus stop opposite.

'What are you two doing?' I shout.

They turn and scream, running towards me at top speed, almost toppling me over.

'Happy birthday!' they shout, balloons in hand.

I grin.

'Be careful!' Hayley swats at Jessica. 'Her arm!'

'It's nothing,' I say, waving my wrist support in her face. 'Just a tiny fracture. I can take it off in a couple of weeks.'

I gesture at the balloons, all foiled and shiny, clearly filled with helium.

'You know I'm sixteen, right, not six,' I laugh.

'Special day, is it, Pillai?' James Godfrey asks, grinning, as we make our way through the playground. 'Happy birthday,' he says, leaning down to hug me. 'We were worried about you, but you don't look that terrible. Not any more than usual, anyway.'

'Thanks,' I smile sarcastically, as my phone buzzes.

'OK?' he says, smiling at Hayley. She smiles back shyly.

I squeeze her hand.

Ash:

they say it's ur bday

I grin at my phone, as thrilled as if he were standing right next to me. We're going to be OK; I just need to see him, and everything will be OK.

Ellie:

it's my bday too, yeah

I wait for a response, but after a few minutes, the girls pull me towards reception, forcing me to put my phone back in my pocket.

'Ellie! You're *alive*,' Jeffrey Dean says, pointing at me; and actually, an awful lot of people are staring at me in this hallway. Like I'm Jesus, and I've just rolled the stone back on Easter morning: back from the dead. I want to print some kind of sign that reads: *NOTHING TO SEE HERE. Fractured wrist, and thirty seconds of cardiovascular collapse.*

'Yup,' I smile, trying to pretend this isn't weird.

'Ellie ... you look like death ...' Billie McQueen intones dramatically, as she eyes me from the centre of the cool girls' wall. 'Hey, Jess,' she says deferentially. 'Love your fringe.' Thankfully Jess's taste in friends has improved since she started going out with Elina. She barely speaks to the McQueen sisters since she came out. Probably because they barely spoke to her, not when it counted.

'Thanks,' Jess says flippantly. 'Come on, birthday girl,' she says, linking arms with me. 'I'll walk you to your form room.'

'Why, thank you, Your Majesty,' Hayley says, mock curtsying, as Jess rolls her eyes.

And it feels like a gift just to have the two of them next to me. To know they're on my side. Although, once again, I realise I haven't returned the favour as much as I should have over the last few months.

'So, um, where's Elina?' I ask, hoping this will lead to some information on Ash's whereabouts.

'Art studio,' she replies, blithely unaware of my digging.

'Cooooool,' I say, gripping the balloon string tighter. 'Is she coming tonight?'

'Of course,' she says distractedly. 'Listen, I'll see you at lunchtime,' she says, looking down at her phone. 'I have to go.'

'What happened to our royal escort?' Hayley mutters.

'Ha ha,' Jess says, mock punching her skinny arm. As she disappears around the corner, I turn to Hayley.

'So . . .' I say, letting the silence unfold, because we haven't talked about what we *talked* about at the hospital yet.

'Yes . . .' she replies awkwardly.

I widen my eyes at her, while I try to untangle the balloons from my wrist.

'I talked to Mum,' she concedes quietly.

'OK,' I say eagerly. 'That's good.'

'This isn't . . . the first time,' she admits.

'Oh,' I reply, trying not to react.

'But I'm going to see a doctor, a specialist this time – and I've started going to a thing.'

'A thing?' I question.

'YES,' she says tetchily. 'A thing.'

'Therapy?' I suggest.

'No.'

'Support group?'

'Sort of,' she says in a small voice. 'And I told James and Benji and Jess. So, you know, you can all keep an eye on me.'

'I'm so proud of you,' I say, squeezing her arm.

'For what?' she says irritably. 'Being a weak, pathetic, cliché, anorexic-bulimic, wannabe actress?'

'Come on, Hayley,' I say, shocked to hear her give such a damning verdict on herself. 'You're not a cliché, you're a human being. Stop being so hard on yourself.'

'Well, you should stop *not* being hard enough on other people,' she says short-temperedly.

'Meaning?' I respond quietly. But I know what she means.

'Where's Ash today?' she demands.

'I don't know,' I reply, embarrassed.

'Hmmm,' she replies, as Shawn appears around the corner – a Dirty-Blond Miracle, come to save me from further uncomfortable truths.

'Ellie!' he says, pulling me into a hug. 'How are you feeling?'

'Like I look. Which is, you know, not great . . .' I semi-joke, because I feel like today is one of those days when, no matter how hard I try, the best I'm going to look is Not That Bad.

'Actually, I feel fine,' I say, staring at Hayley, who's suddenly stood far too close to me, trying to provide some kind of protective barrier between me and the rest of the world; like a princess being protected by a dragon. The kind of princess the prince doesn't even bother to show up for. Which is fine. Because this princess doesn't need dragons or princes. This princess is more than capable of saving herself.

'Are you feeling up to rehearsal tonight?' he asks, smiling.

'It's my birthday,' I say, gesturing towards the balloons. 'We're going out.'

'I'm coming to that too,' he says, nodding at Hayley, who's still nervously pushing away anyone who comes within several metres of me. I feel like doing the same thing for her. 'We can start earlier – straight after school.'

'Um . . .' I say, trying to work out how to say no, while also untethering myself from the balloons before they either drag me up to the ceiling or garrotte my arm.

'See you then,' he says, disappearing down the corridor, giving me no chance to reply.

'I don't know if my wrist . . .' I trail away, my empty words directed at his retreating back. Because I was hoping, at some point, my boyfriend would cease to be MIA and become IA; and that he might want to do something with me after school.

I look over at Hayley, who, while edgy, now also appears to be smirking.

'What?' I say, glaring at her.

'Nothing,' she says, shrugging.

'WHAT?' I demand.

'Nothing,' she says, rolling her eyes. 'It's just you know where you are with that one.'

'What you mean like *James*,' I say bluntly. 'Or *Benji*?'

'Oh, shut up,' she says moodily.

Then she squeezes my arm.

'I'm glad you're not dead,' she says, her face immobile.

'Fractured wrist, thirty seconds of cardiovascular collapse,' I say matter-of-factly. 'I did not almost die.'

'Technically . . .' she replies.

'I'm proud of you,' I say, ignoring her. 'And you're *not* a cliché. You should be proud of yourself too.'

I put my head on her shoulder and she says nothing as we walk the remaining length of the corridor to Mr Gorley's form room. Which is the closest Hayley will ever get to saying 'I'm proud of me too'.

70

The Forever Ellipsis

Ellie:

where r u?

Ash:

· · ·

The typing ellipsis at the top of the screen seems to go on forever.

Ash:

not feeling great. sorry. meet at cinema later?

Ellie:

k

What's an appropriate way to respond to that message? What's the right thing to say? He's allowed to feel ill. He's allowed to not be here today. It's just a stupid birthday. A stupid, nothing, sixteenth birthday that doesn't really matter. I just need to see him. It doesn't matter when that is, where that is.

Ellie:

Ash:

He told me he loves me.

And that has to mean something – right?

71

They Say It's Your Birthday Part II

As soon as I walk into the main hall after school, the band launch into a rendition of the Beatles, 'Birthday'. Jess, Elina, Hayley and James cheer in the background, along with some kids from drama class and a few of the people that hang out with the band, including the delight that is Hannah, who is glaring at me. We've never even spoken, but somehow it's clear she hates me.

Lucas and Elliott are doing some serious guitar swagger, while Benji plays the drums like a man possessed.

They say it's your birthday, Shawn sings scratchily – and man, that boy can sing.

Jess jumps on me, hugging me while simultaneously foisting a box in my direction.

'What's all this?' I ask, happily surprised.

'Your pre-party party!' she says, gesturing to the group while Shawn grins at me.

'Thanks,' I say, hugging her tight. I feel so grateful all of a sudden, so grateful for all of them. 'For this too,' I say, pointing at the box.

'I'd love to take credit for that,' she smiles, 'but it's from Aunty Kitty – your mum couldn't give it you in front of Granny,' she says, raising her eyebrows.

'What is it?' I ask, shaking the box. Why would Mum want me to open it at school?

'Open it!' Hayley squeals from behind us.

I tear at the paper, revealing a pale pink Sculpt box. Inside is the oxblood velvet mini dress I tried on in New York, wrapped in layers of soft white tissue, along with a card.

Don't worry, it was on sale –
and Hope had some friends with a discount...
Aunty Kitty x

The Lennox sisters.

'I wish I had an Aunty Kitty,' Elina jokes.

'Or a cousin with a discount,' Jess says.

'They're both pretty great,' I grin.

'So, you're going to wear it tonight?' Jess says, nudging me.

'It doesn't really go with the shoes I brought,' I say unconvincingly. Because me and this dress – we can't be meant to be. Because me and beautiful things – not compatible.

'That dress will go with *anything*,' Elina says matter-of-factly. 'Just wear it with the Converse you've got on,' she suggests.

I disappear to the toilets and, against my will, try the dress on. It fits perfectly; beautifully. Like it was made for me. Short sheer sleeves and a sweetheart neckline, the length hitting the top of my thigh. Because me and beautiful things do work. And I have to stop telling myself differently.

I take a deep breath and look at myself. Willing my brain to oxygenate. In through the nose, out through the mouth. The day's been fine so far. OK, if a bit weird. It's just Ash isn't here. We've barely spoken in a week, and I don't know how to feel about any of it. So, I decide not to. I decide not to feel at all.

I step out into the corridor and back towards the main hall, where my appearance is met by some seriously over-the-top wolf whistles.

'Ellie,' Benji says, rolling his eyes, and he's standing next to Hayley, looking a bit like she does around me. 'For the next hour, this is still a rehearsal.'

'Say it again. Slower,' I mime sarcastically, as Lucas and Elliott laugh.

'You look nice,' Shawn says quietly.

'Shall we try your song from last week?' Elliott suggests.

'I've got the lyrics here,' he says, putting his battered notebook down on my keyboard stand. And it feels like he's standing too close to me, his breath on the back of my neck, the arm that's holding his guitar brushing against my spine, and it's like the air's being sucked out of me, my heart pulsing like a drum.

I look into the crowd and try to be OK with it. With singing in front of them, in showing them who I am. The only face that seems anything other than friendly or familiar is Hannah, grimacing like the mere sight of me pains her.

So, I close my eyes and wait for Shawn to start singing – and when it's my turn to sing, I open my eyes and stare at him, like he's staring at me, giving me the courage to do this, the courage to keep going.

And I think about Ash, and Rebecca. Hayley, and James. Shawn, and Hannah. And me.

Me.

Not ready for the shallows, not ready for the heights
Don't know if we're ready, just know that tonight
Our mistakes aren't over
Any more than they're made
Tell me the truth
If you want me to stay

72

Your Ex-Lover Is Dead

'You OK, Pillai?' James asks, squashed up next to me in the Uber.

'Fine,' I say, smiling at him. But the smile feels weird and forced, like I'm trying too hard not to scream. I can hear the tiny people in my pores singing.

'I know that feeling,' he says, throwing a look at Hayley in the front seat.

I feel sorry for him, even though technically I *am* him. The one that keeps hanging on, for no fathomable reason.

'Is Ash coming?' he asks uncomfortably.

I shrug.

'You look nice,' he says, trying to make conversation. 'I like your dress.'

I shrug again.

'Excellent taking of a compliment,' he says sarcastically.

'So . . . Hayley talked to you . . .' I whisper.

He nods. 'I kind of had my suspicions. You know she took that time off in Year 9?'

'When she had glandular fever?'

He raises his eyebrows.

'I'm just glad she's talking about it,' he says, examining his hands. I grab one and squeeze it.

'I really like her, Ellie. I mean, I . . .' He gulps.

'I know,' I say sympathetically. 'But she's got so much stuff going on. Now's not the time for her to be thinking about anything except herself.'

He nods.

As we pull up outside Cinema, he turns to me and whispers:

'If he doesn't come tonight, he's an idiot.' Which is when I think: no. I'm the idiot. Because I shouldn't care if he comes tonight. I should care about the people that *are* here.

When I get out of the car and join the back of the queue, Jess grabs hold of me and marches me to the front.

'Ellie Pillai,' she says sweetly. 'We have an area reserved.'

The doorman nods as he consults his clipboard, and Jess turns around and waves to the pre-party crowd, motioning them to come up front.

When we get inside, she's booked an area by the dance floor, a series of booths where she's pinned up posters and pictures and vinyls, like my honorary bedroom. Promo prints of *A Hard Day's Night*, black and whites of Diana Ross, an Oasis album covered in Post-it notes, an advert for a Primal Scream concert – a postcard of Audrey Hepburn singing 'Moon River' in *Breakfast at Tiffany's* and what looks like a film reel of Norma Jean before she became Marilyn Monroe, barefoot in pedal pushers on the beach, staring happily into the camera. On each table is a little stand-up postcard with a copy of the Beatles badge Ash drew me, my name in chaotic red writing, and underneath, in the same print, the date.

I pick up the postcard and turn it around. On the back are a list of songs I love. The Supremes and the Smiths, the Cure, Aretha, Billie Holliday and Radiohead. The La's, Blondie, Robyn, Lady Gaga. Cardi B, Billie Eilish and Gerry Cinnamon. Ellie's Birthday Playlist.

'*Jess* . . .' I breathe.

'It was Hayley and Elina and Ash as well,' she says, smiling.

Don't think about Ash.

'It's so . . .'

'Yes?' she says happily.

'So . . .'

'You?' she questions.

'Yes,' I breathe, tears in my eyes.

'The DJ promised to play some of the stuff from your list tonight,' Elina says excitedly, from behind Jess.

'Do you like it?' Hayley asks, enveloping me in our tall girl, small girl embrace, even though I'm finally noticing how small she is, despite her height.

'Like it?' I whisper into her shoulder. 'I love it. Thank you. Thank you both.' I grab a hand from each of them. 'With everything you've both got going on, I just . . . I'm so . . .'

'OK, OK, OK,' Hayley says, shaking me off. 'Now, everyone,' she says, turning around bossily. 'The Post-it notes on *Definitely Maybe* are for you guys to fill with birthday wishes. There are pens on the tables,' and when I look closer, even the Post-it notes have intricately scrawled handwritten lyrics or lines from my favourite films on them, with spaces above for people to write messages.

'I did those,' Elina says, pointing to the Post-it notes. 'Although Alfie did "help",' she says, closing her fingers around the word. Jess smiles at the mention of her little brother, but my throat feels scratchy. Because I wonder what today would be like if Amis was here to share it. What he'd look like now, and how he'd feel about Phantom Baby.

How I feel about Phantom Baby.

'Thank you,' I gulp.

'Don't cry, Pillai,' James says, rolling his eyes.

'It's my party, and I'll cry if I want to,' I joke, sniffling.

'Damn,' Jess says. 'Should have put that on the playlist.'

Before long, we're all on the dance floor, laughing and singing, and throwing our hands in the air to Gerry Cinnamon, 'Sometimes'; everyone except Shawn and the guys from the band, who are sat in the booths, the very image of High School Cool. And I can't believe they're here for me, that they're My Friends. That I'm quite literally With the Band.

I turn and look at them, just as Shawn looks up and waves at me, gesturing with his hand, asking if I'd like a drink. I smile and nod, overenunciating the word 'Coke' as if he can actually hear me over the music.

He grins and stands up, making his way towards the bar. I turn to the rest of the group and signal that I'm going to see him, but just as I reach the edge of the dance floor, someone steps aggressively in front of me.

'He was my boyfriend first,' she says, looking down at me.

Why is everyone I know so tall? Or am I just really, really small? Like I should I be living in someone's pores.

'Sorry?' I stutter, confused.

'I said,' she says, more pronounced this time, 'he was *my* boyfriend *first*.'

'Hannah,' I sigh, trying not to poke her in the navel, which is roughly the same height as my head. Is she some kind of giant? No, she's on a step. I gather myself up to the fullness of my five feet two inches, and step up next to her. OK, I'm head height with her shoulder. Not better, but not worse either.

'I don't know what your problem is, but Shawn and I are just friends.' She glares at me. 'Whatever's going on with you two is between you two; it has *nothing* to do with me.' I try to walk past her. Like the mature, adult-like sixteen-year-old I am now.

She laughs, but it comes out a snort. One of those derisive ones designed to make you feel small. Up close, her features are delicate; wide eyes and a slim, elegant nose. Her hair is dark and long and pretty, and she's wearing leather trousers and a yellow vest top with Stan Smith trainers.

'I meant *Ash*,' she says deliberately.

'I'm sorry,' I ask, confused. 'What?'

'Last year,' she continues, staring at me. 'We started seeing each other. We went to the winter dance together.'

'I'm sorry,' I repeat angrily. '*What?*'

'Me – and *Ash*,' she says in a tone that suggests I either can't hear properly, or I'm very, very stupid. 'Before you sang him that song . . .'

'*What?*' I repeat like a broken record. 'I'm sorry,' I say, shaking my head. 'I'm confused. You went to the winter dance together? He went with Elina and Jess?'

'I was in the band. We were supposed to meet when I came offstage.'

And now I'm starting to hyperventilate. I can feel sick firing up my throat, like I might spontaneously vomit.

'How long?' I ask, spitting the words out.

'I don't know. Six weeks maybe. Until the end of term, from just after he broke up with Jessica. Although I guess,' she says, motioning over her shoulder to Jess and Elina, 'they were never actually together.'

Oh my God.

The whole time he was talking to me. The two of us, spending all that time together. And I know we weren't *together* together, but he never . . .

'He said you were just friends,' she spits. 'Then he just stopped talking to me – and on the first day back at school, there you were. Holding hands. And I knew you'd been together the whole time – and now you're moving on to Shawn,' she hisses.

'No,' I breathe. 'That's not it *at all*. I didn't *know*. He never said anything to me about you.' And she looks so hurt then, so small, that I instantly regret saying it.

'What about Shawn?' she demands.

'We're . . . friends,' I mutter, looking over at him.

'So, there's nothing's going on between you?' she asks, watching me closely.

I shake my head. A nodding dog from one of those insurance adverts.

'I don't know why I broke up with him,' she says, suddenly melancholy. 'I'm so stupid.'

But I don't know what to say to her. I have lost the ability to communicate.

'I have to go to the toilet,' I mutter robotically.

'Do you think I should I talk to him?' she asks seriously.

'What?' I ask, staring back at her blankly.

'Shawn,' she says again, as if I'm incapable of understanding any of this. Which I am.

'I have to go to the toilet,' I repeat.

I push past her, trying desperately to avoid pushing her off the step, either on purpose or by choice, Shawn signalling to me from the bar.

What.

The.

Hell.

Does any of this even matter? Because Ash isn't here. He's off somewhere. With his ex-girlfriend. The Other One.

Dear gods. Please help me.

Help me find a box. A place I can bury this information. Somewhere so deep down, I never have to think about it again.

I round the corner towards the toilets, trying desperately not to ruin my eye make-up with a big, snotty, blubbery weep, when like a cosmic response from the universe, he's there, holding hands with The Other One, just outside the toilets.

In the background, I can hear the Smiths, 'How Soon Is Now?' One of the songs from Ellie's Birthday Playlist, Morrissey's flat, angry snarl telling me his shyness is criminally vulgar. Damn Morrissey and his stupid, racist nonsense. How can I still love this song? How can it still speak to me, when he hates me? When he hates people *like* me. And I believe, in Mum's therapy world, they would call this *displacement activity*.

'Ellie,' Ash says guiltily, as he turns towards me, letting go of Rebecca's hand abruptly. 'Happy birthday . . .'

And Morrissey is telling me that I could meet somebody that really loves me – and I think: where? Because I thought Ash loved me, but this isn't what you do to the people you love.

'I need to talk to you,' he says, moving towards me. 'I'm . . . I'm so sorry about the accident. I'm so sorry about everything.' He looks sick. Grey and weird.

'Talk to me about what?' I ask calmly.

'I messed up.' He looks at me like he's choking. 'I should have come to see you at the hospital. I should have come to see you at your house. But your dad . . . he was so angry . . . And I know. All of it. Everything. It's my fault.'

My eyes feel heavy. Tired and small.

'You almost *died*.' His hands are shaking.

'A fractured wrist and thirty seconds of cardiovascular collapse,' I reply robotically.

'Ellie, I'm sorry . . .'

'For what?'

'Everything,' he says quietly.

'But you don't want to be with me any more?' I finish. Because I might as well say it. I might as well admit it out loud.

He takes a sharp breath.

'I guess it's a step up from what you did to Hannah,' I say mechanically. 'I mean, at least you're *telling* me you want to break up with me.'

And in the background, Morrissey is telling me that he's human and he needs to be loved.

He shakes his head as I back away angrily.

'Remember Hannah?' I ask sarcastically. 'She told me about last year. About you two going out. About what you did to Shawn, with his *girlfriend*. About what you did to her. Just ghosting her. Kind of like what you've done to me for the last week.'

'That's not . . .' he says agitatedly, starting to pace.

I cut him off.

'It's fine. But I deserve so much better. You two, on the other hand,' I say, looking at Rebecca, 'you two really deserve each other.'

'Ellie,' Rebecca says, stepping forward, and even I have to admit she looks pained. 'It's not what you think.'

'*You*,' I say, rounding on her. 'You don't get to say *anything* to me . . . But, you win. I guess we weren't right for each other after all.'

I turn and walk away from them. Before the snot that's gathering at pace in the back of my throat is finally released, proving once and for all that I am not the mature, adult-like sixteen-year-old I wish I was. Ignoring the fact I've needed to wee for twenty minutes. Because there is no dignified way to go to the toilet now, no dramatic exit, if I have to push past them both and let them see me cry.

I head back towards the booths, to where the whole group have gathered, and grab at my coat.

'What are you doing?' Jess asks, looking up at me.

'I have to go,' I say quietly. Because I have to leave. Right now. Right this instant. Because he's here, so I don't want to be. And I need to pee. Badly.

'What do you mean?' Hayley asks, standing up.

'I just need to go,' I say, trying to sweep past them.

'Ellie,' Ash says, suddenly behind me. 'That's not what happened. Can you just listen to me, please?'

'Oh,' Hayley says angrily, 'so you're the reason she needs to leave. Makes perfect sense,' she says, throwing her arms into the air.

He turns to look at her, his eyes hurt, and I hate that I care about that. I hate that I care if he's hurting.

'I don't want to talk to you any more.'

'You kept telling me you just wanted to be friends,' he says quietly. 'I never thought you'd . . . I didn't think we'd . . .'

'We weren't together. It's fine,' I reply calmly. 'And now we're done, so there is nothing to talk about,' I say, my voice rising a little.

'Ellie – are you OK?' Shawn says, standing up. James is behind him too, and Elliott and Lucas and Benji.

'Do you want him to leave, Ellie?' Benji says, in what I imagine he thinks is a menacing voice. And coming from him, it is relatively menacing. Benji. Benji, who usually just glares at me and mocks my choice of outfit.

'I never wanted to hurt you,' Ash says, staring at me, Rebecca stood a little way behind him.

He just stands there, so she moves forward and takes his hand.

And I can't speak. I can't breathe.

'You should go,' Shawn says, turning to him. And the humiliation of him standing here, while this happens, is the thing that finally breaks me. Because everyone else knows I'm an idiot but him. Because when I sing, when I write songs, I'm special and powerful and favoured, not weak and pathetic and blind.

I want to scream, or shout, or dissolve into dust and watch Rebecca choking on me.

'I never wanted to hurt you,' he repeats, as Rebecca pulls him away.

I back away from them, pushing my way through the dance floor, the sound of Jess and Hayley calling my name ringing in my ears, thanking every god imaginable that I took Elina's advice and I'm wearing my Converse.

It's cold outside, and my bladder is throbbing, full to the brim with Coca-Cola and ginger beer, and maybe a shot or two of vodka, which I won't be telling my parents about – and I can't tell which one I want to do more – cry or wee.

When I get down the road, as far from Cinema as I can without wetting myself, I find a bush and squat down behind it. Which feels like a fitting end to my not-so-sweet sixteen. Squatting in a bush, in the dark, weeing, while my ex-boyfriend's ex-girlfriends (both of them) fight it out for his attention.

Rebecca. Rebecca and her stupid kaleidoscope eyes. I can't believe I held her hair back.

I can feel my phone vibrating in my bag as I pull my pants up. My friends trying to make sure I'm OK. I feel suddenly grateful. Even though my heart hurts. Even though this must be what it feels like for your heart to stop when you're still awake to feel it.

I look down at my phone, and the first message I see is a link to a song from James.

James:

Stars, 'Your Ex-Lover Is Dead'

I laugh. Deep. Right from my belly. Sucking air in through my nose and out my mouth, filling myself up on it. I open my bag and find my earphones, put them in, click on the link and start running. A dinky little pony with a broken heart.

And it's exactly what I need it to be: beautiful guitars and strings and voices, joining together in a melody that takes my heart and my lungs and my mind somewhere else. Music for running away from your ex-almost-lover. Because thanks to a Hello Kitty crop top and a total lack of privacy, he was only ever an almost.

Maybe we were never supposed to be anything more than that. Maybe that's OK.

Maybe this isn't what falling in love feels like – perhaps this is just the falling bit. The falling flat on your face. Then I let myself cry as I listen to Stars say it so much better than I could.

I'm not sorry I met him, but I'm not sorry it's over. In fact, I'm not sorry; I have nothing to say.

And then I think: Mum and Dad are going to kill me for all this running.

73

Not-So-Sweet Sixteen

I don't explain anything when I arrive home, but I think it's pretty clear from my eye make-up that the evening hasn't been a success. Mum keeps attempting to say something, thinking better of it, and closing her mouth again.

'I'm going to bed,' I say, gulping down a glass of water and hoping they can't tell I've had a shot of vodka . . . or maybe several.

'Okaaay.' Their voices echo as I run up the stairs to my bedroom and slam the door behind me, throwing myself on to the bed.

I open my phone and tap into WhatsApp.

Jess:
i'll kill him

Hayley:
not if I get 2 him first

Jess:
i'll kill her

Hayley:

not if Elina gets 2 her first

Hayley:

may have crush on ur girlfriend

Jess:

back off. u've got Godfrey.

Hayley:

...

Jess:

ELLIE R U THERE?

Hayley:

pls don't be upset. he isn't worth it.

Jess:

i'll kill him 4 u. I promise. just say the word

Ellie:

the word

Hayley:

she lives!

Jess:

& she has a sense of humour!

Ellie:

just about

Hayley:

u OK?

Ellie:

just got home. going 2 bed

Jess:

on our way over

Ellie:

i'm fine

Hayley:

we're outside

When I get down the stairs, I can hear them in the kitchen whispering, Mum and Dad hovering in the hallway.

'Everything OK?' Mum asks, looking up at me, her arm cradling the outline of Phantom Baby. Because she *knows*, like a sixth sense, that it's 9.30 p.m. and I'm already home from my Big Birthday Night Out. The one where I begged for a midnight curfew.

'We need cake,' Jess says firmly.

Mum goes into the kitchen and puts on the kettle, briskly taking out the cake we were clearly supposed to eat tomorrow. Hayley eyes it nervously, and I give her a sudden, unexpected hug. She leans in to me, and I lean back, and this is the moment I think I'll look back and remember the most about my Not-So-Sweet Sixteen. Leaning into each other, knowing there's someone there to catch you.

'I will make the tea,' Granny says, appearing out of nowhere. She takes the full china tea set out, spooning sugar cubes into a matching bowl, filling a tiny ceramic jug with milk, and setting them on the table. Then she proceeds to produce out of nowhere a selection of fish cutlets, mutton rolls and patties, while Dad searches through his record collection for something to suit the mood.

He settles on Marvin Gaye, *What's Going On*, one of Mum's favourite albums; and before I know it, the six of us are dancing in the kitchen, Jess and Hayley holding Granny's hands as they roll her arms up and down to the sound of Marvin crooning. Mum and Dad are dancing together, her head on his shoulder, his arms around her ever-expanding belly, while I just stand there, my eyes closed, my head moving from side to side.

There's something so soothing in this sound. Something warm and comforting; the promise that everything will be OK. And I wish Ash was here. I wish his arms were around me like Dad's are around Mum, but I know I'm not alone. I know I'll never be alone.

When Dad drives the girls home, I sit on the sofa between Mum and Phantom Baby and Granny, watching *A Hard Day's Night* for the millionth time, and I just think: God, John Lennon was *hot*.

'They are old,' says Granny, confused.

'They're Ellie's favourite band, *Amma*.'

'Chkkk.'

I excuse myself at the credits and pour myself into bed, trying not to think too much about my heart. And just before I finally give in to sleep, my brain still churning, I look down at my phone.

Ash:
i'm sorry

Ellie:
i'm not sorry, there's nothing 2 say

Note to self: thank James for introducing to me to the most helpful lyric of all time.

74

Monday, Monday

I'd like to say facing him on Monday feels OK. That over the weekend sixteen has set in, and I am now fully mature and capable of seeing him again, without the desire to spontaneously cry, fall apart, or kill him.

But it's not true.

I spend the day avoiding everyone. Hoping to make it all go away. But when I run into him in the hallway, with the McQueen sisters plastered to either side of him like they can just *smell* the drama, I stand there. Staring at him. Like I've been bewitched by the snakes on Medusa's head – which, to be fair, could be Addy McQueen's ringlets.

My mouth just opens and closes like a fish, no sound appearing from within.

Then I feel him. James Godfrey, taking my arm as he pulls me away down the corridor.

'It gets easier,' he says under his breath. 'I promise.'

75

A Girl Called Ellie

My name is Ellie. Ellie Pillai. And I know how it feels for your heart to stop beating. When the pain feels unmanageable and you don't know how to breathe.

But life is short.

And magical.

Sometimes terrifying and occasionally brilliant.

But mostly, life is adaptable.

My name is Ellie. Ellie Pillai.

And I'm not broken, just a little bit bruised.

76

There Was Never Anyone Called Ash

I never thought I'd say thank God for exams – but Thank God for Exams, because I'm too busy to think about Ash, or look at Ash, or discuss Ash. In fact, there is no Ash. There was Never Anyone Called Ash.

'Do you want to talk about it?' Jess asks for the hundredth time in just over a week, while we're sat in my bedroom, revising for French.

'No,' I repeat for the hundredth time, my hair piled on top of my head in a wondrously weird topknot. I've decided a topknot helps you study more efficiently. It quite literally clears your head.

'You know, I don't know *exactly* what happened with Hannah – but they weren't actually going out. It was all very casual,' she says, flipping her fluffy seventies hair – it seems impossible, but Jess appears to have got more beautiful since she fell in love.

'So, he was just casually sleeping with her when she had a boyfriend. That's better,' I say sarcastically. I am a Topknot. I have a Clear Head.

'*She* broke up with Shawn, he didn't ask her to – and it's not like you two were together at the time . . .'

'Um, why *exactly* are you defending him?' I ask, irritated.

'I'm not *defending* him,' she says in a wheedling tone, 'but he was devastated when you were in hospital, E.'

'Maybe he should have come to see me then,' I mutter angrily. And I am now, officially, having all the feelings. All the ones I said I wasn't going to have – and the topknot isn't working. She's broken it. He's broken it.

In with love, out with anger, I remind myself. I heard it on a podcast about heartbreak, and it is now my new mantra.

'Your dad, E, you don't know what your dad said to him,' she says quietly.

'Why are we even talking about this?'

'You were so happy together . . .' she says sadly.

'No,' I say. 'I wasn't. I was insecure, and obsessive, and not a very good friend.'

And she doesn't reply, because she knows it's true.

'I just wish you could talk to each other.'

'Why?'

'So he could explain himself, and you could stop acting like some kind of weird robot. Get some closure.'

In with love, out with anger. In with anger, out with more anger.

'He's going out with Rebecca. Isn't that closure enough? He basically cheated on me – whether you count Hannah or not – dumped me on my birthday, and now he's got my best friend defending him, like he's some kind of *hero*, when he is clearly an ARSE.'

Anger, love, breathing, anger, anger, anger, bloody podcast.

'Sorry,' she breathes, 'the Rebecca thing is weird and unforgiveable. I'm just worried about him. I'm worried about you.'

Worried about *HIM*?

OH MY GOD.

I stalk away from her, ready to explode. 'I'm going to get a drink. Do you want anything?' I say, trying to remain calm.

'Elina's worried sick,' she continues. 'He's not talking to anyone, he's behind on his coursework, he's jeopardising his whole future, and now Rebecca's going back to London . . .'

'London?' I say, turning towards her. 'I thought they were . . .'

'I don't know,' she says honestly. 'Maybe they're going to try long distance or something – maybe they're not even together. No one's talking about it, so who knows,' she says, exasperated. 'Kyra's really worried, Ellie.'

But it's been ten days, and I'm not ready to pretend what happened doesn't matter any more. That the thought of him stringing Hannah along, or the way he's been with Rebecca the whole time we were together, doesn't matter. Because it does, and it hurts, even though I am determined not to let it.

'Jess, I can't talk about this. I need to focus,' I say, looking down at my exam notes.

'I'm sorry,' she says again. 'I know I shouldn't be defending him. I just hate seeing Elina so down.'

I sigh.

In with love, out with anger, in with love, out with anger.

'He hurt you, and I hate him for that. I just feel sorry for him, I don't know why.'

'Because you're a good person,' I say glumly.

'Apparently, I'm an over-empathiser,' she sighs.

'A what?' I say, looking at her carefully.

'I've been talking to people who live with or care for people like Mum,' she says slowly, 'and apparently, I have a tendency to over-empathise. I put other people's needs before mine.'

'That does sound like you,' I say gently, 'but you never told me you were talking to anyone?'

'You had your own stuff going on,' she says, waving her hand dismissively.

'And *this* is why I'm a bad friend,' I sigh. 'Everything you and Hayley have been going through, and I'm upset about Ash. It's not important.'

'Well, you did almost die,' she says, coming to sit next to me. 'And it took a lot for you to be with Ash, I know that. You did this huge grand gesture, then he shows up with Rebecca and starts behaving weirdly. I mean, it was pretty full-on.'

'He was being weird, wasn't he?' I say, putting my head on her shoulder.

'He was,' she says, putting her head on mine.

'But you're OK, aren't you, Jess?' I say, suddenly worried I've missed something. 'At your dad's and everything?'

'I'm OK,' she says, squeezing my hand. 'I miss Mum, but I'll get to see her soon, and things are going to be different. She's getting help, and I'm getting help – and, you know, *Elina*,' and I can feel her smiling through my hair. 'Plus, I love spending more time with the Alfie Monster.'

And I think: we'll be having our own Alfie Monster soon.

'Do you want a drink?' I ask her. Because I think the topknot is also making me thirstier. I mean, I don't understand the science behind it, but I feel very dry, while also quite tearful.

She nods, and I head downstairs to the kitchen.

As I'm pouring us both a glass of juice, there's a knock at the front door. When I open it, Mrs Aachara is on the other side.

'Hi,' I say awkwardly.

'Hi, Ellie,' she says warmly.

'If this is about Ash,' I say tentatively, 'then I don't want to talk about it. I hope that's OK.'

'He misses you,' she says quietly, 'but that's not the reason I'm here.'

'Kyra,' says Granny, appearing out of nowhere. 'Let us have tea,' she says, ushering her in. As I head up the stairs with the drinks, Mrs Aachara turns back to me.

'He really does miss you, Ellie. We all do.'

'Maybe we'll be friends one day,' I smile softly.

And as she walks into the living room and shuts the door quietly behind her, I wonder if that's possible.

77

Rehearse,
Rehearse, Rehearse

Dirty Blond:

gig at cinema fri. rehearsal thu

Ellie:

Dirty Blond:

you'll be fine 😌

Ellie:

. . .

Dirty Blond:

don't overthink it

And I believe, in Mum's therapy world, this would be described as *growth*. Now all I need to do is not think about Ash, or Rebecca, or the fact my heart feels like it's about to freak out by either stopping entirely or moving several thousand times faster than it should. I just need to get through Thursday – or more importantly Friday, at Cinema.

Note to self: stop thinking about Ash Anderson.

And don't vomit. Nerves are not sexy.

78

Tell Me Why I Don't Like Thursdays

It only strikes me on Thursday, almost two weeks after Ash and I broke up on my not-so-sweet sixteen, that I haven't really spoken to Shawn about the whole Hannah thing. I've noticed she's been hanging around his group a bit more, and I wonder whether they're back together.

When I turn up at rehearsal, he's there early as always, setting things up.

'Hey.' I wave.

'Hey.' He waves back enthusiastically, dragging Benji's drum kit out of the cupboard.

'Why doesn't Benji ever do that?' I ask curiously.

'He does volunteer reading with the Year 7s after school on Thursday and Fridays.'

'Oh,' I exclaim. Because this isn't the reason I'd been expecting. It's a lovely reason. One that doesn't seem in line with my expectations of Benji at all. But then my expectations seem to be hugely, catastrophically off these days, because Benji, it turns out, *is* lovely. Checking in on Hayley, sitting with her at lunchtimes, bringing her pieces of fruit and making every effort not to watch her while she eats them.

'I know,' he says, smiling. 'He's actually a really good person, he just doesn't want anyone to know.'

'I think he may have given himself away,' I joke.

'So, how are you?' he asks awkwardly.

'Oh, you know . . .' I trail away.

He says nothing.

'I didn't know anything about Ash and Hannah,' I say, deciding not to ignore it any longer.

He looks embarrassed, and maybe a little angry.

'She wants to get back together . . .' he says mechanically. 'She says she made a mistake.'

'Oh,' I say quietly.

And Ezra Koenig and Danielle Haim are singing that we belong together, even if it means we won't stay together.

'What do *you* think I should do?' he says, not looking at me.

'Erm . . .' I reply, not daring to look at him, 'whatever *you* want to do.'

'OK,' he says, carrying on setting up.

'So, what's the plan for tomorrow night?' I ask nervously.

'The playlist we've been practising – and our song,' he says matter-of-factly.

Our song.

'I'll introduce everything, and do all the talking stuff, you just have to sing – and play,' he says, gesturing at the keyboard. 'OK?'

'OK,' I say, feeling very much not OK.

'You'll be fine,' he smiles.

I'll be fine, I repeat to myself over and over.

And all through the rehearsal, I keep on repeating it. I'll be fine. I'll be fine. I'll be fine.

But when? When will I be fine?

79

Into Your Arms

I'm stood onstage with a sweaty top lip. Moustache free, but most definitely sweaty. The rolling-down-my-face, taste-the-salt-on-my-tongue kind of sweaty; the kind of sweaty Mick Jagger would empathise with.

The boys are tuning their guitars purposefully, while Benji laughs at some inane joke Lucas just told him.

Oh God.

Why are they so cool and non-caring, when I'm so None of Those Things. In fact, quite literally The Opposite of All Those Things. Hot and sweaty and very much caring, of this ridiculously large crowd, that has gathered here to witness my downfall. Because surely I Am Going Down.

I haven't felt this nervous in forever. The flared black trousers I'm wearing with white ankle boots are sticking to my legs, and my carefully curated make-up has a Joker-esque quality that was not part of Hope's vision when she helped me choose this outfit.

I thought I'd started to conquer this. Started to understand that I could use it. Those first moments of feeling displaced and strange and questioning myself. Putting that into my voice; feeling the words, instead of just singing them. But right now, it's pure nervous energy. Sickly and sweaty. Like I'm somewhere I'm not supposed to be.

I can see Hannah at the front of the crowd. It should be her up here – not me. All confident swagger and black eyeliner, that attitude, like you're just lucky to be near her.

'You OK, Ellie?' Elliott asks, looking concerned, while I sweat all over my keyboard.

'Heebeeejeeebeee,' I reply.

'Great,' he replies.

What's he replying *great* to? I just made a series of barely decipherable noises?

How have I not noticed how hot Elliott is? And Lucas? Why is everyone in this band hot except me? Me who is just *literally* hot. Literally. SO. HOT.

'Let's go,' Shawn says, turning to the crowd.

He leans into the microphone, playing a riff.

'Hello, everybody!' he shouts. 'We are BE HERE RIGHT NOW!' and he launches into a cover of the Lemonheads, 'Into Your Arms', as I lean down into my microphone, my fingers just about connecting with the keys, my voice backing his in low, sweet harmonies, singing about how it would feel to go into his arms.

He turns to look at me and grins. Walking towards me, playing his guitar as he's stood facing me, so it feels like it's just him and me – and I can't help grinning too. The sweat drying on my top lip.

When the song is over, we do another four; and after that, it starts to feel a bit like a rehearsal. Because Shawn's doing all the hard work. Getting the crowd to notice us, making it all connect. All I have to do is sing, and play, and pretend this doesn't terrify me. And I'm feeling less HOT, more *hot*, which is exactly what I was hoping for. Because tonight is magic.

But then.

'So, everyone. We have a new member of BE HERE RIGHT NOW. Say hello to Ellie.' And they all chant, 'Hello, Ellie!'

'Say hello, Ellie,' he says, waving towards me, like a circus master towards a dancing bear. I wave.

'Ellie and I have something special we'd like to share with you. Something we've been writing together. Would you like to hear it?'

'Yes!' they all chant.

Hannah shoots me a look. A superior, snarky look that says, Good Luck, Loser. And I think: Not This Time.

'Hello, everyone,' I shout suddenly. 'Has anyone here ever had their heart broken?'

Shawn looks at me, while the rest of the band shift uncomfortably. All apart from Benji, who looks like he's enjoying the ride.

'Come on, people,' I insist. 'Who here has been lied to, hurt, had their heart stamped on, been made to feel worthless and stupid – then had to watch as the person that did all that to them . . . just moved on?'

Someone in the front screams, 'ME!' while a group around them titters and cheers.

'Me too,' I say to the person in the front. 'And we can't be alone, can we?'

'NO,' screams someone from the back.

'And what do we do when we get lied to, hurt and stamped on?'

The crowd starts murmuring.

'Do we fall?' I ask them.

'NO,' they shout in unison.

'Do we let them see us cry?'

'NO,' they scream louder.

'Do we write a song about it, and tell them we're better off without them?'

'YES,' they shriek.

'This,' I say, pointing towards Shawn, 'is that song.'

I turn around and nod to Benji to count us all in.

At the end of the song, when I see Ash standing at the bar with Jess and Elina, I look right at him. Then I look over at her and think: Take That, Hannah.

But she's started crying, working her way through the crowd, as far away from us as she can get. Looking small, and shaken, and like maybe she thought that entire rant was directed at just her. I look over at Shawn, who's staring at her retreating back, biting his lip and shaking his head. He pulls the guitar strap over his shoulder in one light movement, and throws the guitar down onstage, jumping off to run after her.

I look over at the rest of the band, who look somewhere between amused and slightly drunk.

Damn. It's hard to take the moral high ground when you've made someone cry in public. Benji looks at me and laughs, as Elliott walks over to the microphone.

'Back in fifteen, people,' he says lightly.

♡ Song 6 ♡

Verse, Chorus, Middle Eight – Tell Me the Truth

It feels angry, and sad, and happy and haunted. Music to break your heart, and music to fix it again.

Not ready for the shallows, not ready for the heights

And I'm part confused, part pure clarity. Because that's what mistakes are: a learning you can hold in your hand, folding them over and over, until everything makes sense.

Don't know if we're ready, just know that tonight
Our mistakes aren't over, any more than they're made

Because you can love someone before you love yourself.
But you shouldn't.

Tell me the truth
If you want me to stay

80

Tequila

The first person I find once I start looking is Shawn.

'I'm sorry,' I say, grabbing his arm. 'I didn't mean it like that. It was more . . . for someone else. It wasn't directed at Hannah.'

He looks irritated.

'Now she thinks I wrote it just to get at her,' he says, annoyed.

'Well, didn't you?' I say, annoyed at his annoyance. Hannah cheated on him. She is not the victim here.

'It's not as simple as that, Ellie.'

'What isn't?' I say, starting to feel myself getting hot again.

'We broke up. For all sorts of reasons. Then she started seeing Ash, and it hurt. But she didn't do anything wrong, not really.' He's pacing now in his yellow high-top Converse, the ones he told me he always wears for gigs.

'How can you say that?' I scoff. But I'm already losing my edge on this one.

'I don't know, Ellie. Did you actually want to be with Ash then? She said you didn't. That they just kind of tried to make things work, but he was all over the place, and so was she.'

'I'm not sure what you're getting at, Shawn,' I say, confused.

'I don't know either,' he says, throwing his hands in the air. 'I just don't want anyone to get hurt.'

But I think it's too late for that.

'Are you OK?' he asks, walking towards me, suddenly gentle.

'It doesn't matter what happened back then,' I mutter. 'It's about what's happening *now*. Ash and Rebecca, and *you* and Hannah. And *me*, I'm just . . .' I trail away.

'You're what?' he says quietly.

'Everyone I like is with someone else,' I say quietly. 'That's me. Sad Ellie and her Sad Collection of Boys Who Don't Want Her.'

'I want you.'

'What?' I say, turning around.

'Am I one of the boys who don't want you?' he says, suddenly red. 'Because I'm just saying, if there's a chance you *want* me to want you, then I do. I do want you.'

'Shawn, I . . .' And I can feel myself reaching up towards him.

'You two!' Elliott hisses, as his head appears around the corner. 'We need to get back onstage. Now!'

'OK!' I shout brightly, turning around quickly. But I'm shouting too loudly. Like I'm guilty of something and I'm trying too hard not to look it.

As I get to the side of the stage, Lucas shoves a glass at me.

'Drink this,' he says, throwing a drink down his own throat.

'What is it?' I ask, sniffing at it.

'Tequila,' he says, shoving it at me again.

'Lucas, I'm not really a drinker . . .' As in, I'm the kind of drinker that will vomit in your mouth. Or Shawn's mouth, because OH GOD, I think I was about to kiss Shawn a minute ago.

'I don't know what's going on with you two tonight,' Lucas says, and I look over at Shawn, who's already drunk the shot Elliott passed him, 'but I like it. The girl behind the bar just sent us free shots. She said something about *getting* your song.'

'Have another one,' Elliott says, grasping at his throat – and now I can see why. Because my throat is burning – like I've just drunk a shot of fire.

'Oh my God,' I rasp, as Benji laughs. 'That's *horrible.*'

'One more for the road,' Lucas says, drinking another. As they're all drinking one more, I guess I'm drinking one more too.

And while this stuff is seriously gross, something about it makes me feel warm, and a little bit invincible.

I don't need Ash Anderson, because maybe I like Shawn. Maybe I'm going to kiss Shawn and show him my Hello Kitty crop top. Or maybe I won't do that. Because Hope and Jessica and Hayley say no one should ever see my Hello Kitty crop top.

But he likes me. And I like him. Or do I like him? I don't know. I mean, he makes me feel weird and comfortable, and writing with him feels easy and freeing and *right.* Plus, he's kind, and sweet, and sexy. And he has hair. On his head. That's long, and I want to put my hands in it and see what it feels like. Maybe I can move on too. Maybe I can have a Rebecca.

'Ellie . . .'

Because Rebeccas aren't just for Ash. Other people are allowed to have Rebeccas. Other people are allowed to move on.

'Ellie . . .' Lucas hisses. 'Sing!'

Benji is sniggering as Shawn just stares at me and Elliott sways from side to side.

So, I open my mouth and sing. And I try not to think about kissing Shawn. Even though suddenly, I really, really want to.

We get through our set pretty much perfectly, and I lose myself in the music. In how good it feels to be up there.

At the end, when Shawn says goodnight and it's time for the DJ to start playing, someone screams at us to sing our song again; and someone else joins in. The whole crowd are chanting it until we give in, stealing glances at each other over Benji's drum kit.

This time round, I sing to him, and he sings to me. I look at him and he looks at me.

And I don't know whether we're singing about a shared experience, or whether we're just singing for each other. Or if it's both. I just know that singing with him makes everything feel OK. And maybe that's love.

Or maybe it's not.

81

I Still Love You

We walk offstage feeling like gods. Or maybe that's just the tequila. My heart racing, my pulse pounding.

I feel exhilarated and simultaneously headachey.

'Need . . . water . . .' I gasp.

Benji throws his arm around me and squeezes.

'I wasn't sure about you when we first met,' he says, wagging his finger at the end of my nose. 'But I can't remember the last time I had that much fun playing a gig. You're out of control.'

'Out of control?' I say worriedly.

'It's a good thing,' he enthuses. 'That "break-up" speech was hilarious, and then when you forgot to sing for, like, twelve bars . . .' He laughs. 'Let me buy you a drink.'

'NO,' I say, putting my hands up. 'No more drinks for me. Look – did you see where Shawn went?' I ask, looking around.

He looks at me, suddenly suspicious.

'Shawn and Hannah aren't exactly over, Ellie. They're the kind of couple that will never be *over*, if you know what I mean.'

I go as red as it's possible for a brown person to go, and start mumbling.

'And he's definitely not someone you should be using to get over somebody else,' he says sternly.

'Heebeejeebee,' I mutter.

'I'll get you a glass of water,' he says, suddenly kind.

'Benji,' I say, grabbing his arm. 'Thank you, you know, for keeping an eye on Hayley.'

He shrugs.

'The day she fainted,' I ask, 'you said she didn't eat much. You knew, didn't you? You knew she had a problem with food.'

'I guessed,' he says bluntly.

'I don't know how I didn't notice,' I chastise myself. 'I'm such an *idiot.*'

'Takes one to know one,' he says quietly.

'One idiot to know another?' I smile.

'No,' he says, looking me in the eye. 'One person with an eating disorder to know another.'

And finally these heeled boots have come in handy, as I turn to hug him tight, lacing my arms around his neck.

'If you ever . . .' I whisper in his ear.

'I'm good,' he says, putting me down. 'Let me get you that water.'

When he returns, I drink the pint of water in one sitting, and turn back to him.

'I'd better go,' I smile. The tequila's starting to wear off, and I feel cold and confused. 'If you ever need to talk, Benji . . . then you know where I am. I promise I won't tell anyone how secretly nice you are.'

He grins.

He hugs me goodbye, and for the first time ever, I feel like Benji and I might actually be friends. I trail towards the exit, Mum's now appropriated leather jacket over my shoulders, and try to work out whether to try to find Jess. She'll be with Elina, which means she'll probably be with Ash too.

'Are you going?' And suddenly Shawn is stood next to me, holding my hand as I look down at it.

'Hi,' I say, looking back up at him, my hand still in his.

'About what I said earlier . . .' he says, his thumb stroking my knuckles.

'About that . . .' I say awkwardly.

'I like you. I'm not asking for anything to happen right now, I just want you to know that I like you. So, if you wanted to go for a drive, or a walk, or write some music together sometime, that'd be nice,' he says, looking down at my hand again.

But before I can say anything in return, I hear him.

'And I'm the one that's moved on?' he says drunkenly.

I let go of Shawn's hand, and turn to face him.

'You've been drinking,' I state.

'Haven't you?' he asks, swaying slightly. Elina's just behind him, as is Jess, making eyes at me, telling me she's here if I need her.

'I guess I just know when to stop,' I say, turning towards the exit.

'I never wanted to hurt you.' He trips over the words as I reel back around to face him.

'I am so *sick* of people saying that to me.'

'I'm sorry,' he says, head in his hands.

'You always need a back-up plan, Ash,' I say, staring at him. 'First Hannah, then Rebecca, well, I don't want to be with someone who needs a back-up plan, I want to be with someone who wants me. Who really wants me. Who isn't always half in, half out, working out what their other options are.'

'It's not like that,' he says desperately. 'Hannah was sad,' he slurs, 'and I was sad, and it just happened. Then I was too much of a coward to tell her I didn't want it any more. That I never really wanted it.'

'And Rebecca?' I challenge.

'She's my best friend,' he says, looking away.

I turn back around. I can't hear about Rebecca and their incomparable friend-love that no one else in the world is special enough to understand. Not today. Not now.

'She was the one that was there for me,' he says quietly, his voice shaking. 'When your dad said I tried to kill you. When he said it was my fault. That he lost his son, and I almost took you away from him too. That he couldn't look at me. That my dad would be ashamed of me.'

Elina steps forward and puts her hand on his shoulder as I stare at him, no words to offer.

'I just wish I'd told you I love you,' he says, watching me. 'When you were away at Christmas. I didn't know it, but I did. I still do, Ellie.'

'But *you* broke up with *me*.' And suddenly, I'm crying.

'I wasn't trying to break up with you,' he begs. 'I was trying to say I was sorry. I was trying to explain why I didn't . . . why I didn't stay with you at the hospital . . . How I think about it every day. How I hate myself for what I did. For what I didn't do.'

I'm looking down at my feet. Trying to make sense of his words. *I didn't break up with you. I wish I'd told you I love you. I still do.* I can see Shawn hovering next to me, his face expressionless. Jess, looking pained, as she stares at me over Elina's shoulder.

'But it doesn't matter now, does it?' he asks gently. I can see how drunk he is. His eyes glassy, his voice blurred, staring at Shawn.

'I'm sorry,' he slurs. 'I'm sorry for everything, Ellie.'

'Well, sorry isn't good enough!' I scream suddenly. 'You can't do this to me, Ash. One minute I'm happy, one minute I'm not. One minute you want me, the next minute you don't. I'm trying to move on, and you're here, trying to stop me, and I can't, and it's not . . . it's not fair.'

'It's all my fault,' he says flatly.

'No!' I shout. 'Stop feeling sorry for yourself. This isn't you. This,' I say, gesticulating wildly, 'is not *you*. Drinking and not showing up for school, and not even *trying*, and worrying your mother. That's the person your dad would be ashamed of – but it's not *you*. Not if you don't want it to be. And you can blame all that on *us*, or me, but it's on you, Ash Anderson. Who you're being right now, that's on you.'

I turn away from him, bored by this conversation. Bored by his flat, drunk, feeling-sorry-for-himself voice. I turn away from all of them. Because this was the night of tequila, and Benji hugging me, and singing a song I co-wrote, twice, onstage, to an audience that really wanted to hear it. This isn't a night about Ash. Or Shawn. This is a night about something so much more than that.

But even as I'm pushing my way out of the exit, and running, running with all my might towards home, I can feel the anger pulsing in my veins. Anger about everything. Ash and his *I still love you*, and Dad and his *Your father would be ashamed of you.*

And the more I think about Dad, the angrier I feel. His weird behaviour over the past few months. His paranoia and overprotectiveness. His inability to say anything positive about anything.

How could he talk to Ash like that? How could he throw his father in his face, after everything he's been through? He doesn't know anything about Ash. He wanted us to break up. He wanted this to happen.

And I'm thinking of every little thing I'm going to say to him when I get home. Every truth I'm going to force him to hear. I'm thinking about the silence I'm going to give him, for as long as it takes for him to understand that he can no longer control me.

I'm thinking it even as I round the corner and see the flashing lights outside our house. Even as I hear the ambulance cry out as it screeches its way up the street. Even when I see Granny, stood fragile and delicate and shrivelled in her dressing gown, clasping on to Mum, crying.

I'm thinking it even as Mum's turning to me and screaming that we need to get in the car and follow the ambulance. Because it's Dad. Dad's had a heart attack.

And it's only then that I stop thinking at all.

When Your Heart Breaks

It's been twelve hours now, and he's unresponsive. It was a big heart attack. One that should have killed him, but he isn't. Dead, I mean. Just not there. Silent.

All I can see is his chest, rising and falling under the covers, a tube down his throat, a mask covering his face, medical equipment bleeping and dripping, emitting tiny sounds I can't bear to try and understand.

Mum said he'd been quiet. Thoughtful. That he'd seemed tired; but he'd been tired a lot lately, he hadn't been himself. He crumpled over just before bed, his face creased in agony as he clutched at his chest.

Mum's so huge now, she's finding it hard to fit in the hospital chairs. I can see the baby kicking and pushing, her stomach dancing under the lights. All I can think is how it's her and me and him now. The three of us. In this together.

Granny's gone home. The Pillais arrived there a few hours ago. They're setting up camp at the house. Cooking and cleaning and praying and lighting candles. I haven't been home yet, but they came to the hospital first. Crowding around the glass outside Dad's room in intensive care, making signs of the cross and muttering Hail Marys.

Hope just hugged me, trying not to let me see her cry. We're all scared. We're all so scared.

I want to go in and see him. I want to kneel by his bed and tell him I love him. I want to ask him not to follow Richey, even though the Manics were at their best when his lyrics gave them such heart. I want to ask him to come back to us. To please, please come back to us.

'Ellie?' Mum's shaking me. 'Ellie? Are you OK?' I'm crying silently, the tears falling down my face like so many tiny, shiny jewels.

I'm talking to my brother now. My beautiful little brother, who went away too soon. Please, Amis, please send Dad back. Because there's another little boy coming. Another little brother. And he needs his dad.

'I'm fine,' I say, trying to stop the choking sensation in my chest. 'Are you OK, Mum?' I lean over, reaching out for her hand. I have to be strong. I need to be strong.

'Ellie, Dad wasn't telling us something,' Mum sniffs. 'The doctor said he's known about his heart for months now. He's been trying to make himself better without worrying us,' she says slowly. 'All those stupid bike rides and green smoothies and . . .' she's crying now as I lean in to hold her, 'I knew something was wrong. But I was so worried about the baby, about this pregnancy. I've been so caught up in my own problems . . . I didn't see it. And now we might lose him, Ellie. He might already be gone.' The sniffles are turning into full-blown tears, giant wet patches running down her face like a waterfall.

I have to be strong. I have to protect my family. I have to be the glue, like Dad was the glue, when I was falling apart and Mum was falling apart when Amis died. Because this new baby needs us, it needs *me*. And I promise you, baby, whatever happens, I will always be your glue.

'No, Mum,' I say, squeezing her hand. 'He isn't gone. We're going to get through this. Because if this heart attack doesn't kill Dad, then I swear I will, for not telling us all this sooner.' She laughs, the sound of it soothing and rich and thick, like glue.

And twenty minutes later they wheel Dad in for triple bypass surgery. Because when your heart breaks, you have to try and fix it.

83

A Girl Called Ellie

My name is Ellie. Ellie Pillai. And I'll do anything. Anything, gods. If you'll just grant me this one favour.

It isn't a small favour. It's a big one. But I'll do whatever it takes. No boyfriends. A monobrow. I'll babysit twice a week and teach him how to make Lego. I won't roll my eyes when Dad asks me if That's What I'm Wearing Out – when it's clearly What I'm Wearing Out. I'll let Granny braid my hair however she wants, even if it makes me look like a middle-aged Sri Lankan housewife (no offence, middle-aged Sri Lankan housewives, but I'm sixteen). I'll tell Mum I ripped her leather jacket and sometimes, when she's asleep, that I come in and lie next to her, just to know she's near.

Just, please. Please don't let my dad die.

Please, gods.

84

Pill-ay

'Mrs Pilau?' the surgeon asks, holding up a clipboard, flipping pages and looking younger than Dad would probably approve of.

'It's Pill-ay,' Mum corrects her, because our surname is not a type of – admittedly delicious – rice.

'Mrs Pill-ay,' she says, rubbing her nose.

'That's us,' I say, standing hurriedly. I feel like I should be standing. I feel like whenever you hear *news*, you should be standing.

'Your husband's out of surgery and back in his room. Everything went well, and he's currently stable – but we'll know more when he wakes up.'

'So, he's going to wake up?' I say tearfully.

'We'll know more soon,' she says kindly.

'Can we see him?' I plead.

'You can go in and sit with him.' She smiles.

I nod.

'You say it was successful,' Mum asks. 'What does that mean, exactly?'

'It means the grafts were all placed, and we've done everything we can to alleviate any chest pain he may have been experiencing – basically,' she explains kindly, 'we've bypassed the blockages. What we need now is for him to wake up and remain in a stable condition.'

Mum nods as I try to pull her out of her chair.

'The next few days are critical, but the surgery went well. Just try to make sure you get some rest yourself,' she says, motioning towards Mum's baby bump.

'I'm fine,' she says firmly. But I know she isn't fine. We haven't left the hospital in nearly thirty-six hours, and I can't seem to get her to eat.

When the doctor leaves, I turn to her.

'I'll sit with him, Mum. Go home and get some rest. Big Uncle took the car, but I can ask him to pick you up.'

'I won't leave him,' she says stubbornly.

'You need to think about the baby,' I say just as stubbornly. Because once she's home, there is no way the Aunties are going to let her escape without eating.

'Ellie, I can't . . .' she says, wiping her eyes. 'What if something happens and I'm not here?'

'I won't leave him, Mum, I promise. It's just for a couple of hours. Go home and get some sleep. Please.' She sighs.

'My big girl,' she says, leaning forward and tucking my hair behind my ears.

'Should I call Big Uncle?' I ask, looking down at my phone.

London Cousin – Annoying:

any news?? 😔 having 🐀

London Cousin – Annoying:

r u OK??

'I'll do it,' she says, looking down at her feet.

'Better speak to Granny too.'

'I will. I need to stretch my legs. Do you want a cup of tea, *en anbe*?'

'I'm fine,' I smile, as she hoists herself out of the chair and down the hall.

As she heads off, I read the other messages on my phone.

Jess:

is he out of surgery yet?

Hayley:

can i do anything? bring anything? how ru?

James:

u know where i am if u need anything

I reply to Hope first.

Ellie:

surgery went well, mum home soon.

pls make sure she eats

Then Jess.

Ellie:

he's out of surgery. in stable condition,
but hasn't woken yet

Then Hayley.

Ellie:

i'm OK. ty 4 thinking of me

And James:

Ellie:

tx 4 getting in touch x

'I brought you some tea anyway,' Mum says, appearing next to me, sipping from a polystyrene cup. 'It's green.'

'Thanks,' I smile, taking it from her. 'When's Uncle getting here?'

'I'm getting a lift now.'

'That was quick,' I reply. Then I remember, once I was sat in a car with Big Uncle that took twenty minutes to get from one end of London to the other, which I'm told should be impossible. He's freakishly fast, in a slightly dangerous way.

'Maybe you should get an Uber?' I ask, suddenly concerned.

'I'll be fine – and I'll be back in a couple of hours. Do you have money for the vending machine and the canteen?'

I nod.

When she's gone, I walk back up to Dad's room on the ICU ward. He seems so small beneath the sheets, so fragile.

I remember how angry I was with him, how furious, but I never knew what he was going through. Never knew he was in pain; carrying this secret, day after day. It makes sense of everything. How short-tempered he's been. How quiet and far away from all of us, even Mum, who he worships. The fear for the baby, for being young enough and fit enough to be a dad again.

Why didn't he tell us? Why did he have to hide it? It makes me angry again, because it's a lie. The thing he called me out on, when they finally found out I was taking drama last year. He said lies didn't solve anything. He said lies were wrong. But now he's lying here, in this hospital bed – because of a lie. And they say adults *know* stuff. That adults don't make mistakes. But we all make mistakes, everyone.

Like me. Me and my stupid me-ness over the last few months. Obsessing over Ash and Shawn, not being able to see beyond being a girlfriend, or being part of a band. And there's parts of me I'm proud of, like singing, and trying stuff even when it scares me; writing songs, and conquering fears. But there's part of me that knows that being in the band was always about more than that. It was always a bit about Shawn.

People are going through things. Real things. Jess with her mum, Hayley with her eating and not eating, and trying to be in control of things she'll never be in control of. Mum with the baby, Dad with his heart. Ash with his dad, and all the stuff he's clearly still struggling with, Granny with Aunty Kitty, and Aunty Kitty with Granny. And my stuff is real too – but it's not all-encompassing, it's not everything. I want to pull back from it all. See the bigger picture and not just the minor details.

I turn to Dad and whisper to him, not knowing if he can even hear me.

'This baby needs you, Dad. We all do. So you have to wake up. Granny's going to kill you if you don't.' I can feel my eyes filling with tears, but I force myself to hold them in. I have to be strong. I have to believe he's going to be OK.

'I'm sorry,' he rasps.

I look down at him, wondering if it's just my imagination, wondering if a sixties girl group are going to appear while my dad dances around the hospital in a backless green gown.

I can feel his hand clasping mine lightly, his eyes blinking against the light.

I collapse on my knees, my head against his hand, and I let myself cry. For all the fears and worries I've been harbouring. For all the minutes when I thought he might never wake up.

'I love you,' I whisper.

'I love you too,' he croaks.

'I'm sorry,' I cry.

'I'm sorry too,' he says softly.

And the world stops for a minute as I watch his chest rise and fall with every breath. Life is fragile, but it's also robust and resilient and adaptable.

He's going to be OK.

We all are.

85

You Can't All Be in Here

'You can't all be in here!' the nurse cries, exasperated.

The next day, the Pillais come to visit. Technically, they're not supposed to be on the ICU ward, but when it comes to family, this family consider technicalities irrelevant.

'He's my big brother,' Little Uncle says, turning to the nurse conspiratorially. 'He practically raised me. I was a bit of a tearaway back in the day.' Granny *chkkk*s dramatically, rolling her eyes skywards.

'Oh,' the nurse says, smiling at him indulgently. Little Uncle has dimples, and one of those Bollywood-white smiles. I can see where Hope gets her behaviour from. 'I suppose it won't hurt if it's not for *too* long,' she says, winking at him. 'He needs his rest.'

'With you looking after him, I'm sure he'll be on his feet in no time.' Hope turns to me, miming a sick face, while Aunty Christine, his wife, just shakes her head.

The nurse waves her hand at him, and blushes. Which is seriously gross. Old people shouldn't be allowed to blush. It feels like she's thinking something *inappropriate*. Ugh.

Dad's lying on the bed quietly, his eyes open, but barely speaking, while Granny keeps rearranging his pillows. Which looks stressful. For him.

I walk over to him and try to insert myself between them, while he looks at me gratefully.

'What are these people feeding you?' Granny moans.

'He's not hungry, Granny,' I say firmly, as she starts unbuttoning her handbag and rooting around for something to stuff in his mouth.

'I know what is best,' she says irritably.

'The doctors know what's best, Granny,' I say heatedly.

She looks at me, her tiny eyes screwed up in her face – and I can't tell whether she's going to punch me, or cry. It could go either way.

Mum grabs my arm, quick to defuse the situation.

'Ellie, let's get a cup of tea. Anyone? Tea?' She's adopted a Mary Poppins voice, like she's about to burst into song and reappear with a teapot carried by animated birds. 'Wonderful,' she replies to the silent room.

She frogmarches me out of the room, my arm in a vice-like grip, less Poppins, more Maleficent.

'Mum!' I hiss. 'That hurts.'

'Ellie, he's your grandmother's *son*,' she says firmly.

'I know that!' I say, rubbing my arm.

'No. I don't think you do. Losing a child is, it's . . .' She trails away, her eyes blurry. 'It's unnatural. She needs to be able to mother him, Ellie. She needs to feel she can help.'

'But she isn't helping,' I say, annoyed. 'She's making him uncomfortable, and he doesn't want to eat.'

Mum sighs, and stops, turning towards me in the corridor.

'Ellie. Do you know how your grandfather died?'

'A heart attack . . .' I say slowly.

'Do you know how old he was?'

'No,' I admit quietly.

'He was fifty, Ellie. Pretty much the same age as your dad. Be kind, Ellie. Just think about that.'

'OK,' I sigh. I hate it when parents are right.

'Everything OK?' Hope asks, stepping out into the hall.

'Fiiiinnne,' I say through gritted teeth.

'Hope, why don't you go with Ellie to the canteen?' Mum suggests.

'Come on,' Hope says, grabbing my arm. 'I'll take it from here,' she says to Mum officiously.

Mum grins and rubs her arm.

'Are you really OK?' she asks surreptitiously, as we head off down the hall.

'I just,' and my voice is starting to crack now, 'I *need* him to be OK, Hope. I can't lose him. We can't lose anyone else.'

She turns and hugs me violently – and it's just what I need. She's just what I need.

'Everything's such a mess,' I sniffle.

And I tell her about Ash and Shawn, and being angry with Dad and not noticing how sick Hayley was, or how much Jess was struggling without her mum. About how I should have known Vikash was bad news and how we should never have stopped being so close. How all of it's my fault, and I'm so scared about the baby being OK, because I don't know how we'll cope if he's not OK, and how much I miss Amis. Because being in hospital makes me think of him, and it makes me feel sick, because Amis never came out – and Dad has to come out. He has to be OK. Because Mum, and the baby, and me, we need him. And how sad and tired I feel, and how everything feels like it's too much, and I wish I could make it all stop. I wish I could make everything better.

And she just listens while I sip at a cup of tea in the canteen and says, 'You're sixteen. You're allowed to make mistakes – and you can't blame yourself for everything, because it's not all your fault. You can't fix everything, Ellie, as much as you might want to; people have to fix themselves.' And I think: thank you, gods, for giving me this person. And then she says, 'Charles?'

Charles?

I turn around and there he is. Someone good-looking, but far too old for me to be having those thoughts about.

'Hello,' he replies.

'Where's Aunty Kitty?' Hope asks brightly.

'In the bathroom.' He has a slight American drawl, even though the heart of his voice is British and still a little clipped. 'We just arrived from the airport.'

He looks nervous, and a little angry. Ready for a fight. To defend Aunty Kitty against Granny, or me, or Hope, or anyone that might hurt her. I love him for it a little bit. I love the way he so obviously and definitively loves her, with no room for interpretation.

'How's your dad?' he asks gently.

'He's awake,' I smile. 'The bypass went well, and so far, he's stable.'

'I'm glad,' he says kindly. 'We were getting on the flight when he went into surgery. How are you?'

'I'm happy Aunty Kitty's here,' I say brightly.

'She'll be happy to see you too.'

That's when we hear her.

'Ellie! Hope!' she says, descending on us. She pulls us both into her arms, and it's like the icy Aunty Kitty, the one I grew up with, is suddenly gone. Replaced by this soft, sweet, beautiful woman who seems anxious but content. Happy.

'How's your father?' she says worriedly, tucking her hair behind her ears.

'He's OK,' I smile. And she beams, because that one tiny word, 'OK', can mean so much when you fear the worst.

'Is *Amma* here?' she asks, staring at the floor. 'I'll wait here until she's gone. You'll come and get me, won't you?' she says, squeezing my hand.

'No,' I reply bluntly – and I look to Hope for confirmation as she nods. 'You're not waiting in the canteen. Come on,' I say, taking her by the arm, with Hope on the other side.

'I don't want to upset Noel,' she says quickly.

'Dad wants to see you.'   .

'I mean, if *Amma* gets angry. I don't want him to get stressed. His heart . . .' She trails away.

'He'll be fine,' Hope says, grimacing.

When we reach the ICU ward, Charles lags behind us.

'Maybe I should wait here?' he says, catching at Kitty's shoulder. 'After all, I'm the problem.' He gives her a weak smile.

'You're coming,' Hope says, bulldozing the two of them through the double doors.

'She's right,' Kitty says, steely. 'I should have done this years ago.'

As we get to Dad's door, I step forward into the room.

'I brought you something from the canteen,' I announce to the room.

And before I can congratulate myself on my rather pleasing turn of phrase, Aunty Kitty rushes in and throws herself at Dad, crying.

'*Thangacci*,' Dad says, laughing quietly and stroking her hair. 'I'm OK, I'm OK.'

'*Annan*,' she repeats over and over.

'He doesn't look *that* bad . . .' I joke. 'I mean, he *smells* that bad . . .' and I can hear her laughing into his shoulder.

'Ellieeee,' Dad rasps, annoyed.

'Hygiene isn't our top priority right now, but you do have a particularly . . . *pungent* aroma . . .'

I can hear Granny *chhk*ing in the background, while the rest of the family laugh.

'Charles,' Granny says suddenly. 'Why you there?'

'Um, I . . .' he stutters, as he and Aunty Kitty glance at each other.

'It is family only,' she says sternly.

'OK, I . . .' He points a thumb over his shoulder, as if to say he's leaving. Aunty Kitty stands up straight.

'No,' Granny says. 'You come *in*. It is family in here. You are family.'

And the whole room's holding its breath.

'Kitty, we must talk about wedding sari. Best places are in London. New York places are chkkk.'

Aunty Kitty steps towards her, and Granny looks old. Old and small and tired.

'Yes, *Amma*,' she smiles.

'Charles, come.'

He steps towards her nervously. Like he's worried it might be a trick. Like we're all worried it might be a trick. That he's going to lean down into her, and she's going to poke his eyes out with her bony little fingers.

Instead she pinches his cheek. Hard.

'You are a Sri Lankan now,' she says to him. 'Must learn to stand straight. No good this posture. When you are tall, be tall. Stand *up*. But you are a good boy. You will be OK.'

And that's how Charles became Uncle Charles. Or Uncle Charlie, as Hope calls him, and which he clearly hates. Later that night, Hope and I decide it must have been Dad's heart attack that softened Granny. That made her realise she could never have willingly lost one of her children. That what makes us different is what makes us the same. It's also how Hope and I get asked to be bridesmaids for Aunty Kitty and Uncle Charlie's wedding, and how even though my dad's in hospital recovering from triple bypass surgery, all I can think about is having to wear a sari, and what I'll look like standing next to Hope, when I inevitably do.

Ugh.

But for the moment. This has been the worst/best week of my life. Silver linings do exist, and I'm living inside one.

86

Three Tiny Marbles

As Dad starts to improve and moves out of ICU and on to a normal ward, the Pillais, who up to this point have taken over our entire house with a bustle of noise and cooking and praying that has seriously unsettled our neighbours, leave so suddenly, it feels like the work of paranormal forces. Granny and Mum and me are left rattling around the house, like three tiny, nervous marbles commuting back and forth between the hospital and home.

We miss Hope the most. Even though she's blocked the bath with her hair and used most of Mum's favourite shampoo, having her around made us all feel better. Even if it includes making us all watch *Stranger Things*, which literally terrifies Granny. Turns out my cousin has a knack for taking care of people.

But after a week off school, on Sunday night, Mum tells me she thinks it's time for me to go back. Thanks to The Overreaction, and Dad's Heart Incident, I've missed two weeks this term, and she's nervous I'm Not Prepared for Exams.

She's drafted Jess in to keep me up to date on schoolwork, and as a result I have better notes than I could have hoped for. Given the whole Ash and Shawn thing, I was hoping I could stay home until exams start, take them, and wait until they both leave for university – ideally so I never have to see them again or deal with how I'm feeling. But according to Mum, this is Not a Good Plan. I still have almost a term before I get to exams, and all being well, Dad's going to be home soon.

'Pack your bag, Ellie. You can come and see Dad after school tomorrow.'

'Mum, I really think another week . . .' I trail off, looking at her and Granny's faces. They seem to have joined forces since Dad's heart attack, creating a terrifyingly powerful Asian Super Force. Gods help Dad when he has no nurses and doctors between him and them.

'Must go to school, Eleanor,' Granny says. 'Is important time. You want your father to have heart attack again, when get results?'

And Granny goes straight for the jugular; anything I do that any of them disagree with is going to result in this level of emotional blackmail.

Mum rolls her eyes, momentarily breaking ranks with the Asian Super Force.

'Your father's heart will be fine however you do in your exams. But it's Your Future, Ellie. Your Opportunities You'll Be Wasting. Think of All the People Who Worked to Get You Here. Who Sacrificed to Give You This Chance, These Freedoms. Trust Me. You'll Thank Me for This One Day.'

I sigh. She's right. Dad's doing well. I don't need to be at the hospital every day any more, but school means facing things.

'Fiiiinnne . . .' I reply through gritted teeth.

I walk up the stairs to my room and flop on to the bed, trying not to think about double drama in the morning. About seeing Mrs Aachara and having to pretend it isn't weird that she's my ex-boyfriend's mum.

Ellie:
back to school 2m

Jess:

Hayley:
it's still a patriarchal hellhole of despair

Ellie:
not helping

Hayley:
sorry

Jess:
can't wait 2 c u

Hayley:
missed u

Ellie:

Ellie:

worried about seeing ash & shawn

Jess:

will be OK

Hayley:

just focus on u

Ellie:

k. see u at the patriarchal hellhole.

Focus on you, Pillai. Focus. On. You.

87

Back to School

There's this bit in *Grease 2*, which is quite possibly one of the worst films of all time, while simultaneously being one of the best, where the entire student body starts singing a song about going back to school. All buoyant and American with their letterman jackets and quiffed hair and motorbikes. Excited about school. Never in my life have I so wanted my brain to find a way to incorporate a song into my everyday existence. To feel some semblance of joy at the thought of returning to the Patriarchal Hellhole of Despair. But all I can hear the entire bus ride to school is Kevin Whatley describing his penis to Jeffrey Dean, which really doesn't fit with the whole clean living, musical aesthetic of it all.

I plug my earphones in and try to play something to alleviate my nerves. I've put black eyeliner on today and a red lip gloss, as if I'm a suffragette, preparing for battle.

When I see Jess and Hayley out of the window, I wave unenthusiastically.

'How's your dad?' Jess asks, squeezing my shoulders as I step out on to the pavement.

'Better,' I smile. 'He should be home soon.'

'That's great,' Hayley says, enthused. 'You must be sick of that hospital by now.'

'You can say that again,' I say wearily.

'So, I'll take this morning,' Hayley says, turning to Jess officiously, 'and you can take lunchtime. What are you doing after school, Ellie?'

'Are you two discussing who's babysitting me?'

'After school, Ellie,' Jess says impatiently. 'What are you doing? Back to the hospital? Who's taking you?'

'Um, I'll just get the bus.'

'I can go with her,' Jess says, turning to Hayley. 'I'll get a lift home from there.'

They nod at each other, like two parents discussing shared childcare.

'I'm fine on my own,' I state.

They both look at me.

'Fiiiinnnne,' I admit. 'Some company would be *nice*.'

'See you at lunch, Ellie,' Jess says, turning on her heel. Then she turns back and throws herself at me. 'It's good to have you back. I know it's been a horrible term so far, but remember . . .'

'This is our year . . .' I mimic.

'Exactly,' she says, giving me another squeeze.

And I want to believe her, I really do. But it's starting to feel like this year has something against me. Like I've done something horrible to it, and it's trying to punish me.

'So, at my thing,' Hayley, says linking arms with me.

'Your thing?' I query.

'My . . . support group thing,' she says quietly. 'They have this saying.'

'OK,' I say, stealing a look at her, because I'm just so happy she's talking about it; that she's allowing herself to be supported.

'They say, *new beginnings are often disguised as painful endings*, which means, you know, sometimes the hard stuff is the beginning of the best stuff.'

Something about the way she says it makes me turn towards her and hug her so tight. Like she's read my mind, or I can read hers.

'People are staring . . .' she says, deadpan.

'Sorry.'

'Come on, let's go pretend Mr Gorley is normal.'

She pulls me along to form room, and true to her word, doesn't leave my side until lunchtime – when Jess picks up where she left off. And after school, they're both waiting for me, right by the school reception, practically picking me up on either side as they walk me to the bus stop that'll take me to the hospital. Which would all be fine, apart from the fact Shawn stops to offer me a lift, to which I respond heebeejeebeee, which apparently means: yes, thank you.

Note to self: learn to say no. Coherently.

88

Heebeejeebee

'So, how have you been?'

We go together like . . . and Ezra Koenig is singing about bowls and plates again.

'Heebeejeebee.'

'I'm so sorry about your dad. I can't imagine how stressed you must be with exams and everything.'

Days and dates.

'And your mum's pregnant, right?'

Pots and pans.

'But I'm really glad we ran into each other.'

Bottles and cans.

'You know I like you, and I know you've got bigger stuff going on, and I know you and Ash have . . . stuff too. I just, I wanted to say, nothing's changed for me, and I'll wait until you're ready to talk about it – but I don't want this to affect you being in the band, or us writing together. I don't want it to be awkward. Or for you to feel pressured. Just, I'm here. As a friend. But I do want to be more.'

Surf and sand.

'Ellie, are you going to do something other than nod your head and make that weird noise?'

'Heebeejeebee, sorry.'

And I have to stop thinking about things that go together. Because sand doesn't *need* surf. It's nice to have, but not *necessary*.

'But you want some time to think about it?' he offers.

I nod. Because I still like surf. Or at least the idea of it.

'OK, I'll take that,' he says, looking pleased. 'It's not a no.' He turns and grins at me, and for a second, wraps his hand around mine – and I wonder what it would feel like to have it there all the time. How I'd feel knowing I could hold it, any time I wanted to.

'We're here,' he says, pulling into the hospital car park. 'Do you want me to come in with you?'

'No,' I smile. 'I'm fine.' I lean over and kiss him on the cheek – but on further examination, like most faces, his cheek is quite close to his lips. In fact, all I have to do is turn my head a little, and my lips could be right on top of his lips.

And suddenly, they are; his hands in my hair, his fringe caressing my cheek. It feels gentle, and sweet, and a little bit searching, and exactly what I thought it would be, except maybe a little bit better.

'Um,' I say, breaking away from him suddenly. 'I have to go.' Because all I can think about is Dad, waiting for me while I kiss guitar-playing boys with long hair and long legs and Nirvana T-shirts, which is something the old Ellie, the pre-Heart Incident Ellie, would get caught up in, when she should be thinking about other things.

Focus. On. You.

He puts his hand on my cheek, brushing his thumb along my jawline.

OK. Focus on something other than wanting to kiss him again.

But ugh. I'm kissing him again, and it's even better than the first time.

Just as suddenly, I stop.

'I have to go,' I say robotically, withdrawing myself from the car hastily and bashing my head on the door frame.

'Owww!' I exclaim.

Good work.

Slick. Sexy. A smooth getaway leaving him wanting more. Well done.

He grins.

'See you later.'

I wave and move towards the doors, my head somewhere else, until I walk straight into someone's chest.

I look up at them apologetically, still touching my lips from where seconds ago, they were touching Shawn's.

Salt and pepper.

'Heebeejeebee,' I say.

'Hey, Ellie,' Ash says.

89

Does He Love Me, I Want to Know

Damn Ash Anderson and his sixties girl group. Wherever he goes, his stupid girl group follow. Covered in gold spandex, and permanently waving their arms. Why does he make my heart actually *skip*? Like he wants me to land back in the hospital. An overreaction to his stupid wonky smile and green eyes.

I want to hate him. For being an idiot that lied to me about dating Hannah and having a weird inappropriate relationship with his Best Friend/Ex-Girlfriend/Girl with Kaleidoscope Eyes. Or the fact that he's started drinking again when he knows he shouldn't. Worrying his mother and his sister and my best friend half to death because he can't control himself, or he doesn't care enough to even try.

But then, it's the way he listens to Blur, like every word means something to him. Or the fact we argue about whether *Sgt. Pepper* is better than *Pet Sounds*, but he always agrees in the end, because there's not really any contest. The way he paints stuff, like it's his soul he's putting on paper. The way he cares about things so deeply and honestly. The way he cared about me.

'What are you doing here?' I say more harshly than I intended.

'Dropping something off for a friend,' he says uncomfortably.

So, he can *drop something off for a friend* at the hospital, but he can't be bothered to visit his own girlfriend when she's gone into cardiac arrest. Just. Saying.

'Right,' I say, uptight.

'I was hoping I'd run into you . . .' he says, looking at me.

Damn those green eyes and that blue jumper and STOP SINGING I shout internally at the girl group, who've suddenly launched into Betty Everett's 'The Shoop Shoop Song (It's in His Kiss)'.

I *don't* want to know if he loves me. I Do Not Want to Know.

OK.

I do.

Damn. It.

'Really. Why?' I say, trying to feign disapproval, when all I can think about is how I just kissed Shawn, and even though Ash and I aren't together, I feel like I've cheated on him.

'I wanted to say sorry.'

'For what?' I say bluntly.

Or rather: which bit? Not telling me about Hannah last year, or not telling me about Rebecca, or blanking me after the accident. The possibilities are endless.

'Everything,' he says, looking down at his feet. 'But especially that night at Cinema when I was drunk. You were right. I was being an idiot.'

'Oh,' I exclaim. Because I hadn't really expected him to admit it.

'What you said to me . . .'

'I may have been a bit harsh,' I say guiltily.

'No, I needed to hear it.'

'Look,' I say, suddenly ashamed. 'About what my dad said to you . . .'

'It's fine,' he says, cutting me off.

'It isn't. I'm sorry he hurt you, Ash. Your dad would be so proud of you, you know that. The accident wasn't your fault, I know that, and so do my parents. He was just upset, that's all. People say stupid things when they're upset.'

'It's OK,' he says again. 'Ellie, I . . .' he says, taking hold of my hand. 'I meant what I said that night. I'm sorry I messed things up between us.'

'It wasn't *all* your fault,' I admit awkwardly. 'I wasn't exactly honest with you either.' Because I have to admit that. I have to know that by now.

He looks at my hand.

'I just want you to be happy.'

'Oh.' And for some reason I want him to tell me he loves me. That he wants me back and he can't live without me. But he doesn't, because maybe he doesn't.

'How's your dad? How's your mum and your granny and everything?'

'We're OK,' I say quietly. .

He gives me that wonky smile.

'Am I allowed to hug you?'

I try to say no, but apparently I'm no longer capable of that. His jumper feels soft against my cheek, his arms like a duvet. And it feels too easy. Too comfortable. Too dangerous.

He lets go of me suddenly, and I reel backwards a bit.

'How's . . . Rebecca?' I ask clumsily.

'She's back at uni. Doing better.'

'That's great. I'm glad you guys are . . .'

'I'd better go,' he says, throwing his thumb up behind him.

'OK. See you then.'

'See you,' he smiles.

And Ash Anderson walks away. Which is fine. Because I'm fine – and really, I always was.

90

WEDDING

Over the next few weeks, things at school settle down. With exams coming up, and Dad improving so much he's coming home next week, it starts to feel something akin to normal. I hang out with Jess and Hayley and Elina, and sometimes I just sit with James and listen to music, or Benji sits with me and throws bits of paper at me, in what can only be described as an affectionate, if slightly annoying, manner. I rehearse with the band, careful to avoid spending any time alone with Shawn until I work out how I'm feeling; watching Ash from a distance until I can't tell who's avoiding who.

He seems to be doing well. Showing up to school every day, working in the art studio, being kind but un-flirtatious with all of the girls that seem to want his attention. Sometimes he nods hello, sometimes he just looks at me, like he's looking right through me; and it's all OK. It all feels OK. Because while all this is happening, I'm getting to know myself a little better. I'm working out who I want to be. Just sand, no surf. Working on controlling that little voice that tells me what I can and can't do, what I do and don't deserve.

The night before Dad comes home from the hospital, Granny's sat at Mum's laptop, scrolling through Pinterest. She's gone from total disapproval of Aunty Kitty's wedding to total wedding obsession. Now I've showed her how to use Pinterest, she's pinning everything into a folder she's titled threateningly in capitals – WEDDING – and doing her Sri Lankan head shake every few seconds as she says *ah, ah, ah* – as if the images are explaining something to her she never knew before.

'Is it going to be a . . . Sri Lankan wedding then?' I ask cautiously.

'They are Sri Lankan,' she says, looking daggers at me, 'what other kind of wedding it be?'

'Well, technically, Charles isn't exactly . . .' She stares at me, while Mum mimes a head-chopping motion.

'He will wear suit. Is OK. Has Armani. Is fine,' Granny responds imperiously. 'They are having two weddings. One for his people too.'

'What about the bridesmaids?' I ask hopefully.

'Hmmmn. Kitty says no need for sari or salwar. We will see.'

Gods. Help me out here. I'm too short for sari. And I don't have the stomach for the crop top.

'. . . so, how *are* things with Charles's family?' Which is code. For me asking how things are with Granny, and her accepting Charles's family.

'We will all meet soon. When Noel is better. Kitty and Charles will come for weekend and we will all meet. Soon, they be our family too,' she says sternly. And I wonder where this enlightened Granny came from. How she seems so accepting and modern, when just a few months ago, she was screaming about how hard it is, how impossible, for different cultures to mix like this, to accept each other and be a real family.

'Well, I, for one, am looking forward to meeting them,' Mum says brightly.

'Me too,' I concur. 'I hope we get to go to both weddings. I've never been to a Chinese wedding before.'

'Hmmn,' Granny murmurs, as she continues to scroll through Pinterest.

'Should we look for some Chinese wedding inspiration?' I ask casually.

She looks at me over her glasses, and taps her finger on the laptop.

'You type,' she says, gesturing to the keyboard. I type it into the search box, and we marvel over the pictures. 'Mmmn, pretty,' she admits.

'Think how beautiful their kids will be,' I sigh.

'Yes,' Granny says quietly. 'Children are a blessing. Poor Kyra,' she murmurs.

'Kyra?' I ask, thinking I've misheard her.

She looks at me as though this is a completely normal conversational segue.

'Kyra's mother does not see her own grandchildren. Such beautiful children too. Ash is a very, very special boy. His father was a good man. The son is a good man. No matter the colour, we are all the same.'

'Sorry, *what*?' I repeat, astonished.

'You know,' she says, leaning into me conspiratorially, 'Ash's grandmother only seen him twice? Never even come from India to see him when he was born. Kyra is a good woman. Husband was good, but not Indian. It is sad. Is grandmother's job to look after grandchildren. I die without my children,' she says defiantly.

It makes me feel a bit wobbly to think about Ash; about someone not seeing how special he is.

'She struggled without her mother. Without her family. I will never do that to Kitty. That boy and girl, they are lovely. Especially my Ashar.'

Ashar? I never even knew that was his name.

'Every day he came and drove me to the hospital. Every day he brings me food and drinks, and sits with me during the day, even when I say he should be at school. He is a good boy.'

'Sorry, *what*?' I repeat, like a broken record.

Mum's looking at Granny, now miming a head-chopping motion at her, and Granny's looking suddenly sheepish as she starts to scroll through Pinterest with an unnatural amount of interest, murmuring at wedding images in Tamil.

'What do you mean?' I ask the silent room, looking from Granny to Mum in disbelief.

'I'm tired,' Mum says, fake yawning and rubbing her baby belly, while Granny pretends she can't hear me.

'Is someone going to explain this to me?' I ask, annoyed.

'You should talk to Ash,' Mum says, looking at the floor, as Granny picks up the laptop to take to her bedroom.

And that's how I end up sitting alone in the front room, staring at the walls, and wondering how I can ask him when he won't even speak to me.

91

Not a Big Deal

In the morning, Mum goes to the hospital. They have to wait until the surgeon makes his rounds before Dad can be signed off, so I'm hoping he'll be here when I get home – as is Granny, who's been manically cooking since 6 a.m.

I try to get some information out of her about Ash, but Mum's clearly gotten to her first, because she isn't saying anything.

'You need to talk to *him*,' she keeps saying over and over. She's even saying it quietly, which is completely out of character, and possibly out of her hearing range. In fact, I'm not even sure she can hear herself saying it.

For the love of All GODS. Why won't anyone tell me what's going on?

When I get to school, I go straight to the art studio, and find Ash exactly where I thought he'd be, his hand poised over his easel.

'Hello,' I say abruptly.

'Hello,' he says, turning.

'So, what's this about you and my granny?' I ask bluntly.

He says nothing for a minute.

'Your mum said she wouldn't say anything,' he replies, irritated.

'She didn't. Granny did.'

He says nothing again.

I try to outstare him, leaving the silence silent, instead of filling it with all my usual distractions, like saying something stupid or falling over.

'I wanted to help.' He shrugs.

And now I'm genuinely silent.

'I wanted to make it up to you somehow. About the accident. About how I behaved afterwards.'

'Why didn't you tell me then?' I ask, confused.

He shrugs.

'It was just driving your granny back and forth, and your mum sometimes when she was tired or it got a bit late. It wasn't a big deal,' he says, shrugging again. 'You weren't supposed to find out.'

'Why?'

He shrugs again.

The thing is, it is a big deal. Mum's been nervous about driving while she's so pregnant, and her blood pressure's been high so the doctors have asked her to take it easy, but she's still been going back and forth to the hospital every day, with multiple trips to pick up and drop off Granny. Except she hasn't. Because Ash has been helping.

'How long have you been doing it?' I ask quietly. He stares at me, as if willing me to look away.

'I came to see you at the hospital – the day I found out about your dad. I bumped into your mum in the canteen. She said you were upset, that maybe it wasn't the best time to talk to you. She needed a lift home because your uncle had the car – and it was the least I could do after everything you were going through. She seemed tired, so I offered to help out a bit.'

He turns away from me, towards his easel.

'I don't understand why you didn't tell me,' I say quietly.

'It's not a big deal. I really didn't do much,' he says without turning.

And I want to walk away from him, because he's hurt me so much. But instead, I walk towards him. Placing my arms around his middle, my cheek pressed up against his back, listening to the sound of his heart.

'Thank you,' I whisper. I let go of him and walk to the door.

He turns around.

'You seem OK, Ellie. You seem good.'

'I am.' I smile at his green eyes.

'Good,' he says.

'Good,' I repeat.

92

Mrs Aachara

At lunchtime, I avoid Jess and Hayley and the others, because I just need to think.

It's almost the end of term, and it feels like the entire world has shifted. So, I do what I always do in times of trouble: I head towards the music room. To play the piano, and try to understand who I am. But Mrs Mason isn't there, and for some reason the door's locked.

I turn towards the drama studio, thinking I can use the upright by the stage – but as I get closer, I start to worry about running into Mrs Aachara. It's been fine between us, the same really, since Ash and I broke up. She hasn't mentioned anything to me, and I haven't mentioned anything to her; it just feels like there's something unsaid between us, like there's a giant brown elephant called Ashar in the room, and we can't quite escape him.

Just as I decide to head in the opposite direction, I see her. Like the cosmic ghost of a brown elephant I'm finally forced to look at and admit cosmic brown elephants exist.

I turn quickly and try to avoid eye contact. I will myself to the size of one of the people living in my pores. But it's too late.

'Ellie.' She waves, as she sees me up the corridor. 'Have you got a minute?'

'Um,' I say, swivelling to look at her. 'I have to . . .' I attempt to finish the sentence, but it proves too much for my current level of intellect. 'Er, OK,' I give in, through gritted teeth.

I follow her into the drama studio.

'So, how are you?' she asks, sitting down. Oh God, she's sitting down. That means this is going to go long. Like, awkward, sweaty-band-of-sweat-beneath-my-lime-green-bra long.

'I'm fine,' I smile.

'And your parents? Your dad?'

'He's fine,' I say, refusing to sit.

'Granny?' she grins.

'She's good.'

'Great,' she finishes, looking awkward.

I look at her, and decide to say something useful. And non-cosmic-elephant-related.

'Thank you for speaking to Granny about Aunty Kitty. You have no idea how much you've helped.'

'Your grandmother's a good person, Ellie. If she changed her mind, then it was her that changed it, not me.'

'All the same,' I say, finally succumbing to the need to sit.

'I'm glad.'

For a minute or so, we both just sit there, awkwardly avoiding eye contact.

'How's everything going with exam prep? Do you need any help catching up?' she asks kindly.

'I think I'm OK,' I reply slowly; and for the first time since Dad went into hospital, I think I actually might be.

'Well, if there's anything I can do to help, you know where I am,' she offers.

'You could tell me why Ash didn't tell me about what he was doing for my family?' Apparently, I do want to discuss cosmic brown elephants.

She looks taken aback by my directness, almost as taken aback as I feel.

'I don't think he did it for your family, Ellie,' she says softly. 'And actually, it's me who should be thanking you. Whatever you said to him a few weeks ago – he's pulled himself together.'

I stare at her blankly. Still looking for an answer to my question.

'I think he just wanted to prove to himself that he's the person he wants to be,' she offers carefully. 'The person he thinks you deserve.'

'Oh.' And I have said 'oh' so many times today, it may well be my new catchphrase. The previous one being 'heebeejeebee'.

She stands up.

'Remember what I said. If you need to talk to anyone. About school,' she repeats.

And when she walks out the door, I walk over to the piano, and try to remember who I am.

93

Unknown Number

+44 7860 754322:

> i'm sorry for how we left things, ellie. ash never stopped worrying about u, he just couldn't face the hospital after what ur dad said to him. pls don't 4get the last time he was in 1, it was 4 his dad . . . ty for looking after me at cinema. u didn't have 2 to be kind. he was right about u. i was wrong. also – u suit hats better than u think . . . . love, bec x

I consider how to respond.

Ellie:

> ♥

+44 7860 754322:

> ♥

♡ Song 7 ♡

Chaos, Now – Intro, Verse, Chorus, Middle Eight

When I think about Ash, my heart hurts. And the hurt is both good and bad. Learning and growing and becoming the person I know I want to be. It's learning that falling in love is exactly that. Falling. Quickly and painfully and gracefully, and frighteningly, into something you can't quite understand until you get there. *The more I see, the less I know. The more it hurts, the less I feel.*

This song is the sound of knowing, and not knowing. Choosing, but being unable to choose. Of falling once, and not knowing if you want to do it again. If the fall was heavenly or hurtful.

There's a risk in writing songs in D. A risk of sounding unextraordinary, and too familiar. The move to A then G, like a melody you hear in your dreams. But there's a beauty in it too. A simplicity. An ease.

It's about getting it right. Treading the fine line between something simple and something that can give you wings.

Build it upside down, burn it to the ground
It's all chaos now

94

His Heart, Still Beating

When I get home, the whole house feels different. Like someone's thrown the windows open and we're finally breathing fresh air – because Dad's home, lying on the sofa, watching a music documentary about the Clash.

I run in to him. Like I used to when I was little, but in reverse; when he came home and I was waiting by the door.

I kiss him on the cheek; clean shaven and powdery smelling, like a baby. A big, hairy, irritable brown baby. We're going to have a real one of those soon. A smaller, cuter, less hairy and hopefully less irritable, real brown baby. I feel excited about it. Like he's no longer a phantom I don't want to admit exists, but a person, waiting to be known.

'Sit,' Dad commands, shifting himself on the sofa.

I put my head on his chest.

'I'm sorry if I scared you,' he murmurs into my hair. 'Your mother's too afraid to tell me off, in case it gives me another heart attack – but I should never have lied to you both. I'm sorry, *en anbe*.'

'S'OK,' I whisper tearfully; because there was a point when I didn't think he'd ever make it home to us.

'I know I've been difficult over the last months . . .' He trails away.

I snort.

'A bit agitated.'

I snort again.

'A bit short-tempered and unreasonable.'

I snort for a third time. Like I'm turning into a pig.

'You?' I say jokingly. 'No, you've been a joy. A delight.'

'Ellie,' he says warningly.

'Come on, Dad, it was a joke!'

'I know that!' he says. 'I can take a joke.'

I snort again. It could be the replacement for my 'oh' catchphrase.

'I'm sorry if I was hard on you. I've had a lot on my mind, and I took it out on you and . . .'

'Ash?' I finish for him.

'Your mother told me everything he did for us when I was in the hospital. Your grandmother's practically adopted him,' he says darkly. It's true. I have never seen Granny so wholeheartedly approve of anyone so much before in my entire life. She won't hear a word against him. Which is annoying, because we've all grown accustomed to Granny's little zingers; the sharp ripostes and frosty criticisms that seem to accompany her love – but for him, there's none of that. But then, maybe he deserves it. A grandmother that makes him feel like he's worthy of something.

'He's a good boy,' Dad admits. 'I'm glad you have someone like that in your life. I know the accident wasn't his fault. I'd like the chance to tell him that myself.'

413

'He's not exactly in my life any more,' I reply quietly.

'As much as I'm sure he enjoys Granny's company, I'm pretty sure he is,' Dad says kindly.

I put my head back on his chest, and just listen to his heart. Still beating. And I'm not sure anything else matters.

Just that.

His heart, still beating.

95

If Audrey Hepburn Wore Cocoa Biscuit Foundation

At the final band rehearsal before the spring dance, I ask Shawn for a lift home. On the way to his car, he takes my hand.

'Can we talk?' I ask, turning to him.

'Always,' he responds easily.

He lets go of my hand and opens the boot of his car, placing his guitar into it carefully, then turns to face me, his dirty-blond hair grazing his eyes.

What would it be like, to reach up and kiss him? To let his arms tighten around me as he leaned down into me, his hair tangled with my hair.

I try to remember what I need to say. I try to remember he's not Ezra Koenig and I'm not Danielle Haim, that bowls and plates do go together, but they also don't have to.

'Shawn, right now, I just need to focus on my exams, and my family, and me – and I don't think this is the right time to start anything.'

'OK,' he says softly, playing with my hand.

'I like you,' I explain, 'I'm just . . . I'm not ready.'

'Because of Ash?' he asks directly.

'Because of me, and *my* stuff,' I say, suddenly thinking of Hayley and the whole James thing, and how she said she had stuff to deal with. How she knew she had to be there for her before she could be with anyone else. And that's me. I'm her. I get it. Finally. That you need to sort out *you* before you can be anything more, with anyone more.

That's the thing all those movies never tell you. That Holly Golightly was a mess in *Breakfast at Tiffany's*, and it doesn't matter how lovely and funny and gorgeous Paul Varjak was; she would have stayed a mess until she decided not to be: for her – not him. And OK, I'm no Audrey Hepburn. Not unless Audrey lost several inches in height, gained several pounds and wore a foundation shade called Cocoa Biscuit – but I GET IT. I have *stuff*. I need to do me.

'It's OK. I'll wait.' He smiles as he opens the car door for me. And I just stand there, my mouth opening and closing like a fish.

'Come on,' he says, beckoning me over. 'I'll take you home.'

96

Chain Reaction

I'm onstage singing. My hands a blur beneath me as they pound the keys. Lucas and Elliott and Benji are sweating, all of us dripping on to our instruments, while Shawn looks cool, literally and metaphorically, strutting around onstage, his T-shirt sporting Ben Folds Five, *Whatever and Ever Amen*.

I don't know how he does it. How he was born to be up here, his confidence all-consuming.

But then I know it isn't. I know it's hard. I know it takes work. And I think: I want that. I want to put the work in, and get there. That ever-elusive place, where confidence at least looks like it comes easy.

He turns to face me, and smiles. Singing to me, at me: me singing back, harmonising with his scratchy vocals.

I. Am. Ellie. Pillai.

I grin. Because it feels good. Because in a minute our set will be over, and I'll be able to de-sweat myself in the girls' toilets and change into something else.

At the front of the crowd, Jess and Elina and Hayley and James are dancing; no Ash in sight. And I don't know whether to feel grateful for that, or like part of this night is missing, without him here to make it whole.

When we finish, the crowd are cheering, and Shawn and I walk offstage, hand in hand, looking at each other, laughing and exhilarated.

He hugs me.

'That was amazing,' I say, buzzing.

'*You* were amazing.' He smiles – and I can't help but notice Hannah watching us, her eyes following us across the room.

'You should talk to her.'

'We're just friends,' he says, looking at me.

'Where have I heard that before?' I joke. 'Listen, I need to get changed and go see Jess and Hayley. See you later, OK?'

'I'll be waiting,' he grins, and I can't tell whether it's a double entendre or I suddenly have way too high an opinion of myself.

He kisses me on the cheek. I decide it's a bit of a both.

London Cousin – Not Annoying:

how did it go???

I smile, and tap my phone to reply.

'Ellie!' And suddenly Ash Anderson is calling my name as I stand outside the toilets, sweaty and confused, my heart racing.

Why does he make my heart race?

'That was great,' he says, smiling, as he catches up to me. 'You were great.'

'Thanks,' I say awkwardly. I can hear Elina DJ'ing now the band are offstage. 'I was just going to get changed,' I say, turning away from him.

He grabs my hand and turns me back towards him.

'I'm an idiot,' he states, his green eyes watching me.

'Okaaay,' I sing-song.

He exhales heavily.

'I should have come to the hospital after the accident, Ellie. I'm sorry. I just couldn't face it, for so many reasons – but when your dad . . .' He trails away slightly, before looking back at me again. 'I just needed to know you were OK. I needed to know *he* was OK. And I didn't want you to think I was trying to prove anything or make things any different to the way they are now, I just wanted to be there for you,' and my heart is pulsing like a drum. Like Benji's playing it, in that frenetic, slightly aggressive way of his. 'But the thing is,' he says gently, 'I still love you. And I do want things to be different. So, I'm going to prove it to you. To myself. To everyone. That I deserve you, and I can make you happy – that I'm here and I'm not going to be an idiot any more.'

'Ever?' I joke weakly.

'Maybe sometimes.' He smiles wonkily. 'But I'm not giving up on us, Ellie. I'm going to wait, until you're ready – until you know I won't let you down again.'

And suddenly, there's a whole lot of waiting going on.

'Ash,' I say gently; and it's taking every ounce of self-control not to say I love him back. Not to be the Ellie I used to be. 'I care about you so much, but I was insecure, and jealous, and I stopped noticing things when we were together. I stopped noticing my family and my friends, and when people needed me – and I don't want to be that person any more. I need to be someone else. Someone better. Someone's that's enough on their own,' I say, from somewhere.

Because I'm Holly Golightly, but shorter, and darker, and with infinitely more hair in innumerably more awkward places – and I need to work out who I am before I work out who I am with someone else.

'I need to be on my own right now. I'm not ready for anything else.'

'Like I said,' he whispers, his thumb moving across my jawline tenderly. 'I'll wait.'

He holds my hand for a second before turning away, and I walk into the toilets, somewhere between floating and falling, and change into the dress I got for my birthday. The oxblood velvet minidress, which I tainted with tears and weeing in a bush (don't worry, I've washed it since), that deserves to be worn with joy instead of sadness.

I pull it on over my lime-green bra, and add Jess's gold metallic boots, some black eyeliner – and what I hope is some attitude. And I let myself feel the mess of it all. The mess that I am; the mess that will one day make me into the person I know I deserve to be. Because I'm a million strings tied in a million knots, I'm a story I haven't written; and the glory in that, the beauty in that, the joy in that, is right here, in all that chaos. In not knowing who I am yet and putting it together piece by piece.

Because I get to choose.

Then I walk out on to the dance floor and see them. My two best friends. My real love story. The one that starts with me, and ends with them.

I run to them and envelop them into a hug.

'That was so good!' Jess says, squeezing me.

'Proud of you, E,' Hayley says, throwing her arms around me.

'Proud of you,' I whisper back.

'Guess what,' Jess says, leaning in close. 'Don't tell anyone, but Kyra's going on a date with Mr Green!' she whispers.

'What??' I screech, shocked.

'He's *hot* . . .' Hayley says, salivating.

I glance over at Ash as he smiles at me from across the room.

I. Am. Ellie. Pillai.

'But Hayley,' I say playfully, 'what about *James*? And *Benji*?'

'Don't,' she says seriously. 'I'm choosing me.'

'Me too,' I say just as seriously. 'Although Ash and Shawn both asked me out,' I admit. 'Well, kind of . . . in the future . . . maybe . . . I think . . .'

'Hark at you two and your love triangles,' Jess says, smirking.

'We can't all have perfect relationships like *you*,' I say, pinching her.

'OW!' she says, pinching me back.

But I'm so happy for Jess – because she's fallen in love with Elina, and Elina's fallen in love with her back, and it makes me believe that that's possible. That the falling bit doesn't have to end with your face smashed into a pavement.

Then it starts.

The greatest love song of all time. Discordant disco, a wall of glittering, decadent sound. And we start dancing. Twirling on the spot, our heads bobbing to the beat in that intro; Diana's voice breathy and perfect as we hold hands and sing to each other, our very own sixties girl group.

Because it's Diana Ross, 'Chain Reaction'. The sound of falling in love, and losing yourself, and best friends, and being sixteen, dancing in the school hall, while you try to work out who you are and what you want, and whether it's green eyes or blue eyes or nothing at all. And the future's all laid out before us. The future is happening; but we're right here, in this moment.

In the middle of a chain reaction.

I. Am. Ellie. Pillai.

97

A Girl Called Ellie

My name is Ellie. Ellie Pillai.

I was in love with the boy in the yellow rain mac. I fell. Like one of those coconuts in a cartoon, straight on to someone's head, causing a bump the size of a small mountain and a comedy bruise.

And now I'm here. In half. With someone drinking my insides out with a straw.

And all I know is this.

That I don't know *much*, because I don't know *me*.

And you can't fall in love, not really, until you know who you are, and like who you are, and love who you are.

So, I've decided to stop falling in love. Just for a bit. Or rather, I've decided to see whether I'll make it to a second date with me.

My name is Ellie. Ellie Pillai.

I'll let you know how it goes.